Memento Mori

Other Books By Lexi Blake

ROMANTIC SUSPENSE

Masters And Mercenaries
The Dom Who Loved Me
The Men With The Golden Cuffs
A Dom is Forever
On Her Master's Secret Service
Sanctum: A Masters and Mercenaries Novella
Love and Let Die
Unconditional: A Masters and Mercenaries Novella
Dungeon Royale
Dungeon Games: A Masters and Mercenaries Novella
A View to a Thrill
Cherished: A Masters and Mercenaries Novella
You Only Love Twice
Luscious: Masters and Mercenaries~Topped
Adored: A Masters and Mercenaries Novella
Master No
Just One Taste: Masters and Mercenaries~Topped 2
From Sanctum with Love
Devoted: A Masters and Mercenaries Novella
Dominance Never Dies
Submission is Not Enough
Master Bits and Mercenary Bites~The Secret Recipes of Topped
Perfectly Paired: Masters and Mercenaries~Topped 3
For His Eyes Only
Arranged: A Masters and Mercenaries Novella
Love Another Day
At Your Service: Masters and Mercenaries~Topped 4
Master Bits and Mercenary Bites~Girls Night
Nobody Does It Better
Close Cover
Protected

Masters and Mercenaries: The Forgotten
Memento Mori
Tabula Rasa, Coming February 26, 2019

Lawless
Ruthless
Satisfaction
Revenge

Courting Justice
Order of Protection
Evidence of Desire, Coming January 8, 2019

Masters Of Ménage (by Shayla Black and Lexi Blake)
Their Virgin Captive
Their Virgin's Secret
Their Virgin Concubine
Their Virgin Princess
Their Virgin Hostage
Their Virgin Secretary
Their Virgin Mistress

The Perfect Gentlemen (by Shayla Black and Lexi Blake)
Scandal Never Sleeps
Seduction in Session
Big Easy Temptation
Smoke and Sin
At the Pleasure of the President, Coming Fall 2018

URBAN FANTASY

Thieves
Steal the Light
Steal the Day
Steal the Moon
Steal the Sun
Steal the Night
Ripper
Addict
Sleeper
Outcast, Coming 2018

LEXI BLAKE WRITING AS SOPHIE OAK

Memento Mori

Masters and Mercenaries:
The Forgotten, Book 1

Lexi Blake

Memento Mori
Masters and Mercenaries: The Forgotten, Book 1
Lexi Blake

Published by DLZ Entertainment LLC
Copyright 2018 DLZ Entertainment LLC
Edited by Chloe Vale
ISBN: 978-1-937608-83-5

This is a work of fiction. Names, places, characters and incidents are the product of the author's imagination and are fictitious. Any resemblance to actual persons, living or dead, events or establishments is solely coincidental.

Acknowledgments

There's a passage in this book that comes straight from my childhood. River talks about her father taking her into the woods to see the stars. My dad was fascinated with astronomy. I remember vividly him talking about the stars and constellations. Then he explained to me that the light we see is thousands of years old and that many of the "stars" died long ago, their light still traveling the universe. When I was a kid it seemed like a terrible thing. As so often happens, we grow up and live and view the world through different eyes. All things die. It is inevitable. There is no way around it. One day we're here and the next we are nothing but memories, pictures in an album, stories to be told. But those stories, those memories are like the light from the stars. They give us a path to follow. They remind us of the love we were given. Nothing is wasted. Only transformed.

Memento Mori means "remember that you must die." What I've learned over the last months is that it is only in the inevitability of death that we remember to live, really live. It is because this life ends that we should live it to the fullest, love as much as we can. Do one thing that scares you. Do one thing that intrigues you. Do one thing that helps another human being. So that in the end, death is merely a doorway. So that in the end there is only love.

This book is dedicated to my mother and father. They're together again.

For the rest of my life, I will walk in your light.

Sign up for Lexi Blake's newsletter
and be entered to win a $25 gift certificate
to the bookseller of your choice.

Join us for news, fun, and exclusive content
including free short stories.

There's a new contest every month!

Go to www.LexiBlake.net to subscribe.

Prologue

Brittany, France
Eighteen months before

He could still hear the screams, the shouts of the men who'd gone down. Still see the blood as it started to flow. His brother...god, he could still see his brother.

He'd been caught, locked away in his cell and unable to join the fight. Not that he wanted to fight. When the first splatter of gunfire had sounded out, his instinct had been to breathe a sigh of relief. He'd known one way or another it was over. Live or die, he wouldn't be under her thumb any longer.

Someone was finally coming for Mother. Someone was going to save them.

Then his training had taken over and he'd known he had to try or die. Mother didn't accept failure in her boys. It still made him sick, that trigger in his brain that went against all his instincts and told him to obey.

He didn't fucking obey.

"Do you know what happened to the man outside your cell?" There was a massive blond man on the other side of the table from him. He was the one who'd led the charge. He was the one who'd directed his men to secure what he'd called the Lost Boys.

The blond guy was right. He was so lost.

"George? Are you talking about him?" What was the man's name? He struggled with names. Even his own, but then he'd been "born" a fully-grown man, waking up on a hospital bed with no memory of anything before that moment. "He was my brother."

His brother. He'd been there when George had been "born." Mother never brought a new recruit on alone. He'd been there when George had opened his eyes, confusion clouding them. He'd been kinder to George than Sasha had been to him.

And he'd watched as George had realized he couldn't win, as George had done what Mother had taught them to do when they failed.

Clean up your mess. Don't make me do it for you.

He hated Mother. It was easier and easier to shed the skin she'd forced him into. He was one of the bad boys, one of the boys who didn't clean up his mess.

"Yes, that man." The blond dude had been joined by a gorgeous woman with skin the color of velvety night and dark eyes that looked at him with sympathy. Ariel. That was her name and she was some kind of doctor. A shrink, maybe.

How was it that he could remember what a doctor was and that a doctor who studied behavior and the mind was a psychologist, but he couldn't tell anyone what his name had been before Mother had taken his past away?

"George had been on patrol." He said the words with a calm he didn't feel. "He wasn't in his cell when the incursion happened. His training took over when he realized Mother was gone and that he would be taken."

Good-bye, Harvey. We have to clean up the mess. Don't let them take you. I'll see you soon, brother.

"His training?" The doctor looked at him expectantly.

Now was when his training should take over and he should shut up. They weren't allowed to talk about this. They were to be polite boys, to do their duty.

Or someone would beat the shit out of them. Out of him.

16

Because he was stubborn and arrogant and joking wasn't allowed. They were to be serious at all times.

"He killed himself because Mother...the insane lady who kidnapped us and wiped our memories...planted the impulse. Tomas's brother was coming through the doors at the time. We were all taught to not get caught."

"His name is Theo," Blond Dude said.

Yes, Theo. The mission hadn't been about freeing himself. It had been about saving Theo Taggart. His own rescue had been incidental, but then his life seemed fairly random. After all, who would have guessed he would get selected for experimentation? He would bet it was a fairly uncommon thing to have happen.

"George was what the doctor called one of the good ones. He rarely required correction," he explained. "Are you going to kill us?"

Us. He and Dante and Sasha and Tucker were the only ones left. George was gone. They'd lost Charles and Albert during the mission to Dallas to retrieve Robert and Theo—a mission that had gone poorly. He still had the scars.

He wasn't upset at the thought, merely wanted to know if he should prepare himself for execution.

Ariel leaned forward, putting a hand on his. He stared down where she touched him. He couldn't remember anyone touching him with kindness. Not ever. "No. No one wants to hurt you. Any of you."

"Well, I might punch that Russian fucker. He's obnoxious," Taggart said. Ian Taggart. Yes, that was his name. Theo's oldest brother.

"Sasha can be an asshole." He flinched.

Taggart looked at him with serious eyes. "She didn't like you cussing?"

He sat up straighter. He didn't have to follow her rules now. The inkling that this was actually a good thing had started in the back of his brain. Theo and Robert were here and they seemed good. Happy even. Maybe they weren't going to be handed over to people who would toss them in jail for the crimes the doctor had made them commit or vivisect them in order to find her secrets.

17

Maybe the man in front of him meant what he'd said. He'd offered them protection and to help figure out who'd they'd been before.

"She fucking didn't. Bitch. Actually bitches are female dogs and I like dogs. Dogs are cool. I'm not going to insult them by calling her a bitch. She was an asshole. She killed George. She killed a lot of my brothers."

"Damn straight she did." Taggart leaned forward. "No one is going to hurt you here. We're going to take you and the others to London. We have a safe place for you to stay there, and we have a whole team ready to work with you. Ariel is going to help you process what happened and transition into a world where you don't get your ass handed to you on a daily basis. No more drugs. Well, not the kind she used. Like I said, I might tranq up the Euros."

He wouldn't argue about that. Dante was kind of a dick, too.

He looked at the good doctor, the not evil one. "You know the worst part?"

"The torture and memory wipes? I can't imagine how bad it was." She squeezed his hand.

He was done being careful. It was a new world and he was going to be…him. Whoever the hell he was. He made those decisions now. "The lack of hugs."

She gasped a little, her eyes sympathetic. She stood, but before she could move around to embrace him, Taggart stopped her.

He shook his head. "You're going to be trouble, aren't you, you horny bastard?"

For the first time in his memory, he felt a grin slide onto his face. It was over. He was out and he didn't have to go back. She wouldn't come after him again because Mother Asshole was dead and gone and he was free. Free to be stupid and to eat carbs and to be horny. "I think I am going to be trouble. And I'm definitely the other thing, but seriously, the lack of physical affection hurts my heart. I'm very damaged."

Ariel's expression had changed from sympathetic to amused. "I can see we're going to have to work to get you to take your therapy seriously. But for now, I wanted to give you the option I've given the others." She settled back down. "She named you. I thought it might be meaningful for you to change that, to choose your own name."

He considered it for a moment. "No one chooses their own name. Parents do that. The people who are there when you're born select a name. But I hate Harvey. I don't feel like a Harvey. I don't want it because she gave it to me."

"You look a little like a character from a TV show I liked," Taggart said. "Though he came to a bad end. He was a badass though."

"What was his name?"

"Jax."

Yes, that felt much more suitable.

"My name is Jax." He wouldn't forget his fallen brothers. He would remember them and that life was tenuous at best.

Days before he'd prayed for death, but when the time had come, he hadn't the will to do it. Something inside him had overridden the training, the triggers she'd planted deep in his mind. Something inside wanted so badly to live.

He would live in honor of them.

He suddenly couldn't wait to see the world.

* * * *

Creede, CO
18 Months Before

River Lee wanted to shut the world away.

She looked down at the note for the fiftieth time. It was still there, still written in clean, masculine handwriting. The words hadn't changed.

Sorry for this, love, but it's what I do. I regret the timing though. You were a lovely woman. If I had it in me to be a real husband, I would have wanted you as my wife. You're strong. You'll survive.

He'd taken all the money. Her accounts were empty, both personal and business because she'd been stupid enough to give him access to both. After all, he'd been her husband, though now she understood the marriage wasn't legal. He'd conned her for over two years and finally gotten his big payoff when her father had signed over power of attorney and put his entire life savings in her hands.

She'd lost it all. Her father was dying, the cancer eating away at his body and soul. How would she take care of him?

How would she tell him how foolish she'd been?

She put the letter down and thought about calling the police. Who would she talk to? She lived on unincorporated land between Creede and a tiny town called Bliss. She lived in a ramshackle cabin her grandfather had built back in the fifties. Every bit of cash she'd had she'd put into her business.

And now she couldn't work. She would have to sell off the equipment.

She walked out onto the porch, staring at the Sangre de Cristo Mountains all around her. The Rio Grande ran through her backyard. She would call Nate Wright in the morning. The sheriff of Bliss County was a good man. At least he would file a report on the con artist she'd thought loved her.

The man who had betrayed her utterly.

Over the gurgling of the river, she heard the sound of her father coughing. It seemed to rattle the cabin.

At least he wouldn't suffer for long. The doctors had given him three months at most. She could hold everything together for three months, surely. Her father didn't have to know that she'd ruined everything.

She sank down on the Adirondack chair she'd bought when she'd married Matt. There were two of them, and she'd imagined she and Matt growing old together right here.

She watched the river and cried for the longest time.

Chapter One

Bliss, CO
Present Day

Jax stared out the massive windows, his gaze trained on the vibrant colors in front of him. The sun itself seemed different here. Brighter, as if someone had a remote and had turned up the picture clarity. He'd spent all his time inside. His logical mind knew Hope McDonald's compound had been in the countryside, isolated for privacy purposes, but he hadn't been allowed to wander the land. He'd known the white walls of the facility and the inside of his utilitarian cell. Even when he'd been taken someplace new, it had been by plane, the land below so far away as to seem unreal. But this, this was something from a dream, a good one.

Greens so deep they looked like they came from an artist's palette. Massive pines rising from the ground up and up and up into the sky. The mountains dominating everything. And the river. He loved the sound of that river. He'd gone to sleep to the lullaby it created.

He could breathe here. For the first time in his life he felt like he could take a full breath, as though his lungs had been bound and someone had clipped the rope.

"You going to join us, Princess Jax?"

Not that everything was perfect.

"I'm not sure I have anything to add. You have the sarcasm thing down." He kept his eyes on the scene in front of him. He wanted to go out and explore. They'd gotten in the night before, but it had been incredibly dark. He hadn't seen a thing except the stars shining overhead. He'd stared at those for the longest time, too. He'd stood on the big front porch of the house they were staying at, his head dropped back and eyes focused on the way those diamonds sparkled in the deep midnight.

Big Tag had been the one to poke him then, too.

With a sigh, Jax turned and walked back across the great room to join his brothers at the massive dining room table. It was obviously meant for dinner parties and entertaining, but they'd taken it over and turned the whole place into one big conference room.

Story of his life. No matter where he went, the place became somewhere to work, the beauty of whatever space he was in overtaken by charts and laptops and maps to all manner of horrors. In the year and a half since he'd been freed from Mother's tender care, he'd buried himself in work as an investigator for McKay-Taggart and Knight in London, rarely leaving the building known as The Garden. He'd become excellent at hunting down information on the dark alleys of the Internet.

He was rarely allowed outside. Sometimes he felt like he'd exchanged one cage for another.

Still, he forced himself to sit down in his chair across from his current jailor, Ian Taggart. And yes, he knew that wasn't fair. Big Tag had kept him inside because there were several BOLOs and warrants on him. While he'd been Mother's drone, he'd committed any number of crimes for which actual jail would be called for. But small-town Colorado should be different than London. Surely no one should be looking for him here.

Big Tag held up a file folder. "Nothing to add? I thought you were the subject matter expert on this op. Was I wrong?"

"Jax is the one who found the site in the first place," Robert replied. Robert was the one who tried to smooth everything over. In their odd family, Robert would be the eldest brother, the one who kept them together, who took responsibility.

"So he is reason we're here in this shit hole." And Sasha would be the brother everyone wished had been born to another mother. His accent was Russian, thick and heavy. He looked around, his dark eyes taking in the scene.

"It's not a shit hole. I think it's pretty here." Tucker was his favorite brother, his closest friend in the group. But then he and Tucker had been close inside the compound. He and Tucker and George had been a unit. Tucker had been the one to sneak into Jax's cell after particularly brutal beatings. He was an excellent thief and he would show up with things he'd stolen from medical to ease Jax's suffering. Many a night he'd spent under Tucker's care. "It's different from London. I like the trees. I got up early this morning and sat on the porch and there's a couple of chipmunks running around. It was cool at first. I thought they were playing. Then I realized it was chipmunk porn and that dude was not a gentle lover. Like I know it sucks to be a human female sometimes, but think about the chipmunks."

He was also the weirdest of the group.

"Oh, you must be talking about Felix and Finola." The newest guy on the team leaned forward. He'd briefly met the man they called Henry Flanders the night before when he'd let the group into the massive mansion-like cabin after more than twenty-four hours of flights, including a side trip to Dallas to pick up the big boss. Henry Flanders was a blandly handsome man who looked to be in his early- to mid-forties. "That's what my wife named them. And we don't know that there's no consent. That's extremely judgmental of you, Tucker."

He'd heard that Henry Flanders once had a different name. Now he was a mild-mannered husband who ran several earth-friendly businesses and loved his pretty, pregnant wife. But once he'd been a man named John Bishop and he'd been a deadly CIA operative. He'd trained Ian Taggart and Ten Smith.

Now he wore Birkenstocks and apparently didn't mind a little rough sex.

Tucker was shaking his head. "Nope. I bore witness to that scene. No one would consent to that. No one. I've never thought of it before, but I think lube might be the best creation ever. Certainly the kindest."

Big Tag sighed and took a sip of his coffee. "Knight warned me it would be this way. Could we please move on from kinky chipmunks? All you bastards were either too sleepy or too drunk to have this meeting last night. I need a briefing on why I'm here in Colorado when I could be home being used as a stud for my wife's plans to have so many children they form their own army and take over the world. Don't think I'm joking. My daughters have plans. They use those little pony things to lay out the battle maps."

Dante sat back in his chair, his eyes sunken. Of course he'd been one of the drunk ones on the plane the night before. They'd come in on a private jet in a mysterious circuitous route designed to throw off whatever agency was looking for them, the airplane version of losing a tail. The private jet had been loaned to them by the royals of Loa Mali and had come with a fully stocked bar that Dante had done his damnedest to drain. "We're here because Jax enjoys the—what do you call it? Goose chasings. He chases the gooses and we sit and do nothing."

Ezra thought Dante was possibly Romanian. From his accent, Jax believed it.

"It's not a wild-goose chase," a man with a thick Scottish accent said as he walked in from the kitchen. Owen was relatively new to the "family." He'd been born the day of the raid that freed the rest of them. Mother had used him to bring Theo and Erin Taggart to her. She'd kidnapped Owen's mother and sister, using them as leverage to force the man to do her will. Of course, she'd killed them anyway and punished Owen for not bringing baby TJ Taggart along for the ride. Owen was the only one of the group who knew who he was, where he'd come from. But that knowledge wasn't personal. Owen had to read about his history in a report.

Sometimes Jax wondered what his own report would look like. Not that there was more than a blank page on him. He wondered what his real name was, where he'd come from, why he was good with a computer. Other times he realized he never wanted that report. Ever. He couldn't have a great past if he was so

24

easily erased. And yet, he was in charge of looking for something he might not want to find. "The place is real. I've got too much evidence for it to be anything but real."

Sasha shook his head. "I think people who believe in the Sasquatch think same thing."

"Yeah, well there's not aerial footage of Bigfoot," he replied.

"You have satellite footage? Then why can't we simply go to the spot?" Tucker asked. "Why the whole hiding out here thing? Not that this place isn't cool. But why not charge in and get the files and run like hell?"

It was more complicated than that. "I've seen footage, but the actual longitude and latitude was redacted and I can't find anyone who knows the exact location. Apparently if you worked at this base, you were brought in with the tech equivalent of a blindfold. And the majority of the place is underground. The footage is from years ago. I suspect the place is overgrown with vegetation now."

"Why doesn't someone explain what this place is exactly?" Big Tag asked. "And how it's connected to McDonald."

He didn't flinch at the sound of her name, but his stomach did churn a bit. Hope McDonald. Somehow that was worse than Mother. Mother was a monster. Hope McDonald sounded normal. It reminded him that she'd had parents and a family and still turned out to be evil as fuck. "It was originally an underground base built during the height of the Cold War. It was meant to be used to protect military big wigs and their families. Over the years it morphed into a scientific base where certain experiments could go on in secrecy."

Big Tag frowned and opened the file. "So the Agency took it over."

It wasn't a question. The boss knew where to put the blame. "The CIA took over in the early nineties. From the information I've discovered, it was code-named The Ranch."

Henry Flanders's jaw tightened. "I've heard the name before."

Big Tag glanced over at the other former CIA operative in the room. "What do you know about this, John? I'm sorry. Henry. Too many names. I'm glad I never stayed long enough in the Agency to acquire all the names long-term operatives do."

25

A faint smile crossed Henry's face. "Well, the one time I asked you to go undercover you called yourself Frodo Baggins. Seriously. He had a passport and everything. I have no idea how that got by support."

Tag grinned. "Don't tell Charlie because she thinks I was a virgin until I met her, but I was banging the chick in charge of support. It was her idea. She was a geek girl, probably with a lot in common with Finola. And I thought it was quite apropos. You were asking me to escort a shipment of arms into a jihadist camp so we could find information. Believe me. I felt like the dude with the ring."

Jax didn't want to sit and listen to old war stories. He was anxious to get out, to see something that wasn't a club in London or a bank he was supposed to rob. For the first time it felt like the world was right there and he was stuck in here. On the outside looking in. Except he wanted to be outside…

"The Ranch was a black ops site. It was highly classified. I only heard rumors but I suspect it was a medical research facility," Henry explained. "What you have to understand about the Agency is that there are different branches and those branches have many teams and those teams divide into units. It's a big bureaucracy and sometimes one hand has no idea what the other is up to."

"Is that how Ezra ended up getting fired?" Owen asked.

Ezra Fain was their new "dad." If Taggart was the boss, then Fain was the man who watched over them on a day-to-day basis now that they'd left the safety of The Garden. Fain had gone into town earlier to meet with some of the authority figures of Bliss, Colorado. It was all to make sure they could operate in peace. A small town was a good place to hide, but the locals would definitely notice all the new faces. Fain had to make sure their cover would be secure.

"Fain left the Agency because his side of the investigation lost with brass," Taggart explained. "You know every intelligence group in the world would love to get their hands on any one of you. Well, at least on a few of you. Owen is protected by his citizenship. My brother has a verifiable past and connections. But the rest of you have no ties. I can say I think Robert and Tucker

26

and Jax are Americans all I like, but I can't prove it. Sasha, we're almost certain you're Russian, but there are no records. I'm pretty sure Dante was spit from the bowels of hell, hence his name."

Sasha nodded readily. "Yes, this I could believe. What you are saying is Ezra wanted to deal with us one way. Levi Green wants to bring us all in and crack us open until he find out how the drug worked in our brain. The Agency prefer Green's method and that's why Ezra was told to get with program or leave."

Sasha was a bastard, but he wasn't stupid. He'd made the point nicely. "That means we can trust Ezra. He gave up his career to help us. But it also means the Agency probably won't stop."

Dante frowned. "Or this Ezra is setting us all up and we will get into this laboratory and find ourselves being studied."

Jax felt weary. They'd been arguing about Ezra Fain's motives from the moment the man had come on the scene.

Owen stared at the man. "He's not like that. He's a good man. Everyone is working hard to help us. We can't treat them like dirt."

Dante shrugged and stood up, pushing back from the table. It was obvious which side of the argument he was on. "So you say. As for people helping, I don't know about this, either. All I can tell is no one knows who we are and it's been a year and a half. I think they care not much. They're getting free work from us."

"I'm not getting much out of you, buddy," Taggart said. "Jax, Robert, and Owen earn their keep. Tucker is at least somewhat amusing. Sasha is fairly good at communications, even though I can't understand a word he says most of the time. You spend almost all your time drinking and complaining about what's not happening. If you don't like it, the door is that way."

Dante stared at the big boss. "Well, you've taken me to a place where if I leave I will likely be eaten by bear. I think I'll stay. When you need me to kill someone, wake me up."

He stalked away. Dante was so dark. Besides Sasha, he'd spent the most time with Moth…McDonald. Sasha had been her favored son and Dante, well, he'd tried to help Dante, too, but it was like the man welcomed the pain.

Taggart leaned back, obviously tired from the long night's travel and next to no sleep. "Could someone explain what

McDonald's connection to The Ranch is?"

He glanced to the stairs where Dante had disappeared. Dante was sharing a room with Sasha there. Despite how large the house was, they were bunking together. Still, Sasha didn't seem to care that his partner had left. Jax took a deep breath. Tucker was his partner. He couldn't run after every one of his brothers who had problems. He would never stop running. He focused on the issue at hand. "From the information I've put together, The Ranch was abandoned. It sat dormant for years and then it was reopened, but this time the Agency accepted cash for rental space, so to speak. Cash and a glimpse into some of the things certain pharmaceutical companies were interested in developing that might not get by the FDA."

"Why would they research stuff they can't sell?" Owen asked.

"The dark stuff can lead to stuff they *can* sell," Henry explained. "The FDA has all sorts of rules. The Ranch offered them a place to experiment outside the normal spaces and with almost no oversight. I assure you plenty of the drugs we use today weren't developed with kindness in mind. And they can make a ton of money on the Dark Web selling torture drugs to governments and jihadists and drug cartels. There's a whole world under the shiny one we see."

He knew that better than most. "The intel I found has a pharmaceutical company called Kronberg doing research at The Ranch. Hope worked there at the time and I've found records of her flying into Colorado Springs. The flight in and the flight out were months apart. She was here but there are no hotel reservations, no cars booked. I clock her time here during a four-year period at one thousand forty-two days. She was here and she was working on her time dilation drug. I believe her early notes are still in that base."

"Why wouldn't she have taken them with her?" Tucker leaned in.

Henry took that one. "Because if her company was paying for her to have that space, one of the ways they would pay would be in information. The Agency would have kept documentation on all the experiments that went on there."

"She developed the drug right here," Taggart mused. "Her father was a senator before he became a corpse. I'm sure he was the one who put her in touch with the Agency. No wonder they're fighting. They helped to develop the drug. And the timing of her leaving would fit. She left Kronberg when she kidnapped my brother."

"There's more to it. Something happened right before McDonald left for Argentina." He'd spent the better part of the last eighteen months putting this timeline together. "The rumor floating around is that there was a biological incident at The Ranch. They shut it down overnight three years ago and no one has been back since. That's why we need the bio suits, although I doubt there's a real biohazard. I believe that's a smoke screen to keep people out."

"Then what's the real reason they shut it down?" Robert asked.

He'd thought about this long and hard and come up with only one reason that made sense. "At roughly the same time there was a shift in power in the presidency. Zack Hayes was elected and he cleaned house. The Agency got a new head. A whole lot of files were deleted during the regime change, and one of them was all information involving The Ranch. But before that delete command was pushed through, I found evidence that The Ranch itself was closed up and locked down to wait for a more amenable administration. This all went down a few weeks before McDonald shows up in Grand Cayman and steals Theo Taggart and places him in her stable of experiments."

"That's awfully coincidental." Taggart was staring down at the file in front of him like he could change the words on the page.

"Yes, but we're talking about the intelligence world. It's not surprising." He'd learned a lot about this world. "The Agency is good with coincidence."

"What does that mean?" Robert asked.

Robert took point on logistics. He was incredibly good at making sure things flowed smoothly. Sometimes it was hard to believe that once he'd fought on a Dallas street to try to bring Robert back to Mother. He could close his eyes and feel how hard his brother had fought. They'd been standing in the middle of a

29

park with food trucks around them and Robert had battled them all to retain his memory, as sad and pitiful as it was. Jax had been the bad guy that day. He'd been the one on the wrong side, and he'd paid for it in blood and humiliation. He'd watched two of his brothers jump into traffic.

He'd been punished for not doing the same.

"It means that they shut down the project," Taggart replied. "It means that they thought they couldn't do anything with the data at the time. Hayes wasn't supposed to win the election. He was behind in the polls right up until his wife was killed. He was swept into office with a sympathy vote. The Agency hadn't counted on that. I still have thoughts on the assassination of Joy Hayes, but this isn't the time or place to go into that. What affects us is that the Agency thought they would get one president and they got another. The head of The Ranch project might shut it down until such time as they get an administration they believe they could work with."

"I agree," Henry said. "Hayes was not what they were expecting. His election sent ripples through the intelligence community. It makes sense. So they immediately shut down The Ranch and tried to get rid of all evidence that it existed. They buried the research in the hopes that four years from then they might get it back."

"Are you seriously telling me Moth…Hope McDonald's research is still down there?" Tucker had gone a pasty white. "I thought Ezra destroyed it."

This was why he hadn't talked about this project until he had to. He hadn't wanted to worry his brothers. But he knew it was there. All that information, including perhaps intelligence on her early targets, including Robert and himself, was there, deep in the earth waiting to be discovered. The timing was so that there might be information on Sasha, Tucker, and Dante, too.

Ezra Fain had destroyed the later formulas of the drug, but there could be something in the early notes, something that might lead to what no one ever mentioned, what they were all too scared to hope for—a cure.

"Yes. I think the answers we're looking for are all here," he said. "The Ranch is hidden somewhere in the national forest lands. I don't know the exact place, though, and we're going to need a guide."

Taggart closed the folder. "All right, then. Ezra is handling the locals. He's meeting with the sheriff to explain our situation. When we're sure we're good here, he and Robert are going to figure out the best way to begin our search for The Ranch."

Sasha leaned forward. "Is that good idea? Talking to the authorities, I mean. Sheriff is law enforcement, correct? Like old western movies?"

"Sheriff Wright is a good man, and he's been around long enough to know how to handle anything that gets thrown at him," Henry assured them all. "Nate used to be a DEA agent. He understands how bureaucracies work. I trust him and his deputy implicitly. The mayor of Bliss is a former FBI agent. I believe he actually has ties to one of Ian's men."

"And woman. Don't forget Eve. But, yes, turns out Mayor Kincaid used to work with my partner Alex McKay and his wife, Eve, when they were with the Bureau. Alex speaks highly of him. It's why we decided on making our base of operations here and not closer to where the actual site is supposed to be," Taggart explained. "We've got friendly authorities we can be honest with and they'll watch our backs. At least according to Henry they will."

"I assure you, it won't be a problem. No one is going to question you here in Bliss. Well, except my wife." Henry glanced over at the windows. Jax had heard he lived within walking distance of where they were staying. "She'll probably protest the whole thing. She's definitely protesting me right now."

Taggart looked Henry's way. "Did you think about lying to her? I wasn't planning on telling anyone outside of the authorities who need to know. I'm not sure that includes your wife. You know we have a pretty good cover."

They were "reporters' for this mission. They had the press credentials to prove it. For the rest of their time in Bliss, he was Jax Seaborne, a producer for an investigative television show. They were looking into the rumors that the Army had abandoned

31

an old highly classified base that might be polluting the Rio Grande. It would get people talking, they'd reasoned. Coloradans tended to like to preserve the nature they'd been gifted.

Henry had gone pale. "No. I can't lie to her again. Not if I want to keep her. I can't lose her. She's everything to me so I won't lie. She's no threat to the mission. I promise."

As if talking about her had conjured her, a pretty woman with long, dark hair walked in through the cabin's doors. She was dressed in a flowy skirt and a cotton shirt, carrying a basket.

Henry was on his feet in an instant. "Hello, love. Are you all right? Do you need something? How are you feeling?"

She frowned, walking past him. "I made muffins. I didn't know if any of you could cook. I know you don't remember who you are, but I wasn't certain about the other things you might have forgotten. I thought since we'll be neighbors for a while, I would bring you some breakfast. Not that I mean to conform to gender roles, mind you."

"We would never want that, love," Henry said.

Owen stood up, offering his hand. "We would love some muffins, dear lady. And we thank you for thinking of us. We might not remember much after the terrible experiments that were performed on us against our wills, but we know kindness when we see it."

Owen remembered how to deal with a woman, or perhaps he simply had amazing instincts.

It was like Nell melted in front of them, her slightly icy demeanor slipping away, and in its place, pure sunshine and sympathy took over. She took Owen's hand in hers. "Of course. I can't imagine what you gentlemen have been through. I want to do everything I can to help. Starting with breakfast. Please sit back down. I'm sure Seth has some juice. He keeps this place stocked for when he comes home. Please, sit and let me take care of you. Except which one of you is Taggart?"

He'd never seen the big boss look slightly afraid. Taggart was always in charge, but he said nothing as the slender woman stared around the room.

So naturally they all pointed him out.

She gave him a long stare, like a fighter evaluating her next opponent. "I am protesting you, sir. I've looked into your company and I don't approve of your recycling practices nor the body count you've racked up. You are entirely too invested in handguns."

Taggart shrugged. "Well, I tried killing my enemies with kindness. Guns worked better."

She huffed and turned on her sandaled feet. "You and Henry are on your own. The rest of you I'll take under my wing. There's also Holly's banana bread in the basket, though I warn you, it's not vegan."

She strode into the kitchen, Henry following behind.

"I recycle stuff," Taggart complained, his arms over his chest.

"Wait, did she say vegan?" Robert frowned at the basket.

Tucker already had a muffin halfway down his throat.

Jax reached for what looked like a blueberry muffin while Owen was divvying up the banana bread. Sweet, sweet carbs. They hadn't been allowed them while Mother had been in charge. Of course, they hadn't been allowed to do much of anything except be tortured and commit crimes.

He glanced outside again. He couldn't wait to explore.

* * * *

Marie Warner stared at her for a moment, her intelligent eyes likely seeing far more than River wanted her to. She didn't get into Bliss often. Usually she went into Creede. It was slightly closer, but she'd heard Marie took less of a percentage of the real estate sale then normal and would be easy to work with.

"Didn't your father recently pass?" Marie asked.

She nodded tightly, trying not to think about the last year and a half. Her father's few weeks had turned into torturous months, months where she watched him drown daily, where his misery became her daily life, every choice she made with him in mind. Every moment of her life revolving around his death. "Yes, he did, but it was expected."

It had been a relief. And a horrifying loss. How could it have been both? How could she mourn and weep and still feel like a burden had been lifted? How could the quiet in her home be both peaceful and suffocating?

"Hon, that kind of thing can be expected and still devastating." Marie had a gruff voice. She was a solidly built woman in her early sixties, her hair a helmet of steel. "It's usually best to wait a bit before you make big life decisions."

She would love to wait. She would love nothing more than to sit on her porch and let time heal her, but that wasn't going to happen. Her past had caught up to her again.

She'd never gone to see Nathan Wright to talk about what her con man husband had done. She'd put it off and put it off. She could tell herself that the reason had been her father, but it had been shame. Embarrassment.

Now she would pay for it again, but by god, her employees wouldn't. She wasn't going to sell off her business. She had one employee who'd stood beside her through this hell and she'd recently hired two more. Things were starting to look up on that front. She wasn't going to allow her evil ex to screw this up for her. This time, she would fight back.

But she couldn't do that without some cash. She only had one thing left to sell.

"I'm good." She kept every word even, pressing any emotion she felt down. "I've been ready to move for a while now. I don't need all that space. I'm going to move into the apartment over the shop."

It wasn't an apartment. It was more like a storage closet, but it was all she could afford now. She had to choose between her business and her home. She'd only recently managed to get a loan to secure some new equipment. She had to keep up the payments or she would lose it all again.

"I'm glad to hear you're working. You're the best guide around these parts," Marie was saying. "I always feel comfortable telling folks to go to you."

She'd grown up in Creede where her father had worked as a wilderness guide during the summer and in the ski resort during wintertime. She'd taken over his small business at the tender age of twenty and built it up into something that made serious money.

34

Mountain Adventures had grown from a room in the cabin to a big office nestled between the Rio Grande and the National Forest. At one point she'd had ten employees and offered guided tours of some of the most beautiful country in the world.

Unfortunately, one of those employees had been Matt Lewis. Well, he'd told her that was his name. She had no idea what his real name was. He'd romanced her, married her, and looted every dime she had. Every dime her father had worked hard to save.

She'd let most of the employees go and sold that gorgeous office and most of the equipment—the rafts, the skis, and snowboards. She'd moved to a much smaller office and kept only the equipment that was essential to hiking and guided camping. It was the most cost-effective way to keep going. Ty Davis had stayed on, though he had another job. He'd helped her survive.

It still hadn't been enough. She'd gone hungry more than once in favor of feeding her father and getting his medications.

"I'm glad, too. It's been too long since I got out there." She hoped being out in the forest would start to ease the tightness in her chest. It seemed like it was always there now, as though her grief and guilt required a physical manifestation. "I want to concentrate on working. I sold off a lot of equipment when Dad got sick. I hope I can use some of the proceeds of the sale of the cabin to buy it back."

And to have a way to fight her ex.

"Well, if you're sure, but it's a slow time right now," Marie warned her. "There are a couple of places that have been on the market for a while now. I'll come out next week and take some pictures."

Marie would catalog the home River had grown up in so she could sell it for far less than it was worth. Someone would buy it if she was lucky and her childhood home would turn into a vacation spot. "Thank you. Give me a call. I'm spending a lot of time at the office. If you let me know when you're coming out, I'll make sure to be home."

Home. It wouldn't be her home for much longer. She would miss it. She would miss the porch and the tiny kitchen where her father had prepared pancakes every Sunday morning when she was growing up.

She turned and headed out, the easy part of her morning over with. She would love to do anything but what she needed to do now. She would take a group of hypersensitive princesses on an eight-hour nature hike a hundred times before she would do this.

She stopped, staring at the stationhouse. Maybe she should let Matt Lewis have everything. She could walk off into the wilderness and let a bear have her. Then she wouldn't have to let anyone know how stupid she'd been.

"Hey, are you going to finally do it?"

She turned and one of her recent employees was standing roughly five feet away, a reusable shopping bag slung over her shoulder. Heather Turner was a gorgeous blonde in her mid-twenties. She was also willing to work for far less than she was worth. Five months ago, River had hired Heather as a guide. She'd done the same job for a company in her native California, but a bad breakup had sent her wandering. She'd gotten to Colorado and needed some cash so she'd done a couple of temp jobs for River. Now she was full time and living in a small cabin on the outskirts of Bliss.

She was also a good drinking buddy, which was how she knew way too much of River's business. Not even Ty knew the real reason she'd been forced to downscale. She'd told them Matt had taken half in their "divorce." But one night and too much tequila and Heather knew everything.

She shouldn't have talked so much to a woman she'd known for roughly six weeks at the time.

This was what happened when she kept too much inside. River was a powder keg waiting to blow. The trouble was she wasn't sure what would come out—the molten hot lava of rage or pure, unadulterated sorrow.

"I'm thinking about not doing it at all," she admitted. "I'm standing here weighing my need for justice versus my horrific embarrassment."

"Because you trusted the wrong guy? There isn't a single woman on the planet who hasn't done that. Stop being arrogant." Heather moved beside her.

36

"Arrogant?" What was Heather smoking? "I assure you after the last couple of years I've been through, there's no arrogance left in me. Not a drop."

"Oh, that's untrue. Look, I haven't been around for long, but I've spent enough time with you to have figured a few things out. You come off as super quiet and humble, but you're a control freak and that equals arrogance. All the control freaks I know will tell you it's because it's simpler or they just like things a certain way, but it's truly because deep down you think you know better."

Okay, maybe they weren't such fast friends. "I really don't."

"I wasn't saying it's a bad thing. Shouldn't the boss know better? Someone has to take control. Someone has to be in charge. And so far you're a good boss. But there's a flip side. You think you have to be in control all the time and that's not good for anyone. The one time you took a shot at sharing control with someone, he turned out to be a complete asshole. You should have gone after him with both barrels, but somewhere deep down you blame yourself because you should have seen it coming. See, that's kind of the definition of arrogance. You couldn't have known he was lying. You couldn't have known he was a con artist. Did you marry him right away?"

River shook her head, hating the memories rolling around in there now. "No. I was cautious. My father had been sick. We didn't know what it was at the time. I hired Matt because he had excellent recommendations and he knew his stuff. I needed someone to take over the front office when I had to take care of my dad. Matt was perfect. I didn't even say yes to dinner with him until he'd been around for a few weeks. I got to know him. Well, the him he wanted me to see."

"You did everything you should have in the beginning. You didn't rush in. The trouble is he's a patient con man," Heather said. "You have to forgive yourself, and that starts by walking into the office of Sheriff Nathan Wright and admitting you got conned. The reason you haven't done it is you're punishing yourself, and that has to stop."

Was she punishing herself? Had she gotten so mired in misery that she believed pain was all there was? It felt like it. God, it had been three months since her father died and she still woke up in a panic, wondering if he needed something. She felt guilty enjoying the morning without him.

And she felt the loss like a gaping canyon in her soul.

How had she gotten so stuck? Trapped between grief and relief. Unable to truly feel either.

Heather stared at her for a moment. "Or you can go back to the cabin and sit for a while if you're not ready. It won't fix what's wrong with you. I'm going to tell you something, River. I like you. I'm surprised at how much I like you. It's not something I expected."

"You had expectations?"

"Always," she replied. "I'm that girl. I can't help myself. I meet people and usually can sum them up after a couple of minutes. You're different. I met you and thought there was no way we would be friends. You were cold the first time I met you."

It hadn't been too long ago. At first, River had been reluctant to take on another guide, but then the requests had started coming in. She wasn't sure why, but business had rolled in at the end of summer, more than she and Ty could handle alone. She'd had to send the rafters to another company, but she'd taken every guided hiking job she could. Heather had waltzed in with a pack on her back, worn-in hiking boots, and a smile that she couldn't match. Clients loved Heather. She was a born salesperson. A few months later, River had been able to hire on Andy Cox. She now had a small but reliable crew. "I didn't mean to be cold. Dealing with my father's illness was hard. I was his caregiver most of the time. We had a nurse at the very end, but when you hired on, I was pretty overwhelmed."

Those blue eyes of Heather's softened and she put a hand on River's shoulder. "I know, and now I know how hard that was on you. I wasn't close to my dad. I kind of grew up on my own. It made me a little cold, too, until I met the right guy. And then I screwed up with the right guy and found a total asshole."

Sometimes Heather talked about this amazing man she'd been close to years before and then she moved on to her asshole ex. It was something they had in common. Well, the asshole ex part.

She'd never dated a truly amazing guy. They were all over Bliss, but she always seemed to meet them after they found a woman and settled down. Perhaps that was why she'd fallen so hard for Matt.

River stared at the station house. Half a block and she would be standing in front of it. Another few steps past that and she would be inside, and then she would either have to tell Nate Wright how stupid she'd been or look silly standing there and saying nothing.

"Matt deserves everything the sheriff can do to him," Heather said quietly. "And you deserve some peace. You can't have that while he's out there. How much was it this time?"

If she couldn't admit it to her friend, how would she talk to the sheriff? She was here in Bliss because Nate Wright would be infinitely easier to talk to than any of the other law enforcement officers. Wright was an oddball, a former DEA agent who'd moved to tiny Bliss and married a local sweetheart of a woman. And like many of the men of Bliss, he hadn't married her alone. Bliss was what many people called a town of great tolerance. And what many more people called plain crazy. The fact that the sheriff had a wife he shared with the local bar owner, Zane Hollister, didn't bother her at all. She kind of always wanted to high-five Callie Hollister-Wright for roping in such gorgeous men.

Was she really going to allow her anger at herself to hold her back?

"Matt opened a credit card in my name. I thought it would be over, but he spent five grand and basically sent me the bill." She'd been foolish, and it had bitten her in the ass again and again. She had to stop the bleed. "Before he'd only stolen money, not my identity. If I let him, he'll ruin my credit, and I'm kind of running on that right now."

"I've got a little saved up. I know Ty does, too. He doesn't need a place of his own. He sleeps with a new woman every night to cut down on rent and food," she joked, although with Ty it was kind of true. He was known as the manwhore of the county. "Let us help you. I heard the woman who runs the sheriff's office is also an attorney. She could give you some advice. I'll float you the cash to buy a couple of hours of her time."

39

That was sweet of her, but it wasn't necessary. "I have some. I was careful with the money we had left. I have enough to live meagerly on until the cabin sells." She held up a hand because she'd known this argument was coming. "I know what I'm doing. I'm going to sell and use the cash to rebuild the business. I want us ready for summer tourists next year. I want to start up the rafting tours again and then cross-country skiing tours."

All she needed was one good season and she'd be able to grow. The business. That's what she'd concentrate on. She wasn't going to let Matt fucking Lewis beat her. It was time to take the steps to prove she wasn't defeated.

It was time to convince herself she wasn't so broken she couldn't put herself back together.

"I like the look on your face. You look fierce right now," Heather said. "Are we going in?"

She nodded and started to walk toward that station house. It was easier with Heather by her side. She'd pushed everyone away for the last year and a half. She'd taken all the burden on herself when she didn't have to. Maybe it was also time to lean on her friends.

"And when we're done making Matt Lewis's life a complete hell, we can head to Trio and get drunk off our asses and find a hot tourist and get laid. Separately, of course. Normally I wouldn't have to add in that disclaimer, but there's a lot of sharing going on around here. It's a weird town. I kind of love it." Heather turned her face up to the sun as she walked along.

"I'm not sure about that. The part about getting laid. Bliss is absolutely weird." Getting laid was the last thing she needed. Wasn't it? God, she hadn't had sex in over two years. Her body had been nothing but a machine to perform duties, a robotic tool that didn't feel anything but numb.

"Come on," Heather urged. "I'm buying, boss. And I'll totally vet all the guys who hit on you. The chance of us getting lucky has gone through the roof since this morning. I heard a rumor that there's a film crew in town, and they're all gorgeous. According to what I heard this morning at Stella's, they got in last night and they're staying at that mansion cabin on the river. The one the billionaire guy owns. I can't remember his name."

"Seth Stark. He built it recently, but he spends most of his time in New York with his wife and partner." So much sharing. A film crew? She wasn't sure she was ready for that, but perhaps it was time to open herself up at least to the people around her. "Maybe one drink."

Heather smiled and she could swear the man walking past them tripped as he looked at her. Not that she noticed. "Excellent. We'll deal with Asshole Matt and then party."

In front of them, the door to the station house opened and a truly lovely man stepped out. Six foot plus, broad shoulders, and long lines. He wore a T-shirt that covered his big muscular chest and jeans that showed some mileage. She glanced down at his feet. She could tell a lot about a man by his shoes. Cowboy boots. Worn and likely comfortable. He was a man who worked.

He held a hand out to Nate Wright.

"Wow. Do you think he's part of the film crew?" Because if the rest of them looked like him, every woman in the county would be panting after them.

Heather stopped and suddenly opened her bag. "Damn it. I left my wallet. I'll be right back."

Heather turned and jogged back toward the Trading Post, leaving her standing there alone.

Nate glanced over and nodded her way. "How are you doing today, River? I was just talking about you to our new friend here. He's with a film crew. They need a guide to do some shots out near the Needle."

That was interesting. The Crestone Needle was considered one of the hardest climbs in Colorado. "Are you working on a mountaineering doc? I'm sorry. I didn't introduce myself. River Lee. I own Mountain Adventures."

The gorgeous man's eyes were covered by mirrored aviators, but she still could sense a grimness about him. He shook her hand. "Ezra Fain. Good to meet you. Wright here speaks highly of you. And the nature of our film is…well, let's say I can't talk about it until the producers agree to hire you. We've got a meeting tomorrow morning. We'll be going over a list of guides that might

41

be able to handle us."

Yeah, that didn't sound like she was heavily in the running, but then she was small-time now. They would likely go with one of the big operations, and she couldn't blame them. "I hope you find a good one."

"Nice to meet you." Fain tipped his head and started to walk toward a big Jeep.

She looked up at the sheriff, surprised at how her hands were shaking. This was it. She had to tell him.

"Hey, what's going on?" Nate asked, his eyes softening.

She wasn't going to lose it. God, now that she was standing here, she wondered why she hadn't asked for help in the first place. Was she as controlling as Heather accused her of being? Had she gone so far into her shell that this small piece of daylight was causing her to shake?

There was only one way to find out.

"I screwed up, Nate. I screwed up and now he's making me pay."

The sheriff put a hand on her shoulder, his voice low and gruff. He started to lead her into the station house. "Is this about your ex-husband?"

She had to tell him everything. "I don't think we were legally married. He lied about his name. He lied about everything. He took all my money. Almost everything I had, and now he's still trying to con me."

Nate nodded slowly and turned to the blonde who sat at the desk in the middle of the big room. "Come on into my office. Gemma, we're going to need you."

She followed the sheriff inside and for the first time felt like it might, just might be okay.

Chapter Two

Jax stared overhead at the neon sign. Trio. That was a word that meant three. He was going to have at least three beers. Three beers in an actual bar with people who he didn't live with or who had been carefully vetted.

Women. There were women in there. Women who weren't married to members of McKay-Taggart and Knight. Women who might be looking for a man. He made the decisions tonight. He wasn't locked in a room trying to prove he wasn't going to go insane. Tonight he was just a man. He could pretend he was a normal guy.

A normal, spectacularly horny guy.

Tucker stepped up next to him, looking up at the bright light. "There are women in there."

Tucker was apparently horny, too.

"Yes, there are." Women who had no idea what a fucking freak he was. Women who might believe he was a regular guy.

Tucker leaned over. "How do we decide who gets the woman? Rock, paper, scissors?"

He would pick the one he wanted, toss her over his shoulder, and run away with her. That was the instinct humming through his system. Shit. He remembered what Ariel had told him. His caveman self was wrong. He had to find a modern-man self, and that meant consent. He was supposed to get lots and lots of consent. "I guess we let her choose."

"I think we're supposed to do that." Tucker's lips had kicked up in a grin. He nodded toward the entrance as two large men holding hands with a petite woman led her inside. "Maybe we don't have to choose. I overheard that Henry dude saying something about how everyone here is in a ménage. Except for him. And some rich guy. I think the others don't have enough money to keep a woman on their own."

Tucker hadn't been listening to Ariel. "A woman can keep herself. She's not property. We're not supposed to be overly possessive. We're supposed to be nice and polite and sexually generous."

He could handle the sexually generous part. It was the other two he struggled with. He could be dangerously possessive. Not about material goods. He could give up possessions easily. People he cared about were a totally different thing.

Tucker frowned his way. "Your sessions with Ariel are nothing like mine."

He talked a lot to the therapist about women. It went beyond horny though. He felt like something was missing. Something beyond his memory. He felt disconnected. He would give a lot to feel like he belonged somewhere, somewhere other than his sad-sack band of brothers. It wasn't that he didn't care. It was simply that when he was with them, he had to think about what had happened. The tragedy of losing their memories, of being molded by a mad doctor couldn't be dismissed when he was stuck in a room with his brothers. He wanted to figure out who he was without the grim reality of his life hanging over his head.

And he wanted to have sex with a real woman and not his hand.

"Don't do anything stupid."

There was one thing keeping him from marching into that bar and throwing down with the first woman to consent to throw down with him. Ian Taggart was blocking the door.

"You said we could go out tonight." If Taggart took this away from him, he wasn't sure what he would do. He'd been stuck in that house all day and this was the first deep breath he'd taken. He'd walked out on the porch and been surrounded by trees and clouds and rushing water. He couldn't go back inside. Not tonight.

Taggart crossed his arms over his chest. "And you can. You and Tucker have the night off. I argued against the two of you in particular because it's like asking the blind to lead the insane, but Ezra put you two together. Robert and Owen are researching the site with Henry. Dante and Sasha are taking watch this evening. Don't waste your night off. Hopefully we'll find our guide in a couple of days and then we have to work. I know you've been cooped up, but you have to think about every single thing you do out here in the real world."

Something eased inside Jax. He knew it was only a bar and he'd been to the bar at The Garden, but he felt compelled to go inside, to be out on his own.

To meet someone who didn't look at him with sympathy or pure terror.

Please don't hurt me. Please. I have two kids.

His stomach rolled as the vision flashed across his brain. He hadn't meant to scare the teller at the bank in Madrid. At the time, it had made sense to rob the bank. Mother needed money to continue her research.

He shook the memory off. Sometimes he wondered if getting his memory back would be a good thing. Maybe his real life had been terrible, too.

"We won't do stupid things," Tucker assured the big boss.

Taggart stared at him until Tucker started to squirm.

"We probably won't do stupid things." Tucker didn't sound as sure now.

Tucker was his best friend in the world, and he could be such a dipshit. Jax put a hand on Tucker's shoulder, guiding him around the massive mound of sarcasm. "He knows we're going to do stupid shit." He nodded at Taggart. "We won't get arrested. Probably."

"Now that I believe." Taggart stepped aside. "I'm going to

45

hang out with a crazy dude who believes in aliens and who might or might not be one of the world's top minds when it comes to intelligence. And I think I have to eat beets. So you two be here at midnight or I'll kill you."

That gave him five whole hours. Five hours of freedom.

He strode through the double doors and was hit with the rocking sound of music and laughter, the smell of frying food and fresh beer, the sight of women.

He was so fucking hungry.

Play it cool. Don't let anyone know that you don't remember ever being in a public bar. Don't let anyone know you can't remember if you've ever had sex.

"Hey, you remember about the consent thing, right?" Taggart had followed them in.

It was right on the tip of his tongue to tell the man to go fuck himself, but he gave the boss a calm smile. "I do. I'm not going to kidnap anyone."

"We don't do that anymore," Tucker offered.

Taggart's stare moved between them. "Tucker, I believe. You, I worry about. You think you fool me, Jax. You're incredibly good at acting calm, but I know how pissed off you are. I can't figure out if you'll take it out on a woman or find some peace in one. Try really fucking hard to make it the latter because I don't want to have to kill you."

Yes, this was why Ariel had spent all that time going over consent with him. Everyone worried about his inner beast. Fuck up one guy and suddenly he was a pit bull who might need to be put down.

Okay, so it was more than one guy and he'd put all three of them in the hospital, but he wouldn't hurt a woman.

"I'll try not to make you kill me." And he wouldn't find peace. He would find an orgasm. That was all he wanted. One night outside his cage. Oh, it was a nice cage, but he wasn't free to come and go as he pleased. If he ran, someone would chase him down.

He would take his one night and revel in it.

A big hand came down on his shoulder. "You know what I'm going to say, right?"

He'd had this lecture twice already. "I have condoms."

"Because we're not sure what McDonald did to your sperm, man," Taggart snarked. "Those suckers could be as confused as you are."

He would punch the man, but he'd figured out sarcasm was the only way Taggart knew how to show he gave a damn. He'd noticed recently that Taggart was only a sarcastic asshole to the people he liked. If he didn't like a person, he usually went silent and cold. "See, there you go, boss. My sperm probably doesn't even remember what it's supposed to do. It'll get confused on the way to the egg."

"It'll probably try to impregnate her cervix," Tucker said and then a grim look came over his face. "I'm going to grab us some seats."

Tucker walked away, his head hung low. Shit. His night might take a wrong turn.

Taggart sighed. "You'll have to fix that." He looked up and nodded. "There's my date for the night."

"You Taggart?" A thin man with a trucker hat on his head stepped into the bar. He was older, possibly in his mid-sixties, but the man hadn't let himself go. There was a lean strength in the arm that reached out to shake Tag's hand.

"I am. You must be Mel Hughes. If what I suspect about you is true, it's an honor to meet you." Tag shook the man's hand. "Joh…Henry speaks highly of you."

"And you, too." There was something almost innocent about the older man. Although Jax wasn't sure what the hell was under his trucker cap. It looked metallic, like he'd wrapped his head in foil like a burrito and then shoved his hat over it. Weird.

Taggart followed behind the guy with the tin foil and Jax heard them talking about patrolling, but only after Tag had…something about beets. It looked like the boss was going to have a special night. And he was going to spend his night dealing with his crazy, haunted brother. Damn it.

It sucked that the cervix was what did it. He'd been planning on bumping up against one of those things tonight, but no, Tucker had to get all freaked out because he might or might not be evil.

47

He glanced around the small space. Tucker had taken up a barstool and shook his head at the big, dark-haired man behind the counter.

"You do not wish to be drinking? Because you look like man who need to drink."

That was one thick Russian accent. What the hell was a Russian doing in the middle of small-town Colorado? Every instinct Jax had went on full alert. The Agency wasn't the only intelligence group that would love to get their hands on one of McDonald's experiments. The formula had been lost, but it could potentially be hiding deep inside their bodies.

"Maybe a beer," Tucker was saying. "It won't help. Sometimes I wish I could forget all over again."

He was going to murder his brother. He slid onto the barstool next to Tucker. "Seriously?" He turned to the big Russian. "My brother is joking. He's got a memory like a steel trap."

The Russian frowned and leaned forward. "You are not men we're supposed to protect? Keep voices to the lowdown because many ears here. Walls thin. Trust me, I hear every time boss tries to make new baby in his office."

Jax frowned. "I thought we were supposed to be undercover. Now the random bartender knows. Is that why you're doing that crazy Russian accent?"

The Russian looked around. No one was sitting at the bar yet, though there were several booths taken up by couples and families. He seemed to think it was okay to speak more openly. "I have crazed Russian accent because I am from Russia. My name is Alexei Markov. You might know my cousin. I speak much better English than Nikolai."

"Nick?" Nick Markovic was on the London team. He'd known Nick for almost as long as he'd been able to remember. And Nick spoke way better English.

"Yes, Nicky is my cousin. He go into intelligence when he graduate. I go into mob." Alexei held a hand up. "I am no longer mafia man. I am family man. I kill man who kill my brother and now I tends to the bar and to my wife, Holly. She require much tending. I leave bad life but Nicky ask that I help watch over the boys who got lost."

"I didn't get lost. Someone fucked with my brain," Jax replied, bitterness creeping into his soul. Why had they been forced to stay in all day if everyone knew who they were and what had happened to them? He wanted one person who didn't look at him with nauseating sympathy. One person who saw him as a man and not some victim who needed to be protected. Or a bomb waiting to go off. "So the whole bar knows? I suppose that's why we're allowed to be here."

Alexei's dark head shook. "No. Only a few people be knowing. Nicky ask to bring me in because of trust between us. Mayor knows and deputy and sheriff. I was asked to not tell partner, but you will likely meet him anyway. He is doctor. Many people shot here in Bliss. Caleb is good man. He will fix you up when bullets hit. Would you like beer, too?"

At least it wasn't everyone. Jax nodded. "Yeah. A lager."

They'd spent most of their time since their release figuring out things like what beer they liked and what they wanted on a pizza and that *Firefly* should never have been canceled. That was the sum total of his knowledge of the world.

Of course, Tucker had learned something he wished he hadn't.

Alexei turned and moved to pour their beers. The music changed to a slightly louder, rocking country song about someone's tractor. It made it easier for them to talk. He had to get Tucker in a better mood or he'd spend all night morose and worried. Tucker's angst wasn't going to ruin his night.

Jax leaned in. "You're not some kind of evil supervillain."

Tucker stared mulishly forward. "That's not the rumor I've heard."

Five months before, Tucker had been taken on an op with Brody Carter. It had ended in a firefight between McKay-Taggart, the Ukrainian mob, and a bunch of Dutch mercenaries, but before the bullets had gone flying one of the men on the mercenary side had recognized Tucker. The mercenary had called Tucker Dr. Razor because "he cut so deep." Tucker had been morose every since, guilt eating him up inside. "He was probably lying. He would have said anything to get Taggart to not murder him. Have you thought about that?"

"I've gone through every possible scenario. I can't not think about it." Tucker shook his head. "That mercenary knew me. No other explanation makes sense. I know everything about the human body. Did you know what a cervix is? How many single men know what that is?"

"I read about it," Jax admitted. "Penny said something to Ariel about her baby nearly ruining her cervix and I looked it up. Don't do that on the Internet. Some weird shit comes up. Maybe that's why you know."

Tucker leaned in, his voice going low. "And how would I know the heart has four chambers, the right and left atriums and ventricles? The right atrium pulls in oxygen-poor blood and sends it to the right ventricle. The right ventricle sends that blood to the lungs. The left atrium takes the now oxygen-rich blood and pumps it into the left ventricle, that sends it back out to the body. Who besides a doctor knows that shit?"

"People who watch a lot of medical shows, maybe." He wasn't sure how to deal with this. They should have sent Robert with Tucker. Robert was good with all the touchy-feely crap. "Or maybe you've got an evil twin out there somewhere. Maybe he's Dr. Razor and he hated your ass because you were all sunny and shit and that's how you ended up in Mother…McDonald's lab. Have you thought of that?"

Tucker turned, his face freezing in that constipated look he got when he was thinking hard. "An evil twin. You know that would explain everything. He would hate me because I got all the girls and I was probably smarter than he was. Mom definitely liked me more. We both got medical degrees, but I probably had a way better residency than he did."

Excellent. Maybe he could get the night back on track. Not that it appeared there were a ton of good prospects in here, and by good prospects he meant a woman desperate enough to want to possibly sleep with him. All he had to do was convince Tucker that it was a good thing there was an evil copy of him out there somewhere who had betrayed him and given him up for torturous medical experiments and probably wouldn't show up sometime to

50

do it all over again. "See, there are multiple explanations for what that asshole said."

Tucker seemed to calm, his normally sunny air coming back to him. "Yeah. Or that asshole could have been making it up. Or McDonald might have kidnapped me because she thought it would be cool to have another doctor on the team, but she couldn't break me and that's why she erased my memory."

Or he'd been another human being in another life, one who'd done terrible things and for whom this new start was a blessing.

Jax often wondered what things he'd done in his past, wondered if he'd be walking down the street one day and someone would attempt to make him pay for a crime he couldn't remember committing. Or one of the ones he did.

Alexei placed two beers in front of them. "Here you be going. Beer is good for making the bad things seem not so bad. And relax. I am here to watch out for you."

"Are you here to make sure I don't do stupid shit?" Because he really wanted to do stupid shit.

Alexei shrugged. "I am here to make sure you are safe and that no one runs off with you who would like to slice you into small pieces and study those pieces. This is bad way to go. And very messy. I am to keep from making mess."

"But are you to keep us from getting laid?" Jax was willing to speak the guy's language.

Tucker sat up straighter. "Wait, now I was told the only thing I wasn't supposed to do was stupid things. Getting laid isn't stupid, and Candyee told me I was getting good at it."

Candyee, with the double e's. It summed up her name and her bra size. "That's his favorite hooker. Big Tag gave him a hooker allowance after he saved a bunch of people."

Because this version of Tucker was good. This version of Tucker sacrificed for the people around him. Shouldn't that be the only thing that mattered now?

Alexei nodded. "This is good to be knowing, but you should also know there are only nice ladies here. None of them will accept the monies. Give them orgasms and they will be happy. But first you must be seeing doctor."

"We passed all the tests." He wasn't waiting. "And Dante's syphilis cleared right up. I wish there was an antibiotic for his perpetual bad mood."

The door opened and Jax heard the sound of a woman laughing. He turned on his chair, taking in the newcomers.

The laughing woman was tall and blonde, her hair back in a ponytail, but it would likely brush the tops of her impressive breasts. She was tall and gorgeous, and he liked the sound of her laugh and that generous smile on her face.

So why did his eyes move to her shorter friend, the one who smiled, but it didn't come close to reaching her eyes? She wasn't as glamorous as the blonde. Her dark hair was cut in a sensible bob and she wore a plain T-shirt, jeans, and sneakers. She hadn't dressed for a man. She'd dressed to be comfortable. Her eyes came up and he felt like someone had kicked him straight in the gut.

Clear green eyes. Eyes like the forest he'd stared at all day.

"Who is she?" He heard himself ask the question, but he didn't take his eyes off the woman with dark brown hair and a whole world in her eyes.

"Her name is Heather Turner. She guides the wilderness so bear do not be eating her clients," Alexei said.

"What?" Tucker shook his head.

"She's a nature guide." He was starting to understand the Russian. Maybe it was all the time he'd spent with Nick.

"She works with River. River has been guiding the nature for many years. Heather comes to Bliss a few months ago, but they seem to be friends. Heather is fun girl. You will like. Hello, Heather." Alexei waved and the blonde waved back.

"Not that one. The other one," Jax corrected, his eyes still on her. She seemed to have noticed his stare and like a pretty rabbit who figured out a wolf had caught her scent, she'd stopped and stared back. Those eyes looked at him, widening in something akin to recognition.

"Her name is River," Alexei offered. "I don't know you should try to play with her. She has…what is phrase? Been through many sufferings."

He hopped off his stool as she turned from him and followed

the blonde. "I'm merely going to introduce myself."

Tucker was right behind him. "Wait. Are you telling me I get the blonde? Because that works for me. She's fucking gorgeous."

"You can have her. Give her your best shot, buddy." He watched as his prey practically ran away. She moved toward the booths at the back of the bar, passing him without a single look.

Until she got to the booth her friend selected, then she turned and their eyes met again and she sent him the slightest smile.

That smile sealed her fate because there was no way he would let her out of his trap. He would have her. He would be good to her. He would do everything he could to bring her pleasure, but she would be his tonight.

It was time to do something stupid.

* * * *

Heather leaned out of the booth, looking back toward the bar. "Yep, he's still looking this way."

River took a deep breath because she'd just seen the most stunning man. Tall, muscular, with sandy blond hair and green eyes and a jawline so straight she could probably cut herself on it. And scruff. He had gorgeous scruff that would feel perfect on her skin, tickly and arousing. That man had to be the star of whatever film the crew was shooting. She didn't recognize him from a movie or TV show, but there was no way he wasn't an actor or a model. The camera would love him.

Which was an excellent reason to stay away. She could think of another couple of reasons including the fact that she had terrible taste in men. She was in the middle of a legal fight with her asshole ex and didn't need another man who would use her. She'd just lost her father and she wasn't in a good emotional place. She needed to concentrate on her business.

Lots of reasons to not even think about the sexy man.

But the most serious reason was that he hadn't been looking at her. He'd obviously been staring at Heather. Lots of men did. Heather stopped traffic. It had been wishful thinking that made her believe for a second she'd been the target of that completely lustful stare.

His stare had gone straight to her pussy. She'd stood in the doorway for a moment and she'd felt stalked. But in a good way, in a way that led to something she hadn't felt in forever—pleasure.

"Are you going to go talk to him?" She asked Heather. It might be for the best. After her long discussion with the sheriff, she was ready to go home and stare for a while. She wouldn't even turn on the TV, just stare at it and maybe down a bottle of cheap wine and pass out on her couch. That seemed like a proper way to end another terrible day.

But Heather had shown up a few minutes after she'd started her confession and she'd held River's hand while she'd told the sheriff and the lawyer about how she'd gotten herself into trouble and then more trouble by ignoring the first round of trouble. Heather had been there the whole time and it had taken hours and hours. When she'd asked if they could head over to Trio for dinner and drinks, River hadn't had the heart to tell her no.

If Hottie McHotterson showed up at their table and wanted to spend some time with her gloriously beautiful friend, she could ease her way out and head home.

Or she would have to play Heather's wingman. She was fairly certain she'd seen a second man beside the first, though it was hard to see anyone but him. Would she end up getting stuck with fending off Hottie's friend's advances?

"I'll certainly talk to him if he talks to me. It's rude if you don't," Heather allowed, settling back in. "He's talking to his friend. They look super serious. You don't think they're fighting over who gets who?"

Yep, that's what she thought. They were arguing over who got to hit on Heather. Whoever lost that small but meaningful battle would be left with her, and it would almost certainly be the other guy because Hottie was definitely the alpha male.

"I don't think I want company tonight." Was she being selfish? What if Heather wanted company?

Heather sat back. "Then I'll tell them to go away, but are you sure? That man is hot. He looks like he could do some damage, and in a good way. When was the last time you got well and truly laid?"

She felt her cheeks heat. "A long time, and I spent the afternoon dealing with the repercussions of that truly bad decision. I couldn't handle Matt. I seriously doubt either of those two are attracted to me. The last thing I need is another man who sleeps with me when he's not really interested in my body."

Not that her body was all that bad. It fully functioned. It walked. It ran when it had to. It kept her perfectly upright most of the time.

But it seemed like forever since it tensed and then released because the pleasure was so much she couldn't handle another second. Forever since she'd felt hands on her, moving and exploring, touching and letting her know even for the briefest of moments that she wasn't alone. The longest time since she'd lain back as her body pulsed in afterglow.

When she sold her cabin, she was buying a big bad vibrator. She would name it and have a long, happy relationship with that sucker.

"I think you're being pessimistic. Oh, I know you have reasons for it, but if you sit too long in the muck, the muck starts to seem normal." Heather leaned over, putting a hand on hers. "I know where you are. A couple of years ago, I was in this great relationship. I was madly in love. We got married and everything looked perfect. But something went wrong on a job."

"He was a guide, too?" She had to admit, she was intensely interested in Heather's past. Sometimes the gorgeous blonde would stand and stare at the mountains and she would seem so far away. Like she was lost in memory and didn't want to come back.

She nodded. "Yeah. He and his brother. I made a bad call on a rafting expedition. You ever run the Lochsa?"

The Lochsa was a river in Idaho. It was known for its explosive rapids. The river had rapids that ran into other rapids, making for an unending wild ride. It was only for the most experienced of paddlers. It was far from the gentle section of the Rio Grande she used for family expeditions. "Yeah, I know it."

"It had been raining heavily. He didn't want us to go on the river that day, but the sun came out and I decided it was worth the risk. His brother died. He's never forgiven me." Heather frowned. "I probably should have told you that."

The incident hadn't been in her records. River had to wonder how long ago it had been because the references Heather had produced had all been outstanding. "I can see why you wouldn't. I suspect you aren't as reckless now."

She laughed, though it was a rueful sound. "Not in my work but in other ways, I suspect I still am. I told you about the massive mistake I made after my divorce, right?"

They'd bonded over their terrible taste in men. "Yes. But can I point out that he didn't steal every dime you had?"

"Nope, but he's in the business, too, and he made my ex's life miserable. Still does. My point is I know how hard it is to crawl your way out of depression and anger. It's like rapids. You get caught in one and it takes you off course. For a while you don't notice if you aren't careful and then you have to fight your way back or find yourself in a worse position. You're there, River. Are you going to drift off or fight your way back?"

Heather's words sent a shaft of pain through her. Why was everything a fight? It was a child's question. Every moment was a fight. Life was made up of survival and work broken up by moments of peace. But how could she enjoy the peace if she didn't have the fight?

"Ladies, I be bringing gift to you." Alexei Markov stood with a plate in his hand. The big bartender was gorgeous, but then Bliss tended to attract incredibly lovely men. They also tended to be taken, as this one was.

Heather glanced up. "A gift?"

"The mens at bar asked me to send this to you." Alexei placed a massive mound of cheese fries in front of them. "I tell them most mens send women drinks, but they use word *consent* very much."

River laughed, really laughed for the first time in forever. It was good to know Me Too had hit southern Colorado. They'd sent cheese fries as their lure to catch a date for the evening.

Heather's eyes were practically glowing in the dim light. "There's no way we can eat all of this."

"I think they were counting on it," she replied. She wasn't

ready for this. But when would she be? If she never got back out there, Matt won. When she thought about it, not dating was akin to letting the terrorists win.

Not that it would be a date. It would be a lot of watching the hottest man she'd ever met hit on her friend. She hoped Hottie's friend was fun to talk to.

"Alexei, could you invite them over?" She was going to be brave, if only for her friend's sake.

The big Russian walked off and it wasn't more than a minute before they were standing at the booth.

He took her breath away. She glanced down at his feet. Boots, but they weren't the flashy kind worn to show off how much cash a man had. These were well worn, subtle. They were working shoes, like the jeans he wore. Nothing ripped or torn and yet she could tell he'd worn them down to soft denim.

"Hello. I'm Jax." His voice was deep but there was a musical quality to it. She would bet he could sing. "This is my brother, Tucker."

Brothers. They oddly didn't look a lot alike, but she'd seen siblings who she would never have guessed came from the same parents. Tucker wasn't bad himself. Dark, wavy hair any woman would love to have. It was slightly overgrown but did nothing but enhance his male-model beauty. He seemed far softer than his incredibly masculine friend.

Her first impression of Jax hadn't been false. He was broad and muscular, his face defined by stark planes and lines. He looked predatory and hungry.

She could barely breathe. Maybe this was a mistake. She would have a hard time watching this gorgeous man fawn all over Heather. Something about him pulled her in, made her want to forget that she had terrible taste in men. It was like there was some invisible tether connecting her to him.

Except that was stupid because he couldn't be here for her.

"I'm Heather and my very quiet friend's name is River." Heather was smiling that ridiculously sunny smile of hers, the one no man could resist. "Thanks for the fries. You know normally men send over drinks. I'm glad you're so concerned with consent.

57

That's very forward thinking of you."

Tucker shook his head. "We're not allowed to have sex without consent. Do we need a note? Like a contract?"

Jax jabbed an elbow in his brother's ribs. "He's being a weirdo and moving way, way too fast. Sorry about that. He doesn't get out much."

Tucker frowned and said something under his breath that sounded like *neither do you*, but then a sweet smile came over his face. "Sorry. Sometimes my jokes fall flat. Can we please join you? We're in town for a week or so and besides the Russian dude, we haven't met anyone."

"Sure." Heather slid over.

River did the same, expecting Tucker to slide in, but it was Jax's big body that moved beside her. She felt tiny compared to him. She watched as Heather grinned her way as though to say *you were wrong*.

Tucker sat beside Heather and started passing out the small plates.

Jax probably wanted to be able to look at Heather. That was it.

God, he smelled good. She kind of wanted to lean over and run her nose along his shoulder and up his neck. He smelled like soap and fresh pine.

"Can I get you some? I like French fries but they're even better with cheese and bacon. I think maybe everything is better with cheese and bacon, but if you want something else, I'll get it for you. You can have anything on the menu. And I'll buy the wine or beer or whatever. I merely wanted you to understand I don't want to get drunk tonight. I would rather get to know you."

She turned, expecting to see Jax staring across at Heather. Nope. Those stunning green eyes were staring at her expectantly. He had a plate in his hand as though waiting for her permission to serve her.

Her. He was looking at her.

"She does talk," Heather said. "I've heard her and everything."

"Yeah, I would love some." She was hungry, actually. She could take the bacon off. The rest of it was perfectly vegetarian. It was odd. Her stomach kind of rumbled, but in a good way. For the last year and a half it seemed she'd lost her appetite and had to force herself to eat, but tonight she smelled the fries and cheese and wanted.

And she wanted him, too. She wasn't going to lie to herself. This time she would be smart. If he turned out to be a nice guy, she might spend the night with him. Might. And then she would send him on his way because he was a tourist.

She wouldn't fall for him because she wouldn't spend more than a night.

He used his fork to put a thick stack of cheese fries on her plate. "I hope you like them. What do you do for a living? I work in tech for the most part. A little security on the side."

He actually looked interested in her answer. "I'm a nature guide."

His eyes widened. "Seriously? That's sounds interesting. Tell me about that."

She sat back and talked about something other than misery and death for the first time in forever.

Chapter Three

Jax looked out at the tiny cabin in front of him. River's Jeep was open aired, it not being cold enough to put the "top up," as she'd explained. When winter came she would put the hard top on the vehicle, but until then she liked the open air.

He did, too. God, he loved it. He loved the way she drove and the fact that he could turn his head up and see a million stars blinking in the velvet sky above. He'd loved the wind against his hand when he'd stretched it out.

He felt so fucking free.

Beyond that he felt something for the woman beside him. Something he'd never felt before and he wasn't exactly sure what it was. It had caused him to follow her out of Trio when he knew damn well he shouldn't. He was supposed to stay with Tucker until Robert came to pick them up in a couple of hours. He wasn't sure how he would get back, but it didn't matter. He wanted more time with her. He wanted to be alone with her.

River. He even liked her name.

"This place is beautiful," he said when she hesitated.

She nodded but didn't move from her seat. "I love it here. I went to college in Denver, but I always missed this place. When I was younger, my dad had a house in Creede. He started the business there, but when he could, he moved us out of town. My dad was a loner, I suppose. Creede has a population of four hundred and Dad thought that was way too many people."

"I know the feeling. I lived in London for a while. That was definitely too many people." He kept his tone even. It was odd. Now that he was here, that hunger he always felt was tempered by her fear. He'd thought he would take anything offered to him, but he couldn't having met her. If the blonde had offered herself up, he would have turned her down. Over the two hours they'd sat in the booth, eating fried food and drinking beer, he'd figured something out. Some people were more special than others. River was special. He should be more cynical. He could hear Damon Knight telling him to be cautious, but he couldn't make himself do it. Perhaps it was the fact that he didn't have a long well of history to draw from and to teach him that this was likely a mistake.

It didn't feel like a mistake.

"Wow. I've never been farther than Kansas City." She still wasn't moving and her voice had taken on a tremulous tone.

His heart constricted, and it was surprisingly easy to not listen to his dick. His dick was pleading with him to get aggressive. His dick was trying to convince him that if he could get inside her, she would accept him.

Yeah, he wasn't going to listen to his dick.

"If you've changed your mind, I can call my brother to pick me up. I have a phone and so does he. His number is programmed in. I don't want to scare you. I had a good time talking to you tonight. It was one of the nicest nights I've had in a long time." Ever. It was the best night ever. It was the first night he felt normal, though he wasn't exactly sure what that word meant. Comfortable was a better one. That tight feeling in his chest had eased as he'd sat in the booth with River and Tucker and Heather.

Although he'd hated lying to her.

She finally turned, looking at him. Her eyes shone in the moonlight. "You mean that, don't you?"

He wanted to touch her. He'd had to force his hands not to move toward her all night long. The most he'd allowed himself

61

was to have their hips and shoulders touch as they'd sat next to each other. He'd decided it had been a good thing he'd sat next to her because he was fairly certain he had a case of Big Tag's crazy eyes, and she would have seen them had he sat across from her.

"I do mean it. Please don't get me wrong. I want you. I would like nothing more in the world than to take you into that cabin, lay you out, and make a feast of you. I want to kiss you and when I say that I don't merely mean your lips. I want to put my mouth all over your body. But more than I want that, I want you to like me." It was important somehow. He wouldn't see her after tonight, but he couldn't stand the idea that she was afraid of him.

Everyone was afraid of him. Everyone he knew was waiting for his powder keg to blow, but he'd sworn to himself earlier in the evening that it wouldn't blow around her. He would protect her even if it was only for one night.

"I'm not afraid. I'm nervous. I haven't done this in a long time. Not the one-night thing. I've never actually done that. It's the sex thing I haven't done in a while. We were coming back here for sex, right?"

Yep, his dick was trying to take over again. "Only if you want it. River, this is about you. I'll take anything you're willing to give me. If you would refer back to my previous monologue about my mouth on you, you'll understand my motivations. But again, this goes only as far as you want it to go. If all you want is a kiss, I'll be happy to provide it."

What she wouldn't know was this would be his first kiss. Unlike some of his brothers, he hadn't played around with the women at The Garden. There had been a sympathy to the encounters he couldn't stand. It overrode even his horniness. Not that the others seemed to mind. Not all of them, of course. Robert hadn't touched a woman because he was far too interested in Ariel, but the rest had all found women to comfort them.

Jax didn't want comfort. He wanted something more. He wanted…connection.

Beyond that, he wanted a woman to want him, and not because she felt sorry for him.

River had no idea what he'd been through. River didn't

understand how damaged he was. If she let him take her to bed…that was the problem. The word *let*. He didn't want her to *let* him do anything. He wanted her to want him to do all those things that had gone through his head, all the nasty, hot, brilliant things he wanted to do to her.

"I wouldn't mind spending the night with you, but it won't go anywhere."

It couldn't go anywhere. "I'm only in town for a few weeks. And honestly, I have work to do while I'm here. I can't promise you more than tonight."

He'd wanted her to know something real about himself, so he'd broken from their cover story. He'd told her what he actually did. Not that he was a professional train wreck, but that he worked in security and with computers. He'd then avoided talking much about it because he'd been more interested in her.

He'd discovered she'd been through a bad divorce and the loss of her father, though she'd only briefly mentioned them.

She seemed to think for a moment. "I'd like for you to come in. I'm going to be honest with you. I'm hesitant because I'm not sure why you're here."

"I thought I covered that with the mouth on you speech. My dick is interested, too."

She laughed, finally turning to him. "You're an odd man."

So she'd noticed. It hadn't stopped her from inviting him back to her place. He gave the excuse Taggart had told him to give. "I was homeschooled."

She shook her head. "I've known many homeschooled kids. Somehow they turned out normal." But she was laughing. She sobered suddenly as though remembering she shouldn't laugh. "I meant I don't know why you would pick me."

"What does that mean?"

She frowned. "You know."

He shook his head. "No, I don't. If I knew I wouldn't have asked the question."

She stared at him like she was trying to figure something out. Maybe why he was so socially awkward. That could be what that stare was about. He was fairly certain she would run if he explained the situation to her.

Well, River, I'm awkward because I'm basically a few years old. I was born into the body of a horny, apparently picky asshole who can't remember anything past how to rob a bank and play around on the Dark Web. The only people who could have taught me how to function in society are all sarcastic ex-military dicks, so here I am, perfectly incapable of being a normal human being.

Yeah, he wasn't going to say that. He was going to be patient and wait.

"You're gorgeous and I'm not," she said. "That's what bugs me. I've never had a man who looks like you come on to me, and it makes me question why you're here with me instead of Heather. I can see you with her. Not me."

"I wasn't attracted to Heather." He had no idea how to deal with this. How did he prove he was attracted to her?

She gave him that look he'd realized meant someone thought he'd said something dumb. "Everyone is attracted to Heather."

"I barely saw her. I understand that she's pretty, but I wanted you." This was a conundrum. "I don't know how to make you believe me. I paid attention to you the whole time. I tried to be courteous and attentive. Was I supposed to do something else? If you tell me what to do, I can probably do it."

She stared at him for a moment more and he was convinced she would turn the engine over and drive him right back into town. Instead she turned and slid out of the Jeep, grabbing her purse and walking around to the passenger side. She stopped in front of him.

"You're right. I'm making things difficult and it's not your fault. You've done absolutely everything you could to make the evening nice for me, and I'm letting old wounds keep me from trying something new. I'm nervous and awkward and I think the only thing to do is for you to kiss me."

A flash of desire sparked through his body. Kiss her. He could do that. He'd watched people kissing. His last "home" had been a freaking BDSM club. He'd watched people fucking. He'd just never done it himself. He slid off the seat and stood in front of her, almost no space between them. "I'm nervous, too."

"Why would you be nervous?"

"It's been a long time since I did this, too."

"Sure, it has."

She was frustrating. "Why do you think I'm a liar?"

"Because…" She shook her head. "Because I have a hard time taking people at face value. Because I have to sell this cabin. This is going to be one of my last nights here and it's all because I trusted the wrong man and he took everything from me. I'm sorry. I guess I'm not ready for this. You don't deserve someone who can't ever trust you."

"Can you trust me to kiss you? Or maybe it would be better for you to kiss me. I meant what I said. I don't want to take more than you're willing to give. Kiss me. See if you want me. See if this is something you're willing to risk one single night on." He wasn't giving up without a fight. Certainly not because someone out there had hurt her. He wasn't going to hurt her.

"You would do that for me? Let me be in control?"

It would be difficult, but he could handle it. Hell, it might cover some of his awkwardness. His cock was up for the challenge. His cock had begun a low throb in his jeans. Fuck, he wanted her. He'd never wanted anything as badly as he wanted to walk inside that cabin with her, and given that there had been days he'd wanted his torture to stop, that was saying something. "Yes. Anything you want, and we'll stop if you tell me to."

God, he hoped she didn't want to stop. It might kill him, but he was determined to make this good for her. She was confusing and he still couldn't take his eyes off her. He had no idea what it was about this woman that called to him. Though perhaps it was the sorrow he'd sensed in her, as though like called to like. As though if he could put their pain together, it would be eased in both of them.

She reached out and her hand found his, the connection so warm he nearly sighed. "Come inside."

He followed her up the steps, watched as she took out a key and opened the single lock. The door was flimsy, utterly incapable of keeping anyone out. He could kick it in easily. He glanced around. There weren't any other cabins out this far. They'd driven

65

down a long path to get from the highway to the cabin. She was completely alone out here. "I think you need better security."

"From the bears?" She flipped the light on and closed the door behind him. She put her purse down. "Because that's about all you'll see out here. Across the river it's all national forest land. Sometimes during the winter wolves find their way across, but not often. I can handle myself out here, Jax."

He still didn't like the idea that she was out here all alone. Not that he could do anything about it. He had one night with her.

Unless he could see her again. He would get his mission guidelines and then he didn't see why he had to stay holed up in the house. Surely there would be other nights. Unless they found the site quickly and moved out, and then he wouldn't see her ever again.

Which would be the best thing for her. He was a wanted man, and she could be in danger if she got caught up in his life.

"Sorry. In London we had security procedures."

She cocked an eyebrow as she looked up at him. "Really. That sounds fancy."

He doubted the big, burly ex-SAS men who vetted every single person who came in and out of The Garden would like being called fancy. "My boss there was kind of paranoid." He looked around the small space. There was a couch and a thick area rug covering the wood floors. To his right he could see the kitchen and a hallway that likely led to her bedroom. "This place is nice. It's sad you have to sell it."

The light in her eyes dimmed and he wished he hadn't mentioned that again. "Yeah, I wish I didn't have to either, but I don't want to talk about that now. I want to forget everything for a while."

"I want that, too." He wanted to forget that he'd forgotten, to forget all the things he didn't know, and feel like he was more than half a man for one night. "I'm going to sit down on your couch. When you're ready, come and sit with me and we can talk or kiss or touch all you like. I want you, River. I want you very badly. You can't know how much."

He moved into her small living room, settling himself on the couch. It was leather and comfortably worn in. There was a lounge chair beside it, the only two pieces of furniture in the room. Between the chair and couch sat a small table with a lamp and the remote to the TV. He was surprised how nervous he was. He'd faced down some bad shit and not had his heart race the way it was now.

Because he hadn't cared. When he'd had a gun in his face, he hadn't cared if the man on the other side pulled the trigger. He hadn't cared if Dr. McDonald got the dosage wrong and he never woke up. He hadn't cared if the building fell down around him that night Taggart had raided.

He cared that she liked him. He cared that she enjoyed the time she spent with him. Damn, but he cared that he got to touch her, to taste her. Not some random female. Her.

She turned and moved toward him, taking a deep breath as though girding herself to do something. He thought she would move to his side, but she stood in front of him and then lowered herself onto his lap.

He let his arm wind around her waist and prayed she didn't notice how hard he'd gotten. His dick had gone on full alert. Soft. She was soft in his arms, her weight comforting to him. He could easily pick her up and take her wherever he wanted. He was bigger and stronger on every physical level, but she'd placed herself on his lap. She'd made the choice to try with him.

He couldn't take his eyes off her. He had no idea what had happened to make her think she wasn't sexy, but he intended to fix that. "I want you to kiss me."

She twisted in his lap, her ass moving against his dick. Her hands came up, framing his face, and she leaned in. Soft lips brushed his own, sending pure electricity through his system. He closed his eyes and let the feeling flash through him while River gently kissed him. He followed her lead, somehow synching with her movements. His hand tightened on her waist, pulling her closer. Her breasts brushed against his chest and he could feel his cock pulsing with need.

It was going to have to wait because he wanted to enjoy this. He wanted this to last all night long. Over and over she brushed her lips against his, the sensation arousing and frustrating because he wanted more.

He wanted her tongue rubbing against his like a cat in heat. He wanted to take over and show her how good he could make it. She didn't feel sexy? When he found the right spot, he could make her *know* she was sexy. He could learn her body so well he would know exactly how to touch her to make her scream out his name.

Instinct was sweet. He might not remember having sex before, but his body knew what to do. His body was heating up, going primal.

"I want to touch you." He whispered the words against her mouth, practically breathing them into her.

"Okay." She was breathy.

"Do you know how soft you feel to me?" He let his hand run up her arm, finding his way to her neck.

She rested her cheek against his. "I don't know that I want to be soft. I need to be strong."

"Just because something is soft doesn't mean it isn't strong. Soft is nothing but the opposite of hard and, River, opposites attract." He lifted his hips slightly, not wanting to hide his erection anymore. She was here in his arms and she should know exactly how much he wanted her.

She gasped and then moved her head back, looking at him with those deep green eyes. "I think I would like for you to kiss me now. I was afraid I couldn't handle you, but I can and that means I want to know how Jax Seaborne kisses."

He had no idea, but he was more than willing to find out. He pulled her close and got ready to find out exactly how good life could be.

* * * *

It was his sweetness that did it, that made her give over to him. She knew what she liked and it wasn't to be in control. She wanted him to take control. Not because she wasn't a feminist, because she was wired that way, wired to enjoy having a man dominate her sexually and not anywhere else.

It was precisely why she should have walked away from Matt and quickly. Matt's desire had been nothing like this. It had been a lazy thing, an afterthought. At the time she'd believed it had been normal, but this…oh, this felt real. This felt primal and exciting. This felt like everything.

It was how odd and awkward Jax could be that drew her in. Someone that gorgeous should have had practically everything handed to him on a silver platter—especially women. He should know exactly how to seduce the woman of his choice, but Jax just laid it all out there, no hiding behind flirtation, no trying to disguise what he wanted.

She wasn't sure she could believe he was real. She might wake up and find out the whole day had been a dream, but she was going to stay asleep as long as she could because she hadn't felt this good in… She'd never felt like this.

His arm around her tightened and his free hand moved to cup her jaw as he started to kiss her. He moved slowly at first, a slight hesitance. And then she could feel his confidence take over, his mouth moving more surely. She wrapped her arms around him, loving how warm his body was against hers. He surrounded her, trapping her in the cage of his arms, but it was a cage she had zero interest in breaking free of.

The kiss deepened, his tongue running over her bottom lip. A shiver went through her. She opened her mouth and felt his excitement as he took the territory she'd ceded. His tongue invaded, dominating hers and turning the kiss wild. His arousal fed hers, sending desire through her body and silencing all those questions going through her brain. This was exactly what she needed. She needed to stop thinking and let him take her some place she'd never been to before. Like a hike through a virgin forest. No one else could know what it meant to be here in this moment with him. No matter what happened later, she would always have this night.

One last sweet memory from the cabin she'd grown up in.

"I want to touch you. I want to feel your skin against mine." He whispered the words against her cheek between kisses that trailed toward her neck.

The open honesty made it easy for her to agree. She leaned back, drawing her T-shirt over her head. She wore a plain cotton bra and wished she owned something sexier, but she was a utilitarian kind of girl. It didn't seem to bother Jax. His eyes were hot as he stared boldly at her breasts.

"You are the most beautiful thing I've ever seen."

She shouldn't believe him. He was merely trying to get into her panties, but something about his reverent tone made her toss aside her cynicism. "You're not bad yourself, Jax. I suspect you're going to be gorgeous without your clothes on."

His face went blank and he stared at something over her shoulder as though he couldn't meet her eyes. He was silent for a moment and worry crept back into her before he spoke again. "I have scars. I didn't think about that. I didn't think you would see them. Now that I say the words out loud, I realize how foolish it was to think that. Of course you'll see them if I take off my shirt."

The words sounded dull coming out of his mouth. She hated how blank his eyes had gotten. "I don't mind a few scars. I have scars." She pointed to a small line across her collarbone. "I got this one when I was twelve. I was riding on this dirt bike my dad got me for my birthday. I wasn't paying attention, clotheslined myself on a low hanging branch from a pine tree. I've got more on my legs, and a pretty nasty one on my back."

"I don't want you to see me like that. I don't want you to pity me."

How bad was it? What had happened to him? She wanted to press him but remembered how good he'd been with her. She moved so he couldn't not look into her eyes. "You don't have to do anything you don't want to. Leave your shirt on or we can turn out the lights. But you don't have to. I want to see you however you are. I think you're gorgeous. Even if your body is a mass of scars, I'll still think you're beautiful."

He was back to looking at her breasts. That was a good thing. The hollow look in his eyes had gutted her. Lust was way better. "How about we agree to not talk about them? The scars, I mean. I would rather think about you. But if they scare you, if you change your mind, I'll understand."

He tugged his shirt free from his jeans and dragged it overhead, exposing his torso. He tossed the shirt to the side. The light from the lamp illuminated his skin, giving a golden glow to the evidence of his pain.

She had to stop her jaw from dropping. His chest…his muscular chest was covered in vicious scars. It didn't look like there was an inch of his skin that hadn't been harmed. Were those burns?

"My back is worse," he admitted quietly.

How had he gotten those scars? Torture was the only word that came to mind, but it had to have been an accident. These weren't decades-old scars. She suspected some of them had been made in the last few years. He didn't want to talk about them.

He wanted her to ignore them, to pretend they weren't there. Hadn't she wanted the same thing? To pretend she hadn't fucked up her whole life?

She shoved all her questions aside and touched him, running her hand over his chest like it was perfectly smooth. It was time to stop being tentative. He needed to know she wanted him. She leaned over and ran her nose along his neck. He still smelled like soap, but now she caught a hint of arousal. Was his cock already weeping? It sent a rush to her pussy. She didn't need to know how he'd been hurt. She only needed to let him know he wasn't any less sexy for those scars.

A shudder went through him.

"That feels so good." His hands were back on her, keeping her close. His eyes closed like he wanted to enjoy the sensation, the feel of her hands on him.

He was right. It felt incredible. Her mouth found his again and she felt him relax. It had been too long since she'd felt close to someone. It made her realize how much she'd pushed away, even her friends. She used to be affectionate. She'd let Matt take that when he'd taken her money and her future. She had to fight to get all of herself back.

This was definitely worth fighting for. His tongue played lazily against hers as his hands started to fumble with the back of her bra.

Unfortunately, the clasp wasn't back there. She waited until he came up for air. "It's in the front."

His head came up, his chest moving against hers. "What?"

Her nipples were hard as rocks. The idea that he was about to put his hands on them nearly made her moan. "The clasp is in the front."

He shifted and that was when she started to go backward, falling inevitably to the floor. She gritted her teeth, ready to have the breath knocked out of her. Yep, she was a graceful swan. Jax moved quickly, his hands finding the back of her head, sheltering her. He twisted and wound up taking the brunt of the impact. Not that they'd gone too far, but he'd reacted like they were taking a serious dive.

She ended up on top of him, chest to chest.

"Are you all right?" He let his hands drift over her shoulders, checking for damage.

He was the one who'd taken the fall. Yet she found it hard to breathe as she looked down at him. She should have rolled off him, but she found herself shifting to her knees and straddling that part of him that seemed to honestly want her. He'd done everything she could think he should have done. He'd been patient and kind, taken care of her. If he turned out to be an asshole at least she'd done her due diligence. She was above him, looking down at the sexiest man she'd ever seen, and she was ready. Ready to take another shot at everything.

She flipped the clasp of her bra open and eased it off, letting him see her breasts. "I'm more than okay. I think you should do all those things you promised me."

She wanted it all. She let go of her inhibitions, of her fear, let go of anything but the expectation of pleasure.

Jax looked down at her, naked hunger in his eyes, and she realized this would be a night she would never forget.

Chapter Four

He was going to die. His dick was going to explode and things would get messy and he would die happy because she was simply stunning. She loomed over him, her eyes focused.

And she wasn't looking at him like he was something to pity. Those eyes were lit with lust.

They were in perfect accord because lust was first and foremost on his mind. Her breasts were lovely, round and perky with tight nipples he couldn't wait to get his mouth on. Of course, he should probably touch her with his hands first. She'd given him permission.

He reached up, cupping her. He'd been right about how soft she was. Her skin was like silk, and for the briefest moment he wondered if he shouldn't let her go. She was perfect. Those tiny scars did nothing to mar her. But he'd seen that brief flash of horror when he'd taken off his shirt. She'd covered it quickly and then she'd touched him like she couldn't stop herself, but he'd had the momentary worry that she was Beauty and he was a beast. He let that thought go now because there was none of her previous hesitance in the way she moved now.

Her eyes closed and her head dropped back as he stroked her

skin. Her hips rolled and there was no way she didn't realize she was sitting right on top of his cock. She had to feel it, had to know how close he was to rolling her over and shoving himself deep inside. She wasn't afraid of him and she wasn't doing this out of pity. She wanted him, and that was the first thing that made him feel like a man and not some lost fucking little boy.

He rolled her nipple between his thumb and finger. Those nipples had peaked, begging for him to play with them. He could do that. His mind had gone into pure tunnel vision. There was nothing in the world except her. Everything else fell away and all he was left with was the feel of her, the slow dance they were caught in.

He let his instinct lead him, rolling her over and pinning her to the ground with his body. Her eyes opened in surprise, but there was no fear in them. Her gaze softened and body bowed, offering herself up to him. All that sweetness was his for now.

He lowered himself down and kissed his way from the curve of her neck to that sweet nipple. He pulled it into his mouth, lavishing it with affection. Every moan he heard seemed to spark deep inside him, transforming him into something more than he'd been before he'd touched her.

"Jax, please." Her hands were in his hair, moving restlessly. "I can't stand it."

He ignored her. He would never brush off a request for him to stop if she didn't want him, but even he knew what she was asking for with her breathy moans. She wanted him to move this train along, to take her. She was impatient and that was a beautiful thing. But he'd promised her something. His mouth everywhere. He would lick and kiss every inch of her. It would take far longer than this one time to truly map her body, and that was exactly what he intended to do.

He moved to her other breast, unwilling to leave that sweet bit unloved. He tongued her before biting down lightly. Gently, just giving her the edge of his teeth. The hands in his hair tugged and pulled, she squirmed under him, but he didn't give in. He merely moved down her body.

"Oh, Jax. Are you really going to…"

He kissed her belly and down to the top of her jeans. "Fuck, yeah, I am."

She gasped, squirming again like she couldn't make herself stop moving. "You should know I'm messy down there."

He could smell her. It made him feel feral, primitive. This was what Ariel had talked about. It would be hard to stop now when the prize was close, when his heart beat in a primal rhythm. "I want you messy. Sex is messy."

He knew that somehow. Sex, when done well, involved a lot of mess, both physical and emotional. He knew that last part because he was already coming up with a hundred reasons to change his mind about leaving her at the end of the night.

He unbuttoned her jeans, getting to his knees and dragging them down her body. He needed her naked, needed to see the evidence of her desire for him. Sure enough, he could see the wet spot on her underwear and it sent another surge through his cock. He could take her then and there and she would be perfectly happy. Or he could indulge himself.

He'd learned not to be impatient. Life was far too short to not take advantage of every good thing that came his way, and she was such a good thing. She might be the best thing. He would soak in every moment he had with her, taking in memories to get him through the bad times.

He eased her underwear off and tossed it to the side. She wouldn't need it again tonight. He would keep her naked. He stared down at her, letting his mind memorize the sight of her against that rug, the light from the lamp turning her skin a rosy gold. Her legs rubbed against his like she couldn't stand the thought of not touching him. She was gorgeous. He'd thought the woods outside the cabin they were staying in were lovely. They had nothing on her. Round breasts, gently curving hips. She was petite but there was an athletic feel to her body. Like he'd said before—soft and yet strong. She could handle him. Could she handle his damage?

He put a hand on her, right between her breasts, dragging it down the length of her torso until he cupped the mound of her pussy. For the first time since that moment he'd woken up in a too-bright room, Sasha staring down at him, he was happy he didn't remember anything else because this felt new and fresh and meaningful. He had no idea who he'd been in the years before, but he liked who he was now because her eyes had come open, widening in wonder as he stroked her.

If he knew who he was, he wouldn't be here with her. He wouldn't be experiencing this for the first time with her.

He wanted to be with her.

He lowered himself down, needing to connect with her in every way he could. The urge to put his mouth on her was overwhelming. He wanted to surround himself with River—her touch, her scent and god, her taste. This needed no prior knowledge. This was something he instinctively knew how to do.

He licked her, his tongue finding her clitoris and lapping at the jewel. She bucked up, but he was ready for her. He held her down, pinning her to the floor. "Stop moving or I'll tie your hands down. Don't think I won't do it. I might not know a lot, but I'm good with rope, baby."

"That should worry me." She went still. "But somehow it just gets me hotter. What are you doing to me?"

He was making a meal out of her, that's what he was doing. "I'm enjoying every inch of you, and don't think you'll get rid of me so easily. I've changed my mind. One night isn't enough." He licked at her, moving to her labia and exploring. "Let me stay with you tonight. We'll sort the rest out in the morning. I don't know when I'll have to leave Colorado, but I want to spend time with you while I'm here."

"Yes," she said. "Stay with me. You can stay here if you like." Her body shuddered as he speared her with his tongue.

She tasted like honey and perfection, like nothing he'd known before. He couldn't get enough of her. He spread her thighs, wanting more. He fucked her with his tongue, his dick throbbing with jealousy. His dick would get its turn, but for now he needed to taste her orgasm.

He found her clit again with his thumb and rubbed while he fucked up into her pussy with his tongue. She shuddered and then he tasted fresh cream. It coated his tongue as she came apart, his name on her lips.

In that moment it didn't matter that Jax wasn't his name, or perhaps it was in that moment that Jax finally became his name. Hearing it from her lips made it real to him after all these months.

His body felt electric as he got to his knees. Pants. He needed to take off his pants, and then there was the condom he had to deal with. His hands shook as he fished it from his back pocket before shoving his jeans down and freeing his dick. He ripped open the packet and managed to do what he needed, trying not to think about the fact that he'd practiced on a fucking banana. The thought made him laugh because how many other thirty-something guys in the world had to take a sex education class taught by former commandos?

She was smiling when he moved over her. "I love your laugh."

He rarely laughed. "You make me happy, River. And I meant what I said. I don't want a one-night stand."

"Then we'll have to move this to the bedroom." Her arms drifted up. "And next time, you're taking your pants off."

But not this time. He couldn't. He was far too desperate to have her. He lined up his cock and pressed inside her. Pure pleasure nearly made his eyes roll in the back of his head, but he forced himself to focus on her. The orgasm he'd given her made her slick, but she was still shockingly tight around him. He was shoving his cock into a warm, wet vise, and his brain could barely handle it.

His body took over, finding a rhythm and riding it. He gritted his teeth, trying to hold out to make the moment last. River's legs wound around his waist and her whole body tightened as he fucked deep inside her. He felt her pussy clamp down and there was nothing else he could do. He lost control, pounding into her as the orgasm hit him, frying his brain and sending shockwaves through him. Nothing had ever felt as good as that moment when she wrapped herself around him, when he emptied himself into her.

Jax dropped down, covering her body with his. He didn't bother to hold his weight off her. She'd accepted him, still was as her hands stroked down his back. She wasn't thinking about how to "help" him or how damaged he was. She was basking in what he

77

could give her.

And what she'd given him was nothing short of miraculous. He sighed and let his head rest against hers. He would text Tucker and tell him he would check in tomorrow. Surely everything could wait until the morning. He wanted all the time he could get with her. It wouldn't hurt the mission for him to sleep in her bed, holding her close and waking with her. It couldn't hurt anyone.

He kissed her lightly, pleasant lethargy taking over. Could anything be better than to lie with her, warm and happy and sated?

"I'm going to make you pancakes in the morning," she said with a smile.

Yep. Life was pretty perfect.

* * * *

He came awake with the absolute certainty that someone was in the cabin. He wasn't sure why he knew it, he simply followed instincts honed from all his time in the bunker with McDonald. There had been nights when he would wake up and know someone was there. He would try to stay still, but he would open his eyes and there would be Mother. She would stare at him while he slept, likely thinking of all the torture she would put him through when he was awake.

Jax pushed the memory aside, his whole body on alert, listening for any sound that would give away where the intruder was. It wouldn't have taken much to get inside the cabin. He'd secured the front and back doors as well as he could, but he hadn't had a lot to work with. There was a single, simple lock on each door, and a hook on the screens. It was nothing he couldn't get through in roughly three minutes if he took his time and picked the locks, a few seconds if he kicked the door in.

Everything was perfectly silent except the sound of the river rushing past. It gurgled and churned, a soothing sound he would miss when he left here. If he followed it several miles to the south, he would be at the big cabin where his brothers were being housed, where Taggart was probably coming up with some punishment for disobedience.

There hadn't been physical punishment at The Garden, but that had been Damon Knight's choice. It had been explained to each of them how important it was to follow the rules when they were out in the world. There would be fallout for defiance. There always was.

It would be worth it. He would take whatever pain was coming his way because she was the best thing that had happened to him.

The cabin was still and silent. Maybe he'd been wrong. Paranoia was one of his closest friends. He glanced at the clock on the nightstand. 3:43 a.m. They'd moved into the smaller of the two bedrooms sometime after midnight. She'd given him no reason why she wasn't staying in the master, but he could extrapolate. Her father had died recently. She wasn't ready to take the room over yet, but they would need a bigger bed if he was going to stay here.

He might stay here forever.

The slightest creak of the hardwoods forced his attention back to the matter at hand. That hadn't been the house settling. Someone was moving carefully out in the living area. Adrenaline started to thrum through him.

Breathe in. Breathe out. Remember the layout of the cabin.

He eased his arm from under her head, careful not to wake her. The last thing he wanted was to scare her. He could take care of the intruder and then wake her up to call the authorities. Or he could kill the intruder and toss his body in the Rio Grande and go back to bed.

As quietly as he could, he stepped into his boxers and moved out of the room.

The master was across from the bedroom he'd shared with River, the bathroom to his back. It was no more than ten steps from where he was standing to the living room and the kitchen beyond. He clung to the shadows, listening intently to try to figure out how many intruders he was dealing with. He hadn't been given a sidearm, but he didn't need one. He preferred hand to hand, genuinely enjoyed the feel of fighting an opponent with nothing but strength between them.

79

"Ow, damn it, Dante," a hushed voice said. "You couldn't have mentioned there was a table there?"

"Not my problem," Dante replied and he wasn't whispering.

Damn it. No fight for him, and he couldn't throw his brothers into the river however much he wanted to. He strode out, not caring that he wasn't even half dressed. Dante and Tucker stood there in the darkened living room, though it appeared Tucker had brought along a flashlight. He clicked it on and shined it right in Jax's eyes. "Hey, put that thing down. And keep quiet. River's sleeping."

"Certainly. We wouldn't want to wake your girl. She's probably had a rough night." Dante chuckled. "I hope you had fun, brother. It's time to go. Robert has the car outside."

Tucker frowned. "I tried to tell them you would come back in the morning, but Ezra was insistent. He doesn't think we should be out all night. He wasn't particularly happy you picked up a chick. Although, when you think about it, you're the one who got picked up since you don't actually have a car or a place to take her or well, anything else it takes to have a girlfriend."

That hurt more than it should.

"She is not girlfriend. She's some chick he banged," Dante said. "I always knew Jax was the smart one. He finds woman he doesn't have to pay. He finds slut instead of whore. Saves him money."

He didn't realize what he was going to do until his fist met Dante's jaw. Dante could be a dick about women, and the idea of him even thinking about River made Jax crazy. "Don't you ever use either one of those words in my presence again."

Maybe he would get that fight.

Tucker had the good sense to get in between them before Dante escalated the situation and River walked in to find a brawl occurring in the middle of her living room. The game might be up when she met the assholiest of his brothers.

"Hey, keep it down," Tucker said, his voice low. "You know what Robert said. We're supposed to get him out of here as quietly as possible."

"I'm not leaving." He took a step back. "I texted you and told you what I was doing."

Tucker nodded. "Yes, and then Ezra turned on the GPS on your tracker and told us to get you. We're not allowed to be out on our own. I got a horrible lecture and I've been told Big Tag is going to have more to say in the morning when he's sober again. Apparently you can see aliens way better when you drink a shit ton of whiskey. Big Tag is a weird drunk. Like you almost can't tell, but then he calls his brother and asks for a grilled cheese delivery. Sean Taggart was pissed."

He didn't have time to listen to one of Tucker's rambling commentaries. "I don't care. I have to get back to River or she'll wake up and wonder where I've gone."

Tucker sighed. "I'm sorry this didn't go the way you hoped, but we have to get home."

Home? It was a laughable word. "That massive cabin is not our home. The Garden wasn't our home, Tucker. We don't have a home. Those places are nothing but a way to keep us locked up so we won't hurt anyone."

Dante rubbed his jaw. "This is the first thing I've agreed with you about. But there's nothing we can do now. If we leave, we'll be picked up by the police, who will place us in jail, or the Agency, who will likely make the McDonald bitch look like a baby."

He didn't like agreeing with Dante. He ignored the man and turned back to Tucker. "I'm not leaving her. I told her I would stay and she's making pancakes in the morning. If you want to, come by around nine or ten and you can drive me back then. But Ezra needs to know that I'm not going to ignore her. I'm going to see her again."

Dante groaned. "One taste of pussy and he's a duckling following her around."

"I can slit your throat while you sleep," Jax vowed.

"I would love to see you try," Dante snarled his way.

Tucker was back in the middle again, pushing them away from each other. "Stop. We're all going to get into serious trouble if we wreck this lady's house. Jax, I'm sorry, but we have to go. It's late and we've got an early meeting. We start this op in a couple of

81

days. With any luck we'll be done and out of here in a week. It's not a good idea to get involved. She's going to get hurt. When we started the night out, you remembered that little fact."

"She's a nice woman. I like her." *Like* was another ridiculous word to use. He craved her. But it wouldn't do to let Dante know it. Dante liked to play games. Oh, he never took them too far, never enough to get him kicked out, and he took his beatdowns with surprising aplomb, but Jax wasn't about to hand the man another weapon to use against him. "I told her I would be here in the morning. I think I should honor my word."

They would have to carry him out of this house. He wasn't going to disappoint her. She'd had enough of that. When they weren't making love, they'd talked. She'd talked. He'd listened and held her. She'd told him a bit about how hard it was to lose her dad, how she still expected to wake up and hear him.

He might not be able to stay with her the way he wanted to, but he could keep one promise he'd made. He could make sure she woke up warm and safe, and he could watch as she made breakfast for them. He could eat her pancakes and kiss her, maybe convince her to sit in his lap and watch the morning pass. It sounded like a perfect way to spend the day.

"He's not going to listen," Dante said. "We should go."

"We can't go without him." Tucker was insistent. "I don't know Big Tag the way I do Damon, and I absolutely don't know Fain. I don't know how he'll handle us failing. We can't fail."

Because failure in Mother's world meant death, or something so close it felt like it. Something that would make a man wish for death.

"It's not the same." He prayed it wouldn't be, but his gut churned at the thought. No one had tested Fain yet. They'd been on their best behavior. What would Fain or Big Tag do if they caused trouble?

Dante had moved behind him, seeming to go toward the door. "These men talk a big game, but they wouldn't hurt us. Still. I don't like to fail."

Jax hissed as something bit him on the arm. He looked down and realized it hadn't been a bite. Dante pushed the plunger on a hypodermic needle. "What?"

The world immediately went fuzzy.

"Damn it, they told us that was for emergencies or if the lady turned out to be an Agency plant," Tucker complained. "Do you have any idea how heavy he is?"

The words were fading as he hit his knees. Pain flared, but it was nothing compared to his anger. His choice was being taken away again, but this time she would be the one who got hurt.

As the world went gray and then black, he wished he'd never seen her, never pulled her in. He didn't regret touching her, but his hands couldn't touch her without his world touching her. He couldn't bring her into his fucked-up world.

"Grab his clothes," Tucker was saying. "We're not supposed to leave anything behind."

It had been ridiculous to think he could even have a night's peace. That kind of thing wasn't for a man like him.

The world blinked out, his last thought being that he would always be alone.

Chapter Five

River reached across the sheets, stretching to find Jax. Her body felt pleasantly used, like she'd gone on a long run. She'd definitely gotten a workout the night before. After he'd taken her on the living room carpet, he'd picked her up, carrying her to the bedroom. He'd made love to her again on the double bed in the room she'd grown up in, his legs hanging off the end because he was too big. For the bed. Not for her. He was exactly the right size for her.

He'd held her until she'd fallen asleep. She'd laid her head on his chest and listened to the strong beat of his heart. That was the important thing. The fact that his chest was a mass of scar tissue didn't mean his heart wasn't strong, wasn't capable of caring.

She opened her eyes, daylight streaming into the small room. The place beside her was empty. Had he gotten up already? She frowned, looking around the room. It wasn't such a surprise. He couldn't have been comfortable in the double bed. He was a king-sized guy. He'd had to scrunch himself up to fit on the mattress. He was probably in the shower, using the hot water to work the kinks out.

River slipped out of bed and immediately smelled coffee.

He was a keeper. He could make her scream in bed and knew

how to use the coffeemaker. She'd taken a chance the night before, but it was going to work out this time. She merely had to temper her expectations. He wasn't staying around forever. They would have a few weeks, maybe.

Of course, he'd changed his mind about the one-night stand pretty easily. She needed to stop being so pessimistic. Who knew where it could go? He had a phone. He'd used it to text his brother that he wouldn't be going back to the place they were staying at. It wasn't hard to keep up a connection if a person wanted to.

She threw a robe on and walked down the hall, ready to start the day differently than she had for the last several months. She stopped, realizing what she hadn't done. It happened every single morning for the last couple of years. She would lay in bed and wait for it, wait for the wretched coughing sound that accompanied her father's waking up. It signaled the peace he'd found in sleep was done and his misery continued. She would lie there and listen for it and put off hope for another day.

Even after he'd died, it was the first thing she thought about every morning until this one. This morning she'd woken up thinking about Jax.

There it was—that guilt she felt every time she remembered her dad was dead. She didn't want to feel it today. Today she wanted to make some changes. It started with cleaning out his room and moving into it. She'd thought she wouldn't make the move because she was selling the cabin, but Jax would be far more comfortable in there.

It was time to look forward and not to the past. It was time to try to live again, and it started with having a cup of coffee with the single most gorgeous man she'd ever met.

She strode into the kitchen and stopped.

"Hey, you. I thought I'd make some coffee. How was the hottie? Tell me you didn't drop him off at his place. I talked to his brother for hours so you would have time with him. That boy is weird. Not like scary weird but still weird." Heather stood in the middle of her kitchen, pouring coffee into a mug. She finished filling one and held the pot out. "Want some?"

"Where's Jax? Did he let you in?" The minute she asked the

question she realized how stupid it was. If Jax had let Heather in she wouldn't have asked if she'd spent the night with him.

Heather set the pot back in its cradle. "The door was open. I'm sorry. I didn't see him. Maybe he's out for a run or something."

He wasn't out for a run. He'd been wearing boots. No one ran in boots.

She glanced around the living room. He'd tossed his clothes off. His and hers. Hers were still on the floor but his were gone. His boots weren't sitting near the fireplace, as they'd been the night before. He'd taken his things and left.

"You were expecting him to stay?" Heather's voice had gone sympathetic.

"He said he would." A familiar numbness washed over her. Ah, humiliation. Her old friend. He'd either tricked her or changed his mind.

Why? She'd been more than willing to accept a single go. She'd requested it, actually. He'd been the one who told her he was staying.

Heather frowned. "I didn't see a note or anything. Are you okay? You went pale."

Because something else—another reason for his lies—had just gone through her brain. "Have you seen my purse?"

Where had she put it?

Heather moved out of the kitchen, joining her in the living room. "You don't think he rolled you. He wouldn't."

Oh, but she'd learned that even the sweetest faces could hide opportunistic assholes. There it was. She winced. She'd zipped it up the night before but it was open now. "Someone went through my bag. Damn it. I'm such an idiot."

"What's missing?" Heather knelt down beside her.

She quickly went through the whole bag. She didn't have much in it. Keys. A brush. Her wallet. All her credit cards were in there, and so was the ten dollars and twenty cents she'd had on her last night. Her cell phone was there. "He didn't take anything. I wonder if he saw how little cash I had and took pity on me."

"Or you forgot you left it open and he didn't touch it," Heather offered.

But she was sure of that. She remembered zipping it up after she'd put her keys in there. She stood. Still, it wouldn't do to argue with Heather. It only made her look even more like a fool, and she felt that enough. "Maybe so. Anyway, what are you doing here? Do you need something?"

He was gone and he hadn't even left her a note. At least Matt had written her a note when he'd left.

God, she had to stop that. She'd slept with the wrong man. At least this time she hadn't married the asshole and handed over everything she had to him. She just wouldn't learn.

"I came by because Ty said we've got a meeting with a big client," Heather explained, looking at her like she wanted to get back to the Jax subject.

She couldn't let that happen. If she did, she might break down. She wasn't going to cry over a one-night stand. No way. He'd gotten what he wanted. She'd been willing to do anything he wanted to her sexually. She'd been compliant, and that had likely been his point. She'd thought he was awkward, but he'd turned out to be a master manipulator. Was he pissed off that she hadn't had anything valuable to steal?

Anger was better than sorrow. Anger felt good.

"What client?"

"It's the film crew I told you about."

"Yes, I met one of them. A guy named Ezra," she replied. She was surprised they wanted to talk to her.

"They need a guide," Heather explained. "Ty set up a meeting and called Andy and me. I said I would get you on my way into the office. It's a lot of money, according to Ty. They want two units, one guide a piece full time for a week or two."

That would cost a fortune. That kind of money would let them buy some winter equipment for the upcoming season. "What's the catch?"

She shrugged, moving back into the kitchen. "None that I know of. The meeting's in an hour. We're supposed to meet with the production crew. If you don't think we can handle it, I'll call and have him cancel. They can use High Country Adventures."

"I thought that's who they would go with." High Country was

a much bigger firm located in Del Norte. They would be better equipped to handle a big venture.

She poured a second mug. "According to Ty, they want us." Heather passed it to her. "Although they're going to have to go without me. I have to run into town. My brother needs me to wire him some cash."

She hadn't known Heather had a brother. "Sure. We can handle the meeting. I'll let you know how it turns out."

Jax worked security, not for the film crew. Although that had likely been a lie, too. He and his brother were con artists. They had likely moved on to a more target-rich environment. Had he waited until she'd gone to sleep, looked around for something to steal, and then called his brother to pick him up? She was damn lucky he hadn't taken the Jeep.

Stupid. Stupid. Stupid.

"There might be an explanation." Heather stared at her with sympathy. "You never know what's going on in a person's head. Sometimes circumstances make things appear worse than they are. He might have started off the night planning on staying and something happened to Tucker."

"How was Tucker when you left him?" She and Jax had left Trio around eleven, leaving his brother and Heather still talking.

Heather's mouth twisted in a grimace and she had her answer even before the words came from her friend's mouth. "He was fine. Like I said, a little on the crazy side, but sweet enough."

"So you didn't even think about sleeping with him?"

"Ew. No." Heather seemed taken aback by the thought. "I mean he's attractive enough, but he's not my type. I'll be honest, after my husband left me I made a couple of bad, self-destructive choices. I'm not looking for a lover. I'm trying to find myself for now. The Tuckers of the world need to find another love goddess." She nodded. "He actually called me that."

The brothers seemed to have selected an awkward-nerd vibe to reel their marks in. "It doesn't matter. He doesn't matter. You should go and deal with your brother and I'll get ready for the meeting."

"Wow, he did a number on you." Heather set her mug down.

"River, you can't blame yourself."

"I'm not. I blame him. But like I said, it doesn't matter. We need to get moving." She wanted to be alone. It wasn't fair to take it out on Heather, but she'd been the reason River had gone to Trio in the first place. She could be waking up after an uneventful night to the exciting news that they might land a big gig. As it was, she couldn't get excited about the job. She could only think about how stupid she'd been to listen to him.

I want to put my mouth all over your body. But more than I want that, I want you to like me.

Sure he did. He'd sized her up and figured out exactly how to take her down.

A sad expression took over her friend's face. "I wish I believed that. Don't hate me, River. I wanted to see you smile, and he did make you smile. I'll let you alone but if you need me, call me. I'll be there. I want to be your friend, but you have to let me in."

"I appreciate it." But she'd let too many people in and they'd fucked her over. It was time to start being smart. "I'll call you and let you know how the meeting went."

Work. She would focus on work. What happened last night meant nothing. It was sex and that was all. She should thank him for showing her how good it could be.

It had felt like more than sex. It had felt like connection, like communion, like for once someone truly understood her.

And that was why she failed. She was getting rid of all the romantic bullshit in her life.

"Bye." Heather walked out, her disappointment obvious.

She was alone and that was a good thing.

She heard Heather's SUV pull away.

Yes, alone was good.

* * * *

Jax came awake slowly, consciousness coming back in bits. His first thought was complete terror. His head wasn't clear. He tried to stay still, but the minute he moved he felt oddly disconnected

89

from his body. Odd? It wasn't odd to him. How many times had he woken up trying desperately to find his balance because he'd been used to test some drug?

Had it been a dream? The small freedom he'd had? Was he back in the lab? If he opened his eyes would he see that bright light that meant he'd been recycled again? How many times had he gone through it? How many times had she plunged that needle into his arm and erased all that he was?

She wasn't going to take River away from him. No. She wouldn't take that night away, wouldn't make it blink out of existence like it hadn't happened. He punched out, determined to catch anyone who would try to put that needle in his arm. He could remember River. It was foggy, but he knew it had been real. She'd cuddled close to him, letting him hold her, letting him be her lover, her man.

"I can't handle this drama, man," a familiar voice said. "We didn't bring Ariel with us, why?"

"Robert didn't want her in danger," another voice said. Fain.

"I'm too old for this shit." Taggart was definitely the other voice.

His head was so foggy. What had happened? One minute he'd been happy and warm, with her clutched close to him, and the next he'd been here, fighting his way back to consciousness.

"You're definitely too old for rotgut whiskey," Fain was saying.

"I told you. It was supposed to keep the aliens away. I'll take it over the beet juice I had to drink any day of the week. Hughes is completely insane, and I like him. He's my new favorite person," Taggart replied.

Jax's stomach rolled and he stayed still, not wanting to puke.

"Is he the real Hughes? Fuck, I thought he was a myth, man," Fain continued. Why couldn't they have this conversation elsewhere? "He's so classified I couldn't get his records even when I had clearance. Do you think he knows about the rumors? About the lieutenant? I have to admit. I see a resemblance."

He groaned as he remembered what had happened. It came back to him in flashes. Tucker had tried to talk him into coming back to the cabin and then Dante… Fucking Dante. He punched out as if the fucker was here.

"Chill out, Jax. You're safe and shit, though you are in trouble. I wish we had a doghouse I could put you in. I distinctly remember telling you not to do stupid shit." Taggart stood over him. "Though apparently all the puppies were dumb last night. I did not tell Dante to use that cocktail on you. It was there in case your date for the night turned out to be an Agency plant. We've heard a rumor there's at least one in town, and he or she has been in place for a while. They know we're going to try to find McDonald's research."

"I told you it could be a trap." Fain looked down at him. "You okay? That dosage shouldn't have made you sick. I can call Tucker in, or there's a doc in town we can get."

He sat up. He was in his room but it looked like Tucker had already cleared out. Taggart sat on the second bed.

"I'm fine." If they were both here, it was likely time for punishment. It was best to get that over with. "Where do you want me?"

They would do whatever they were going to do and then he would start planning. He would get away, but he needed to be smart. He needed to talk to River and make sure she would go with him. It would take some time, but he could get them new IDs. He could find a way to get his hands on some cash and they could run. He would tell her everything. He wouldn't lie to her again. But he had to be patient. The good news was his patience meant he would have time to plan Dante's brutal murder.

But first he would take his punishment.

"Why does he have that look on his face?" Fain leaned against the desk in the room. "Look, man, you can't kill Dante. I know he's an asshole, but he's been through a lot. You should know. I promise I'm going to let him know that if he pulls something like this again, I'll send him straight back to Damon, who'll find him a place by himself."

"He thinks we're going to hurt him now," Taggart said quietly, those icy blue eyes regarding him solemnly. "He doesn't trust us and he might never."

"Why would we hurt him?" Fain asked before shaking his head. "I'm not McDonald, man. I did send Tucker and Dante to get you, but I did it because I got word about the Agency plant. Hate me all you like but I did it for your protection. There's no punishment except to ask you not to kill Dante."

"And the only place I want you is in the shower because, dude, you smell like sex. We have a meeting soon," Taggart said, not unkindly. "Come downstairs because the mayor thinks he's found someone for us to hire to handle the walk in the woods. The mayor, sheriff, and a man named Stef Talbot are coming in to brief us about the town and the company we're working with. You're going to run point with them. And not killing Dante isn't your only punishment. Nell Flanders made breakfast. Yep. It's tofu, and we're not allowed to not eat it or Henry will kill us. He's incredibly good at internal decapitation so I'm going to give it a try. I already told Charlie when I get home she's to greet me with three pounds of bacon."

Jax looked back and forth between them, trying to figure out if they were lying to him. Maybe they were into mind games and they would let him get comfortable before pulling the rug out from under him. "No punishment?"

"Did you hear the part about the tofu?" Taggart asked. "And I'm pretty sure Robert used all the hot water in the house, so you're in for a few chilly moments."

He wasn't about to get his ass kicked. He could handle the shower. "I want to see her again."

He was pushing his luck.

Fain sighed. "I understand, and if we can make that happen, we will. Take your shower and after the meeting we'll have a talk about this woman of yours. We have to vet her."

He nodded. He got the need to check into the background of anyone coming into the group. It was something he would have done anyway because he wanted to know more about her. And he definitely wanted to know more about her ex-husband. There was more to the story. He could feel it. She said she lost everything in the divorce, but she'd been lying. Or rather hedging. There was something she wasn't telling him, and he bet he could figure it out.

"Jax, I would never punish you physically," Fain said quietly.

"I might punch you if you annoy me," Taggart admitted. "But I'll also expect you to punch back. Not today, though. Seriously, that whiskey had something else in it. I need some coffee. Surely there's some coffee that harmed no indigenous peoples around here somewhere. See you guys downstairs in half an hour."

Taggart put a hand to his head and found his way out.

"You're safe. Well, safe from us. None of us is safe from the Agency or the Collective or any number of assholes who are after us," Fain said with a weary sigh.

It was easy to forget how much Fain had given up to lead them out into the world. Ezra Fain had been the Agency's golden boy at one point in time. But he'd been forced to make a choice: bring in the men McDonald had experimented on so the Agency could find out more about her work or keep them safe. He'd been disavowed for his choice.

"Thank you, Ezra. Thank you for helping us." He was fairly certain no one had said that to him. Sometimes he thought they were still too mired in their own misery to see the good things that could happen to them.

Fain's stare found the window, looking out as he spoke. "I know what can happen when the Agency takes control of things they don't understand. Levi Green is an asshole looking to move up, but there are people in the CIA who mean well. That's what I've learned over the years. You can mean well and it still falls apart, especially if you don't listen to the people around you. Even when you're in the middle of the fight, you can't see all the possible outcomes. I thought about it, you know."

"Thought about turning us in?"

"*Over* would be a better word," he replied. "After what happened in Mexico, I sat down and weighed the pros and cons."

He'd read about the operation in Mexico. Levi Green had tried to use Kayla Summers as a path to get into The Garden and to gain access to the Lost Boys. Kayla was former CIA. Up until a few months before, she'd worked at McKay-Taggart and Knight and she'd been a good friend to them all. She'd been sent to spy on a Hollywood star who supposedly had connections to a drug lord. It

93

had all been a setup and Ezra had a hand in saving her. Now she was married to the same star she'd been investigating and Ezra was on the outside. And Levi Green had proven he could weather any storm.

"There was a huge fight at the Agency about how to handle you," Ezra continued. "Some wanted to bring you in, protect you, try to figure out who you are, and if we couldn't, train you and give you new lives as operatives."

Because they would likely make excellent operatives. They'd been trained to obey. They didn't have loyalties to anyone but themselves. It was pretty much what Taggart was doing. "And the other faction?"

"Would study you. I worried you would end up in a place like The Ranch. They shut down one site to keep an unfriendly president from discovering it, but that doesn't mean there aren't others. The Ranch was simply on the books. There are black ops sites out there that are so dark they're rumors even to operatives. That's why I made the decision I did. That's why I walked away. I fought with some people I respect. Hell, I broke with them over this, but I thought they were being naïve."

How much had Ezra given up? "Were you friends with Levi Green?"

He shrugged. "We came up through the ranks together. He's not the naïve one, Jax. He knows exactly what he's doing. Somewhere along the way, he started to hate me. I'm not sure why since I'm the one who did everything wrong. It doesn't matter. All that matters is we're safe for now, and we keep our eyes open. They'll come for us at some point. We have to be ready. See you downstairs."

He turned and walked out

And Jax got up and headed to the shower, a bit of his balance restored. He didn't have to run. He did have to find a way to get to River and explain what had happened. How did he explain? Tucker had an emergency. That would work.

He could protect her. He could still see her. It was all he could ask for right now.

But damn that water was cold.

* * * *

He was still thinking about River an hour later as he sat at the big dining room table. He'd been fed a tofu scramble by Nell Flanders and he hadn't hated it. He'd noticed that River hadn't eaten meat the night before. She'd carefully picked her way around the bacon on the fries, and when they'd ordered dinner, she'd had the black bean burger. He could give the veggie stuff a try. He'd been rewarded with the glowiest smile from Henry's wife when he'd praised her cooking. And Henry hadn't looked like he wanted to punch someone. Nell had even given him a hug before she'd left because she didn't want to know anything that might violate someone's human rights. That was when Henry had gone back to frowning.

"Jax, this is Rafe Kincaid." Taggart introduced him to a tall, dark-haired man in slacks and a button down. "He's the mayor of Bliss. Rafe, this is Jax Seaborne and Robert McClellan. They're going to be running the two teams searching for the site."

The mayor gestured to the men he'd brought with him. "Good to meet you. This is the sheriff, Nathan Wright. I believe he met with Mr. Fain yesterday, and this is a very prominent member of our community, Stefan Talbot."

"By prominent he means rich as fuck," Taggart said, holding out a hand. "Good to see you again, Talbot. I probably would have visited Bliss earlier if that one there hadn't been so sneaky."

Henry Flanders grimaced. "Well, if Stef had hired you when Laura had a serial killer after her, you probably would have figured out I wasn't dead."

The sheriff took his Stetson off as he sat down across from Robert. "I'm glad it's all out in the open now. I mean, I always knew Henry was hiding something."

Stef Talbot snorted. "Sure you did, Nate. Caleb knew. Gemma knew. You didn't know." The dark-haired man nodded his and Robert's way. "Welcome to Bliss. Don't mind the murder rate. It's been going steadily down."

The sheriff's eyes widened. "Since when? Since Henry and

Logan killed half a cartel in the backyard?"

Talbot waved it off. "That was forever ago."

"No," the mayor argued. "It was like five minutes ago. It only seems like it's been forever. Honestly, around here we count a week without a crisis as a win. But hey, now apparently we're going to have CIA hanging around, so I expect another bloody battle at any moment."

They started arguing about the town's worst murder spree, but Jax was thinking about River again.

He couldn't call her because he'd been too dumb to get her number. It would be okay. He would go out to her place after this meeting was done and they had everything set in stone. He could find his way back there. It was good to have a plan. He'd already texted the smartest woman he knew to get her advice.

Kay, fell for a chick here in CO. Spent amazing night with her. Promised to stay and then buttfuck Dante drugged me and hauled me out of her bed. Can't tell her that. How to make it better?

It had been mere seconds before Kayla Summers-Hunt had written back in a flurry of hearts and starry-eyed emojis.

So happy for you, babe!!!! Flowers work. And chocolate. Show up on her doorstep and beg her forgiveness and you'll be back in. Promise. Also oral is good. Lots of oral.

He could do that. He liked oral. He kind of thought he was pretty good at it, too.

"Jax, I get that you're all a flutter now that you've managed to get a girl to kiss you and shit, but could I have your attention?" Taggart's sarcasm let him know he'd probably missed something important.

He glanced around. Yep. Everyone was staring his way. Someone had taken a map out, circling the possible site of The Ranch. They appeared to have moved on in the conversation. He put his phone down. "You have my complete attention."

He would find someplace that sold flowers. What kind of flowers did she like? Flowers were supposed to say things. Red roses symbolized love. Deep crimson were used for mourning. A lavender rose could mean love at first sight. That would work. Or not. Yeah, that might come off as crazy and stalkerish. He'd been given strict instructions not to stalk people. Not for sex reasons. Murder reasons were okay, but only if the victim was cleared by Fain. Yellow was for friendship, but he didn't want to get stuck in a friend's zone the way Robert was with Ariel. Nope. Definitely not yellow. That way led to frustration and more cold showers. But orange… yeah, orange was for desire and enthusiasm. He enthusiastically desired her.

Where could he get orange roses?

How the hell did he know so freaking much about flowers?

"Yeah, I totally have your attention," Taggart snarked.

He was off his game. He was usually much better at seeming like he was paying attention than this. "I'm looking right at you, Tag. What more do you need?"

"You're looking at him with a goofy grin on your face," Robert pointed out. "She was good, huh?"

He was pretty sure the grin came off his face. "She's a nice lady."

Robert's eyes widened. "I meant that in a perfectly non-sexual way. Sorry, man."

"Could we get back to the meeting at hand?" Henry asked. "I need to spend some time with my wife before we go out to Mountain Adventures."

That name triggered something. He couldn't quite remember what though. He was too preoccupied with how much he knew about flowers. Everything. He knew that marigolds needed sunlight. Lots of sunlight. Coneflowers also liked the sun, and they attracted butterflies. Lily of the Valley was said to have been around since 1000 B.C. and had a sweet scent. How did he know that?

Ezra looked down the table to the mayor. "Do we have all the right permits in place?"

Kincaid nodded, sitting back. "We've filed everything under the name of the fake production company."

"It's not fake, according to the government." Finally he had something to add. He'd spent weeks making sure their cover would hold. "If you look into the records you'll find that First View Productions has been around for three years. We specialize in

97

investigative reporting. I even invented an IMDB page for us. It'll hold up to pretty close scrutiny."

"Chelsea vetted it," Taggart said. "My sister-in-law is one of the best hackers on the planet. She says Jax's work is excellent. That doesn't mean it will get by the Agency, but I also don't think they're going to storm the town. There's a reason we came here. It's actually closer to our target to be based in Creede."

"I brought them here because even the Agency will hesitate before launching an all-out assault on this town," Henry explained. "Mel alone would make them think twice. And it doesn't hurt that they now know I'm alive and here. We don't have to worry about a frontal assault. They'll come at us soft. They'll embed someone who can feed them intel. We need to look at anyone who's come into town in the last few weeks."

"I don't know of anyone who moved here that recently." Talbot looked thoughtful. "The doctor's nurse has been here less than a year, but she came in with Gemma and there's zero chance she's CIA. There's a new waitress at Trio, but she's been here for a couple of months. River's hired a couple of people on in the last six months."

The sheriff shook his head. "I had Gemma vet them both. Andy's Canadian. He came down here a month ago. Heather's from California. She's been here for almost five months. We get a lot of tourists. It's easy to rent a cabin long term around here. I'll ask Marie if she's heard of anyone renting lately and look into them."

The sheriff had said the one thing guaranteed to get his attention. "River?"

Ezra slid a file his way. "Yes, River Lee. She runs Mountain Adventures. I need you to do a quick workup on her. She's going to be our main guide, but her assistant manager, Ty Davis will probably run the secondary unit. You're our expert on The Ranch. I want you working closely with her and Robert will work with Ty."

Shit and fuck. He felt his face go red. Okay. It was okay. He could handle this. He could tell her he'd lied because too many women thought because he was a producer that he could be a ticket

98

into Hollywood. She was so beautiful she could be an actress. He wanted her to like him for him. That could work, right?

Also, my brother got sick in the middle of the night and he's a baby so that's why I left without leaving you a note. I mean, he could obviously drive since I didn't walk five miles home, but he was sure he was going to get sick.

He was fucked.

"River knows these woods like the back of her hand. She grew up here and her dad started the company," the sheriff was saying. "The former sheriff agrees with me that she's the perfect person for this job. Rye Harper has known her for years and says she's solid. She runs a small operation and she's had some financial trouble lately. You might have to pay her upfront so she can outfit everyone properly, but she's the only one I would trust with this. She's worked with law enforcement before. When we have to find a missing hiker or climber, she's the first person we call, and that includes park rangers."

"I like the idea of working with a smaller company. I want to make sure we can buy all her time for the next couple of weeks," Taggart said. "You've already set up the meeting for this afternoon, right?"

Robert leaned in, looking at Jax with worried eyes. "Are you okay?"

There was nothing for it. He couldn't hide what he'd done because she was going to be pissed to see him. Or maybe she wouldn't care that he'd left and then he would be the one upset. "Boss, remember when you told me to not do something stupid?"

Taggart's face went blank and then it fell. "Tell me she wasn't the woman you spent the night with."

"I really wish I could." Not that he regretted the night. Merely he regretted that this would make things harder. "And I might have told her I work security. Which is not technically a lie."

Ezra shot him a look that could have frozen fire. "It's also not your damn cover."

He felt like a complete idiot. "I wanted her to know something true about me. I like her. She invited me to stay with her while I'm here. That's good, right? She offered that after we made love, so she must have liked me. Of course then asshole Dante carted me out without leaving a note. I might have promised her I would stay until morning."

The sheriff groaned. "Are you serious? River's got abandonment issues and she has a serious problem with anyone lying to her. Her ex-husband…hell, apparently they weren't even legally married…he conned her out of everything she had. Left her high and dry and selling off everything she could to pay her father's medical bills. She's going to be pissed."

"She's going to be hurt," Talbot corrected.

Taggart's head hit the table. "Just when I think you guys have hit the absolute height of idiocy, one of you reaches for the stars."

Ezra turned to the sheriff. "Is there anyone else who can do the job?"

He wasn't about to get her fired. Damn it. She needed the money. "I'll work it out. I'll find a way to make her forgive me. I promise. I'll make this right."

"She's really the only person I would hire," the mayor added. "You could go with one of the bigger companies, but they'll likely have other clients. You can buy all of River's time. I thought that was what you wanted. She's the only one who can promise you privacy and her complete attention. Perhaps you should change out your lead. You've got six men, right?"

Oh, that was not happening. "No one knows this project like I do. I can find that site. Also, she's already met Tucker, too. If you get rid of both of us, you're down to Robert and Owen and Sasha and Dante. Owen flips his shit at the thought of bears. Sasha claims he's never camped before—like he would remember—and if you try to put Dante anywhere near her, I'll kill him myself. Boss, let me deal with this."

"If it comes down to it, I'll go in with River and Jax can work with the second," Robert offered.

"Or I can handle it." He wasn't sending Robert off with her. Days and days alone in the wilderness, exploring the land and sleeping in tents. Relying on each other. Nope. He sat up straighter. "She liked me. I'll make her like me again."

Ezra and Taggart exchanged a look. Taggart finally sighed and put his head back down.

Ezra nodded his way. "All right. We meet with her team at three. Come up with something good, man."

"I think money could work," the sheriff said. "If she's upset about working with her one-night stand, pay her more. Her ex recently opened three accounts in her name and she's now fighting another twenty grand in debt. I'm working with her on the problem, but she needs cash."

"Or she needs someone who can make his life hell." Jax felt the anger start low in his gut. No wonder she'd been wary. "I'd like a name, please."

The sheriff frowned. "I think that's something I should take care of."

"He'll find and destroy the asshole," Robert offered. "It's a hobby of his. He works out and ruins the lives of people who piss him off. That's how he spends his days. He can do things you can't. Unless you don't think this man deserves it."

It was good when his brother actually backed him up.

"I'll have my office manager send you a copy of the file." The sheriff stood up. "River will take care of you and I'll have my men be on the lookout. The only people who know about this op are the three of us, Alexei, my deputy, Cam, and Henry and Nell. I am worried though that there will be some suspicious people once Nell starts refusing to talk."

"Refusing to talk?" Ezra asked.

Henry got the most wistful look on his face. "It's her way of protesting us lying to the town. She's got a truthful soul."

"Thank god I fell for a girl who loves drama and guns," Taggart said, getting up. "Come on, Henry. Let's go see if your wife can cure my hangover."

"She's got a great cure for that." Henry followed him. "It does involve some chanting though."

"How did you ever run a black ops unit?" Taggart was poking at his old mentor as they walked out. "You know what you need when you're black ops? Bacon, man. You need a shit ton of bacon."

While they walked out, Jax got back on his phone. This would take more than a text.

"Jax? Hey, what's going on?" Kayla answered on the first ring.

"Things just got more complicated." There was no one in the world he would trust more than Kay to advise him. After all, she'd had to lie to her lover once, and Josh Hunt was now her husband.

"Okay," she said. "Did you hear me about the oral?"

He sat back and listened.

Chapter Six

"You okay?" Tyler Davis was the very definition of sunny blond, though in a masculine package. He always had a smile and it drew every female within a ten-mile radius to him. He also had a libido that meant he rarely turned one away.

River gave him what she hoped was an "everything's okay here, I didn't get my heart broken again" smile. She didn't want him to know that it took everything she had to stay sitting in her chair. She wanted to get out into the forest. Alone. She needed that quiet time to process what had happened. "Of course. What do we know about First View Productions?"

The man who'd helped her through the last couple of years sank down into the seat across from her desk. The Mountain Adventures offices weren't huge, but she still maintained a private office. Ty was a man of many talents—as a lot of female tourists would attest. Like many of the people in her generation, he had more than one job. He was one of two of the county's EMTs, worked at the ski lodge as their in-house medical tech during the winter, and took shifts with her all year long. How the man found the time to sleep with an army of women, she had no idea. "I heard a rumor you met a new friend last night."

Damn Trio. If she'd wanted privacy she should have gone to Hell on Wheels. Trio was one of the epicenters of Bliss gossip. She should have thought about the fact that the minute she left the bar with Jax, everyone in town would know. She decided to go for a casual cool. "It was nothing, really. I'm not planning on seeing him again."

"What did he do?" Ty asked, sounding way more serious than she was used to hearing him.

"What do you mean?"

Ty leaned in, his voice taking on a much deeper timbre than usual. "I mean you walked in here looking like someone kicked your dog. You haven't had one since Jango died, so I assume that long face is about something your date did last night. I want to know what his name is and where I can find him."

"Whoa, slow down there." She'd never seen him get so steely eyed. Ty was laid back. He wasn't the kind of guy who typically got into fights. "What's this about?"

Andy walked through the door, his lanky body in cargo shorts, a T-shirt, and hiking boots. Andy had been added to the team after everything had gone to hell. "Has Ty gone all commando on you? He heard a rumor that you got a little something something last night, boss, and he's all kinds of worried about it. He thinks he didn't do enough to Matt when he left."

She didn't like the way this conversation was going, but she was curious. "Do enough?"

"Revenge stuff," Andy explained as he sank onto the second chair. "He thinks he should have taken Matt and cut him up into tiny pieces and fed him to the bears."

"No, the bears did nothing wrong, and that asshole was so full of himself he's probably toxic. Burying him would have been a good idea though. Preferably alive," Ty said, his jaw tight. "I didn't know what he'd done until later. I thought you two broke up because he wasn't man enough to handle taking care of your dad, but…"

Humiliation swept over her. Yep, it was not her day. "How did you find out?"

She'd been careful to keep it from her staff. Well, from the guys. She'd told Heather, and that might have been a mistake. When the hell would she learn? When she'd had to let go of everyone except Ty, she'd promised she would hold herself apart. She'd done a damn fine job of it until Heather had hired on. Loneliness had become her weakness, as last night could attest.

Ty sighed and turned a nice shade of red. "Your dad told me a few weeks before he died. I don't know if you remember, but I came over to sit with him so you could go into town. He asked me to watch out for you. I didn't know what Matt had done, River. I thought the business had gotten into trouble and you had to sell things off because of your dad's treatment. Damn it. I should have asked more questions."

Her dad had known? She'd definitely tried to keep her situation from him, but she'd also had to spend hours on the phone trying to clear up all the debt Matt had left her with. Her dad had probably heard more than she thought he had. The cabin was small. He'd probably heard her crying.

Her father had died knowing how she'd fucked up.

"Dad shouldn't have put that on you, Ty."

"Yeah, he should have," he argued. "We're friends. You and me and Lucy, we grew up together. I should have handled it back then and I will definitely handle it now. You're like my sister. I need to be a better brother."

She and Ty and Lucy had gone to school together, taking the long bus ride each day to the Monte Vista school. They'd been the outcasts, huddled together to survive in the beginning. She'd always thought Ty and Lucy would get together, but they were still merely friends. River had drifted away from them over the last few years. Why had she done that? Matt had been good at separating her from her support system. "I appreciate that, but I'm fine. I spent some time with a tourist. Like I said, I won't see him again."

Andy frowned. "Bad lay, huh?"

He'd been spectacular. The man knew what he was doing. Her skin still tingled thinking about how he'd touched her. Like he was exploring something amazing for the first time. Like he couldn't stop himself.

You're so soft.

She needed to be hard. "It was definitely a mistake I won't make again. I'll hire a pro next time." That was good. She would go super salty and pretend like she hadn't woken up half in love with the man. "Now when are we meeting the production team? Are they serious about the pay? Because this is more than we would normally get for a couple of days' worth of guided camping. What's the catch?"

She'd learned there was always a catch.

Ty stared at her for a moment, like he wasn't sure he should let the subject go, but he finally passed her a file folder and sat back. "They're legit. They've done a lot of work with Canadian TV stations and a couple of documentaries specializing in how man is fucking up the environment."

"Have you watched any of them?" Film types always thought everyone should know their "work." She'd had business dealings with several of them. Hollywood had come through a couple of times in the last ten years. Some had been easy to deal with. Others she'd kind of wished she could have left out in the wilderness.

Andy snorted. "Hell, no. You know Ty can barely make it through a cartoon without falling asleep, and I'm not into documentaries. Now if they were doing a movie about an innocent pizza delivery boy who finds himself invited to a sleepover with three scantily clad sorority girls, I would be all in."

"I don't think anyone's going to be filming porn in the Rio Grande National Forest. I think they prefer valleys," she quipped. She glanced down at the printouts. It looked like this production company wasn't into the entertainment side of the business. They were known for visceral documentaries.

"Heather watched a couple," Ty said. "She thinks they do good work. Is there a reason she's not here? Is she not going out with us?"

She'd noticed Ty preferred to let Heather deal with setup, but he would have to handle it today. "She'll back me up, but she's got a family issue to deal with."

Andy shook his head. "I thought she was an only child and her parents were out of the picture."

She wasn't going to blame Heather for keeping quiet about

family issues. She herself should have been way quieter. "Apparently she's got a brother and he's a handful, so I need you to help me take notes. We'll have to use some of the down payment to get new equipment. They're not coming in with anything except their production stuff. The good news is it looks like they work light."

Ty nodded. "They want to go in two-man crews. Basically a cameraman and a producer. That's far easier than a pack of ten of them. And it's good, too, because this is some delicate land. I don't want to piss off the rangers by hiking a massive group through there."

She sat back, looking at her two employees thoughtfully. "We need this job, guys. We might be able to get back on our feet sooner than I thought. I would love to be able to equip for winter."

"If we've got the right equipment, I know the owner of the ski lodge I work at would let you do signups." Ty seemed eager to do anything he could to help.

Was there a way she could save her cabin? She hadn't actually put it on the market yet. If this job paid and she didn't spend a dime on herself, she might be able to scrape by this winter and put off the decision about the cabin.

A bell chimed, signaling someone had walked into the building. She glanced up and Nate Wright walked in, followed by the man she'd seen walking out of his offices the day before. Fain, he'd called himself. Ezra Fain. It was good to know Nate was on her side. Apparently he was the one who'd gotten her the job or he wouldn't be here with the crew. A massive blond god of a man wearing aviators strode in behind them.

Not that she hadn't learned her lesson about gorgeous men. He might be nice to look at, but this was nothing more than a job. At least both men looked fit and ready to spend some time hiking.

"How does Henry Flanders fit into this?" Andy had turned, too, staring at the group as they filed in. Henry was speaking to the Nordic god.

Ty shrugged. "No idea. You know there's a rumor out there now that Henry used to be some kind of cop, right? I have a hard time seeing that."

107

She couldn't see it either. Henry Flanders was a pacifist. She could maybe see him trying to change an attacker's mind with a thorough discourse about the nature of good, but she couldn't imagine the man hurting someone. "I think that's a rumor. Like Mel's aliens. I'm sure Henry's with them because they're environmentalist documentarians. Nell likely had a hand in this, too. You know her roots go deep in that community. We should go out and greet them. We can use the planning room. I'd like to know where they're going to want to film and if they've got all the proper permits."

The last thing she needed was to get in trouble with the park rangers.

"I checked their permits myself," Ty explained, opening the door and letting River walk through.

Henry was the first to turn and greet them. "River, I wanted to introduce you to Ezra Fain. He's the head of the team. We also brought out our lead and secondary producers. This is Robert McClellan, who'll head the second team, and Jax Seaborne is in charge when you're in the field."

She stopped, the whole room going cold. She willed herself to wake up because this couldn't possibly be happening to her. He wasn't standing there looking at her with those gorgeous puppy dog eyes. Lying eyes. He'd told her he worked security. If she'd thought for a second he was with the film crew, she would have gone home alone. She wouldn't have had a one-night stand with someone who might employ her at some point.

Of course, she also had promised to stop sleeping with liars and thieves, and that hadn't worked out for her.

"River, it's good to see you. Could we talk privately for a moment?" Jax stepped up to her, a look of concern on his incredibly handsome face. His voice went low. "I'd like a chance to explain."

She bet he would. "I'm sorry, gentlemen. Ty spoke too soon. We're booked up for the rest of the season."

"No, we're not," Andy said, scratching his head in confusion as he looked around as though trying to assess the situation.

Ty stepped up beside her and it was obvious he'd figured out something was wrong. "It was entirely my mistake. I didn't check the calendar."

The blond hottie in the back groaned. "Can we skip all the posturing? Jax fucked up and pissed you off, and how much is it going to cost to get you to deal with him? You should charge the fuck out of us because he's going to be obnoxious as hell since I sent his brother to force him out of your bed, and he's been pissy about it ever since. He's crazy about you, and by crazy I mean mentally unstable."

Jax frowned at the man. "Really? You're going that way?"

"After the night I had, I got nothing but honesty," he said. "I also invested heavily in Adam's new company and they just made a shit ton of cash, so I need the write-off, man. Believe me, I usually go with the lowest bid, but this was a lot of money. I slapped Adam upside the head enough times over the years to make him really smart. I can give the money to the IRS or to the nice lady who might save you from wildlife."

She hated feeling like the butt of the joke. It was obvious they all knew about the night before. Had Jax gone around getting high-fives from all his friends? Had they laughed about it until they'd found out she was the guide? "I'm sorry. I can't do the job."

What amount of money was worth her pride? God, she had so little of that left. Shouldn't she protect the tiny bit that was still hers?

Andy was frowning. "I thought we needed this job."

Ty sent him a look that should have singed him. "We don't."

Nate stepped up. "I don't know what happened, but we should talk because I think this could be good for you."

Jax pushed past him. "Please let me talk to you, River."

"There's nothing to talk about," she offered. "It's simply a scheduling problem."

No one would believe it, but she wouldn't see them again after today. She would stay out of Bliss for a while, too. She would definitely sell the cabin. Maybe it was time to pull up stakes and move. She didn't seem to have much luck here anymore.

Henry pulled a notebook out of his jacket pocket and grabbed a pen from one of the counter tops. He jotted something down and passed her the paper. "Ask for this."

She glanced down and her heart threatened to stop. There was a crazy large number on that piece of paper. "Are you serious?"

Ezra took the note from her hand and nodded. "You got it. Do you want a check or a wire transfer?"

Six figures. More money than her cabin would ever bring in. Definitely more money than her pride was worth. "I'll take the wire transfer."

Even Ty was nodding. He'd seen the number on that piece of paper. "Yep, I think that solves our scheduling issues. Let's take this into the conference room."

Her stomach twisted but she had to stay cool. Jax was nothing but a regret and she had a job to do. "Gentlemen, if you'll follow Ty. We'll get this thing started."

They all moved into the small planning room, but Jax held back.

Andy was a looming presence at her side, but she had to deal with this now. If she was going to take all that pretty money, she had to deal with the reason she was getting it. "I'm fine. Could you give us a moment?"

Andy stared at Jax. "Are you sure?"

"I am. Go and start mapping out some of the production sites for me." She needed to set down a few ground rules. He might not have planned on ever seeing her again, but he would have to now. Perhaps they could come to a mutually agreed upon plan for survival.

The door closed behind Andy and she was alone with Jax.

"I didn't want to leave you last night."

Sure he didn't. "It's fine. It was a one-night stand. There's a reason it's called one night and not one night and half the next day. Now do you want to join the rest of them so we can get down to business? I'm going to assume since you're here that you feel like you can be professional around me."

"Not at all," he replied. "But I'm not all that professional in the first place. River, I didn't want to leave you."

"And yet you managed it brilliantly." The bitter words came from her mouth before she could force them down. She shook it off, hoping she had a professional smile on her face. "I'm sorry. I shouldn't be sarcastic. Like I said before, I was having a rough night and I did something out of character. You saved me the embarrassment of waking up with a stranger in my bed."

Except he hadn't felt like a stranger. Being with Jax had felt natural, like something had finally gone right and she was home again. Something had eased inside her, that tight place she'd had since the day her world had fallen apart. For that whole night she hadn't thought about anything except him, except how good he made her feel. For the first time in forever, she'd felt like she could breathe.

He went still, his gorgeous face falling. "Why would you be embarrassed?"

Because she'd gotten taken again. Because she'd been stupid enough to believe his act. "Like I told you last night, it's not something I do often. I've never actually done it. I got emotional when I shouldn't have. I woke up this morning and I was happy I didn't have to face you."

"I woke up this morning in a panic because I wasn't with you."

He said the weirdest things. He was trying the socially awkward hot guy thing on her again. She couldn't let it work. She couldn't do what she wanted to and reach out to him. "It's all done now."

His hands were fists at his sides. "I don't want it to be over. I don't understand. I know I screwed up. I get that. I said I was going to stay and then I didn't, but that wasn't my fault."

She couldn't help but ask the question. "Oh, really? Did someone show up and drug you and drag you out?"

He seemed to struggle with that. "Would you believe me if I said yes?"

She wouldn't believe him if he told her the sky was blue. "Nope. And again, it doesn't matter because we're going to put it behind us and move on."

His eyes were steady on hers, like he worried if he blinked she would disappear. "I don't think I can."

She had to lay it all on the line for him. "Then we need to find

111

another guide. I'm not falling for this again, Jax. I'm not stupid. I know you went through my purse before you left. Now I'm not sure why. Do you roll people for cash for fun? Because it seems like you have a pretty nice job. A job you lied about."

His eyes widened. "I didn't do that. I swear I didn't. River, I'm not like that. I know I lied about my job, but there's a reason for that. I absolutely didn't touch your purse. I...I didn't mean to hurt you."

She shrugged. "You didn't. It's all good."

"It doesn't feel that way." He carefully measured his words, each one coming out in a calm but confused tone. "I'm not good at this, but even I can tell your words and your expression don't match. You want me to think you're cool, but you're mad at me. You're so angry with me."

She was angry about a lot of things. "No matter how I feel, I can be professional. Do you want to tell me about the sites you want to shoot at? I was told this is a documentary."

He moved in. "I want to talk about us."

She took a quick step back, unwilling to let him get a hand on her. "I'm done talking about us. There is no us and I've told you that several times now. If you keep asking me, I'm going to assume you're harassing me."

"And I'm not supposed to do that." He looked so fucking lost, like he didn't know how to go on. "I'm sorry. I wanted to wake up with you. I loved our night together. It was the single best night of my life."

"Sure it was."

He stepped back, his shoulders slumped. "If you had any concept of what my life is like, you wouldn't question it. If there had been any way for me to stay with you, I would have. I'll behave any way you would like me to from here on out. I don't want to make you uncomfortable. This op is important to all of us. I've been working on it for as long as I can remember, but I'll let my brother handle it."

Something about the way he'd moved away from her made her change her mind. She knew she should take any out she could get with him, but the almost shame that had come over him gutted her. And the fact that she was going to make a fortune off this job. "I'm fine working with you as long as you understand the boundaries. We'll be out there alone some of the time. I'm not going to sleep with you again."

He nodded but didn't look at her. "All right. Like I said, I'll behave however you like."

"Then let's join the others and get started." She moved toward the door. It was better this way. She wasn't sure she could stand there with him another minute without losing her damn mind and reaching out for him.

When she got to the door, he rushed by her, opening it for her, his eyes meeting hers. She could have sworn there was pain in those gorgeous orbs.

She pushed the thought aside. She wasn't going to think about his weird, beautiful self again. But as she sat down at the head of the table, she couldn't help but wonder what the hell he'd meant when he'd called this job an "op."

She wasn't going to look his way. Even when he was the one talking, she would pointedly open the folder and brush through the pages, keeping her eyes on anything but him. It was easier that way. She was still trying to find a way out. The money was incredible, but she worried if she actually went out into the forest with him, she'd screw up all over again.

Because even though he'd lied to her, he was still the single most delicious man she'd ever set eyes on.

"We've got two basic tracts we want to search," he said, passing out the folders. "I've included maps and the grid pattern we'll use if River thinks it's a workable solution. You'll note that they're both deep in the forest. They're off the beaten track. We'll need to take along everything we need to survive for the days we'll be in there. We can take a Jeep part way, but then the terrain is such that we have to go by foot or helo."

Helicopter? He used a surprisingly militaristic vocabulary for a film producer. "I would prefer not to use a helicopter. First off, we don't have a lot of them out here. They're mostly used for search and rescue. We would have to borrow one or at least use their landing sites."

"We've already discussed and discarded the idea of choppers," Fain said. "Too much attention. We want to keep this low key."

She frowned as she looked over the map, her mind putting the land into the right places. "A couple of these places are no-gos. This is all public land, but not every acre is usable by the public. There are places in the Rio Grande Forest where camping isn't allowed. You seemed to have found most of them. We can't even hike through some of this."

There might still be a way out. If they couldn't get into the place they were trying to film, there was nothing she could do about it. She wasn't going to break the law.

Ty was staring down at the map, pointing to a big swath of forest in the middle. "This whole area is off limits."

And there was the catch. There was nothing out there for them to film with the exception of moose and elk and the occasionally cranky bear. A couple of the spots were designated refuge areas.

She'd known it was too good to be true, rather like the man running the meeting. "What exactly are we looking for, gentlemen? I was told this was about the environmental impact of big business on the national forest land. There's no big business out here. Unless you count Marie and Teeny. They're talking about opening a used bookstore. Between that, the tea room, and the Trading Post, they're kind of the captains of industry around here. I seriously doubt they're dumping trash and used tea bags deep in the forest."

"Absolutely not," Henry said. "They follow all of the best recycling practices. They would never pollute anything but the air." He shrugged. "Marie has a potty mouth at times."

She gave him her best stay-on-task stare. "I'm serious, Henry. What's this actually about?"

The golden god of a man who she'd found out was called Taggart set down his coffee mug. "It's about all those zeroes you just got."

Nope. She wasn't going there. It was important to set some ground rules right up front. She'd done this job long enough to know that some clients weren't worth the trouble. "Zeroes are nice. Truth is better. Look, I need the money, but I also need to keep my business. You seem to think you can walk in here, flash a ton of cash, and get me to do anything you want. I won't do anything illegal and I won't do anything unnecessarily dangerous. And *I* make the call as to whether or not something is dangerous. You are not the expert, Mr. Taggart. I am."

"I'm a former Green Beret. I assure you, I know a thing or two about surviving," he shot back.

"And if I need someone to save me from bad guys, I'll give you a call. If you knew how to handle those woods, you wouldn't need me. You would lead this party yourself." If there was one place she still felt confident, it was in the wild.

His lips turned up in the faintest grin. "I'm far too old to rough it. I like beds and I swore I'd never eat another MRE again. When we take the kids out, my wife and I are all about the glamping."

Fain snorted. "Sure you are."

Taggart chuckled. "Charlie glamped my rig up. We get Netflix in that sucker. Oh, we put the kids in a tent with one flashlight between them because they need to learn to survive. We already did that. That's why the puppies are running this show. Their backs can handle it."

She wasn't sure that man took anything seriously. "I have to know what I'm taking us into. You're holding out on me and that makes me worry. If I can't trust you out there, there's no amount of money that will get me to risk my crew on this mission of yours."

"It's not a mission," Fain insisted. "It's a film."

Taggart sat back, those ruthlessly intelligent eyes watching her. "We have all the proper permits. I'll give you copies and you can make calls if you like. We've made all the arrangements with the National Forest Service. I assure you, those tracts of land aren't off limits to us."

"And that scares me, too." She wasn't getting a filmmaker vibe off these guys. Only the fact that Henry Flanders was in the room kept her from walking away. Otherwise, she would be worried she was getting the wool pulled over her eyes again and she was being asked to work for the mafia. She could see the big guy running some American wing of the Swedish mob. Did they have a mob? Didn't everyone have a mob? "No one gets these permits with the exception of scientists."

"Or documentarians trying to prove that there's a secret CIA black ops site deep in the forest." The words dropped from Jax's mouth like a boulder.

Or a landmine. Yep, she was standing on a landmine, and if she moved it would explode. "The CIA doesn't work on American soil."

Taggart stared at Jax, an arctic look in his eyes. "I thought we were going to keep that secret."

"She needs to know that this is dangerous. I'm not letting her walk into this ignorant." Jax turned to her. "This team was put together because of the potential danger the job holds. Most of us are ex-military. We're all trained. Every single man on this crew can handle himself, and we can protect you. What we can't protect you from is whatever the hell is in that building."

"Could I take this moment to remind everyone in here that you all signed nondisclosure agreements?" Robert asked with a grimace. "We're going to take that seriously. You are not allowed to talk about anything that happens during this expedition, and that includes what goes on in this room."

They were all frowning at Jax, but she was grateful at least one of them was telling her the truth. Why did it have to be him? She wasn't going to soften. Just because he was telling the truth now didn't mean he wouldn't lie later. She should have known this would go south when they'd had her fill out as much paperwork as she'd given them. "We know how to be discreet. This is not our first nondisclosure."

"Yeah, I once took a group of swingers out into the woods, and I've never talked about that," Ty offered with a shudder. "I really try not to talk about it. Or think about it."

Taggart snorted. "I'll remember that." He sighed and seemed to relax. "Well, go on then, Romeo. The floor is yours."

The sarcasm didn't seem to faze Jax. He turned toward her, his gaze serious. "It's called The Ranch. The Agency used it to house medical experiments they wanted to keep off the radar."

A chill went through her. "This is starting to sound like a conspiracy theory. Like a medical Area 51."

His gaze didn't waver. "If this is nothing but a conspiracy theory, then you've got nothing to worry about and we're out a ton of cash."

"I'm struggling with the idea that the actual CIA is here in Colorado," Andy said. "I thought they worked in places like the Middle East. Aren't they spies? Why do they care about medical stuff?"

It was a good question. "Isn't the CIA supposed to protect us from foreign attacks?"

"The CIA's mission is to gather intelligence that will protect our country from all kinds of attacks," Fain said. "Everything from physical terrorist attacks to cyber attacks to foreign governments manipulating our systems for their own gain. The question is always how to do it. Sometimes they try to protect in extremely ruthless ways. And I assure you they have an interest in all things scientific and technological. The Agency knows the future of warfare will be on two fronts—the cyber and the biological. The time for big bombs is over. Bombs are for terrorists. Viruses are the new Manhattan Project."

"And drugs," Jax added. "Pharmaceuticals can be used to keep a population in line. Drugs and other therapies can make soldiers stronger."

"Eugenics is back in play," the man named Robert said. "Originally it was a way to manipulate the human gene before birth to make the human race stronger. It was perverted by the Nazis to build the master race. Now we use it to make sure our kids have blue eyes and not brown. But the Agency would use it to make their soldiers better, faster, stronger."

She'd landed in some kind of sci-fi story. "How would they know who is going to grow up to be soldiers?"

"Not all DNA is manipulated before birth," Jax said with a gravity that scared her.

"And they're doing this in my backyard?" It was almost incomprehensible. She lived here to be away from all the crap that

117

came with large populations of humans. She turned to Nate. "Do you believe this is true?"

Nate nodded. "Yes. I do. I also believe that these men will do everything they can to protect you. There are rumors that The Ranch has been abandoned because the current administration would likely have a problem with what went on there."

"They shut the whole thing down overnight," Jax explained. "And from what we understand they haven't been back. This was a site that housed roughly twenty labs and everything that goes with medical research."

"Like medical waste?" Ty asked. "But they would have gotten rid of that, right? We have regulations."

"And that's why it's a black ops site," Taggart pointed out. "No oversight. I assure you the EPA isn't watching them. The EPA has no idea they exist. Neither did the Bliss County Sheriff's Department."

"We might have had something to say about it," Nate agreed.

"It's beyond mere medical waste. It's everything that goes along with having a bunch of humans and animals in a closed space for months or years at a time." Jax's fingers drummed along the tabletop. "All those systems are degrading by the day. Our research indicates that The Ranch has been closed down for roughly three years. They left everything. All the doctors and staff were taken out, but we believe everything else was abandoned."

All those chemicals. They would have used generators and chemical toilets and god only knew what else. Nature had a way of encroaching. Years of disuse would lead to ways in and out. It would affect the wildlife and the biosphere. It could be worse. "It might affect our water supply."

Experimental drugs could seep into the water table, finding their way into the reservoirs.

Andy looked a little pale. "I think this is bigger than we can handle. You need to get the authorities involved."

Nate's brows rose. "Am I chopped liver?"

Andy frowned and pushed away from the table. "No, but you're a small-town sheriff and this is a big-time problem. This could affect everyone in this part of Colorado."

"Which is precisely why we're asking for your help." Jax sounded entirely too sensible. "We have to find the site and document it. Otherwise they'll continue to let it decay or they'll do something more drastic. Fires are common in this part of the country. A nice fire could potentially destroy all the evidence. Oh, it could also decimate the forest and possibly kill off the towns around it, but that's what the term *collateral damage* was invented to describe."

She couldn't get out of this.

She would be stuck out there with him, and she couldn't pawn it off because what he was doing was important. It was critical.

Her heart sank as she forced herself to look at him. She was trapped and there was no way out. In this particular game, she'd lost the second round, too.

She didn't have high hopes for a third.

Chapter Seven

Several hours later, Jax zipped up the lightweight windbreaker Teeny Warner swore would keep him warm during the cool nights out in the forest. He looked at himself in the mirror. There was a hollow look in his eyes that never seemed to go away.

He thought seriously about smashing that mirror into pieces. It had been so long since he'd had blood on his hands. Mother had been right. It was really the only thing he was good at.

"Robert said you flat out told River what we were looking for. You told her about The Ranch?" Tucker was wearing the same jacket only in blue instead of black. "I thought we weren't supposed to do that."

They had a shopping list of personal items River thought they would need for the expedition. She'd handed him the handwritten list at the end of their meeting. She'd had a hollow look in her eyes, too.

Had he put it there?

"I wasn't going to lie to her. I hate the fact that I already did." He shrugged out of the jacket and into the second one he'd been given to try on. It fit better than the first. He hated clothes shopping. When he'd been rescued, he'd come out of the facility with nothing but the white T-shirt and gray pants he'd been given to sleep in. They all wore the same things. No one was different in

Mother's world. The evil doc had believed in equality among her soldiers. Everyone got the same torturous drugs and the same utilitarian clothes to wear. Two sets of PJs. Two sets of fatigues. One pair of boots. Five pair of boxers and socks. He'd left it all behind except for what he'd worn out of the facility. He would have left that behind, too, if Taggart hadn't forbidden nudity on his private plane.

At the time he'd thought he would buy all new things. It had felt like a fresh start. So why when given the choice did he always buy the most utilitarian thing he could? There were lots of colors, but he'd picked up the black and navy blue. All of his T-shirts were plain. Now he owned three pairs of jeans. Four plain T-shirts. One pair of slacks with three collared shirts in neutral colors.

There was very little color in his world. He'd loved the fact that River's offices had been brightly painted. The walls had been a sky blue, covered with pictures of the adventures she'd led. He'd stared at them for the longest time. She had a whole wall of memories.

He only remembered pain and one night with her.

"I'm sorry about last night." Tucker unzipped his jacket and put it on the buy pile. "Can we talk about it now or are you still ignoring me?"

What the hell other color would he get? And Tucker was right. He couldn't ignore him forever. "It was stupid to think it could work out."

He'd hated how distant she'd been. Hated how she'd looked at him and reminded him how many times she'd asked him to stop talking about their non-relationship. She'd left him no way out except to leave her alone.

She hadn't looked happy alone.

"Did you hear the part where I was sorry?" Tucker was staring at him in the mirror.

"You were doing your job." The job was pretty much all any of them had. Even Dante.

Tucker's jaw firmed, a stubborn look coming into his eyes. "I won't do it again."

Now Tucker had his back? "You won't have to. I told you

121

she's done with me."

"She doesn't have to be."

He turned because that hadn't been said by Tucker. That optimistic statement had come from a feminine voice.

Tucker's whole face lit up. He went from grim to hopeful in a second, reminding Jax of how Tucker could find the light in any darkness. "Heather, it's good to see you. We missed you at the meeting. Were you looking for me?"

Heather stood a couple of feet away, a bag in her hand. She'd obviously been downstairs shopping. The Trading Post was Bliss's all-purpose store. The grocery and household goods were on the first floor. The second floor contained clothing and sporting goods and an odd collection of miscellany. He had to wonder if she'd heard them talking and headed up the stairs.

Heather stepped forward and ruffled Tucker's hair like he was a puppy. "No, I didn't, sweetie. I told you. You are far too young for me."

"We don't even know how old…" Tucker began with a frown. "I mean you don't know. I could be far older than I look."

She smiled vibrantly and shook her head. "Not a chance, buddy." She turned to Jax, her smile fading. "You fucked up. River has been screwed over one too many times. She'll take anything you do and twist it into something bad. She's looking at the world through poop-colored glasses, if you know what I mean. I came looking for you because I need to know if I should kick your ass or help you out because you're dumb as dirt."

She was giving him a chance? A tiny kernel of hope kindled inside him. "Dumb as dirt."

"Whoa," Tucker intervened. "He's not dumb. He wanted to stay with her, but we had an emergency back at the base. I had to come get him. He's our computer and security expert. He was the only one who could deal with the problem."

She crossed her arms over her chest. "All right. I can understand an emergency. Why not leave a note?"

Dante had fucked him over. He wouldn't be in this situation if he hadn't been drugged and dragged out. "I didn't think about it at the time and I'd forgotten to get River's phone number. I meant to go by after the meeting with our guide. Surprise. I'm with the film crew. So is Tucker. We didn't talk about that because we've gotten burned by women who thought we were Hollywood types. We're not, though we do know some actors."

Her brow arched. "You do?"

This really was part of their cover. Over the years McKay-Taggart had done some bodyguard work for stars and royalty. "One of our best friends is married to Joshua Hunt, and we've worked with Lyle Tarpin before."

Her eyes went wide. "The action star?"

He nodded. "Yes. He's a pretty cool guy. We did a couple of pieces on the king and queen of Loa Mali, too. But we mostly work with journalists. I would never want a woman to sleep with me because she thought she would get something out of it beyond an orgasm and my deepest affection."

"I am not as picky," Tucker offered. "I'm cool with whatever she gets out of it."

Heather ignored him. "Okay. I accept your explanation. Are you still interested in River?"

"Yes." He'd been trying to find some way around her *we can't talk about our relationship* edict. It was making him crazy. He finally kind-of, sort-of had a relationship and he definitely wanted to talk about it. "I like her very much. I'd like to spend time with her."

"She has an ex," Heather began.

Jax nodded. This had been his morning project. "Yes, I believe I've found all his aliases. The wire transfers should go through tonight. I've set it up like a line of dominoes. They'll start falling at nine p.m. Central time. I located him in Omaha. I don't want him going into a physical bank. He'll have to call customer service."

"I'm sorry. What are you talking about?" Heather asked.

He'd thought it might be the only thing he had to give River. A little revenge. A lot of justice. Sometimes they went hand in hand. "The sheriff gave me her ex-husband's name. By the end of the night, River will have her money back. Probably more. I don't know how much he stole from her so I took everything. She also

123

now owns a nice one bedroom in Midtown Manhattan."

Heather's jaw dropped open. "Are you fucking with me?"

"He never fucks around about ruining lives," Tucker explained solemnly. "Dante should be glad he doesn't have an internet footprint or Jax would have come down on his ass. Once a member of British parliament called our friend Kayla a cow and Jax doctored up a video of him screwing farm animals. He didn't get reelected."

"Tucker, new friends." Tucker had absolutely no discretion. Not that he was ashamed of what he'd done. That PM had also screwed over more women than Jax could count, and Me Too hadn't started at the time. It had been up to him to deal out some justice.

"I like you, Seaborne. I'm going to take you under my wing," Heather said. "First we're going to dress you better. Then we're going to do a couple of things that will make River's heart melt and get you right back in her bed. Tell me something—was your revenge on Matt all financial?"

That would be far too easy. "He might find himself with any number of arrest warrants in most of the cities he would run to. And I might have tipped off the cops in Omaha to the illegal drugs he has in his apartment."

"Did he have illegal drugs?" she asked.

"He will after the PI I paid gets through," he said with a shrug. "I've learned one lesson. If you're going to take someone down, take them all the way down. He won't hurt another woman again."

Heather sighed. "I did not expect that. You're going to make this hard on me, aren't you?"

"I'll make it quite easy. I'll do anything you tell me to do if it gets her to like me again." He wasn't going to be stubborn about anything but getting her back.

An oddly wistful look crossed Heather's face. "I do like a man who knows what he wants. River is a wonderful person. She's a little lost right now. I think she needs you."

It hurt to hear that. There was an ache in his chest thinking of her adrift. "I know how that feels."

She picked up the jacket he'd tried on. "I think we're going to trade this in. I saw a nice green one. It would go well with your eyes. And we're going to tighten up those jeans."

He put himself in Heather's capable hands.

* * * *

River sat in the booth at Hell on Wheels and stared down at the beer in front of her.

"Are you sure you don't want to go to Trio?" Sawyer asked, his brows drawn as he looked at the two of them. It wasn't every day the owner of a business tried to get less business. Then again, she wasn't the usual client here. She glanced around. It was past nine and the crowd was starting to pick up. The booths were all full and the bar was getting there. A group of rough-looking bikers had come in five minutes before. They'd ordered beers and whiskey and started to boldly check out every woman in the place. Heather had already turned down three different men and they'd only just sat down. "I don't have any of that fancy wine you like."

Sawyer owned Hell on Wheels. The bar had been handed down from his grandfather who had started it on unincorporated land fifty years before. Sawyer hadn't bothered to update the décor. It was a dive and proud to be one. If a night went by without a fight, it was a miracle. She was hoping for a miracle tonight. And by fancy wine, he meant the kind that used a corkscrew.

"The beer is fine. You know, if I didn't know any better I would think you don't want us here, Sawyer." She didn't need to deal with his overly protective instincts tonight. She needed a beer. It had been one more tough day to get through. One more day when she would go to bed alone and worried about how to get through the next.

His normally hard face softened slightly. "You know that's not true. But I also know how nights here can go. I don't want you caught up in that. Trio would be far more peaceful."

It wouldn't be peaceful for her. She would look at the booth where she'd spent the night cuddled against Jax's warm body, trying to make sure she didn't get a mouthful of bacon.

"We won't be long." She wasn't even sure why she'd decided

125

to come out tonight. Something about going back to her cabin, back to the silence and the odd mix of regret and fear and calm. In the cabin alone she had to mourn, and she was so sick of mourning.

"I promise to watch out for her," Heather said.

Sawyer shook his head. "Yeah, that's what I'm afraid of. I don't like the feel of the crowd tonight. Things start going south in here, you two head back to my office. And if any asshole won't take no for an answer, let me know."

He stalked back behind the bar, pouring out a whiskey for a blonde in a barely-there miniskirt. Hell on Wheels was starting to fill up with a crowd that wouldn't be caught dead at family friendly Trio. If Trio was a pub filled with happy tourists and familiar locals, Hell on Wheels was pure bar. Most of the people who walked in came alone, looking for someone to spend some time with or a way to forget all the things that were wrong with their lives.

She belonged here.

What was Jax doing tonight? She'd sent him off with a list of things he would need for the couple of nights they would be out in the forest. She would do the heavy lifting when it came to shopping for equipment, but the nights were getting cold and he would need more than the light hoodie he'd come with. He'd told her he didn't own a coat. Who didn't own a coat when he lived in London?

"What were they like? The film crew, I mean." Heather sipped on her vodka tonic. "Andy said they were all dicks and that he could legally disclose that. I wasn't sure what he meant."

Because she'd missed that meeting. "I can't legally tell you until you sign the paperwork. Let's just say they're interested in protecting what they're investigating. It's more complicated than we thought, but we're still doing the job. And they weren't all that dickish."

She was already softening. Give her a couple of hours and all her good sense flew out the window. She'd barely managed to not call Jax back and let him explain. Would she ever learn?

"Really? Andy particularly hated the head producer guy."

"Taggart? He wasn't all that bad. I talked to him after the meeting." He'd been sarcastic as fuck, but there was something about the man that made her think he was honorable. He'd thanked her for challenging him. He'd told her he didn't trust anyone who kissed his ass.

Heather shook her head. "No, the other one. Uhm...the Fain guy. That was his name, right?"

Ezra. He was an enigma. "He was pretty quiet, actually. If I had to guess, he has as much power with that group as Taggart does even though he doesn't flex his muscle as much. He seems incredibly smart, but he doesn't talk a lot. He's hot, though. They're all hot. Could they not find any plain guys? Speaking of, you know just because it didn't work out with me and Jax doesn't mean you have to dump Tucker."

Heather sputtered, patting her chest until she could breathe again. "No. You misunderstand, my friend. I'm not interested in Tucker. I prefer my men a little rougher, if you know what I mean."

River preferred Jax. Well, she preferred the idea of Jax. Why had he turned out to be such a liar? "Well, you won't have to worry about him. You'll be leading the group with Robert and Owen. Robert seems solid, very smart. Owen has a Scottish accent that would melt the panties off most women, and he's a flirty boy."

"I'm not most women." Heather sat back, glancing around the bar. "Trust me. Those guys will get an excellent guide and nothing else. I did catch a glimpse of the maps when I dropped some supplies off earlier. I was surprised. It looked like some of those places are off limits."

The off-limits sites wouldn't be roped off, but all the experts knew where not to go. The rangers would patrol those sites and they would escort anyone in violation out of the forest. They would not be welcome back in. "They had permits."

She'd called and the paperwork had held up. They were going in on scientific permits.

Heather seemed to think about that for a moment. "I guess that's what Andy was upset about. I don't know him all that well. He's kind of a loner, but I do know how much it annoys him when

127

he feels like protected sites are trampled on."

"I think I'll let Andy watch the offices while you and I head the two teams and Ty stays at base camp. Do you think Andy's ready to be in charge of the office?"

Heather shrugged. "It'll be fine. Though I do wonder how much we know about him. He doesn't talk about himself."

"We're a weird group. Most of the people I worked with over the years have more in common with Andy than you or Ty. The kind of people who like to spend long periods of time in the wilderness tend to be loners. I don't talk a lot, either." She took a sip of her beer. After all this was over, she would take a trip by herself. She would have the money to take a few weeks off, find a good trail and hike. There were places where she could walk for days and not see another soul.

Maybe then she could find a way out of this cage she was in.

"You can talk to me, you know." Heather leaned over as the jukebox started playing, the sound of classic rock filling the room.

"There's nothing to say."

Heather glanced up as the door came open, a cool breeze sweeping through the room. "Well, maybe that will give us something to talk about."

River turned slightly and frowned. Jax had just walked through the door and he wasn't alone. Tucker was with him along with Robert and Owen, who she'd met earlier in the day.

She couldn't catch a break.

And it wasn't like he could walk in looking like hell. Nope. He had on a pair of Levis that managed to sit low on his hips and hug his ass. No man should have an ass like that. Muscular and round, and he hadn't minded when she'd held those cheeks in her hands as he'd driven into her, making her scream out his name.

"Are you okay?"

She kind of heard Heather. Mostly she heard the way Jax laughed at something Owen was saying to him. He didn't smile a lot. There seemed to be a shroud of sorrow around him sometimes, but when that handsome face split into a grin it was like the sun came out.

He turned and then the smile was gone as he caught her gaze.

She turned back to Heather as fast as she could. Maybe he wouldn't come over. Maybe he hadn't noticed that she was drooling and making an idiot of herself when she'd told him she wasn't interested in him anymore.

"He's totally coming over here, and he's got his band of man hotties with him. Do you think they would be upset if I called them a man squad? And take a deep breath. You're super flushed right now," Heather said.

Crap. Crap. Crap.

Why did she hate the fact that he'd stopped smiling when he'd seen her? Why did that make her ache? She'd tried to tell herself it was a good thing that he'd shown his true colors, but now she wasn't sure what those colors were. He'd been so sweet earlier in the day. He'd seemed earnest and real, but then, like he'd said, he knew a lot of actors.

"Hello, River." His voice was deep and rich.

She loved the sound of it. She bet he could sing. "Hi. I didn't expect to see you here."

"Would you like us to leave?" He stared down at her with sad puppy eyes. Gorgeous eyes. "I didn't come here to make you uncomfortable. Big Tag and Ezra gave us the night off. We thought we would have a couple of drinks."

Heather sat up. "Is the whole gang here, then?"

He shook his head. "The bosses are hanging out with Nell and Henry. Big Tag complained about tofu, but it was actually pretty good. I'm not minding going vegetarian. I think I might try it for a while. Sasha and Dante are hanging around the house."

"The house being that massive cabin on the Rio Grande?" Heather asked.

Billionaire software developer Seth Stark had spent his summers in Bliss when he was growing up. When he'd decided to settle down and get married in true Bliss fashion, he'd built a massive cabin on the banks of the Rio Grande outside of town. It made sense they were staying there. She hadn't heard about the Movie Motel being full.

He nodded. "Mr. Stark is in New York and graciously allowed us to stay. It was good to see you, River. We'll grab a six pack and head back to our place."

He didn't get out much. The way he and Tucker talked, their bosses kept them inside most of the time. She wasn't sure why. Possibly the delicate nature of this job. If she had to stay inside all day she would go stir-crazy. She couldn't help but think about the way he'd stared up at the stars the night before. He'd tilted his head up and there had been a look of wonder in his eyes. Like he'd never seen the sky before.

He'd looked at her that way. Like he'd never seen a woman before and couldn't take his eyes away. In that moment, she'd felt beautiful.

"You don't have to leave." She couldn't send him away. "I was almost done."

"We just got here," Heather complained.

Now if she retreated, they both suffered because she got the idea Jax would be hurt.

If he could be hurt by her leaving, if he was capable of that kind of emotion, he wasn't exactly a ruthless bastard, was he? "We can share the bar. We're going to be sharing the woods in a few days anyway."

The smile that rocked her damn world was back. "Thanks. And yes, we will. I got my jacket today. And some socks. Mine all had holes in them. I think Owen does the laundry wrong." He stopped, his expression turning a bit sheepish. "You don't want to hear my laundry stories. I'll go hang with my broth…the guys. See you later."

He turned and there was his backside. He did not skimp on the glute workouts.

"You're flushed again. Should I check your temp?" Heather looked like the cat who had lapped up all the cream.

"No." She sipped on her beer, determined not to look their way. "And you're a terrible wingman."

"I'm an awesome wingman," she argued. Heather didn't seem to mind looking at the group of hot guys. "I think you're wrong about Jax. I think he's a nice guy. Can I ask you a question?"

"I get the feeling you're going to ask it even if I say no."

"Was he bad in bed?"

River sighed. "He was perfect. He was amazing. I didn't take exception to anything but the fact that he felt the need to lie to me. And he went through my purse."

"You don't know that he did that. I've thought about this. The door was slightly open when I got there. What if it was a raccoon?" Heather asked. "Have you confronted him about it? We know he didn't take anything."

Was she really certain she hadn't unzipped her purse sometime that night? She'd had her mind on other things and she'd had a couple of drinks. Nothing had been missing.

Heather seemed to sense that she was wavering. "Would it be so bad to spend time with him while he's here? He's going to be in town for a few weeks. Why not enjoy him? Are you afraid you'll fall for him?"

She'd already fallen for a version of him.

Heather leaned in, her voice going low. "You never have any fun. You never let go, River. How can you get back into the groove of life if you keep running away from it? Do you want to be stuck forever?"

"No." She couldn't stand the thought of staying in this place, this bland, colorless existence she'd been living in since she'd realized her father was dying. She hadn't even cried. She'd buried him and shed not one tear. She hadn't cried in the last months. Numbness had taken over and all she'd felt was regret that she couldn't mourn the father she'd loved because she'd spent so much of her soul serving him in his last days, watching that once mighty man grow small and confused, crying out like a child in the night.

The evening before had been the first time she'd felt alive in forever.

Could she handle it? Could she enjoy Jax and not expect anything but a good time?

"I'm not ready." It hurt to say the words. She wanted to walk over and pretend she was that girl, pretend she could have fun, but she wouldn't. She would get in too deep with him. She would need him and she couldn't let herself need anyone else. Maybe not ever again.

Watching her father die seemed to have killed something

131

inside her, too.

Heather put her drink down. "All right. Well, we'll sit here for a bit and then we'll go back into town. I'm sorry. I worry about you."

She was trying to be a good friend, but River wasn't sure she wanted to feel close to anyone right now.

Melancholy stole over her as the song changed to a ballad.

She glanced over and Jax had taken a seat next to the blonde at the bar. He was turned away from her, talking to his brother, but the blonde was staring openly at his back. River realized she'd probably looked a whole lot like that when he'd first walked in.

It looked like the blonde had a friend. A busty brunette walked in from the back of the bar where the bathrooms were. She stopped and stared and then seemed to have a whole slutty conversation with her friend using only the powers of their skankiness.

Damn. She wasn't that girl either. She didn't judge anyone for how they dressed or who they consensually slept with.

"Uhm, maybe we should go." Heather was staring at her like she'd grown a couple of heads.

Her purse suddenly vibrated. "Why?" She reached in, not wanting to take her eyes off Jax. Maybe this was exactly what she needed. She needed to watch him pick up another woman. Or two. They were two sexy women. Sure she thought they didn't need to show their hoochies off every time they bent over, but that was their choice. And maybe they had particularly overheated hoochies that required more air circulation.

Or they were skank hos.

She didn't even look to see who was calling, simply slid a finger over the screen to accept the call. "Hello."

They were circling him like two bedazzled sharks. He was talking to Tucker. Owen seemed to have figured out there were women in the bar, but Jax hadn't even noticed them. The blonde tapped on his shoulder and he turned, shook his head and turned back to Tucker.

"What have you done to me, you bitch?"

She started at the sound of that familiar voice. "Matt?"

"You know exactly who this is."

Heather's eyes had gone wide. "Your ex?"

She nodded. "Why are you calling me?"

"Because I'm on the run, you vindictive bitch. Did you think I wouldn't figure out it was you? Where did you put it? That was two million dollars. Two million fucking dollars I worked my ass off for."

"I have no idea what you're talking about but if you call me a bitch one more time I'll hang up." She should hang up anyway, but she was curious. He sounded angry and panicked. There was a part of her that kind of loved that.

Heather had moved out of the booth, leaving her alone.

"You stole my money. How did you find those accounts? Where did you put it? I can't even figure out how you did it. Look here, River, I played nice the first time," Matt growled over the line.

"By stealing everything my father and I had? Didn't seem nice to me."

"By not hurting you, sweetheart," he explained. "I didn't see reason to but I'm rethinking my position now."

"I haven't touched you, Matt. I did report you to the authorities since I got that lovely bill for twenty grand. You're still stealing from me," she said, indignation growing.

"I'm going to kill you if you don't put my money back."

A big hand covered hers and before she knew it that callused masculine hand was lifting the phone away from her.

Jax stood at the end of the booth, his eyes icy as he put the phone to his ear. "Hello, Mr. Lewis, or should I call you by any of your various aliases? I assure you I know them all. My name is Robin Hood. Yeah. I'm the one who stole your money, and I'm giving it back to every person you ever conned. And if you call River again, we'll take this fight of ours from the virtual world into the physical one. Yes, I would like that, too. Let me make this plain. If I catch you having any contact with River again, I'll kill you myself. And yes, I know where you live. I'm sending someone by in the morning to have a talk about other reparations." Jax sighed and pulled the phone from his ear. "He hung up. It must have been something I said. Or maybe it had something to do with

133

the police sirens I heard in the background. I can't be sure."

"What did you do?"

"I might have tracked your ex-husband down, found all his bank accounts, and had them wired to yours. How much did he steal? We didn't get around to talking actual numbers."

"It was around two hundred thousand."

One muscular shoulder shrugged. "Now you have two million. Interest."

She felt her jaw drop. "Jax, you can't do that."

"'Course he can," Owen said in his thick Scottish brogue. "He's good with a computer and he's got a wicked sense of justice. Dante was saying his email got lit up with something called furry porn. I gotta think that was you after the way Dante hauled you out of River's place last night."

She couldn't even process that bit of information. "What do you mean you took his money and gave it to me?"

"I hacked his bank account and transferred it to you. I would say it's simple, but it's actually quite difficult. You see, there's a firewall I had to get through," Jax began.

Why was he being deliberately obtuse? "Why would you do that?"

He loomed over her, his eyes warm now. "Because I wanted to make sure he can't hurt you again."

How did he think this was going to be okay? "That wasn't your call, Jax."

"Hey, you should leave the angry chick alone and come hang out with us." The blonde had gotten off her barstool and stood behind Jax, putting a manicured hand on his shoulder.

He gently brushed it off. "I'm sorry. I can't talk right now. I need to explain what I did to River." He turned back to her. "I didn't like what Matt Lewis did to you and the cops weren't doing anything about it."

"And they weren't going to," Heather said under her breath.

"I went to Nate," she said with a huff. What had Jax done? "You have to put the money back. I'm going to get in trouble."

"Why would you get in trouble for taking back your own money?" Jax asked.

He was being naïve. "I assure you Matt will have a way to make it look like I stole it. It's what he does. He's a damn con artist. He's a criminal."

"It's okay. I've thought about that, too. The police are on their way to his place right now." Jax's eyes opened wide and he jumped slightly before turning to the woman behind him. "I did not give you consent to touch my bottom, ma'am."

Oh, she was done with Blondie. "Get your hands off him."

The brunette was suddenly by her side. "Says who?"

"Well, him for one thing." Heather moved to River.

She might have to rethink the idea that Heather was a bad wingman because it felt good to have some backup. Especially since Jax looked slightly confused as to what to do. He was frowning. He'd apparently ruined her ex-husband's life with a few keystrokes and then threatened to violently murder the man, but a woman getting too aggressive made him stop.

Because he wouldn't hurt a woman. Because he'd been raised to be a gentleman.

Everything he'd done the night before had been with her comfort in mind with the single exception of leaving her alone.

"Is there some kind of problem?" Sawyer was a massive presence even among the big guys.

"No problem." Robert seemed eager to step up and deal with the situation. "We're going to leave and go to the other bar. You know the one where we don't get in trouble. I believe I might have mentioned we should go there instead of here since we were specifically told not to come here in the first place."

"Who told you not to come here?" Sawyer frowned Robert's way. "And what the hell's wrong with my bar?"

"And there is definitely a problem," Tucker said. "Because Jax did not give consent to have his ass cupped. He's saving that for River. My ass, on the other hand, is perfectly single and available for cuppings."

Owen winked at the skanks. "Mine, too, loves."

"I don't think he minds." The brunette put one hand on Jax's chest and the other clearly on his ass. "He's just playing hard to get. He loves this."

She wasn't sure why her hand was suddenly in the brunette's hair, but she found herself dragging the woman away from Jax. "He said no. He doesn't want you to touch him."

The brunette yelped and then tried to dig those claws of hers in and chaos erupted in the bar. One of the bikers threw a punch Sawyer's way for no reason River could discern, though she was distracted at the time since Blondie decided to defend her friend by jumping on River's back.

Heather was right there. "Got this."

She was like a freaking ninja. Heather pulled the blonde up by her hair, dragging her off. "I'm going to teach you not to touch a sister's property, my friend."

Jax stepped in front of her, taking a punch in the back from the brunette that had definitely been meant for her front. If he felt that punch, he didn't show it at all. He simply put his hands on her arms as though bracing her. "I am very confused about how to act in this situation."

"I'm not!" Owen grinned and threw himself right in the middle of a mass of punching bodies.

Robert threw his hands up and waded in while Tucker shook his head and went back to the bar.

Sawyer had a biker in a choke hold. "Really, River? I did not expect this from you. Get her out of here. Now."

Jax lifted her up and she found herself cradled against his big chest. He held her close, protecting her from the chaos. He moved through the fight around them, gracefully dodging every stray punch and kick that came their way.

"I can't leave Heather," she shouted over the wails. She glanced over his shoulder back to where they'd left her friend.

"I'm good!" Heather had the blonde on the floor and was going after the brunette. "This is excellent stress relief. You two have fun."

Tucker held up his beer as they walked by. "I'll make sure she gets home okay."

"See, she's fine. Come on. I have a present for you." He strode out into the night and she wondered how much trouble she was in.

She was pretty sure it was a lot.

Chapter Eight

"You have to put me down now."

Jax kept moving. He wasn't putting her down until they were well away from the dive bar from hell. Maybe dive bar *in* hell. Wasn't that pretty much as far as one could dive? Damn, but he'd been tempted to make the same jump his brothers had.

If she hadn't been in his arms, his hands would have been shaking. Walking away from all that violence had been hard. He'd been conditioned to do violence, and it had been far too long since he'd had a taste of that particular drug. Someone always broke up any fight he'd gotten into when they'd lived at The Garden. They'd always joked about the time Dante had snuck out to find a prostitute. What they didn't talk about was the fact that after he'd had the woman, paid for her services and walked away, it hadn't been enough. He'd walked straight into a pub and gotten himself arrested. By the time Damon had found him, Dante had a broken nose and an arrest for assault. He'd had a satisfied smile on his face when he'd gotten back, a dark look that made Jax wonder if any of them was salvageable.

When that first punch had been thrown this evening, his instinct had been to walk into it, to take it and let it fuel a nice long session of brutality. Maybe at the end he too would have that smile.

He couldn't let River see that part of himself. Ever. He had to tamp it down.

"I'll let you go when we get to my car." Every word was hard because his brain was on the sounds coming from behind him. There were the shouts and low moans of someone in pain. Crashes and the shattering of glass. How much blood was flowing now? He hadn't missed the way Owen had leapt right into the middle, his eyes flaring with glee.

Nor had he missed how hollow Robert had looked as he'd given in. God, he'd brought Robert into this. He was a selfish shit.

He hoped Tucker was still on that barstool. His brother had walked away, but not before Jax had seen how his eyes had glazed over, likely remembering all the times the doctor had pitted them against each other, forcing them to fight until everyone was bloody and battered. She'd called it "bonding time."

"You should take me to my Jeep." Her arm had drifted around his neck, balancing herself. "Are you all right, Jax?"

He stopped and forced himself to take a deep breath. "I'm okay. I...I struggle with violence."

Struggled not to commit it. Struggled not to glory in it. When he'd been in those fights, nothing had mattered. He hadn't cared whether he won or lost. If he won, he'd be praised. He'd been given an extra ration of food. If he died, well, if he died, he didn't wake up the next day.

For those moments, he didn't have to think. He only had to react, and that had been the only times he'd felt free.

"You didn't sound like it when you were talking to my ex-husband. Though he wasn't legally my husband. He lied on the marriage certificate."

He'd thought about this as he'd searched the web for the man who'd ruined her. He didn't like to think about the fact that she'd loved the fucker once, but she should know he understood. "You went into the marriage with the best of intentions. He was your husband. We put far too much emphasis on legalities."

"Yes, I can see you don't mind legalities much." She was back to sounding pissed off. "He's going to find a way to come after me."

"He can't from jail, and I have something for you in my car." He'd done everything Heather had told him to do, including making a special stop at the Bliss Veterinary Clinic. He'd spent the whole early evening plotting and planning how to get back into River's good graces.

It had oddly been a nice night. It had felt good to think about her, act in her best interests. He'd felt...clean.

She sighed in his arms. "I don't think this is a good idea. Look, I forgive you for leaving last night. It's fine. We had a good time, but we're working together now."

He stopped in front of the big SUV Robert had brought them all out here in. Jax had forced Robert to park next to River's Jeep, as though their cars being close meant they would be, too. The back window was open halfway but there was no sign of the extra passenger they'd brought along.

"We're walking through the woods together. It's not like I'm your boss," he replied.

She crossed her arms over her chest, staring him down. "No, it's like I'm your boss when we're out there."

He needed to make this plain. He wanted no obstacles in the way in case she changed her mind and decided to jump his bones. When he'd walked in earlier, he could have sworn the woman looked at him like she wanted to eat him alive. "This is not the same situation. Believe me, I looked it all up. I read several scholarly articles concerning relationships between contractors and contractees. And technically, Ezra and Big Tag are the contractees. They're the ones putting money in your account."

"Oh, according to you, you did that, too."

He felt a smile slide across his face at the thought. "But that wasn't about a job. I did that one for free, baby."

She stared at him, the moment elongating between them and giving him hope. There was no distaste in her gaze. But then she blinked and the moment passed. "You have to put me down now."

He didn't want to, but he set her on her feet.

She put her hands on her hips, a light coming into her eyes.

139

"Tell me it was a joke."

"It was a joke." He was supposed to try to give her what she wanted. Heather had been explicit in those instructions. He was supposed to do almost everything River wanted right up to the point where he took control and gave them both what they needed.

She took a deep breath. "Thank god. Who did you get to call me because he sounded exactly like Matt."

He'd sounded like a nasally douchebag. Hopefully he was currently in police custody whining at them. "That's because it was Matt."

She stilled, a suspicious gleam in her eyes. "So you know Matt."

"Only because I stole two million dollars and a bunch of property from him," Jax admitted. "And set him up to go to jail for quite a long time. He should be there right about now."

She stared for a moment. "Tell me you're…oh my god, Jax. You really did it."

"I did. He deserved it and now he won't hurt you or anyone else again. Also, your credit rating is now perfect. I believe I mentioned I'm good with computers."

"You didn't mention you're a black hat hacker."

"Because I'm not. I use my talents for good." Now. And it wasn't like he'd had a choice before. When he'd refused to do what McDonald wanted, someone got hurt, and it usually wasn't him. The doc had been smart enough to figure out that he would take any beating she could dish out and not move at all. Ah, but when one of his brothers was taking the beating for him—that was the way to get him to cave and quickly.

"I don't know who you are." She pulled her phone out of her pocket, the screen illuminating her face in the darkness. Her finger swiped and moved until she finally gasped. "There's two million dollars in my account. Well, two million two hundred thousand and change. Holy shit."

"No one is coming after you," he said quietly. He hadn't expected this response. He'd thought she would be happy. "I've fixed the banking records, too. You sold the big office building two years ago. If anyone looks casually, that's when the deposits were made. No one will question it."

She stared at her screen as though she couldn't quite believe what she was seeing. "I don't understand. They have records."

"And I changed them. Obviously it won't stand up to intense scrutiny, but why would you come under intense scrutiny?" He didn't like how far away she was. "I can put it back if you want, but he'll use it to hire a good attorney and he might get out. Then he would likely come after you and I'll have to kill him. Did I mention that I have a problem with violence?"

She shook her head. "I don't know what I want to do right now. I still can't believe you did that. Two million. It didn't all come from me. How many of us did he trick?"

Finally something he could do. "I can find out. I can find them all and use the money to make their lives better. Would you like that?"

The faintest smile crossed her lovely face and then it was gone, replaced with the uncertainty he'd found in her eyes so often. "I don't know. I have to think about it. How did you even find out about Matt?"

"You mentioned your ex-husband. I'm a good investigator. It's what I do." It was what he did now. "I was trying to do something good. I don't like it when people take advantage of others. We should all live and let live. Well, until someone's an asshole and then I have to deal with it. River, I would like to spend some time with you."

Her eyes widened in the moonlight. "I think that's a bad idea."

He moved in, invading her space. If she told him to back off, he would, but he had to try. She didn't back away so he stayed close. He needed to remind her exactly what he could do for her physically. "I think it's the best idea I've had all day."

Her head tilted up, her voice on the breathless side. "Since you stole two million from my ex and set him up to go to jail, I would have to say…" She huffed out a laugh. "I was going to say you don't have a lot of good ideas, but I like the idea of Matt enjoying some prison time. Can you really find the other women he conned?"

He reached out and she didn't move away when he touched

141

her hair, smoothing it back. Just touching her calmed him. He wasn't thinking about the fight now. There was nothing in his brain but her and how soft she felt under his hand. "I promise I will. I have friends who can help me, too."

"I would like that." She nodded, her eyes on him.

He leaned over and his lips were almost against hers when something barked behind them. River started and turned.

The puppy he'd adopted earlier in the day had two paws on the window, his face pressed against the glass, eager eyes open wide. He barked, a little yelping.

River gasped, reaching in and gently pulling the dog out. "You have a puppy. Why would you bring a puppy to a bar?"

"Because he's a gift for you."

The puppy was already madly in love. He licked at River's hands, face, neck. It must be nice to be a dog because he just got to lick River all he liked. The dog didn't need consent.

"What?" She glared his way but still held the puppy close. Her hand went over the dog's thick fur. "You can't give a pet as a gift unless you know the person wants one. It's not like this is a bracelet. This is a living thing that requires a lifetime commitment."

Heather had told him she needed a pet. On the night they'd met, River had mentioned she'd lost her dog a few months before she'd lost her dad. Heather had said a lot of things about how surrounded by death River had been, and now she needed life around her. "You like dogs. You talked about Jango last night and you sounded like you missed him. I know I can't replace him, but this guy needed a home and you need someone to watch out for you. I know he's tiny, but he'll probably bark a lot. I don't like the thought of you out there all by yourself. Anything could happen. Even a small dog can help scare off a person who's trying to get into your cabin."

"Small?" She held the dog up, inspecting him. "You have got to be kidding me. This dog is a St. Bernard mixed with a Great Pyrenees. This dog is going to be massive. This is an overgrown cuddle buddy."

And that was where he'd made his mistake because he'd kind

of meant for the dog to be the security system and he would be the overgrown cuddle buddy.

"What are you looking for, Jax?" She held the dog close again.

How to answer that question. He rather thought she might run if he told her the truth. He was looking for a reason to keep going. He was looking for something good to hold on to. He was looking for something to answer his suffering with—a balance to all his pain. "I want to spend time with the most beautiful woman I've ever seen."

She shoved the dog at him. He found himself with ten pounds of scrambling mutt.

"I'm not buying your bullshit." She reached into her purse and came out with her keys. "The dog is cute, but I don't have time for a pet right now. I hope you two will be very happy together."

The dog whined as though realizing a good thing was getting away.

"I don't think Big Tag will let me keep him." He was confused again. He'd been honest with her about how beautiful she was. He'd taken revenge on her enemies. He'd done everything Heather had told him to and given clear signals that he was more than willing to do what Kayla had told him to do. He couldn't simply perform oral sex on her in the bar parking lot. He'd done everything he could do to convince her to let him back in.

Where had he gone wrong?

He had to come to the reasonable, logical conclusion that she didn't want him. The reasonable, logical thing to do would be to go back into the bar and find another woman.

He didn't want anyone but her. He worried he might never. He'd been surrounded by lovely women before, but River was the only one to move him. Big Tag would likely slap him on the back, tell him he was the memory equivalent of a toddler and he should give himself time, but her rejection caused an ache in his heart he hadn't expected.

He watched as she opened the door to the Jeep and hopped in without looking back.

The Jeep roared to life and she put it in reverse, dirt and gravel crunching around her tires. She didn't have the hard top on so he could see her plainly. Her dark hair had escaped from the pony tail she'd had it in before the bar fight. It swirled around her shoulders as she shoved the Jeep into first gear. She stopped, her head swiveling around so their eyes met, and he stood there feeling as stupid as he ever had in his short life. And that was saying something because he so often felt like a moron.

He was stupid because he memorized her in that moment. He memorized how her eyes flashed in the moonlight, how her lips trembled like she had something to say. Later, he would make up all the things she could have said to him. Things like, *I forgive you, Jax. Get in the car, Jax. Run away with me, Jax.*

"Good-bye, Jax." She put the Jeep into first gear and drove away.

And he was left with a whining dog. A dog who knew damn well things hadn't gone the way they should have. Things had taken a bleak turn and they were both screwed.

Disappointment sat in his gut. He would drop the fucking mutt right where they were standing and let it fend for itself. It would probably get eaten by something out here, but that was kind of the way of the world. That was the natural order of things. The soft got eaten to make the strong stronger.

He would walk back into the bar and do what he should have done in the first place. He would beat the shit out of whoever he could, let them beat the shit out of him. He wouldn't think about River again.

The dog whined and he made the terrible mistake of looking at it. Right in the eyes. Right in the big, dumb, trusting eyes. The dog leaned over and licked him on the cheek, nuzzling him and asking for affection. Begging for it, really. The dog was too stupid to know that he was a train wreck who had nothing to give anyone at all. The dog only knew he better find someone to love or the world would be a cold place.

Jax sighed and put the animal against his chest, trying to calm him down. "Big Tag's going to kill me, buddy."

He knew how hard the world was. Maybe the dog never had to know. Maybe the dog only had to know affection and kindness. Maybe the natural order of the world sucked and he could fight it in any way he could, his strength protecting the weak.

The dog whined again but settled in his arms.

"Yeah, I'm going to miss her, too."

Twin lights nearly blinded him as a vehicle turned into the parking lot. It took him a moment to realize it was a familiar Jeep.

River frowned at him. "Just get in. Get in and bring Buster with you."

She'd come back for them? But she was totally wrong about the name. "The doc told me his name is…"

"His name is Buster," she growled.

There were times when he should simply agree. "Absolutely. He is obviously a Buster."

Her expression changed slightly, her eyes softening. "This is about sex. Just sex."

But it wasn't. Even he knew that. Again, it was time to agree. "Just sex."

He climbed into the Jeep beside her, Buster in his arms. He would take anything she gave him.

For now.

* * * *

She put the Jeep in park and slammed out of the driver's side door. Stupid. Stupid. Stupid.

She was the single stupidest human on the planet. She had been out. She'd been free and clear and he wouldn't have called her again. If she'd driven away, he would have taken his intensely adorable dog and his hot bod and gone his own way. Maybe he would have gone back into the bar and taken up Blondie on her aggressive offer. But no. She hadn't driven all the way home. She'd stopped first and told him good-bye. She'd stared at him standing there with the cutest little fluff ball she'd ever seen. He'd looked hopeless and yet he'd clutched the dog gently.

And she'd still managed to drive away. Only to U-turn and come back because she'd realized she would never, ever get that image out of her head. She would go to her damn grave thinking about that man and that dog and what could have happened if she'd been the tiniest bit brave.

She turned and found Jax standing behind her, still holding on to Buster. The whole way back to the cabin, they'd been silent. Jax had tried to talk once, but she'd shut him down. He'd gone quiet and she kept her eyes on the road. Only once had she looked over and then she'd found both man and dog hanging their heads out, smiling into the wind.

If she let herself, she would fall head over heels in love with them both, and that wasn't going to happen. "I want sex."

"I would like that, too."

She shook her head. "No, stop. I'm giving you my terms. We're going in that cabin and we're going to have sex, and then you are going to take Buster and go back to your place."

He frowned. "I don't have a car."

Not her problem. "Fine. You can call your brother."

"My brother might be in jail after that bar fight you started."

He had a point. "You can call a…." There was no taxi service in Bliss. He couldn't walk all that way. "Fine. I'll drive you back, but you have to take the dog."

Buster was squirming in his arms. "You don't like him?"

The way he said it was like he was asking if she liked him. Like he was some gorgeous boy asking what he'd done wrong that she couldn't like him anymore.

It made her soften. "He's sweet, but I can't keep him."

And she couldn't keep Jax.

"My boss will be upset. I'm not supposed to have a dog." He breathed long and deep. "But I can't take him back. I think he would get confused. Maybe Big Tag'll kick me out. It wouldn't be so bad. I've got a coat now. I agree to your terms."

Terms? She'd given him terms? She guessed she had. "Good."

"I have terms of my own."

It had been far easier the night before. The night before they'd simply fallen into bed. This negotiation thing was weird and disconcerting, but she'd started it. "All right."

"You'll see me every night you can while I'm here."

She shook her head. "I don't think that's a good idea."

"Neither is me walking into that cabin with you when you

won't open yourself up to me again. I'm not even taking a risk here. You won't like me again. You've made up your mind. Now you've decided to use me for sex."

"That's what you're using me for, too."

"No," he argued. "I've thought a lot about this and I was never using you for sex. I like it, the sex, that is. But I was using you because I'm desperate to feel close to someone. I knew the minute I saw you that I wanted to be close to you, to get to know you."

Sweet words, but she wasn't sure she could believe them. Still, it wasn't like the sex had been iffy. It had been spectacular. It had been addicting. If she went into it knowing they had an end date, she could protect herself. Besides, if there was any way she could find Matt's other victims and help them out, shouldn't she take it? "If I say no to your terms I suppose you'll back out on helping me disperse that two million you reclaimed."

He hadn't really stolen it. He'd released money that had never been Matt's in the first place.

"I'll do everything I can to help you and the people he hurt. Even after we move on from here, I'll stay in touch," he promised. "I'll find them all. I swear this to you. I want you to sleep with me because you want me. Even if it's only sexually."

"That's all it can be." She made her decision. "All right, why don't you stay here with me while you're in town."

A slow, sexy smile curled his lips. "I will. And one more thing, I have to insist on. I'm in control. I want you to follow my lead when it comes to sex. I want to talk about it more than we did last night."

The idea of him taking control made her far more excited than she was comfortable with, but then nothing made her comfortable right now. "We talked a lot last night."

"Yes, about trivial things, and I loved talking to you. I want to talk about sex. I want you to tell me what you like and what you don't like. I want to know what your fantasies are."

She might have given up on fantasies long ago. "I want to be out of my head for a while. I don't want to think, Jax."

"You don't have to think about anything but me and what we're going to do together." He frowned. "This is very hard to do

147

when Buster is trying to lick my mouth."

He was. The pup was desperately looking for some affection, and it was obvious Jax was, too. Yet he didn't toss the dog down or even ignore him. He would be a good dog owner. Matt had always complained about Jango. He'd argued they should put him down far before it had been necessary. Somehow, she doubted Jax would have done that. Somehow, she could see him helping her take care of the dog she'd raised from a puppy. "Did you get him a crate?"

He nodded. "The vet gave me a list of things and the ladies from the Trading Post helped me find it all. He's got a crate. It's small though. I wish I'd bought a big one now. It's inside your place. I put all of his stuff in there. You'll have to let me know if I got everything we need."

He had to be joking. The door looked fine. He had the weirdest sense of humor.

"I'm sure it's perfect for now." She reached a hand out. "Puppies need smaller crates. We'll get him a bigger one later on." She stopped. He wouldn't be here when Buster got big. "I mean, I'll help you. I've raised dogs since I was a kid. You help me with the revenge thing and I'll help you with Buster. Let's go inside. And Jax, you can't break into my place."

"But I did and quite easily." He followed her up the steps as she put the key in the lock. "I picked that lock in under thirty seconds. It'll be better next week when the new door comes. A sickly kid could kick yours in."

He was right about that, but she wasn't sure she liked him butting into her...she stopped and stared at the living room. The place was filled with candlelight and someone had changed her utilitarian pillows and the plain quilt on her couch for gorgeous, overstuffed luxury throw pillows and a soft-looking blanket.

Someone? "Jax, what did you do?"

"That depends," he said, studying her. "Do you like it? Because if you do then I found some stuff that I thought you would like. I didn't throw anything out. It's all in the closet. I'll change it back if you don't like it. Of course, if you don't like it, then we should call the sheriff because someone broke in and left all this shit."

148

If he was playing her, then he'd gone all in. "How did you get this done in a day? Half a day, really. And I love it."

She hadn't realized how big a difference a small change could make. The candles made the room look totally different from the one she'd spent months and months existing in. This room was full of warmth and life.

Jax had given that to her.

"The candles are fake. I would never have lit all of them and then walked away. That goes poorly. Believe me, I know. I got creative in The Garden once and that was a fun night. People get so pissy when they get wakened in the middle of the night by sprinklers coming on."

"I like it." She turned to him. "Tell me you're not playing me for some weird reason I can't understand."

"I'm not playing you."

"Then I think you should put the puppy in his crate and kiss me." They had a few weeks. She would revel in him. And she wouldn't get attached to the dog.

Or the man.

She promised.

Chapter Nine

Maybe it had been the candles that did the trick. He would have to thank Heather for suggesting that he do something to liven up River's living room. She'd explained that River hadn't changed anything in the cabin in years, and apparently that was important. He wasn't sure why shiny throw pillows and a super soft faux fur blanket put a smile on her face, but he was happy it was there.

Wait until she saw what they'd done to her utilitarian bedroom.

She'd asked him to kiss her. It was his time now. She'd agreed to his demands and that meant he was taking over.

"Take off your clothes, River." He knelt over and opened the crate he'd purchased. Buster wiggled and squirmed, whining a bit. He looked so sad when he managed to turn and look out of the cage. Damn cage. He hated leaving him there. When he was house trained, that dog wouldn't see the inside of a cage again. Jax passed a chew toy to Buster and he settled down.

He turned and River was staring at him. "Your clothes are still on."

"It's weird to undress in front of someone. I thought we would do what we did last night."

"What we did last night left you with the completely wrong impression that I wasn't serious and that's why we are in this situation in the first place. So we're going to do it my way." He hadn't known he had a way, but this seemed a little like computers. The doc could erase his mind, but he learned again and quickly. "I would like to see you naked. I have friends who are into a lifestyle called Dominance and submission. I'm not as invested, but I thought you might like to play. I know I would."

She bit her bottom lip, a sure sign that he'd made her nervous. "That sounds kinky. I've heard rumors that Stef Talbot does something similar. I don't know if I want to try that."

"Is he married?"

She nodded.

"Does his wife seem like he grinds her under his boot?"

A wary smile crossed her face. "She practically glows."

Thank god Talbot wasn't a douche. "You can stop me at any time. You can say no. I won't press. I'm asking you to take off your clothes for two reasons. The first is that I think you're gorgeous and I want to see you naked again. The second is that you need to learn how gorgeous you are. You need to stop seeing yourself as something less."

She hadn't done the things he had. She'd lived a good life. He had to believe that if he was good, he could have good in his life, too.

"Do you think your brother is going to need you tonight?"

"I've worked out all the problems." Tucker was going to cover for him. And Dante, well, Dante would be far too busy dealing with the laxative he'd slipped into his drink. Dante wouldn't be drugging him again anytime soon. "I'm not leaving again, River. You said I could stay until we need to move out. I'm going to stay unless you don't want me to. Now do you want to sit down and talk about this or do you want to take off your clothes and let me look at you."

"I wanted you to kiss me."

She was frustrating, but he could be patient about this. He moved in, looming over her and loving how she turned her face up.

He cupped her cheeks and let his mouth find hers. She needed to take it slow? He could do that. Long, slow kisses that drugged him and made his head fuzzy. Over and over, he brushed his mouth on hers. Those petal-soft lips tempted him in ways he'd never imagined and his cock hardened. He licked that plump bottom lip, requesting an invitation in.

Her lips parted, flowering open for him, and he took the territory she'd ceded.

Her arms drifted around his neck and her tongue slid against his, shy at first and then boldly playing. That was what he wanted, her in the moment with him. He wanted them completely together, no pain or loss between them, no misunderstandings or insecurities. Just Jax and River and connection.

He lifted his head, breaking the kiss, but not the contact. He rested his forehead against hers. "Take your clothes off for me. Show me how gorgeous you are. There's no place for fear here. You've seen me. You've seen my scars and you didn't flinch, baby. Don't think I'll do anything but love the way you look. It's anticipation. When we start, I'll get too excited. I won't stop and look and enjoy watching you. I'll be far too busy licking and sucking and fucking. Think of it as a good meal, the best. It's like the meal you get after you've starved for a couple of days." Or weeks, in his case. "You know you should take it all in. You should see it and smell it and taste it for all it's worth because you might not get another one."

Her hands moved from his shoulders down to his chest and she sighed. "You know exactly how to get to me, Seaborne."

"Jax." Seaborne was something they'd made up a couple of days ago. It meant nothing. Jax had been given to him by Big Tag. No one named themselves. It was a part of the human condition. One was born and named. Jax was his name.

Her hands moved on him restlessly, like she wasn't sure where to put them, but she knew she wasn't going to stop touching him. "Jax. You know how to get to me, Jax. You always know what to say."

"Maybe because we're alike." He couldn't tell her how he didn't know shit because he'd literally been born an overgrown toddler. She wouldn't find that sexy. But there was truth in what he'd said. "We have a connection, you and I. I felt it the moment you walked into Trio."

She was quiet for a moment and then she stepped back, breaking their contact. "I did, too."

Her hands went to the hem of her T-shirt and then she pulled it over her head. She worked quickly, tossing it aside and taking off her bra. "Better?"

Her breasts were exposed. Hell yeah, that was better. They were perfectly made, delicate and round, and her nipples tight. They were a lovely pink and brown and ready for his attention.

But still, not where he wanted her to be. "Better. Take off the jeans and we'll talk."

He took a step back, letting her know this was serious. He meant business, though only because he thought she needed it. She didn't understand how gorgeous she was. She'd made him feel normal the night before and he wanted to return the favor. He knew he was a freak. He was covered in scars and yet she'd ignored them all. She'd pretended like his skin was smooth. She'd kissed him and lavished her affection on him and it was his turn to let her know the truth.

She was perfect.

With a frown, she kicked off her shoes. She pushed at her jeans, pulling her underwear down with the pants. She chucked them to the side and seemed to stand tall in front of him.

Brave woman.

Lovely woman.

She was sheer perfection, standing there with her nipples upthrust and her pussy on display. Her dark hair gleamed in the light and her legs were together in a way that made him want to ask her to sink to her knees and show him her pussy, but he was being patient.

For now.

"What did you like about last night?" He had to talk to her or he would fall on top of her and not get up again. If they only had a few days together, he wanted to know her.

What would happen if they succeeded? What would happen if

153

the answers were in that building? It could be mere days before he found some answers about who he was, who he'd been. What if the doctor had a cure? What if he could take it and remember everything that had come before that moment he'd woken up in a cold, white room?

He shoved aside the thought, concentrating on her.

"I liked everything except the way it ended, and I guess that was really more about waking up without you."

Finally some truth. She had a whole bunch of walls he needed to either break through or climb over. "That won't happen again. You are so lovely. Turn around for me."

She frowned but did it anyway. "This still feels weird."

It didn't feel weird to him. That ass was damn near perfect. He stepped in, his hands twitching with the need to touch her. He let his palms find her shoulders and felt the muscles there immediately relax. She needed touch to feel connected to him. He could give her that. He could engineer their time together so he could always have a hand on her, always let her know that he was there.

He kissed the top of her head as he brought her back against his body. "Tell me how you feel right now."

Her head fell back against his chest as he let his hands roam, cupping her breasts. "I feel good now. I didn't like standing in front of you naked. It made me feel like you were judging me."

"Never. I was admiring you. If you like, I can let you admire me." She didn't seem to mind his scars.

"I guess I don't think there's much to admire. I don't think about my body like that," she admitted with a sigh as he rolled her nipples between his thumbs and forefingers. "My body always seemed like a tool. I stayed fit because my job requires a ton of hiking and physical activity. I never thought of myself as sexy."

"I think you're very sexy. I think about having sex with you a lot."

She laughed, the sound magical to his ears. "You're such a weirdo. No one admits that."

He would get self-conscious but her words didn't match her actions. She was rubbing against him, her ass nestling against his cock like she was inviting him to play. "I am a weirdo and I do think about having sex with you. It's all truth. I think you like weirdoes."

He ran his hands over her skin, keeping her close to him.

She nodded. "I think I do, too. You make me feel things I've never felt before."

She couldn't know how true that statement was for him, too. One of the reasons he'd made sure this place was secure was the fact that it had been the first place he'd found real joy. He couldn't stand the thought of anyone desecrating this space or hurting this woman.

He let his hand trail down, finding the mound of her sex and teasing at it. His heart thudded and his cock jumped when he realized she was already wet. "Is that for me? Maybe I'm not the only one who thinks about sex."

Her hips flexed, pressing her pussy against his fingers. "I never did before. I'll be honest, my sex life wasn't that great. Masturbation was better than real sex because at least I knew I wouldn't stop until I got myself off."

"He didn't make you come?" It made him even happier the man was likely behind bars. Matt Lewis had done far more damage than merely taking her money.

Her breathing picked up as he started to rub her clit. "No. He never took the time you seem to. I thought maybe it was me, that I was a little on the cold side. Okay, I didn't think that. He might have told me that when we fought. God, I hate that I stayed with him, let him manipulate me."

He was not letting her go there. He rubbed in circles, stroking her, feeling all that creamy arousal coating his fingers. "You have to let that go. You have to forgive yourself. You had good intentions." Spending most of his short life in therapy had taught him a few things. He had a lot to forgive himself for. Maybe if he could convince River, it would help him find his way. "Forgive yourself and let yourself try again. Explore with me. Let's see how good we can make this."

"Yes." She shuddered against him. "Yes, Jax."

She might be saying yes only to sex, but he planned on being sneaky. He wanted her. He wanted her for far more than a few

155

nights. His exploration would go beyond her body.

But it was a good place to start.

He picked up the pace, rubbing her, allowing her hips to set the rhythm. He kissed the shell of her ear and his free hand cupped her breasts. His dick was dying, but there was no way he would stop. Giving this to her, letting her know how hot she could be, that was a gift to him, too. He wanted to be the one who showed her how sexy she could be, how amazing they could be together.

A low moan shuddered from her and she shook in his arms. He gently bit her earlobe and she came, calling out his name.

Satisfaction washed over him. He could win her back. Now it was time to take Kay's advice. River sighed and was relaxed as he hauled her up into his arms. He held her against his chest and strode toward her bedroom.

* * * *

She was making a huge mistake and she wasn't going to do a thing about it. River felt floaty and melty and other soft–y words that women who'd just had crazy orgasms used to describe themselves.

She was a perfectly competent woman and if anyone had asked her, she would say she was confident. At least she had been before Matt. But she'd never been comfortable in her own skin. It was nice to be naked with Jax. She'd never simply stopped and let herself feel during sex. She worried and overthought and sometime in the middle of it all got bored and started thinking about her job or what she needed to do around the house.

There had been not a thought in her head except Jax.

He strode through the cabin, taking her into her bedroom where it was obvious he'd done some redecorating. Nothing permanent. He had to have purchased all the battery-powered candles in the county. He'd added more candles here and changed her bedspread to a decadent comforter he placed her on. She was surrounded by softness. It wasn't something she would ever have bought for herself. She would have convinced herself her old threadbare quilt was good enough, but she sighed at how good it felt to be pampered.

"You were busy today."

"I plan to be busy tonight," he said, tugging his shirt over his head.

He thought she was lovely? She couldn't even come up with a word for him. He was beyond hot. The scars that marred his body didn't detract from how blessed Jax was with beauty. She watched as he shoved out of his jeans. She wanted to ask him how he got all those scars. They were on his torso and back, and she'd seen some on his thighs. But nothing where a person could see them. If Jax wore shorts and a shirt, he would look normal.

"I wanted to do something nice for you." He was still in his boxers, though they hung low on his hips.

She was fairly certain her mouth actually watered at the sight of him. It was time to forgive him. "If you need to leave, write me a note. Okay?"

He nodded, looking oddly solemn. "I promise, but you should know I don't want to leave. Give me your hand."

She might have balked at the command in his voice before he'd given her an orgasm, but now she simply did as he asked. She offered him her left hand. He brought it to his mouth, placing a kiss on the inside of her wrist. And then he drew it back, slipping a silk knot over her wrists. He'd been very busy.

"I did not have those on my bed earlier today." She wasn't afraid. Maybe she should be, but would a guy who was going to hurt her have gone to all this trouble?

She wasn't sure she wanted to live in a world where someone could kiss her like Jax did and want to hurt her.

"You have them now." He leaned over and brushed his lips over hers. "We don't have to do this if you don't want to, but I think it will help you stay in the moment. I want you to forget about everything that's wrong in your world and I'll do the same. This is our time and it's important." He moved to her other hand. "I've tied this lightly. All you have to do to get out is give it a hard tug. When you trust me, I'd like to handcuff you and blindfold you so all you can do is feel what I'm doing to you."

She would be completely at his mercy. Could she trust anyone so much? Of course if anyone had asked her a week ago if she

157

would go to bed with any man, she would have laughed and said no.

And now she'd agreed to sleep with this one, to be with him while he was here. They had days and days to get to know each other, to trust each other. Days to get addicted to the man.

"Now spread your legs for me."

So she would be laid out for his pleasure. She moved her legs apart, well aware of how vulnerable she was. Tied up, and she could see the way his cock was poking at the fly of his boxers, trying to get out. It would be good to give back to him. Then he would hold her. He seemed to like to cuddle afterward.

Except he didn't shove his boxers off and thrust inside her. He took her ankles in his hands, spreading her legs wide. He climbed on the bed, his muscular body between her legs, the look in his eyes nearly singeing her.

He was going to do that? She wasn't sure she could survive having his mouth on her. "It's okay, Jax. I don't need any more foreplay. I'm ready."

"I'm not." He leaned over and licked her, his tongue lapping.

She suddenly couldn't breathe and she couldn't move because if she pulled too hard, the ties would come undone. Damn him for thinking of that. It forced her to stay still, to concentrate on her body.

"I told you I was going to take control." He put his nose right in her pussy, breathing her in like she was the sweetest smelling bouquet. He made it hard to be self-conscious. How was she supposed to be worried about how she smelled or how messy she was down there when he was feasting on her?

Pleasure coursed through her, bringing her arousal right back to life. She'd thought she was done for the night, but he proved her wrong again.

"While we're together, I'll do this whenever I like. I'll ask you to spread your legs so I can get my mouth on you, so I can taste you because I love how you taste. I love the fact that all this cream is here because I got you hot." He sucked on her clitoris, a brief caress that made her gasp. "I'm going to slide right inside you. You'll take my cock easy tonight because I made sure you're ready."

She'd thought she was ready before. Now all she was ready for was another orgasm.

She felt him slide a finger inside her. It wasn't enough. Only his cock would be enough, but he knew what to do with that damn finger. It curled up inside her and rubbed the exact right place. The buildup was swift, her body already primed.

And then he pulled away, standing up and leaving her empty.

She nearly screamed, but he was shoving his boxers down, freeing his cock.

"I can't wait." He reached over and grabbed a condom.

He'd prepped her room for sex. "You were sure of yourself."

"I was optimistic." He rolled the condom on his dick and moved between her legs. He stared down at her for a moment, like he was memorizing her body.

And then he was on her, moving to cover her. She could feel his cock pressing at her pussy. He thrust inside her and she watched the way his face contorted with pleasure. He held his weight on his hands, his hips moving as he thrust inside her. He moved with slow deliberation, every thrust and retreat pushing her higher and higher. His head was down and she realized what he was doing. He was watching his cock disappear inside her, watching as he took her.

She watched, too. His dick was so big it looked like it wouldn't fit, but he'd done his job well. She was slick and ready, pulsing for him. There was something deeply erotic about watching his dick disappear and reappear, glistening with her arousal.

"It's beautiful," she said.

His eyes came up, meeting hers. "It is. This is beautiful. You're beautiful to me, River."

He flexed inside her, finding the same place his finger had before, and it was enough this time. This time he didn't pull away.

She gasped as the pleasure took her for the second time that night. The world floated away as Jax pumped into her, rubbing her just the right way that left her squirming and desperate for more. It was almost too much. Instinctively she fought the ties that bound her, and sure enough, they came apart and she could hold on to him like he was the only real thing in the world.

His eyes widened and then closed, his face so gorgeous as he took his own pleasure.

He dropped down, letting his weight fall on her. His arms went around her, holding her close. "Next time I'm tying them tighter."

He started to kiss her again, melding their mouths in long, slow kisses.

Next time, she would let him.

* * * *

River woke up alone in bed. Again.

It was okay. She'd told him he could leave. He'd promised he wouldn't, but what had she expected? She had no doubt she would find a note somewhere and the next time they met up, he would be perfectly polite.

He'd probably taken Buster, too. Damn, she should have thought about that. The puppy had cried in the middle of the night and she'd been surprised when Jax had rolled out of bed, taken the dog out, and come back to bed with the puppy.

He's lonely. I can't stand to think about him out there all alone.

He'd let the dog sleep on his chest.

It had damn near melted her heart, but she'd still woken up alone. The house was going to be so quiet. She wondered if Tucker or one of his friends had come to pick him up. Maybe he'd walked Buster all the way back, jogging along the river in the early morning light.

This was what she'd asked for. Nights of crazy, kinky sex, and then they would go their separate ways and pretend like it hadn't been hot between them, like she hadn't poured everything she had into making love with him. She should call it sex, but it hadn't felt like sex.

She sat up in bed. She had a lot to do and for the first time in a long time, she didn't have to worry about having the money to do it.

Thanks to Jax.

How did one thank a man for turning her whole life around? She hadn't even gotten her mouth on his cock. Every time she thought about trying, he would have her pinned down, his cock inside her. She never thought she would be so frustrated because she hadn't gotten to give a guy a blowjob.

He was a giving lover. She sighed. Maybe he would show up tonight. She would welcome him. She'd set up the guidelines and she had to be a big girl and live with it.

Would he bring Buster?

"Buster, you have to poop. Stop trying to fight the bugs and void your bowels," a low voice said. It was coming from outside her window.

She found her big, fluffy robe and pulled it around her and stepped up to the window, peeking through the blinds.

Jax stood in the middle of the green grass wearing nothing but that perfectly fitting pair of Levis that rode low on his hips, showing off how much time the man spent in the gym. Buster romped on the grass, apparently trying to fight a butterfly. He growled and jumped and looked godawful cute.

"Why do you not simply pour vile medicine in the dog's beer?" a deep voice asked. He had a thick accent that sounded Eastern European. A dark-haired man stepped in from the front of the yard, a frown on his handsome face.

For a second she was gripped with fear. The man looked so angry.

Jax simply grinned, his hands on his hips. "Rough night, huh, Dante?"

The man named Dante shot Jax the finger. "Fuck you."

The potential for violence was thick in the air. She started to fumble to draw the blinds up so she could let that jerk who was threatening Jax know he wasn't alone. What was that man doing here? Was he part of the film crew? She hadn't met him.

Dante prowled closer to Jax. "Do you know what I did to that bathroom? It will never be the same. Big Tag claims he will never go into it again. It is haunted now. Haunted with much pain and

161

regret."

Before she could manage to get the window open, Jax was doubled over laughing and Dante shook his head.

"You are a bastard, Jax." He chuckled. "You have to give me a little of whatever you used. I swear Sasha goes around looking…what is the word? Constipated. Yes, he looks constipated all the time. You forgive me now? We are even?"

Jax didn't look up, merely nodded his head.

There was a knock on her door. She started. Who the hell was in her cabin?

She opened the door and Tucker stood there.

"Hey, we brought some bacon but then we realized we have no idea how to cook it. The instructions are a little vague and Jax told us not to burn anything down. After what he did to Dante, we're all tiptoeing lightly around him. Dude got mean. Do you know how to cook bacon?"

She stared at him for a moment because she could hear people arguing in the background, and they weren't all speaking English. "How many people are in my cabin?"

Tucker smiled, an open expression that made her wonder why the hell Heather had let him go. "Everyone. Well, almost everyone I know. Big Tag spent the night in some bunker preparing for the oncoming alien invasion and Ezra is brooding somewhere, but the nice lady who usually makes our breakfast has a doctor's appointment and honestly, she wouldn't make us bacon. When we asked her to, she protested us."

Ah, so Nell was their nice lady. "I'm a vegetarian."

His face fell and he looked down at that bacon like it was a lover he'd lost.

"But that's my personal choice. My dad was all carnivore and I cooked for him. I can certainly teach you. It's pretty easy." She wouldn't buy a pound of bacon, but she also wouldn't toss it out if someone wanted to eat it. Nor would she protest. "I'm not vegan like Nell. I love cheese far too much. Come on. I'll show you how to make it in the oven and then I'll make us some scrambled eggs, too. I think I've got some muffin mix somewhere."

Someone had made coffee. The heavenly smell wafted

162

through the cabin as she followed Tucker into the front room. It was filled with men. Incredibly hot men seemed to be everywhere.

The big, gorgeous Scot had taken up residence on her couch along with a dark-haired man who was shaking his head.

The man she hadn't met pointed toward the television. "They wear all the protective gear. In my country, we did not need these things. We play sports like men."

"Ah, but you wear knickers, too," the Scotsman snarked. "Real men let their willies get a nice breeze when playing."

"I'm never playing basketball with you again," Robert said from the kitchen. "Not now that I know you go commando."

Owen looked up, winking in a way that let her know he was having fun teasing the guys. "Thank the lord, a pretty face. Please save us, River. We're so hungry and not a damn one of us learned how to cook."

"Speak for yourself," the dark-haired man said. "I can microwave any number of things. I do not need woman. The rest of you are sad men, unable to even care for yourself without woman around."

Owen nodded. "Yes, what Sasha said. Totally unable to take care of ourselves." His voice went low, slightly seductive. "Utterly dependent and on our knees begging the beautiful lady to not let us starve."

Oh, he was a charmer. "Stella would love to feed you. She has a diner in town."

Owen's lips quirked up in a sexy grin. "Oh, but Ms. Stella ain't sleeping with our brother. We made a deal a long time ago."

Tucker took over. "The first one of us to find a woman had to share."

Given where she lived, she felt her mouth drop open. "I'm sorry, what?"

Robert shook his head. "Not like that. Not like Bliss share."

"What exactly are we talking about?" Jax stood in the doorway, Buster in his arms. For a gorgeous man with a ball of fluff, he was quite intimidating. He stared at the men in the room, his eyes all steely. "Because I can promise you despite the place we're in there's not going to be any sharing."

"No one thinks you will share woman with us," Dante said, walking in behind him. He was rolling his dark eyes. "But if woman can cook, we do need help. Tucker turns into a whiny beast when he's hungry. I can't stand it. He won't talk about anything but his gut. How he ever survived I have no idea." Dante sat down next to Owen. "Keep your hands to yourself, Scot. I happen to know that Jax's revenge is very terrible." He shook his head, pointing at her TV. "Why do Americans need so much protection?"

Robert stepped up. "Because we're intelligent. You guys are like rams butting heads. And you're one to talk, Sasha. You want to wear a fucking bulletproof vest everywhere."

Sasha shrugged. "I am very wanted man." He winked River's way. "By everyone. I also believe in using protection, unlike our Dante. How is venereal disease?"

"*Baszd meg*," Dante replied with a sneer. "And it has cleared up nicely."

"I'm perfectly venereal disease free," Tucker told her. "If you want to pass that on to Heather, I would appreciate it. Big Tag made sure all the hookers were healthy."

"Excuse me." He couldn't have actually said what she thought he said.

Robert shook his head. "How do I get you to stop talking about hookers, man? I told you no one wants to hear about your hookers."

"Nell told me we have to call them sex workers," Owen added helpfully. "And if we get the chance, we're supposed to help them unionize."

They were all insane.

Jax had moved to her side. "I'll get them to go to the diner in town. I'm sorry. They showed up this morning. I'll get rid of them."

But she was laughing because they really were insane. And funny. And full of life. She didn't understand half of what they said. These guys were obviously bonded closely and had a lot of inside jokes she didn't completely get, but they were making her morning.

Buster wiggled in Jax's arms, pushing his nose her way. She took the puppy from him.

"He pooped," Jax informed her.

"Rule number one, guys, stop talking about poop." She looked at Tucker. "And sex workers and chlamydia."

Dante shrugged. "It was syphilis. Doctor say he has not seen this for many years. My hooker was very exotic."

"All venereal diseases," she said, biting back a laugh. "Now let's talk about breakfast."

Jax followed her into the kitchen. "Are you okay with this? Because I can get rid of them."

"I don't want to be gotten rid of," Tucker said, looking at her over the bar. "I want to hang out here for the day. Ezra thinks things could get nasty, and I want some fun before they do."

"Nasty?" It was hard to concentrate when Buster was trying desperately to give her as many kisses as he could.

"The weather," Jax assured her. "It's supposed to rain pretty hard."

Ah, she did know that much. "Yeah, I saw the forecast. I don't think we'll be able to go into the forest for a couple of days. Then we might want some time for the ground to dry. Setting up a tent in the mud isn't fun."

She wasn't upset about the bad weather now. Now, a few days of rain meant more time with Jax. And his weird pseudo family.

She turned on the oven. "Someone's going to have to take this one if I'm going to cook. And you guys are cleaning up."

Robert took Buster. "I like dogs. Hey, buddy. And I'm excellent at cleaning things up. It's kind of become my job around here."

Tucker grinned and sat down at her bar. "I'll watch you cook."

Jax sent him a nasty look.

Tucker slid off the barstool. "Or I'll watch the game where people hit each other and throws balls around. I'll do that."

Jax put his hands on her hips, dragging her close. "And I'll help you cook. Teach me so I can feed you in the mornings. After all, you satisfy me at night. I can do the same the next day." He leaned over and kissed her. "Good morning, River."

165

Oh, he was going to kill her. Her stupid heart actually fluttered. "Good morning, Jax."

He kissed her again, slower this time, and she knew she was in way too deep in this particular pool.

And she didn't even want to get out.

Chapter Ten

Jax looked out at the rain and kind of wished it wouldn't stop falling. It had been two days since that morning when he'd woken up and River hadn't kicked them all out of her cabin, and it had been the best freaking two days of his life. He'd spent all his time with her. His brothers showed up for breakfast, and Tucker and Robert usually showed up for dinner. They'd gone out the night before, squeezing into a booth, with Heather along for the ride. Jax had sat next to River, sliding his arm around the back of the booth. It was a protective gesture. Well, that's how she'd taken it. He'd rapidly learned that they could interpret things two completely different ways. She'd taken that arm around her as protective and it totally was. He was protective of her. He was also insanely possessive of her.

He didn't like the way one of her employees watched her. Ty treated her like a sister. Heather was obviously her best friend. But Andy was another story. When she wasn't paying attention, Andy had a dark stare that made Jax wary. Perhaps if that same intense look had been in the man's eyes all the time, he could have chalked it up to being his personality. But when River turned and looked at the man, he became smooth and laid back, his face changing with the ease of an actor.

He didn't like Andy. He didn't like that Andy was currently walking around with Heather and River selecting camping gear.

"Hey, did you find the torches?" Robert walked up, pushing a basket. "I mean flashlights. I spent too much time in England."

Jax turned from the window. They were currently in a large sporting goods store in Alamosa, almost fifty miles from Bliss. The front of the store boasted two large bay windows that looked out over the parking lot. He could see River's Jeep, though it had the hardtop on it. He'd hated that. He liked driving with the wind whipping around him. "I put them in River's basket. She's looking at tents. She said campers usually bring their own and the one she's got is meant for one person. It's not big enough for more."

He took heart in that. She was buying a tent they would sleep in together. They would be out in the woods for a few days and then he had a decision to make.

How much did he tell her? She knew what they were looking for. She wouldn't be shocked when they found it. But she also wouldn't know what they were really searching for.

"You look like someone kicked your best friend," Robert said. "Since I happen to know Buster is perfectly fine and no one has kicked Tucker since the soccer incident of yesterday, I have to figure this is about River. Have you changed your mind about her?"

"Nope."

Robert nodded as though that had been the answer he expected. "Then you're worried about what happens when we leave this place."

No one said Robert wasn't a smarty pants. "A week or two isn't enough. How do I know if I should stay with her? Hell, would I even be allowed to stay with her?"

"I'm sure this is where Ariel would explain to you that what you're feeling isn't truly real. You're imprinting on a person who's being kind to you. That's not truly love." Robert frowned.

He didn't like the sound of that, but he was fairly certain that was what Ezra and Big Tag and the other guys thought, too. He was some idiot duckling following the first person he saw. "Is that what she told you when you said you cared about her?"

Robert sighed. "Yes. She gave me a million and one explanations for why I feel the way I do about her. Desperation is a word that came up more than once. I'm sure she would say the same thing about you and River. You haven't known River very long and you've never been in a relationship before."

"That we know of." It haunted him, the idea that there could be someone out there who had depended on him, that he could have a wife and kids. He'd sat in bed thinking about it, thinking about what would happen if somehow his history was in that buried facility.

Robert was thoughtful for a moment. "We're fairly certain McDonald was careful with how she picked her subjects. It's hard to completely erase a human being from existence. If you had a wife, she would have told someone you were missing. There would be traces of a search for you somewhere and Miles would have found it."

Adam Miles was an expert on missing persons. In their case, instead of trying to find someone who was gone, he was trying to piece together the identity of a person who had none. He'd been frustrated so far. What Robert said made sense. "McDonald wanted subjects no one would miss. Subjects without close family. That's worse in a way."

Because he'd apparently had no one to miss him when he'd gone away. He'd been alone in the world.

"There are a lot of scenarios," Robert said. "But the most likely one is that you were alone and you worked for a Collective company or you were military. Hope McDonald's father was a senator and he served on the Armed Services Committee for years before he died. We know he had deep ties with some of the darker elements of the intelligence community."

"So he could have easily made someone disappear. Especially if no one was looking for him." He shook off the emotion. He had other bad shit to think about. "I don't care what Ariel would say. I know how I feel about River. I don't know if it's love or not, but I like her. I want to spend time with her. I care about her."

169

He couldn't use the "love" word. It hadn't been long enough and it was a word he didn't totally understand. Caring was better. He cared about what happened to River. He cared about his time with her.

He cared about her enough to fight with Ezra over her. Big Tag had simply shaken his head and tried to explain that it wasn't worth arguing over since it was obvious Jax's dick was in charge now.

He'd explained that if Ezra wanted him to stay at the big cabin and not with River, he would have to drug him again and drag him out and lock him up. That was when Ezra had walked off, cursing under his breath.

"I think Ariel is trying to let me down easy. She doesn't feel the same way about me." Robert crossed his arms over his chest. "She's wrong. I care about her and it's not because she was nice to me. A lot of women have been nice to me. I admit when I first got out, I was needy. I probably still am, but that doesn't mean I can't have feelings for her."

"That was obvious when you flipped out because she wanted to leave The Garden with us." Ariel had wanted to come along on this trip, to stay close to her patients and offer help to Ezra and Big Tag. Robert had vociferously objected. He'd been told to call it an objection instead of a hissy man fit. But Jax knew a man hissy when he saw one. "I think it was a mistake. You should have let her come with us. It's been perfectly quiet. I think Ezra might have overstated the threat. There are a lot of ways they can get Dr. McDonald's research that has nothing to do with kidnapping one of us and running tests. Ariel would have been safe."

Robert shook his head. "You're wrong. They will come for us at some point. They burned Ezra because he wouldn't turn us over. Bliss is a safe place. The fact that Henry is here will make a lot of people think, not to mention the sheriff and the others. We're good while we're in town. If it's not the Agency, then it will be someone else. And they'll use the people we care about. I can't risk Ariel. She might not care about me, but I'm fairly certain I'm in love with her, and that means protecting her at all costs. And that's why when you're out in the woods with River, I want you to think before you make a single move. The Ranch is a powder keg and it's waiting to go off."

He understood why Robert thought that way. "Because you think there are warring factions inside the Agency."

"Yes, that's what Ezra firmly believes, and Big Tag backs him up," Robert continued. "The Ranch is something neither have been willing to touch. It's like they agreed to forget it existed until the administration changes and they can fight over it again. President Hayes is considered a do-gooder who won't get his hands dirty. When he's out of office, they'll go to war over the information contained in that facility."

"How many eyes do you think they have on it?" The conversation was making him uncomfortable. Was he taking River into something he couldn't handle?

Robert sighed. "I don't know. I only know that we're opening Pandora's Box when we walk in there, and we better be ready to take care of whatever comes out. I want you to trust your instincts out there. We don't have CCTVs in the forest. We can't watch you. You'll be on your own and you have to make the decision whether the mission is worth the risk or not."

"Don't you want to know who you were?" Sometimes it was an ache inside his body. For now, River filled it in a way nothing ever had before, but he worried what happened if he stayed with her long term. He couldn't avoid telling her what had happened to him forever. She would wonder why he had no family, why there was so much he didn't know or understand. Right now she simply thought they were weird coworkers and that Tucker really was his brother. How would she feel if she found out the truth?

And he had to wonder if there was anyone out there, anyone at all who'd loved him, who missed him.

Robert stared at the parking lot. "I'm not sure I want to know. I can't get my memories back. I don't think any of us is like Theo. He doesn't remember everything, but he knows who he is. He can remember the important stuff about his life before."

"I think I did something with flowers. I know a lot about them. Sometimes I get flashes of my hands in the soil, planting something."

171

A faint smile lit Robert's face. "I get those, too. I think we all do. I think mine is from childhood. Either that or I like to hold hands with giant women. When the sun hits my face in just the right way, I can feel a hand in mine, and in my mind I look up and see a face, but she's backlit by the sun. I can't make out her features, but that feeling…I'm safe. I'm loved. I think she was my mother."

He knew some of the others had flashes. "Maybe we'll know one day. I don't know how I feel about that either. There's this whole world out there and I can't see it, but I know it could affect the world I have now in ways I can't imagine. I don't want Tucker to ever find out."

Because he was worried about what Tucker would do if he ever remembered he'd been Dr. Razor.

"I can't see it," Robert admitted. "I know what that mercenary said. I know Ezra knows more than he's saying, but how could he be so different? Sometimes I think what McDonald truly did by pulling our memories out by their roots was to strip us down to the essence of our souls. She took us down to the core essentials of ourselves. I can't see how a man whose soul is so full of light becomes someone who tortures people."

But Jax could. "He goes through torture himself. He gets kicked again and again and again and he's given nothing to hold on to. We had each other in there. That was her real mistake. She called us brothers. And some of us turned on one another. Sasha…I still struggle to deal with him."

Sasha had been the most brutal of them all. When they'd been forced to fight, Sasha had reveled in hurting the rest of them. While Jax had fought to survive and nothing more, Sasha had fought to win and had enjoyed standing over his opponents.

"He's been better since we've been on the outside," Robert said. "I don't know that we should blame anyone for what we did inside. We would all come out looking bad."

Would it ever end? He'd had two days of tantalizing peace, but the past was out there. The trouble was he couldn't prepare himself for it. There was a monster waiting and he wouldn't see it coming until it hit him in the face.

172

Robert stiffened beside him. "Jax, stay calm."

That was when he realized he'd been so lost in conversation with Robert that he hadn't seen the men coming up behind them. Big Tag would have his fucking hide for this. He was definitely thinking with his dick, and his dick wasn't very security minded. In the reflection from the glass in front of him, he could vaguely see a man behind him. He could definitely feel the press of something against his spine.

"Keep quiet and do everything I say or I'll take you out right here and now," a low voice growled.

A gun pressed against him and it looked like asshole number two had Robert.

Yep, he was going to get his ass kicked for this.

* * * *

River hated big box stores, but they sometimes came in handy. The Trading Post could order much of the equipment she needed, but it would take at least a week for shipping, and Ezra had made it plain that he wanted to be able to go the minute the weather cleared. He was paying for the expedition, hence the trip to the massive outdoor and sporting goods store.

"This one is super easy to set up," the salesman was saying. "It's a pop-up tent, but it's quite roomy."

Heather frowned. "It's also super easy to fall apart. I don't like that company. They cut corners."

Andy nodded. "Heather's right. I recently read an article about that particular company outsourcing a bunch of its manufacturing work to third world countries. They're using sweatshops and child labor. Nell Flanders was protesting them a couple of weeks ago. I'm not sure how she thought protesting them at the Trading Post would do much, but the woman is serious about protesting. She had signs and everything. Did you know she carries an emergency bullhorn with her?"

River shook her head at the salesman. He was only doing his job and that was to push whatever they had the most of. There was also the fact that she was a woman looking for camping equipment.

173

All male salesmen seemed to think they could quickly get rid of her. "We're going to look for a little while. Thank you. I'll let you know when we're ready to get serious."

The salesman sighed and strode away. And River resigned herself to being here for a while. She'd hoped they could get out of here quickly. She wanted to get back home. The rain would stop in a day or two and they would have to get to work. She'd grown to crave the quiet time she had with Jax. They'd spent the last two days cuddled up on her couch with Buster, watching movies he'd never seen. The man worked in the entertainment industry, but he'd never seen some of her favorites like *Titanic*. He'd teased her terribly when he'd gotten all emotional and pretended like he didn't know the whole ship went down.

She had fun with him.

Tomorrow she was going to ask him if he would help her pack up her father's things so they could redo the master bedroom and move into it. It was time. She still felt numb when she thought about her father, but Jax was slowly defrosting her.

She resented the fact that she had to spend one of her precious days with him shopping for equipment in a massive store where she wasn't even sure where he was because they'd split duties and she hadn't ended up with him.

Not that it made sense he would go with her to make the big decisions. He didn't know a lot about camping. He was better with a list of the incidentals they would need.

"All the really good stuff has to be ordered," Andy said, flipping through one of the numerous catalogs the store offered. "Are you sure we can't put this off a couple of days? If we pay the rush fee on these, we can probably be ready by next weekend. I would feel better going out with the best, and after what these dudes are paying us, we should be able to buy the Cadillac of tents."

"I don't think they want to wait and that's one of the reasons they paid so well," Heather commented.

Andy shut the catalog and turned to her. "Have we thought about this?"

She'd thought about it a lot. She definitely wanted at least one larger tent. Jax couldn't fit into some tiny thing. He would need some room. And they couldn't make love in a single person tent. He was inventive and liked to try new positions. She wasn't about to inhibit his creativity by shoving them in a tiny tent where he couldn't maneuver that big, sexy body of his.

Yep, she was getting hot right here in the middle of the store. The night before he'd drawn her up on her hands and knees and taken her rough and hard. She'd simply ridden the tidal wave he created every single time he got his hands on her.

"I've thought about it. We can get serviceable equipment here and still have money to buy some excellent stuff later on. We can always sell this equipment as long as we take good care of it."

Andy's eyes came up. "I wasn't talking about the stuff. I was talking about the job itself," he said, leaning in. "Do we want to get involved with something like this? This is the freaking CIA we're talking about."

She wasn't sure they weren't going on a wild-goose chase. It was another thing she'd thought long and hard about over the last few days. "I think maybe these guys are putting too much stock in rumors. The Internet is full of them. The world seems to run on conspiracy theories these days. If you ask me, I would bet we're going out there and we'll find some abandoned ranger post from the forties or a shelter someone built. Those aerial photos don't show much more than what looks like a metallic roof."

"I think River's right," Heather chimed in. "We're going to spend a bunch of days hiking through the wilderness, and I bet we find some guy's illegal hunting cabin and all we'll get from it is stale chips and warm beer and a warrant for the dude's arrest. I'm not worried about it at all. Now let's talk about something way more fun. Your new puppy is so cute. He's going to be big. He'll do well out here. Someone knew what they were doing when they picked out that dog."

Yeah, that sounded suspicious. She'd wondered if Jax had some help. He'd managed to walk into town and somehow know exactly where to go. "First off, Buster belongs to Jax, not me." Although she was rethinking that. Jax was on the road a lot. How would he take care of a massive dog? She couldn't stand the thought of Buster in a crate somewhere or boarded at a vet's office. Maybe she should offer to keep him and when Jax had time, he could perhaps come into Bliss and visit. But she wasn't going to admit that yet. "Did you go to Noah's and ask for the biggest walking pile of fluff he could find?"

Noah Bennett was the county's vet. He was also known for being able to pair strays with their perfect pet companions, and yes, he put it like that. He firmly believed people were the ones who needed pets, not necessarily the other way around.

Heather had the good grace to at least blush before she admitted guilt. "I might have asked Noah to start looking for you. I know you wanted time, but it can take time to find the right match. Buster had come in a couple of days before and I was trying to figure out how to broach the subject with you. When Jax asked me how he could properly apologize, I took the chance. I think you should seriously consider keeping him. Jax, I mean. I know you're going to cave and keep Buster."

Andy crossed his arms over his chest, his irritation obvious. "Could we get back to the situation at hand? Am I the only one who wants to know more about these people before we waltz out into the woods with them? How about we run a background check? Do you think it's a good idea to let Heather or yourself go out there alone with these guys? I think I should go with you if you insist on going at all."

She'd made this decision days ago. They would hike out together, find a rough base camp and then leave Ezra and Big Tag and the others there. She would take Jax and Tucker with her. Robert and Owen would be with Heather. Ty would stay at base camp and Andy was going to run the office while she was gone.

Andy didn't agree with the plan. He thought the women needed protection from the dangerous film crew. So far the only danger she'd detected was that Tucker whined when he was hungry and Big Tag could lay the sarcasm on pretty thick. Though she did worry about Dante and Sasha a bit, but she wouldn't be alone with them. As long as she gave Jax enough kisses and Tucker enough food, she would be okay.

"Somehow I think if Jax was going to attack her, he would

have already done it," Heather pointed out. "And I'm comfortable with Robert and Owen. I do think I'm going to hike out early and they can meet up with me. Robert knows what he's doing. I talked to him last night and he's obviously spent some time camping. I want to scout the area before I bring them out there."

Jax had admitted he didn't know a lot or she might do the same thing. "You think Robert can find his way to you?"

"I'll give him the coordinates. There's a known wolf pack in the space we're exploring. I want to get in there and make sure we're not tromping all over their territory. They can get aggressive if we go into the wrong places," she said.

"Another reason to take me along," Andy pointed out.

She shook her head. "I need you to answer the phones."

"Let Heather do that," he shot back.

Heather's shoulders squared, her eyes flaring. "You misogynist. Are you too good to answer the phones, or is it that your penis makes you better in the field than me?"

He winced but didn't back down. "I don't want you to get hurt by men we don't know. That's all I'm saying."

They were giving her a headache. She kind of wished Andy had been with them on the night of her big bar fight. He might not question Heather if he knew how good she was at getting other human beings in headlocks. "Heather's been in that part of the woods. She took those biologists out there when they were tagging the wolves. You've never been there. It makes no sense to have you do it and we need Ty at base camp in case something goes wrong. You can either answer the phones, or not and we'll shut down for the time we're out in the field."

"Good," he said. "I'll go with you."

He didn't understand a thing. "No. You'll look for another job. I can't run this place like a democracy. I need someone to answer the phones and keep the office open. If you can't do that, I'll have to hire someone else."

His face went red and he turned on his heels. "I think I'll go see if Ty needs help. I'm obviously not wanted here."

"Damn it. Andy, please wait." She couldn't afford to lose anyone, and he'd been helpful.

He stopped but didn't turn around.

Heather huffed, but it was a conciliatory sound. "I'll go see if Ty and the others need help. River, I'll watch the phones if I need to. Andy, I'm sorry. I know you're trying to watch out for us, but I truly feel I'm the best person to take them out there. I've become an expert over the last couple of months. I spend a lot of time in the forest. And I'm quite good at self-defense. River is, too. We'll both have rifles and several people know where we'll be and who we'll be with. I don't know how to be safer than that."

She walked back toward the sleeping bags where they'd left Ty going through the selections.

"I'm not trying to be difficult," Andy said, finally turning around. "I just think we're going into this blind. I think waiting a few days and maybe doing a background check into these guys could be helpful."

"We sort of go into everything blind if you think about it," she replied. "We don't background check our clients. They can always lie to us."

"But the client is usually a family or a bunch of dorky thrill seekers," Andy pointed out.

He was missing a couple of salient points. "And those thrill seekers can be dangerous. They don't listen to us. Do you remember the guys who said they were only going out for a pleasant bachelor weekend and they ended up taking a shit ton of peyote and we found one of them talking to a tree he thought was a Smurf?"

Andy chuckled. "Yeah, I do. It was like herding cats getting those assholes back to Bliss. And then there's the damn Squatchers."

Squatchers were a special brand of nature enthusiast. They firmly believed Bigfoot lived in the national forests and the government was hiding an entire species for some reason. Like any group they could be a ton of fun to work with or a massive pain in the ass. "It's like that, except this time we have the sheriff and the mayor and Henry backing them up. I trust Henry."

His jaw went tight. "I don't know if we should. I've heard so many rumors about him. Someone told me he used to be CIA and he faked his own death."

It was the single most ridiculous thing she'd ever heard. Henry was a pacifist vegan who worshipped his wife. He'd been a history professor at one point. He certainly hadn't been some killer spy. "I've lived here all my life. This whole place thrives on crazy rumors. Mel believes his girlfriend's sons are half alien. You can't listen to rumors around here. Or you should listen to them because some are funny as hell. You can't take them seriously, though."

"But don't you think it's odd that there's a rumor about Henry Flanders being a former CIA operative and then we get a group of men who come in here looking for a CIA base?"

"In the middle of national forest land." This was precisely why she was worried about what the producers would do when they couldn't find what they were looking for. Luckily, she'd had Gemma go over the contract and they couldn't get their money back. She wasn't responsible for their delusion. "The CIA doesn't work on American soil. Jax and the guys are chasing a story but that doesn't mean the story is real."

Not that she'd said anything to Jax. The last thing she wanted to do was argue with him. He'd been so serious, she couldn't burst that bubble until she had to. She'd already thought about how to handle his disappointment. She would be as good a girlfriend as she could.

God, was she thinking of herself as his girlfriend? She was setting herself up for some serious heartbreak, but she couldn't seem to stop.

Andy's mouth was a flat line as he seemed to think about his next method of attack. "Did you notice that Taggart person had a gun?"

It did not surprise her in any way. "He's from Texas. I'm pretty sure they all have guns."

"Fain was carrying, too."

She hadn't seen any evidence of guns, but it also wasn't illegal. "I understand if you don't want to work with them. But I trust the sheriff and Henry Flanders. I absolutely trust Nell. If she honestly thought someone was in danger, she would be protesting in the streets. She's not. She's been making breakfast for the guys."

Until the last few days when she'd apparently been a bit under the weather and River had taken over that job. She didn't mind. It gave her a chance to get to know Jax's weird friends. They all called each other "brother," though she knew only Tucker was his real brother. They seemed like an incredibly close group.

Not a one of them set off alarm bells except for Dante, and he wasn't around a lot. He seemed darker than the rest, though he and Jax were okay now.

"There's nothing I can do to change your mind?" Andy asked. "To let me go with you?"

She was at a loss for what to do with him. "I'll be fine. I do know how to handle myself. And we'll have walkies. I'll call Ty if things go wrong and we'll talk at regular intervals."

"What could go wrong?" Ty walked up with an order form in his hand. "We've got permits. Do you want me to talk to some of my ranger friends? Not Kendra, though. I'm kind of hiding from her. Turns out she doesn't understand the meaning of one night only."

She rolled her eyes. "You have to stop that."

He shrugged. "Can't have the one I want. Might as well play the field."

"You've played the whole field, Ty. All of it. It might be time to play with yourself," she said. More than once she'd had to deal with a client who decided to try to take Ty home as a souvenir. "Or let me get you a blow-up doll. And Andy is worried about our clients. He thinks they could be dangerous."

"I'm sure they are," Ty replied. "Big Tag is ex-military. I'm sure of it, and I bet he wasn't a foot soldier."

Andy pointed at Ty, obviously happy to have someone who agreed with him. "See. He didn't talk about that."

"Yes, he did." Had no one been listening at the meeting? "He mentioned he'd been a Green Beret. And Ezra was in the Army, too. It's where they met, I assume."

Ty held up his hands. "I wasn't saying that made him dangerous to us. Not at all. He seems pretty cool, actually. Though every time I walk out the door and he's there, he tells me to use a condom for some reason. He's weird, but cool. He told me to double wrap yesterday. I think he was talking about my dick."

It seemed as though Big Tag had already figured out who Ty was. "Look the only reason Ty is going to be at base camp is the fact that he's an EMT. If something happens out in the woods, he could be helpful."

"And if he gets called away on an emergency?" Andy asked.

Ty handled that one. "Elena is on call all next week. And before you ask, I have not slept with her." He cleared his throat. "She has informed me that she doesn't play for my particular team. Or I guess play *with* my team. Anyway, she's going to handle everything that week. I'm good to sit in the woods with the guys."

She turned to Andy. "I know you're unhappy but I sincerely hope you can accept it. I would hate to lose you."

He held his hands up. "I've done everything I can. If it goes to hell, I'm not responsible. I'll answer the phones."

At least they'd gotten that out of the way. "Good. Now about these tents."

Twenty minutes later she'd found the tents they needed and had her order form in hand. The staff would pull the orders and she would pay for everything. It was time to find Jax and Robert and get out of here. She could still make it back to Bliss in time to head out to Trio. There was a band there tonight and she wanted to dance.

God, she *wanted*. She'd been numb for so long that wanting to dance and sing and drink and feel alive was the most amazing feeling ever. She wanted. She suddenly wasn't simply moving through her days, surviving.

Jax had given her that.

Where the hell was he? She glanced around. She could only see Ty. He'd stayed with her. Andy had wandered off and Heather had gone to look for Jax and Robert.

She looked at Ty. He shrugged.

She pulled out her phone and winced. Naturally it was dead. She hadn't put it on the charger. "I don't suppose you put Jax's number in your phone."

Because she hadn't memorized it. She touched his picture in

her contacts and he answered. They'd taken the picture two days before.

"Sorry," Ty said. "He doesn't call me. I think he knows who he wants to deal with."

She'd taken a lot of pictures of Jax, as though she could trap this moment in time, hold it close to her when he was inevitably gone from her.

She glanced out the big window.

Was Jax leaving? She caught sight of a group of men walking past the front of the store.

She'd only gotten a glimpse. "Can you handle the purchase order? I'll be right back."

She strode toward the front of the store, curious about where her boyfriend was going.

Chapter Eleven

Jax moved past the corner of the mega store, praying River hadn't noticed him leaving. Not that it had been his choice, but the last thing he needed was to add River to the equation. If one of these assholes got his hands on her, Jax wouldn't be able to fight. He would give them anything they asked for as long as River was alive at the end.

This was what it meant to have a true weakness. He would fight for his brothers, but he would lie down and die for her.

At least the rain seemed to have stopped. The clouds overhead threatened more storms, but for now only the ground was wet.

"Any chance you want to explain why we're being kidnapped?" Robert was rock solid.

It was sad but he ranked his brothers in the order in which he would like to be kidnapped with. Dante was last because he was the one most likely to give anyone up to save himself. Robert was the top of his list. Robert was cool under pressure.

"Keep moving, asshole. You know exactly why we're taking you," the man with the gun pressed to his spine said. "The group paying us wants you alive, but they'll take your corpses, too."

"Did you miss something, Jax? I thought you kept up with all the Deep Web conspiracies to vivisect us." Robert was going to do something, likely the minute they got out of view of the parking lot.

"There are so many of them. It's hard to keep up with." Adrenaline started to pump through his system. Robert would make a move soon or he would. He would have to stay calm and not get lost in the fight. He couldn't lose it if River had a chance of seeing him.

"We can do this easy, man." The guy behind him had a deep voice, the better to threaten him with. "Or we can do it hard. We're taking you to a private airfield. You're going to take a little knockout drug and when you wake up they'll do some tests. You're some kind of medical freak or something."

They would do far more than run a couple of tests. Whoever "they" were, they would likely lock he and Robert up and study them in the worst possible ways. He would be held in a cage again, away from the sun and the stars.

He couldn't do it. He couldn't go into that cage again.

He tamped down the panic. Big Tag would find them. He'd promised. If it all went to hell and they ended up taken, he would survive.

But it wasn't going to get that far. His hands twitched, ready to work.

They rounded to the back of the building. There were huge trash bins, massive stacks of broken down boxes at the back of the store. It was quiet out here, the only sound the hum of enormous air-conditioning units. There was an eighteen-wheeler parked in a loading zone, but no one was out here now.

A hard shove to his back kept him shuffling along. It was obvious where they were going. A big black van stuck out like a sore thumb among the SUVs and Jeeps and trucks. A third man opened the back and he held zip ties in one hand.

He would be hog tied and bound for some lab if they didn't do something and quickly.

But neither he nor Robert were carrying.

There was the sound of a ping and then the man escorting Robert was on the ground.

They weren't carrying but someone was.

Jax brought his elbow up and back, meeting with his attacker's solar plexus. There was a groan and the man's hand moved. He twisted his body, instinct taking over. He'd been born knowing how to do this. He hadn't known his name or who his people were, but he'd known how to fight. He kicked his assailant, sending the man to the ground. He fell on his back, his head cracking on the hard concrete.

Robert was on him in an instant, getting the gun in his hand. "Get the driver."

Jax turned in time to see the driver raise a pistol. Before he could get the shot off, there was another ping and the man's head suddenly sported a neat red hole in the center.

Jax turned again, trying to figure out who the hell was firing. How many people were after them? Were they caught in between two groups who wanted to open them up and find out all their secrets? He caught a shadow moving from behind the truck.

He was about to run after the man who'd helped them out, but Robert was cursing.

"This one's dead, too. Damn it." Robert got to his feet. "He hit his head when you put your foot half through his torso. Who the hell was the shooter? How many are we dealing with?"

He shook his head. "No idea. I only saw one and I didn't see much more than a shadow. Should I go after him? He can't have gotten far. Did Ezra send someone to watch us?"

Robert was staring at the space where the shooter must have stood. "No way. If that had been one of ours, he would have come to help us clean up the mess. Damn it. I wish we had one to question. I would like to know who they work for."

He could figure out who they were and who they worked for, but he would need time and some information. They had bigger problems right now. If anyone walked out, the cops would be involved, and they weren't in Bliss where the sheriff would help. "We need to get the bodies in the van and then look for any type of ID on these guys."

He strode back to the van and hefted the driver's body back inside. They would have to take the whole thing with them. Or rather someone else would because he and Robert needed to return to the store.

"Jax?"

His heart threatened to seize. River was coming and if she made that turn they would have a lot of explaining to do.

Robert winced. They were surrounded by dead bodies neither one of them wanted to explain to River and she was about to turn that corner. "You need to distract her. I'll get the bodies in the van and meet you inside. I'll call Tag and let him know we need a cleaner."

Jax ran, sprinting toward the building. He got there just as she rounded the corner.

"Hey," she said, frowning at him. "What are you doing out here? I thought I left you with a list."

They were way too close to the scene of his most recent crime. He did the only thing he knew would distract her. He kissed her, swift and hard, his hands dragging her against his body as his mouth made a meal of hers.

Her arms came around him as she softened and gave over.

"I should have known I would find you two making out," Heather said. Jax looked up and she was shaking her head. "You know you can do that at home. We're supposed to be working. Where the hell did Robert get off to? And I can't find Andy, either."

He ignored her, staring down at River. "Sorry, baby, Robert got talked into helping a guy change his tire. He'll be back in a minute. I need to go and finish out my list."

River shook her head, laughing. "I should have known better than to send you off with Robert."

Heather rolled her eyes. "I'll do it. But if Andy's flirting with some chick, I'm not doing his work, too."

She turned on her heels and strode away.

River took his hand. "Come on. If we hurry we can get back home and take Buster for a nice long walk before we go out tonight."

If she'd been a couple of minutes earlier, she would have walked right into the killing field. They'd been lucky. Someone had been watching out for them today, but who knew what would happen tomorrow.

Did he have any right to bring her into this?

He forced a smile on his face and followed her, his brain whirling the whole time.

* * * *

Six hours later, River let her arms drift up around Jax's shoulders as music pulsed through Trio. The band played a slow song, one that made it possible for her to get close to her man. Her kind of awkward, but still crazy hot man. He couldn't dance. Not at all, but she loved that he tried for her.

He kissed the top of her head as the music changed. "I'm going to grab a beer, baby."

She couldn't seem to stop dancing. "Feel free. I think I'll stay here a while."

He looked around, nodding to Robert and Owen. Owen moved closer to her as though acknowledging that he would watch over her. Not that she needed anyone to watch her. She wasn't the one who wandered off every time a stranger needed help.

Owen could dance. Robert wasn't bad, but he didn't have Owen's natural rhythm. Still, she couldn't help but think Jax had perfect rhythm when it counted. In bed.

She moved to the music. It was like her body had come awake after a long sleep. She felt different. Somehow these days and nights with Jax had brought her back to life. She didn't spend every waking moment thinking about what she'd lost and plotting and planning a way to survive. The simple joys of life were pleasurable again, like waking up and rolling into his arms, taking the puppy outside for a walk, even going into work felt new.

It was as if the clouds had parted and she could see the sun for the first time in a year and a half.

It made her realize how deep she'd gotten into her own problems, her own darkness. Jax had forced her into the light again. It made her look at everything differently.

Andy bopped around the Harper twins, who were dancing

with their wife, Rachel. He waved her way. At least there was a smile on his face now. The drive back from Alamosa seemed to have done wonders for him.

"Hey," he said, shouting over the music. "I wanted to apologize."

She moved to the back of the dance floor where she might be able to hear him. It did not escape her notice that one of the tourists immediately moved in on Owen. He was grinning as she twerked, his eyes wide as though he'd never seen a woman shake her ass before.

The whole crew knew how to do the wide-eyed thing to perfection. It had every single woman in the bar panting after them, but she'd noticed Jax could shut a chick down. He did it politely, but he was quick. Her bar fight might have taught him that she could defend her territory.

"What did you say?" She'd thought he'd apologized, but she could hear that again.

A sheepish expression crossed his face. "I'm sorry about earlier. I'll watch the phones and keep the office open. Heather kind of read me the riot act on the way home. She's right. I'm being overly cautious. We should get this job done so there's no way they can ask for the money back. We need it. It'll get us through the winter and we'll be in good shape for the summer season. With the sun out this afternoon, it should be dry enough to go in a day."

She hated the sound of that. A little more than twenty-four hours left before she had to start her job. If they found what he was looking for quickly, they had maybe three or four days before he would head back to LA.

How was it going so fast? She couldn't think about it now. She had to live in the moment. "I'm glad. I think you'll see it's going to go well. Where is Heather? I thought she was coming with us tonight."

He shrugged. "She said she had something she needed to handle. She dropped me off at the office and headed out. I think she's got some kind of secret lover or something. She rushes off at the oddest times and she will not be upfront about where she's going. Don't get me wrong. I love that girl. She's awesome, but she's weird, too."

She wasn't sure she agreed about the secret lover. Heather seemed deeply in love with her ex-husband, but Andy was right about her regular disappearances lately. She was always careful about work. "I think she's got some family issues, but she's solid. She's missed some client meetings, but I can't imagine she'll miss the actual job."

She glanced over. Robert had walked off the dance floor and was talking to Jax, though he didn't look happy about whatever Jax had said.

"Well, I'm going to head home. I'll walk. It's not far." Andy lived in a rented cabin in the valley. It was roughly a half a mile from the center of town. "I'll see you in the morning."

She gave him a smile and turned her attention back to the band. Jax looked like he was having a serious talk. She decided to give him some space.

"You having fun?"

She glanced up and into the eyes of a handsome man. He had warm brown eyes and the kind of scruff one got from careful grooming. He looked a bit out of place in his dress shirt and smart-looking suspenders. He was wearing a shiny pair of loafers. Definitely a tourist, and one from a big city. He was a hottie, for sure, though he had nothing on her Jax. Jax didn't bother with fashion and she would bet this man read *GQ* and kept up with a better skin care regime than she had. Still, with the music playing and the world seemingly softer than it had been before, she grinned up at him. "I am having a blast. Are you here with your family?"

The band slowed down, the song changing to a ballad. Owen pulled the blonde close, getting his hands on her. She looked up at him with a seductive smile. It looked like Jax wouldn't be the only one getting busy tonight.

"I'm here for you, River."

A chill went across her skin. She hadn't told him her name. "Who are you?"

He reached in his pocket and passed her his identification. "I'm the man who's going to save you from a whole lot of jail time. Your boyfriend has been lying to you. He's not who you think he is and he's going to lead you into trouble. Come with me and I'll show you exactly who the man you call Jax Seaborne is."

She carefully read the ID. It looked real. A hollow opened in her gut. Could this be happening again? "I don't believe you."

This was some kind of trick because she couldn't go through this again. But then hadn't she been waiting for the floor to fall out from under her since the moment she'd woken up and he'd been gone? Maybe she'd been waiting for it since the second she'd realized he "wanted" her.

"I'll show you his arrest warrants," the man replied, a humiliating sympathy in his eyes. "Or you can keep going down the road you're going down and face the consequences. Shouldn't you know what they are?"

"Consequences?" Should she run back to Jax? Beg him to tell her this was all some mistake? He had warrants? For what?

She might think this was some play by her ex-husband, but he was sitting in a jail cell. He didn't have any money left to hire a hit man. He wouldn't know Jax's name.

But this man obviously did. She handed him back his very official-looking badge.

"The consequences are far-reaching, and they affect more than you." He held his hands up. "I'm not here to hurt you. I promise. I'm the only one willing to tell you the truth."

"Jax told me what he's looking for." And he'd told her it could be dangerous.

"But he hasn't told you why," the man pointed out. "I'm sure he gave you some story about how he's filming urban legends." He studied her intently. "Or perhaps he's trying to expose some environmental issue that no one knows about. Ah, that's it. Clever, but then he's working with the best. Ezra Fain isn't who he says he is either. He's a disgraced CIA operative who's willing to start a war that could burn us all down. I'm here to stop it and you're the only one who can help me."

She stared at him for a moment.

He stared back. "I'm also the only one who can keep you out of jail."

Did he know about the money Jax had stolen? It was sitting in her bank account. It would look like she'd taken it.

What would she have given for an authority figure to have shown up looking for Matt before he'd taken everything from her?

"Who are you?" She couldn't seem to wrap her brain around what he was saying. It wasn't possible.

"You can call me Mr. Green," he said solemnly. "Or Levi, if you prefer. Please come with me. I can save you a lot of trouble."

She glanced back and realized she knew nothing about her lover.

It was stupid. She should run back to Jax, but the weight of her own history made her turn.

She walked straight over to where Ty was sitting. "I need a favor."

Ty looked up, his shoulders straightening. "Of course."

She pointed back at the man who claimed to be a CIA employee. "I'm going to leave with that man. His name is Levi Green. If he murders me, memorize his face."

Ty's eyes widened. "Whoa, are you sure?"

She had to come up with a good reason on the fly or Ty would insist on going with her. "I'm planning a surprise for Jax and he's going to help."

Ty grinned. "Because he got you Buster? I should have known you would feel the need to pay him back. What are you doing? Setting up something hot?"

She smiled, praying it reached her eyes. "Something like that. I've talked to Mr. Green on the phone before, but a girl can't be too careful."

"Well, he's probably been caught on the security cameras. He's pretty stupid if he's planning on hurting you," Ty replied, nodding over at Green, who gave him a jaunty wave and didn't try to hide his face.

"I'm sure it will be fine. I'll be back in a while." She turned and walked to where she'd left Green. She'd done everything she could to be safe, but she had to know. "I'm ready."

She followed Levi Green out of the bar and worried her world was about to crumble around her. Again.

Chapter Twelve

Jax sat in the back booth at Trio, watching River dance with Robert and Owen. They were grooving to a fast beat, River moving with perfect grace. Jax had already figured out he was a terrible dancer, but he did like swaying with her in his arms. What he didn't like was the new information they'd discovered about their would-be kidnappers.

"I think they were working for someone inside the Agency. From the information Robert was able to get us, we've identified all three. They were mercenaries. They offered their talents on the Deep Web," Big Tag said, his voice low. "My working theory is someone from the Agency hired those assholes. They had a private plane waiting and the flight plan indicated they were going to a facility in Mexico City."

"I happen to know Levi Green has ties there." Ezra nodded. "I knew they would come at us one way or another."

Tucker took a sip of his beer. "If they come for me, I'll go with them. I've got a subcutaneous tracking unit in my butt. It might help to know where they're set up."

They all had trackers. Every man who worked deep cover for McKay-Taggart and Knight had them.

Big Tag snorted, a sound he managed to make authoritative.

"Someone might think you've got a martyr complex. And if it's the Agency, they will pull that tracker out of your ass long before they take you to their leader. The Agency has a big book on me. I assure you, they know I microchip my operatives. If they come for you, I expect you to fight like hell. But damn, leave one of them alive, unlike Jax there."

He held his hands up, offering his only defense. "I only killed one of them. Someone else took out the other two."

Ezra nodded. "Yes, and that's what worries me. We knew the Agency would come. I'm more interested in the identity of our helpful sniper."

Jax had been thinking about it all afternoon. He'd gone over it in his head again and again. They wouldn't stop coming after him and at some point, they might get River. "I caught a glimpse of the dude. He moved fast. I think he was using the eighteen-wheeler as cover. My question is how he knew to be there at all. I think he might have been following those guys."

"Why?" Dante asked, sliding into the booth. He'd left Sasha at the bar where the man was downing vodka and talking animatedly to Alexei in rapid-fire Russian. It was good to know someone could put a smile on Sasha's face. "Why would this man follow hired thugs and then not take you out when he has the chance? He didn't try to kidnap either of you. It makes no sense."

That fact had been bugging him all day. "I don't know. Maybe he wasn't ready to make a move, but he wasn't willing to give up the prize to someone else."

"Did you see a face?" Big Tag asked.

He shook his head. "I saw a shadow. It all happened very quickly and then I had to deal with River. I thought about going after him."

"How can you be sure it was a him? We can't assume we know anything at all about this person." Big Tag leaned over. "I want to rerun all the background checks on River's employees."

He hadn't considered that it could be a woman. Tag was right. That was a mistake. In his world, women could be as deadly as any man. And the idea that Tag brought up made his stomach clench. "You think we should be worried about River?"

"Not River," Tag replied. "Henry thinks River is exactly who she says she is, and I trust his instincts. He's not sure about the others. He hasn't spent much time with them."

Ezra nodded in agreement. "I want to interview them all personally. I haven't met this Heather person. I personally have my questions about both Andy and Ty."

"Ty spent time in Virginia." Dante had helped with the background checks.

"He went to college there." Jax didn't think there was anything sketchy about Ty. He'd grown up in the area, was childhood friends with River.

Dante shrugged. "The Agency recruits from colleges from time to time. It would have been easy for him to make some contacts. There has to be an insider. Otherwise, how would they know where you would be?"

"Andy's been trying to get River to rethink working with us." She'd told him about her conversation with Andy when they'd taken Buster out earlier that afternoon. "He's been on her about it for days. He's telling her not to trust us."

And River hadn't listened. River had chosen her lover over her friend and employee. She'd chosen the lover who was lying to her. How would she feel if she learned the truth? How would she feel if she knew he was taking her into something more dangerous than she could imagine?

Tucker sat back. "I'll watch him. I'll tail him for the time being, see where he goes and who he talks to. I'll try to dupe his phone."

"Not you. He knows you," Dante said. "Sasha and I will follow him for a couple of days and we'll keep track of him while you're in the woods. Although I would much rather follow the woman. Heather is quite lovely."

"I'd just like to *meet* the woman," Ezra admitted. "She's conveniently gone any time I go to the office."

"They don't spend a ton of time in the office when they don't have to." Jax couldn't believe it was Heather. "She's nice. She's the reason River gave me a second chance."

Heather had walked him through everything. She'd been the

one to find Buster and the one to tell him where River would be that night.

"She could have motives we don't understand because we don't know who she really is." Big Tag had his phone out. "I'm going to have Hutch run everything again on River's whole staff. I don't like the fact that those mercenaries knew where you were going to be. River decided to go shopping this morning. It wasn't planned."

He didn't like it either. God, how would River take it if Heather or Andy were CIA plants? Both had been hired in the past year. They could have been embedded because of Henry Flanders's former life as John Bishop. The Agency would want someone watching him in an attempt to figure out if he was a threat. Or someone could have been playing a long game of chess, positioning pieces in anticipation that Ezra would make this move. Or perhaps they were here to make sure no one got into The Ranch.

He didn't like any of those choices and hated the idea that River was going to get hurt. "I think we should find another guide."

Tag cursed under his breath. Dante sighed. Ezra simply rolled his eyes.

Only Tucker backed him up. "I think Jax is right. This is too dangerous. She doesn't know what she's getting into."

"She knows a hell of a lot because Jax's dick told her," Tag retorted. "Your dick got us into this. There's no going back. The fact that those three assholes tried to take you today makes it even more important to get into that facility and try to find any scrap of intelligence we can. Or do you want to live in The Garden for the rest of your life? I love a good dungeon, man, but not even I want to be stuck in one twenty-four seven for the rest of my life."

He'd considered it, but she was more important. "I'm not willing to put River at risk."

Dante stood. "Then you should have thought about that before you started fucking her. If she won't go, I'll walk into those damn woods myself. We're close and we'll never get closer. I'm not going to allow your cock to fuck this up for the rest of us."

Well, it was good to know how Dante felt.

Robert moved in as Dante stalked off. "What's he so pissed about?"

Ezra stood. "He's pissed because Jax has decided to tank the op."

Robert's eyes widened. "What? No. Not when we're so close. There could be a cure in that research."

"There's no cure," he shot back. Robert was being naïve. "McDonald didn't want a cure. She wanted soldiers without conscience, without any kind of loyalty except to her. She wanted to build us from nothing. She was never going to say 'hey, you've done your share, here's your history back.' When she was done, she would have had one of us put a bullet in the subject she was finished with. She wasn't ever going to waste time on something she wouldn't use."

"And if her notes have something that leads to figuring out who we are?" Robert's eyes held a hint of desperation. "Our histories could be there."

"I don't think we want to know who we were," Tucker replied. "I know I don't."

"Well, I do," Robert shot back. "Even if it's bad. I want to know. I want to remember my mother and father. I want to know if anyone ever loved me. We can protect River but if you won't go, I will. I'll go all by my fucking self."

Well, he was pissing everyone off, but he had to think about River.

Tucker put a hand on his shoulder. "I understand. You have to watch out for her. When you care about a woman, you take her safety seriously. Robert's being a hypocrite. He wouldn't even allow Ariel to come with us."

Robert snorted derisively.

Ezra leaned over. "I understand why you're scared, but this is going to happen one way or another. You can be with her in those woods or you can leave her out here in Bliss alone."

Tag's eyes were steely as he looked at Jax. "I think what Ezra is trying to say is she's on their radar now and there's no going back. It's precisely why I thought this was a bad idea, but I do get it. If my Charlie walked in, it wouldn't have mattered how dangerous the situation was. I would have taken her because you get one shot. You need to make a choice. Do you want to be her man or do you want to play it safe? You can get her off their radar, but it's got to be public and nasty."

"What do you mean?"

"He means you have to break up with her because someone is watching us," Robert replied. "You have to let everyone know she means nothing to you. Otherwise she'll always be in danger."

"Or you love her enough to take the risk," Big Tag said without an ounce of his usual sarcasm. "Women are funny creatures. When they love someone, they tend to risk everything. Most of the women I know would rather go down with their man than live a safe life without him. We're trained to sacrifice, but if a woman loves you the last thing she wants you to do is sacrifice her."

"But how will you feel if you get her killed?" Robert asked, his voice tight with emotion.

"She can get killed without you," Tag challenged. "Not a damn thing about this life is guaranteed. Whoever is watching us might not care that you break her heart. They might decide she could know something and off her just in case."

"Or you could realize that you barely know her." Ezra seemed taut, like a bowstring pulled tight, ready to go off. "You could be logical and choose your job because you don't know this woman. She could choose her job over you. Very likely she would. She could be using you for any number of reasons. We'll take care of her out in the field. Unless you choose the first option and break up with her tonight. We're in a public place. Pick one of the single women here and fuck her. That'll end the relationship and let every person here know you don't care about River. I don't think they'll come after her. She's got people who care about her and they would ask questions if she disappears."

He didn't want another woman. He was worried he might never want anyone except River again. "I couldn't do that to her."

She'd been hurt too many times.

Tag nodded. "Good. Then we'll proceed, and you can make

the decision at the end of this which way to go. If you decide to stay here with River, Henry can watch your back. You can watch his. Honestly, I'm worried about him now that the Agency knows he's alive."

Stay here with River? Was that worth taking a chance with her life? Or should he utterly ruin the trust she'd placed in him? Wasn't it better to be alive and hollow than dead? Surely she would move on.

Or would she? How many times could she get kicked before she stopped getting up?

Or he could tell her everything and show some trust in her. But that would mean betraying his brothers.

"Trust your instincts, Jax," Big Tag encouraged.

"My instinct is to tell her the truth."

Ezra's eyes closed. "You can't."

"He can if he's careful about it," Tucker offered. "The bad guys already know everything about us. Why are we hiding it from people we care about?"

"Because again, we can't trust her staff." Ezra stood up. "We can't trust her. I've lost everything because of a woman before and I assure you I didn't think she was capable of doing what she did when I met her. I took one look at that woman and thought the whole world revolved around her. She was the sun in my fucking sky and she took everything from me. Ian, did you think Charlotte was dangerous when you met her? Did you think she would blow up your career?"

The faintest hint of a smile crossed Tag's face, like he was remembering something private and precious. "Oh, yeah. I knew my baby could do some serious damage from the moment I met her. Hurricane Charlie rocked my world, and not always in a good way. I loved her anyway. Look, man, I don't know what this chick from your past did to you, but after everything these men have been through, if they've got a chance at something resembling happiness, I say take it."

"Let's talk about it." Tucker sent him an encouraging smile. "I'll go grab Sasha and Dante and we'll order a round of beers and figure this out. I'll let Owen know what's going on and he can distract River for us. There's not as much at stake for him. He knows who he is. I don't have a problem with her knowing what happened."

"I don't either, but I think we should still go forward with the mission. I think if she's in, she's in. You'll hurt her far more if you break her heart. Let her make the decision," Robert said.

Jax stared at him. Tucker was right about Robert's hypocrisy.

Robert shook his head. "It's not the same. Ariel doesn't love me. We're not going to be together. I can't ask her to risk anything."

Tag made a vomiting sound. "I need another beer. Where's Mel when I need him? I would like to be abducted by aliens now, please."

"You're the worst about this," Ezra pointed out. "You are the most gossipy asshole I've ever met."

Big Tag and Ezra started arguing over whether or not he was a meddling old man, but Jax was looking for River. He glanced out at the dance floor. The song had slowed down and couples swayed in each other's arms. Well, the ones who weren't threesomes did. There were a surprising amount of thruples out on that dance floor, two men surrounding a single female. He caught sight of Owen, his hands on a pretty blonde's hips as he swayed to the music.

"Where's River?" He stood up.

"I'm sure she went to the bathroom or something," Robert replied, but he stood up as well.

Tucker was beside him, looking out over the crowd. "I thought she was dancing." He waved Owen over.

The big Scot frowned but moved their way, gently disentangling from his dance partner. "What is it? I was making time with…I can't remember her name, but she was definitely into me. It's the bloody accent. Makes American ladies go crazy."

"Where did River go?" Surely she was at the bar or she'd seen a friend.

Owen shrugged. "No idea. I thought she went to find you."

He moved toward the front of the bar, scanning the tables and booths. He found Ty sitting next to a pretty brunette. "Have you seen River?"

Ty's lips turned down. "Nope."

Oh, he was lying. Even he knew that. He had to get the information out of River's employee as quickly as possible. "Ty, it's important. I need to find River. There might be a problem. Please. I need to see her now."

Ty sat up, his expression changing to concerned in a heartbeat. "She's going to kill me. She said she was planning a surprise for you and some guy was going to help her."

"What guy?" His heart started to beat heavy in his chest.

"No idea. Never seen him before." Ty stood, worry suddenly clouding his eyes. "Is she in trouble? She did seem tense, but I thought she was trying to keep her surprise a secret. You don't think she was lying, do you? Look, I know River. She wouldn't do that. If you think she's covering up some kind of date with this guy, you're wrong."

He wasn't worried River was planning on cheating on him with some random asshole she picked up in a bar. He was worried the asshole wasn't random at all. River would be the ultimate bargaining chip for him. Still, he couldn't have Ty getting messed up in all of this. He needed to concentrate on finding River, not be worried about saving the civilian if things got nasty. He plastered what he hoped was a casual smile on his face. "I think he's probably one of my bosses. They mentioned they might stop by to check in on how things are going. I'll see if I can find them."

Ty nodded, obviously relieved.

"I'll go with you," Ezra said. "I'd like to know if our friend is here, too."

Jax leaned over and whispered to Robert. "You and Big Tag check the rest of the bar. Send Owen out back. I'll go out the front. Ask Alexei if there are cameras anywhere that might have caught them."

Robert nodded and went back to the table to talk to Big Tag and Owen.

Jax led the way outside, Tucker and Ezra following.

The night was quiet around him, the streets eerily empty after the raucous party in the bar. She was gone.

He had to find her. He had to.

* * * *

River stared at the pictures in front of her, trying to reconcile the image with the vision in her brain. She understood on a logical level that it was Jax. He had the same straight jawline, his hair flowing to the nape of his neck in the same semi-curly wave. His sensual lips were present. It was the addition of the AR-15 and the wretchedly angry look on his face that threw her off.

"I don't understand."

Levi Green pointed to the photo. "That image was taken off CCTV in Madrid during a robbery. The bank was small and local, just like this team likes it."

He started a long recitation of the crimes Jax and the others had committed, but River couldn't take her eyes off the photos he'd lain out on the desk of his motel room. She'd followed him back to the Movie Motel at the edge of town, well aware that she was trailing after a complete stranger who might or might not be a serial killer. If he was, his MO was outstanding because she'd been caught from the moment he'd mentioned he could save her from almost certain personal and financial ruin.

He hadn't been able to save her from getting her heart ripped out of her chest again.

"Why would they rob banks?" She knew it was a stupid question but she had to say something.

"Money, of course." Mr. Green laid out another several photos, each more damning than the next. "I've run the numbers and I believe over the course of two years, Jax and his 'brothers' managed to hit seven banks on three continents to the tune of roughly three million dollars. These are copies of the warrants for his arrest in Europe and South America. The group is careful in the States. They don't spend a lot of time here."

She shook her head because it was all too much. There was a grainy photo of a man holding a gun to a crying woman's head.

How was it possible that was Jax? Maybe he was acting. They were a film crew. Maybe he'd done some work as an extra.

"Do I need to show you news coverage? I have a file on my

201

computer." Green's voice was gentle but relentless.

"If he's such a bad man, why don't you arrest him? The sheriff of the town vouched for him. And my friend Henry said he was okay."

"Do you mean John Bishop?" He had another file in his hand. He opened it, showing the CIA credentials for the man named Bishop. It was a younger version of the man she knew as Henry Flanders. He was younger and harder, his eyes flinty as he stared out. She knew she should wonder if the documents were faked, but the truth was there in his eyes. The man in the picture was cold as ice. And yet it was clearly Henry.

All those rumors were true.

Mr. Green stared down at her, sympathy plain in his gaze. "You are surrounded by wolves, River. The man you know as Ezra Fain used to work with me."

"I'm sorry. I'm confused. His name isn't Ezra Fain?"

"His real name is Beckett Kent, but he's gone by many names over the years. He used to call himself Mr. White when he ran black ops missions. Ian Taggart worked as an operative for a time as well. He was the Agency's go-to guy for wet work. Do you understand what that means?"

It meant he had a lot of blood on his hands. "I don't understand any of this."

"You don't have to know the finer points to understand that you should never have been placed in the middle of this war. No man who cares about you would do this to you."

She was starting to get the feeling Jax didn't care about her at all. He'd needed her for something and he'd found a way to make her do his bidding. Still, he'd told her some of the truth, right? "He told me about the CIA and that this place he wants to find was run by them."

Green nodded as though he'd known that was coming. "Yes, but he's not trying to save the environment. When The Ranch was closed down, the Agency locked everything inside that facility. They evacuated the employees and sealed the building shut. Everything that was being worked on is still in there, and that includes some serious research. I believe they are trying to gain access to the research of a doctor named Hope McDonald. She was murdered by Taggart's sister-in-law, though he would have done the deed himself."

Who the hell were these people? It was surreal. She'd sat and had dinner with a killer? "I don't know that I believe any of this."

"It's easy enough to look up. Take your phone out and search for the world's most wanted criminals."

Her hands shook as she did what he'd told her to do. It took a moment to pull up. She selected the first website in the search and there he was. He had no name, was merely known as a member of a gang labeled the Professionals, but it was obviously Jax. Tucker and Dante and Sasha were on the list of internationally wanted criminals. Robert was missing, as was Owen, but they probably hadn't been caught on camera.

Bile hit the back of her throat. She looked at the second site and he was there as well.

He was a criminal, and not the kind who sat behind a computer, though he did that, too. She had two million in her account that he'd stolen from her ex-husband. Was she laundering money for him? Would she look in there and find the account empty and her fingerprints all over the records?

She thought she'd been conned by the best, but Matt had nothing on Jax. Jax had managed to do more damage in a few days than Matt had done in years of marriage. She might never recover from this. God, she might go to jail. "He put a bunch of money in my account. He said he stole it from my ex-husband."

"The con artist?"

It shouldn't surprise her that he had a file with her name on it. The man seemed to know everything about everyone. He was a master at finding out dirty secrets. "Yes. It happened a couple of days ago. He said Matt had stolen money from a lot of different women and that he would help me find them and get it back."

How naïve was she? Now that she was saying the words, she realized how stupid she sounded. Why had she believed him? She'd bought every lie he'd told her.

"It's possible he took it from your ex," Mr. Green allowed. "It's also possible this is another way they're laundering the money they stole. You could be in a lot of trouble. I can help you."

She went quiet, trying to find that place deep inside her head where she could be cold and logical. "He wants this research so he can sell it?"

How could he be so sweet? So thoughtful?

"There are dangerous secrets in that facility. Do you understand what I mean when I call it a black ops development site?"

She thought she did, and it meant Jax's group was involved in something incredibly dangerous. But then he also robbed banks, so he likely considered it all in a day's work. "They were developing weapons?"

"Yes, and running experiments that would likely make Joseph Goebbels blush. It all sounds horrible, but the Agency will do anything to defend this country. What Ezra Fain and Taggart want to do is tip the balance of power. When they do that, there will be all-out war inside the CIA. The Ranch needs to stay closed."

"He'll still try to find it." She was speaking, but she couldn't feel anything. She'd gone numb, a comfortable cage she'd been in for the last eighteen months.

"He won't succeed without you. Their time is limited. Have they been pushing you to go? They can't stay here in Colorado for long. They have to keep moving."

Because they were criminals. "Why don't you arrest them? Why don't we walk to the sheriff's office and tell him?"

"I assure you Nathan Wright knows exactly who Jax and his group are. John Bishop would have told him." He held out a hand, staving off the question she'd been about to ask. "Wright is a do-gooder and they've convinced him that what they're doing is for the betterment of everyone. I could call in the police, but the truth is I would rather convince them to turn themselves in to the CIA. They have information that would be dangerous if it got out. We could try to take them in, but Taggart has surprisingly strong allies. Again, that group of men is part of the balance I'm trying to keep."

The door swung open and Heather stood there, a pistol in her hand. River got to her feet, shocked at the sight of her friend. She was aiming for Mr. Green's head, but he was cool and calm.

"I should have known you would show up. Were you hanging around outside the bar, watching him with longing eyes?" Mr. Green asked. "You must have freaked out when you realized he was coming into town. Or have you solved your problems?"

Heather frowned and the gun came down to her side again. She pointedly ignored Green, coming in the room toward her. "River, come with me. I need to talk to you. You can't trust this man."

How had Heather tracked her down? Why had she pulled a gun on a CIA agent?

Mr. Green shook his head. "Oh, Solo, I'm not the one she can't trust and you are on the wrong side of this fight."

Heather had a hand on River's elbow, trying to guide her toward the door. "Come on. We need to get out of here. I'll explain it all to you when we get back to the office. Don't believe a word this man said."

But Levi Green might be the only one who'd given her a single bit of truth. She pulled her arm free. "No. I'm staying here." She turned to the agent. "Can you help me?"

She had to get that money out of her account. More importantly, she needed someone who would believe that she hadn't put it there.

A triumphant smile crossed his lips. "I can. I can tell you everything. I'll start with your best friend's real history. How long have you been here? You look good, by the way. I'm glad you went back to blonde. It suits you."

"How do you know Heather?" Suspicion played through her.

"She's the Agency operative sent to make sure we don't get to The Ranch," a deep voice said. "Hello, Solo."

Ezra Fain moved into the room, his eyes on Heather.

It looked like Green was right. She was surrounded by wolves.

Chapter Thirteen

Jax knew the minute he saw River's face that everything had gone to hell. She looked pale, her eyes tight. She looked through him as he crowded into the room behind Ezra, Tucker behind him.

"River, are you all right?" He moved past Heather, trying to get to her. "Why did you walk out of the bar? Did that man hurt you?"

He'd been sick with worry, imagining every terrible thing that could happen to her.

She looked at him like he was a bug she was ready to step on. "Don't come any closer."

She moved nearer to the man in the suspenders. Levi Green. Ezra had cursed his name as they'd jumped into the SUV and headed over here. He'd received a text that had him calling for Jax. Apparently somehow Heather had gotten Ezra's phone number and she'd been the one to send the information on where River had gone.

Ezra had gone positively arctic. "Are you working with him?"

The question had been directed at Heather, but it was Levi Green who responded. The man casually closed his laptop. "She's absolutely not working with me or I suspect you wouldn't be here.

Solo there must have been stalking around outside the bar. She's good. I didn't see her, had no idea she'd embedded herself in this town."

"Who the hell is Solo?" Tucker seemed to be following the conversation far better than Jax was. He couldn't take his eyes off River.

"Heather," River said quietly, her eyes on anything except him. "She's apparently some kind of super spy."

"Oh, she's a legend in our business." Levi seemed to be the only one having a good time. He leaned against the desk, not concerned at all that his room had been invaded. "Her name is Kimberly Solomon. You see there's this driving test you take when you're being trained to be an operative and she managed to make it through the course ten seconds faster than anyone else. Hence, all we nerds in her class like to say she did the Kessel run in twelve parsecs."

Like *Star Wars*. Kayla had watched it with them. He caught a glimpse of a stack of papers on the desk. River must have been looking through them.

"She's also called Solo because she likes to work alone," Ezra said. "She certainly doesn't like to take anyone's advice. River, can we go back to your office? Whatever this man has told you it's not the whole story."

"River, let's go somewhere and talk." His whole body was tight with fear. He couldn't lose her. In the brief amount of time he'd known her, he'd become a different person. For the first time in his short life, he knew what he wanted. He wanted her.

Her eyes finally came up. "Are you or are you not wanted in several countries for armed robbery?"

The bottom dropped out of his world. She knew. She knew the things he'd done.

She would never forgive him.

"River, Beck is right," Heather…Solo…began. "There's far more to this story."

Shame coursed through him, a familiar drug. "I did everything he told you. I did it all."

"You didn't have a choice," Tucker insisted. "None of us did."

River seemed to get some of her confidence back. Or perhaps it was rage fueling her. She stepped up to him, her face an angry mask. "When were you going to take that money back? Would you have tipped the police off or were you simply using me to launder it? I bet the money you paid me for the job would vanish, too. It was easy to offer it when you have someone who can take it back with a couple of strokes of the keyboard, huh?"

It was worse than he'd thought. "I would never take your money. Never. I gave it to you."

Ezra's jaw had dropped. "You did what?"

Yeah, he hadn't exactly run his plans by the boss, but he would have to deal with that later. "I wouldn't take it back."

Levi had a smirk on his face. "Oh, Ezra, are the boys feisty enough for you? I told you this was a mistake. You gave up your entire career to save a bunch of dumbasses. Jax here stole two million from River's ex-husband. I suppose as grand gestures go it was an excellent one. But I have to wonder if he wasn't planning on taking it all back."

"I was surprised you're still going by Ezra." Solo's eyes had gone wide. "Beck, come on. Even after all these years?"

"Is my brother still dead?" Ezra shot back.

He had no idea what was going on with those two. His brain was looking for any way out. It was obvious Levi was doing anything he could to damage his reputation with River. She never had to know who he'd been. That's what he told himself.

"Please talk to me." He couldn't seem to stop trying with her.

She turned to Levi. "Can you save me from him?"

The agent shrugged. "I don't have to now. My job here is done, sweetheart, though I might stick around to see the fallout between those two." He pointed to Ezra and Solo.

River shook her head as though trying to clear it. "You said you could help me."

Jax couldn't let that happen. "You don't need help." He needed to get her out of here. If he could get her alone, maybe he could explain. "You need to talk to me. Baby, I can explain."

She didn't even turn around. "You're not going to help me? You told me you could fix things."

"I'm not sure what I would do to help you. It's not like I can go to the cops. We don't want them to know about Jax's existence," Levi replied as though he was talking about the weather and not people's lives. "You're not going to take him out into the woods. That's what I needed you to do. I doubt he'll be able to find it on his own. Besides, I think they'll have to move on soon. I believe MSS knows where you are, my friends. You got a visit today. Didn't you?"

Well, now they knew who'd hired the mercenaries.

"God, you're such an asshole, Levi," Solo said between gritted teeth. "Are you trying to tell me the Agency knew Chinese intelligence was on their way, but they didn't do anything? I had to stop it, and I barely managed to take them out before they got away with Jax and Robert."

And now they knew who the helpful shooter was. Solo must have seen them being taken and known what was happening. He would thank her except River was looking at her like she didn't know the woman.

"The faction I'm working for doesn't want The Ranch opened," Levi replied. "They want to wait. If MSS wants to come in and stop that, we're open to working with them."

Ezra shook his head. "And this is why I left."

Levi pointed his way. "You left because you've gotten naïve in your old age. The world doesn't work the way you want it to so you walk away. We make the hard calls. We do the dirty work so the rest of those idiots out there can sleep at night."

"You were willing to sacrifice lives," Ezra shot back.

"*Was*? Oh, I am still willing to sacrifice. I'll sacrifice them all if it keeps my country safe," Levi replied. "I'll burn it all down to do my job. In that particular way I'm much more like Solo than I was ever like you. Solo knows that sometimes you gotta break a couple of eggs to make that omelet, don't you, babe?"

Ezra's face went a bright red and he launched himself at Levi, moving with all the grace of a charging rhino. Jax pulled River into his arms because she was in the line of fire. Ezra's big body shoved into his, sending him off balance and he twisted, taking the brunt of the fall as the small room exploded with violence. He

209

could feel her shaking, her arms wrapping around him as he cupped her head in his hands. Ezra punched Levi right in the face, putting him on the ground. There was a crash as the lamp on the table hit the floor and broke into pieces. Jax hissed as a piece of glass struck him in the arm.

Tucker moved in, trying to get between the fighting men. He took a kick to the gut as Levi started to fight back.

"Can't handle the truth, can you, Ez?"

Ezra said nothing, merely hauled him up by his suspenders and drilled a fist into his gut.

"Stop it." Solo stepped over Tucker, trying to get to Ezra. "You have to stop, Beck. He's not worth it."

Jax wasn't waiting for them to resolve their differences. He got to his feet and hauled River up. He wasn't taking no for an answer in this case. Everyone in the fucking room had a gun, and he wouldn't risk her getting caught in the crossfire of people who obviously had their own issues to work out.

She buried her head in his neck, her arms around him as he carried her out. There was a movie playing on a screen outside the parking lot. Some old black and white romance played out as he walked her away from the room. He could still hear the sound of something smashing and Tucker yelling.

He would take her back to her place and they would talk. He would find a way to make her understand. He had to.

"It's going to be okay." She felt right in his arms. He realized this was what he'd needed from that first moment he'd woken up in that bright white sterile room. He'd wanted this feeling. To love and protect someone. To feel like he was a part of something good. He was a part of Jax and River and it was all he needed. He didn't fucking need what had come before. That was the past and it didn't matter. She mattered.

"Put me down."

He didn't stop walking. He would walk her back to the bar and get her Jeep. "It's okay."

"It's not okay." Her arms had come down from his neck and she stiffened, making it difficult to carry her. "Put me down now, Jax, or whatever your name is. Put me down or I'll start screaming.

You might have the sheriff of this county in your pocket, but I assure you I can find another. I can find someone who'll care about what you've done."

All she would have to do was call Interpol or the FBI and he was sure they would come running. "There's an explanation."

"I don't want to listen to it. I don't want you touching me."

He set her down, drawing his hands away. He couldn't force himself on her. He'd had all his choices taken from him. He couldn't do it to her, not even the small ones. "Please, River. I'm asking you to listen to me. Look at me, baby. Look into my eyes. I'm crazy about you. I would never do anything to hurt you. I was talking to Tucker tonight about telling you everything. I couldn't because it's not just my secret to tell. The others are involved."

She stared up at him, her eyes shining with unshed tears. "Is he really your brother?"

God, she would ask that now. "Not by blood. Or hell, I have no fucking idea. Maybe he is. That's the point. I don't know."

She shook her head. "No. I'm not letting you tell me some pack of lies. You should write, Jax. You tell an amazing story. God, do you even care about what could have happened to me? If the feds come after me for the money you stole, I'll go to jail. I'll lose everything. I just got the business back on its feet. It's all I have left. I'll lose the cabin and the business and it's all I fucking have left of him."

Her chest was heaving, emotion coming off her in waves.

He'd done this to her. He was the reason she couldn't breathe. He was the reason she thought she would lose the last memories of her father.

"Please let me take you back to your Jeep. Please. I can't leave you alone to walk back there. I won't talk to you again. I won't bother you and I'll do whatever you want me to with the money, but I can't send you out alone."

Her hands were fists at her sides. "You don't get to ask me for anything."

"I'll take her home." Solo stood a few feet away, her jaw tight and shoulders squared.

Ezra walked out behind her, Tucker following. "You sure

211

you're not going to stay here with your boyfriend?"

Solo's face fell. "I was looking for solace, Beck."

"You call me Ezra," he replied. "When you made the decision to not pull my brother's team out of the mission in Africa, you killed him. But when you decided to fuck Levi Green, baby, that's when you killed Beckett Kent."

She closed her eyes as if she were in pain. "Get in the car, River."

"Fuck you all." River turned and started walking.

She was walking away from him and he wouldn't see her again.

He started to walk toward River. He would follow her home if he had to. He would keep his distance, but he would make sure nothing bad happened to her. Nothing else bad.

Solo put out a hand, stopping him. "I'll take care of her."

River turned. "You will not. You're a liar, too."

"I might be a liar, but I'm also your friend. And I can do what *he* can't." Solo moved in behind River and had her arm in a lock before she could take another breath. "I can force you."

Anger thrummed through him. It didn't matter that she was female, Solo had her hands on River, and not in a comforting way. "Let her go."

River started to move toward Solo's SUV.

Ezra stepped in front of him, putting a hand on his shoulder to stop him. "Let her go. When Solo gets it in her head to do something, nothing stops her, and I don't want to have to call the doc after she's done with you."

Tucker stood beside him. "We can't let her walk away with River. Jax needs to talk to her. We can tell her the truth."

She wouldn't listen, but he had other problems. The person she thought was Heather was actually an operative. She could hurt her or take her someplace where they would question her. "I want River out of this."

It was the only thing he could give her at this point.

Ezra looked him straight in the eyes. His nose was swollen and he would likely have a hell of a black eye in the morning. "She won't hurt River. She's honestly our only shot at getting this thing back on track. I might have personal problems with Solo but she's a solid agent. She likes River. She won't hurt her and she won't let her get into a situation where she hurts herself. Please trust me, Jax."

He nodded tightly, watching Solo move River into the car. He stood there as the headlights came on and they drove away.

Everything he wanted was in that car and she wouldn't come back.

He'd lost her.

"Who is Solo to you?" He heard Tucker ask.

Ezra turned away and for a moment Jax thought he might not answer.

"She's my wife."

He knew he should feel something, some deep compassion for Ezra because the words had come out his mouth hollow and dead.

But all he could think about was River and the fact that he would never see her again. He moved when Tucker put a hand on his shoulder.

"Come on," his brother said. "Let's go back to the cabin and talk this out. We'll find a way."

He got in the car, but stared straight ahead, the beauty of the world around him duller now that she wasn't with him.

* * * *

River felt the car moving but it seemed like she was still stuck in that small motel room. She knew the town was flowing around her, passing the Trading Post and Stella's, but all she could see were those photographs. The proof of his lies would be in her head forever.

It was obvious Levi Green was an asshole, but he hadn't made up the arrest warrants. He couldn't control the Internet. Jax had admitted it. Oh, he'd claimed there were reasons, but she didn't need reasons.

"You don't understand what Jax has been through." Solo sat stiff in the driver's seat, her normal grace seeming to flee in the face of the drama of the past few moments.

213

"I don't care." She was sure every criminal had a story about how he'd gotten to that point. No tales of Jax's shitty childhood could justify his crimes.

"You do, but you're in shock. I get that."

She needed to make a few things plain. "I meant what I said. You're fired. I don't want to see you in the office again."

"Going to play the tough chick, huh? Let me tell you something, sister. You can't play that role any better than me. I've played that role for years and it's cost me everything."

As long as she was stuck here, she might as well ask a few questions. "Was that man your lover?"

"Beck was my husband." She shook her head, never taking her eyes off the road. "The man you know as Ezra Fain is named Beckett Kent. My legal name is Kimberly Solomon Kent, though I'm sure he would say I stole his name, too."

"I don't care." She didn't want to listen to anyone else's sad story. She had her own to think about.

Jax had been so sweet, so perfect. She should have known. She should have understood that first night. There's no way a man like that wanted her.

Something about him had called to her. It reminded her of a moment she'd had long ago. She'd been in the woods, hiking a trail by herself, and she'd come face to face with an enormous buck. She'd been stopped in her tracks, shocked by how large and pointed its antlers were. The buck had huffed and then settled down, staring straight at her. And she'd had a moment of perfect clarity. That buck had been alone in the world, too, searching for something that would keep it going, that would make existence simpler. Every creature on the planet wanted life and peace, craved it, and not a one ever got it, not really.

She'd looked into Jax's eyes and seen the connection.

How could it have been a lie?

Why couldn't she feel the pain? That scared her far more than anything else. She'd gone numb again. Ty once told her the worst wounds were the ones that were so painful the body couldn't process them. He'd treated a man one time who had broken his leg so badly it had twisted off at the knee in a partial amputation. The man had lain there in the snow insisting nothing was wrong with him.

He hadn't felt the pain, as though the universe knew he would die and gave him the gift of a few final agony-free moments.

Was some essential piece of herself finally dying? Would her heart beat on, missing the source that animated it?

"River, I know you're angry, but I need you to listen to me. My ex-husband is a good man."

"Then why did you cheat on him?" She wouldn't stop talking and they had a few minutes until they reached Trio. Why not turn this around on the woman who'd pretended to be her friend?

Solo's hands tightened on the steering wheel. "I never once cheated on him. I didn't look at another man. From the minute Beck walked into my life, he was the only man for me. Levi was a friend and after I got the final divorce papers, we went out drinking and I woke up in bed with him. It was stupid and wrong and I didn't know Levi would use it against him. But this is not about me."

"Oh, I disagree. I think this is all about you. It's not about me. I'm utterly incidental in this game you've been playing."

The bar was up ahead, but Solo stopped at the corner, turning in her seat. "It's not a game. It's serious and we need you. I can take them in, but I don't know the location. I've looked for The Ranch several times myself, but I think you'll know how to find it."

"I believe I'll skip this job." She wanted to get as far away from these people as she possibly could. She would close the office and pack up her Jeep. She would let Marie put the cabin up for sale and then she would hit the road. "You feel free to do anything you want with that band of criminals. But don't you dare try to talk Ty or Andy into it. I want them out."

"I know Levi got to you. He's excellent at his job, but his job is to sometimes take the truth and manipulate it to suit his purposes. He told you that Jax was wanted, but did he explain why?"

"I assume he's wanted because he robbed a fucking bank." She didn't even recognize herself. She didn't curse like this. She

215

didn't sound monotone and dead.

Solo leaned closer. "But you have to ask why he robbed it."

"No, I don't. There's no justification."

"The world is not black and white. You've lived a nice, cushy existence here, but Jax came from what I can only describe as hell on earth. What he's been forced to live through I can't even imagine."

"I don't care." She couldn't allow herself to care or feel. She couldn't give herself even the tiniest crack or she would find a way to run through it and she would fall back into the trap. She would trick herself again and there would be no going back.

Solo shook her head. "River, this isn't you."

A thought occurred to her. How had Solo found them? How had she known where they'd gone? "Did you follow me from the bar or did you put something on my phone the morning after we met Jax? Something that made it so you could listen in or find me."

She'd thought it had been Jax who'd gone through her purse, but there was another player in the game now. It made sense when she thought about it.

Solo didn't bother to blush. "After I found out you were getting involved with the Lost Boys, I knew I had to have a way to track you. Yes, I duped your phone that morning and I should have been way more careful about it. I've been with you for months and I gave you your privacy until it became dangerous for you to have it."

"Well, thank you for allowing me some fucking privacy." Had Solo listened in on her conversations? Seen the flirty texts she'd sent to Jax? Or the other things. "Hope you liked the pictures of my boobs I sent him. Maybe he'll have some fun putting those out as revenge porn."

"He would never do that. And I'm sorry, but god, River, I've seen you come alive in the last few days. I've seen you glow. Do you want to lose that?"

She'd already lost it. "How long have you known him? Did you set up our meeting that night?"

Had she been led like a lamb to slaughter?

"I don't know him or any of them personally," Solo admitted.

"Beck was wrong about my mission. The truth is I was sent here to make a report on Henry."

"Who used to be an assassin." It seemed like Bliss attracted them.

"He was an operative and a damn fine one," Solo replied. "Levi was right about one thing. We do sometimes have to get our hands bloody to protect people. I think Levi's taking it a step too far, but you cannot judge Bishop. He's saved more lives than you can imagine, but I get you're not going to listen to anyone tonight."

She wouldn't listen to them ever again. She slid out of the SUV. "I don't care why you were here. I don't care what you're doing with Jax."

"Do you know what they call Jax and his team?" Solo asked.

"I don't care." She would keep saying it until she believed it.

"The Lost Boys. Think about that, River. Think about everything he's said to you, everything he's done for you. When you're ready, I'll let you read my files on them and you'll understand what his very short life has been like."

"It's not that short," she shot back. Jax was at least thirty.

"It's shorter than you can imagine," Solo said. "It's more violent and abusive than you can imagine. But he survived and the fact that he could fall in love with you, that he or any one of them got out of that life with the capacity for kindness, is a miracle. I know why Big Tag called them the Lost Boys. He was being sarcastic, but it fits them. And what you have to remember is that anything that's lost can be found again. God, I have to believe that. You found yourself again with him. Don't give that up because you're afraid. Don't live the rest of your life without compassion, without forgiveness, without love."

River slammed the door closed and walked toward her Jeep, Heather's words ringing in her ears.

Except she wasn't Heather. She was someone named Solo and River was alone again.

Chapter Fourteen

"All right, I think I have this figured out," Tucker was saying the next morning. He stood in front of a large board he'd decorated with pictures and a whole bunch of strings connecting names and faces. He'd spent a good portion of the previous evening making his reminder board.

Jax barely looked up from his computer. He hadn't slept, hadn't eaten. Didn't want to. He wondered if she was going to keep Buster or if she wouldn't want him now. Would the puppy be another casualty in his never-ending drama?

He'd found some peace with her. For a few days he'd felt normal, better than normal. He'd been important to her and he'd been good at making her happy.

Now when she looked at him, she would see nothing but a criminal, a con man who'd lied to her. He wouldn't even have a good place in her memories.

Oh, but she would be everything to him.

Owen put his hands on his hips, looking up at the monstrosity of a conspiracy board Tucker had spent all night putting together. "So Heather is really named Kimberly, but she likes *Star Wars* and has a nickname."

218

"I think whoever gave her the nickname liked *Star Wars*," Tucker corrected.

"And Ezra was Mr. White but then he was Ezra who was actually his dead brother who Solo killed but his real name is Beckett Kent?" Robert scratched his head, trying to follow.

Tucker nodded. "Although I bet she didn't, like, put a bullet in him. I think she screwed up an op and Ezra blames her. And Levi Green is a mystery. If I'm right, then his real first name is Levi, but I don't think he's a Green. It would be pretty coincidental given the revolving color code names the Agency uses."

"You missed one of his names." Dante wrote something on a sticky note. He slapped it up next to Green's face. It read *DICKHEAD*.

It was fitting. Jax had called that asshole about a hundred nasty names in his head. "Do we know if Ezra killed him?"

He hadn't seen a body. They'd left directly after the incident with River, and Ezra had closed himself up in his bedroom. Jax had been too shocked to think about anything but the fact that River was driving away. The worst had happened. River knew about his crimes and she hadn't waited for an explanation.

Big Tag chose that moment to walk in, carrying a coffee mug in his hand. He stopped and stared at the big wall. There was a picture of him with the names *Ian Taggart*, *Big Tag*, and *Satan* connected with carefully lined string. He nodded. "That's fair. And Levi is alive. Too many witnesses. If he's still at the motel this morning, I think I might have a chat with the fucker myself."

"We can't kill him." Ezra walked in and slumped into a chair. "If we kill him, we bring the Agency down on our heads, and we would likely implicate Henry as well. Is she here yet?"

Big Tag shook his head. "She said she's on her way."

That got Jax sitting up straight and paying more attention. "Who's coming? Did someone talk to River?"

He was well aware he was making an ass of himself, but he couldn't help it. He was the sad-sack, pathetic SOB who would likely spend the rest of his life hoping to catch a glimpse of her or hear someone say her name.

"He's talking about Solo," Sasha said with a long sigh. "Or

Kimberly. Or Heather. I need fucking note cards to keep up with this shit. Could you all wear name tags, please?"

Big Tag stared at the picture of Solo for a moment. "This is your ex-wife? You know who she looks like, right?"

Ezra's eyes narrowed. "She looks like Solo."

Big Tag snorted. "She's a fucking dead ringer for my sister-in-law, Mia. You either like shopping at the same store or you have never gotten over this one, buddy."

"I'm not going to talk about my ex-wife." Ezra crossed the great room to pour himself some coffee.

"He told us she was his wife last night. Not his ex," Tucker pointed out. "Did you forget your divorce? It's cool because I forgot my name, so we're on the same page. Also, I'm sorry I hit on her. I didn't know she was your wife. I just thought she was a hot chick, and as long as Jax was getting some…you know how it goes."

"I didn't forget a thing. You misheard," Ezra bald-faced lied because Jax remembered exactly what he'd said.

And it was a good thing Solo was coming because she'd taken River home. She could at least assure him she'd been okay.

Of course, he might be able to do that himself. He pulled out his phone and there was nothing on it. No flirty texts or pictures that got his heart racing. Nothing at all. He pulled up her name and wondered if she'd blocked him already.

I hope you made it home all right. Do I need to come and get Buster?

He stared and saw the floating circles that let him know she was replying.

He's mine and I'm keeping him. Don't you dare come after my dog. I'll shoot you if I see you again.

It was good to know she was still mad.

Fuck. What the hell was he going to do now?

There was a knock and Sasha opened the door, ushering Solo in.

Big Tag nodded her way. "Hello, Mia. I'm sorry. I meant Kimberly. You look an awful lot like my brother Case's wife. Ezra back there had a thing for her. Followed her all over the globe."

220

Solo's eyes found Ezra. "I didn't know you dated."

Ezra shrugged as he took a seat again. "I didn't know you gave a shit. And I didn't date Mia. I was her bodyguard for a while. She's a lovely woman. Case hit the lottery with that one. She's a journalist and a philanthropist. She does a lot of good in the world."

"The comparison being I do a lot of bad, I'm sure," Solo said. "I didn't come here to fight with you. I came here to figure out what you're going to do now."

"How about you explain to us what you were doing here in the first place," Ezra demanded.

"I was sent here by the Agency to discern what Henry is doing here." Solo sat down beside Jax. "John Bishop was a legend at the CIA. When he resurfaced after his incredibly well-done fake death, there were people who worried he'd turned. There were a couple of factions with the Agency who wanted to send in an assassin."

"They sent in you, didn't they?" Ezra said, his eyes on his ex-wife.

"I'm not the assassin, Beck. And I think I've given them enough evidence that Bishop didn't fake his death in order to start a life of crime," Solo said. "He's here because he fell in love."

Sasha stood. "I have things to do. If we're leaving soon, I want to be ready."

Dante stood with him. "I'll be in my room. I can't handle all the love shit. I'm calling Damon. I want to go back to The Garden. We made a mistake following Fain."

Owen sighed and pushed his chair back. "I'll make sure they don't do anything stupid." He nodded Tucker's way. "But I do like the soap opera playing out here, so I expect notes from you, mate."

Ezra took a deep breath as they left the room. When Big Tag started to stand, he put a hand on his arm. "Let them go. I promised them something I might not be able to deliver. If they want to call Damon and head back, let them."

"There was a reason we left England," Big Tag replied, but he settled back in. "It's dangerous for them to stay in one place for too long. As we learned yesterday. That fucker Levi has us in a corner."

221

"I think we can still run this op." He wasn't going to give up on finding the data they needed. He was the one who'd screwed everything up. He hadn't lost River only to run away without the one thing they needed. He turned to Ezra's ex. "You can take me in. We go in this afternoon and we won't leave the forest until we find it. Everyone else stays behind to deal with MSS and Levi Green. We go in light and fast and they might not know we're gone."

Solo's fingers drummed along the conference table as she gave his plan some thought. "Don't worry about MSS. My boss has taken care of the problem. We can focus on the op."

A brow rose over Ezra's left eye. "I don't suppose you want to tell me who you're working for."

She sent him a tight smile. "I'm afraid that's classified. I do know the woods. I've spent a lot of time in them. I have a camp of sorts over the first ridge. It's the perfect place to spend the night. It's got a good view."

"And by view, she means a view of Henry's place," Big Tag corrected. "Henry's cabin is next door."

"Henry is Bishop." Tucker smiled like he was the smartest kid in the class.

Jax ignored him. "We have time to hike before it gets dark." He frowned as a thought occurred to him. "Or not, since River has all the equipment."

"I have some," a new voice said. Henry Flanders strolled in through the back of the house, having come in from the side door. He was the massive cabin's caretaker while its owners were in New York. His wife was with him, though she looked a bit pale. She carried a basket in her hand. "I've got a lightweight tent and enough supplies to get you through a day or two. The sun's going to be out all day and that should help dry the ground."

Nell placed the basket on the table with a wan smile. "I made some muffins. I also made a batch of protein bars, too. They're good hiking fuel."

Henry took a deep breath. "I think I should be the one to go. Ms. Solomon, if you're not afraid to work with me, I'll go with you and the rest can stay here. Mr. Green won't expect me to be the one going in search of The Ranch."

Nell paled visibly.

Jax couldn't let that happen. Henry was already in trouble because his wife hadn't known about his past. And she was pregnant. She didn't need to worry about what would happen if her husband got caught. "No. The only reason you're here and not in some Agency detention center is the fact that you have stayed out of the business."

"I went to Mexico earlier this year to help out an old friend," Henry answered. "I'm sure that was enough to put me back in the crosshairs. Wasn't that around the time you were put on assignment, Ms. Solomon?"

A wry smile lit up Solo's face. "Not at all, and unless Beck there put you in his report, the Agency doesn't know about that. You were the one who saved Kayla Summers and that hottie actor of hers. I should have known it was you. Levi didn't mention you at all in his report. Likely because he wanted to keep that information in his back pocket."

"Or because it happened very quickly," Henry replied. "I pretty much walked in and started killing people. He ran as fast as he could. Levi always did have excellent survival instincts."

Solo's eyes rolled. "He wrote you up but in his report you were a minor player and he shot you."

"He didn't shoot Henry. He fucking shot me," Ezra complained.

Solo lost a bit of her smile. "Yes, he didn't mention that part. The point is Jax is right. Henry Flanders is not of interest to the Agency anymore. I've made a recommendation to leave you alone and let John Bishop be a star on Langley's wall. It ends there if you let it."

Henry reached down and tried to take his wife's hand.

She shifted away from him, turning to go into the kitchen. "I'll make some tea to go with the muffins."

Henry sighed and sat down. "All right, but I think if you're going to make this op happen, you need to head out at night and work fast. Once you're in the woods, they won't be able to follow. I doubt Green is a mountain man."

Ezra shook his head. "No. Solo isn't a true guide. She grew up on the Upper East Side. What she's good at is imitation. Jax has never been in the forest before. I'm not risking my men so Solo can play whatever game she's playing."

"I'm trying to save you, you dumb bastard. I stayed on because I heard a rumor that you were going to come for The Ranch," she said. "I think you've got a leak in your group. The only reason there's not a bunch of soldiers surrounding the place is the fact that they would have to let President Hayes know in his daily briefings, and then he would start asking questions. I think Jax and Henry are right. You do this quick and quiet and you might get out whole. They're afraid of Hayes. One of his closest friends from childhood used to work for the Agency. He only left a couple of months ago and he still has friends on the inside. They have to play this as carefully as they can. If it's a choice between letting the information go or risk letting the fact of The Ranch's existence get to the White House, they'll cover their asses and start planning ways to pin the blame on someone else."

"I concur," Big Tag replied. "Though I think someone should send Connor Sparks a heads-up at the end of this."

"Only if you want a war," Solo shot back.

"We know which side you'll be on," Ezra replied.

He was sick of the fighting. "Stop it, both of you. I'm going in and I'm going tonight. I'll go alone if I have to. I think I should. I think I want to keep the Agency as far away from this as possible."

"I can take you out there, Jax," Solo insisted. "I did grow up in Manhattan, but I'm perfectly competent in the woods. I've spent months here learning. We'll be fine."

But he couldn't trust her. "You have people you have to answer to. I won't put the mission at risk."

"I'll go," Robert offered.

Big Tag shook his head. "We need to be seen around town. Levi might be gone or he might be here, but I assure you he has people watching. If two of us go missing, they'll start searching. He knows how hard Jax took the breakup with River. We say Jax is butt hurt and whiney and won't come out with us."

He wasn't sure he liked the sound of that, but he wasn't in a position to argue. "I'll go alone. I'll be fine."

"You won't." Solo stood up, facing him. "The woods are dangerous. You need a guide or you could die out there."

He needed River, but he wasn't going to get her. "I'm going. You can help me by prepping me or you can leave."

Henry's eyes were somber as he sat back. "You have a grid of where you think this place is? Let's eat some breakfast and then lay out a map and see what we've got."

Solo had her hands on her hips. "I'm not sending him out there alone. Beck, you can't do this."

Ezra stared at him for a moment. "Are you sure, Jax?"

He had never been more sure of anything in his life. "I'm going."

Ezra turned his attention back to his ex-wife. "You can help him prep or you can leave, and if you walk straight to Levi and tell him what we're doing, I'll be the one who comes after you, and it won't be for a tender reunion."

"But if he dies, you'll blame me. Can't you see I'm trying? Please talk to me, Beck. I miss you. I know I screwed up, but there has to be a way to make you see that it doesn't have to be the end of us. Let me take Jax out. Let me find this for you," she pleaded.

"I can't trust you. I can't trust anyone who still works for the CIA. I'll let you spend the afternoon prepping him and you can help with logistics, but I won't send him out there alone with you." Ezra stood, his decision obviously final. "I'm going to see if Dante and Sasha have calmed down and then I'm taking a shower. You guys eat something and we'll meet back here in an hour to start our prep."

Solo stared as he walked away.

Tucker picked up a marker and started writing on his sticky notes again. He pasted it on the line that connected Solo to Ezra. *Whole lotta drama*, it said.

"You know that's true." Big Tag seemed like the only one who was finding it all amusing. He strode over to Solo. "I think you should stay. Also, look up Mia Taggart. You'll be surprised at the resemblance. Now I've got to go call my wife and fill her in. I left her alone at home with three kids and a massive dog who pees

225

every time someone walks in the door. The least I can do is let her know Ezra has a secret ex-wife who is obviously going to cause loads of trouble."

"I'm not trying to cause trouble. I'm trying to keep him out of it," Solo said.

Tag shrugged. "Where's the fun in that?"

He walked off as Robert joined Tucker, adding to their wall of drama. Solo glanced at the door as though ready to leave now that her plan had failed.

"You can't help Ezra if you walk away," Henry pointed out. "You made the right call when you came out of cover to try to counteract Green's effect on River. You made the right call when you saved Jax and Robert. Make it now. Help us even if Ezra doesn't want you to."

Solo seemed to settle in. "I'll do what I can. And I know no one will believe me but I intervened for River's sake. It wasn't about any mission. It was about helping my friend."

Jax took the opportunity to ask what he really wanted to know. "How was River when you left her?"

Solo's face softened when she turned to him. "She was devastated and confused. I think she needs some time. I tried to talk to her, but I'm not her favorite person right now. She wouldn't listen to a thing I had to say. I'll try again this afternoon."

"She still won't listen. She was lied to." Nell placed a tray with a pot of tea and several mugs on the tabletop. "The person she thought she knew was someone different. It's difficult to find trust again."

Henry's jaw tightened. "Are you done, sweetheart? You can rest for a while before Caleb comes to check on you."

She glanced over at Tucker's wall. It was easy to see she didn't find it amusing. "I think I will. I might go into town for a bit. No need to come with me. I can see you're needed here."

"I'll walk you back." Henry was at her side in a flash.

She shook her head. "No need. I'd like to be alone for a while."

"I'll walk you back and then you can be alone, Nell." Henry's tone brooked no arguments. "The ground is soft and you could fall."

She turned and started to walk out but didn't argue when Henry put a hand on her shoulder and led her out.

He was left alone with Solo.

"Jax, let me take you out there. I know I'm not anywhere close to River's level of expertise, but I don't think you know all the dangers you could face in those woods. Beck isn't thinking straight. He's letting our past color everything."

But he had to trust Ezra. Solo hadn't walked in and introduced herself. She'd done everything she could to protect her cover. Now that he looked back at it, she'd been excellent at avoiding the one man in their group who could have identified her. "I take it all those times you couldn't make meetings, you were trying to make sure Ezra didn't catch a glimpse of you."

Her face fell as though she knew she was losing the battle. "I had a job to do. When my boss got the intel that Beck was on his way here, he asked me to stay and watch from a distance. I was supposed to report back on what he's doing. I haven't and I won't, though I'm certain Levi will already have filed something. I'll figure it out. I'm pretty good about smoothing things over. I did it the whole time we were married."

"Why did you befriend River?"

"You're going to keep asking questions until I look as bad as possible, aren't you? Well, I'm not going to lie. I got a job with her because she was hiring and it was an easy way to blend into town. At the time, she was distracted. Her father was dying and her husband had been gone for a while. She needed help so she didn't look too closely at who she was hiring. It gave me a reason to be in the woods if anyone caught me. Nell likes River. When Nell likes someone, Henry follows. I befriended her because it was my job to do anything I had to do to get the information I needed."

On some level he understood, but this wasn't some random op. He couldn't ever be ruthless enough to view a person as nothing but a piece on a game board. He'd been a pawn and he couldn't handle the idea that River thought he'd treated her like that, too. "I wasn't going to let River be hurt. I was getting permission from the others to tell her the truth. I always told her as

227

much of the truth as I could. She was so cold when she looked at me. At me? She looked through me. It makes me wonder."

"If she cared about you?" Solo asked slowly. "I know she did. She's been more open and happy since she met you than I've ever seen her. I'll be honest. At first, I didn't like her. She was cold and shut down. Then I realized why. Watching someone you love die will do that to you. Eighteen months and every day she had to get up and take care of someone else. Every day she had to feed him and take him to the bathroom and clean him up. Every day she watched him get weaker and more miserable. I don't know that she's come out of it yet. When you get that overloaded emotionally, it's comfortable and safe to be numb. It feels good to not feel."

"She rarely talked about her dad." He knew her father had died, but she hadn't talked about it past the fact of the matter.

"I think when she found out about your past, she closed herself off again. She'd been opening up in a way I hadn't seen before. She slammed that door and went back to the place she knew was safe." Solo's voice was soft, sympathetic as she spoke. "I think she'll come around."

He stared out over the lawn where Henry was walking his wife toward their small cabin, the tension between them easy to see. "I don't think she will. I think she'll be like Nell. I think the only thing holding Nell to her husband is the baby she's carrying."

Solo sat back down with a weary sigh. "I hope not because if those two can't make it, there's no hope for the rest of us."

There wasn't any hope at all for him, but he could help his brothers. "I'm going to do it."

"All right. If you're determined to go alone, I'll help you as much as I can. First off, I can promise you won't need that bio suit. The Ranch was sealed but it's perfectly clean. And I think I have an excellent point of entry. No one will think you would go in from there. I have to warn you, it's a little odd."

Jax poured the tea as Solo started to talk about the mission.

* * * *

228

River watched Buster chase after his own tail and kind of wished she could be a dog in the next life. Buster had been despondent the night before when she'd come home and let him out of his crate. She'd held him but whenever she'd put him down, he'd run around and around the cabin looking for Jax. He'd whined and cried until she'd picked him up and taken him to bed with her.

This morning Buster was happy and playing, perfectly adjusted to the new normal.

She was not. She hadn't slept, didn't want to eat. God, it would be good to cry. She simply couldn't. The world was dull again and she hated Jax for reminding her how much color there was when looking at it with new eyes. She was back in this gray place and she worried she might never come out of it again.

She'd sat and stared at the TV, the morning news not sticking to her brain in any way because all she could think about was the way he'd looked as she'd walked away.

The man was good. She would give him that.

She'd even answered his stupid text about the dog. She'd started to type back that she didn't want anything from him, but then she'd glanced over and Buster had looked at her with big doggy eyes and she'd known she couldn't lose him, too. Buster would be the only thing she took with her, the only proof that she'd been with Jax for a brief time.

Would Buster like the city? Would he like being stuck in a tiny apartment where he would need to be in a crate most of the day?

God, she was going to miss this place.

"Hello."

River turned and forced a smile on her face. Nell Flanders was pedaling her bicycle down the path. There was a basket in front and it would have some treat for her. At least once a week since her father had been diagnosed, someone from town would show up offering food and help. She'd felt so alone, but now she realized she hadn't been. Rachel Harper would show up with a casserole one day and Holly Burke would bring them banana bread another. Nell had organized the food for her father's funeral. Of course, it had been the woman named Solo who'd sat in the funeral home and held her hand.

She wouldn't see Solo again, but Nell was one of the kindest human beings she'd ever met. It was hard to believe that she was married to a man who'd been a deadly operative. Henry looked like the history teacher he professed to be. But then she'd proven to not have good instincts when it came to dangerous men.

Did Nell know her husband's past? Fear struck her in that moment because she couldn't be the one who broke her friend in that manner. She froze at the thought of being the person to tell Nell Henry wasn't who he said he was. But didn't she deserve to know?

Fucking Jax had screwed her over again.

"You don't look happy to see me," Nell said, not unkindly. "I heard you had a rough night. I brought you some herbal tea. I was in Colorado Springs with Henry a few days ago and picked some up at the sweetest little tea shop. I thought you would enjoy it. Henry. Should I call him John now? I don't know. He still looks like a Henry to me. At least your formerly violent lover only has one name. Well, that he knows about."

River breathed a sigh of relief. "You know."

Nell parked the bike and plucked the bag of tea from her basket. "About Henry's former occupation? I've known for a bit. I was very foolish. I didn't even suspect he wasn't exactly what he said he was. But then a drug cartel showed up on our doorstep and Henry murdered them all. Now, in his defense, they were planning to kill all of us, and I've thought a lot about the fact that his preferred method of murder is actually quite earth friendly. He's very well versed in the art of internal decapitation. They say it's quick and painless, so there's that."

She shivered. "You're taking this well."

Nell grew somber. "No, I'm not. I'm not taking it well at all. I'm making him sleep on the couch, and I don't know that I can ever forgive him."

"For being a killer?" At least someone understood.

"For lying to me about it. I'm not as naïve as he thinks I am. I know there are things in this world that are so evil they require men who are willing to fight them. They can't fight terrorists with light. I know he protected us. I fight my fight and he fought his. Why wouldn't he tell me?"

There was only one reason she could think of. Henry had been with Nell for years. From what she understood, he'd changed his whole life for his wife. He wasn't working an op or biding time. They were having a baby together and it was all Henry could talk about. "He was afraid. He loved you and he was scared of losing you."

"Yes, I suppose he was." Nell passed her the tea and then knelt down and smiled as Buster did his best to lick the newcomer all over. Naturally Nell didn't even try to stop him. She simply accepted his affection with a smile. "Have you thought about the fact that Jax likely lied to you for the same reasons?"

Oh, that trap had been cleverly sprung, but they weren't in the same position. Not even close. "Henry worked for the CIA, and while I might think that's a sketchy job, he wasn't a criminal."

Nell picked up the wriggling puppy and Buster seemed to relax as though he knew he was being handled by someone who loved animals. She stroked his fur as she spoke. "I thought you had been told the truth."

"Yes, I was. The active CIA agent explained the whole situation to me. Jax and his friends are wanted in a whole lot of countries for any number of crimes. I only heard about robbery and some Internet crimes, but I'm sure there will be a murder in there somewhere."

"Oh, I'm certain Jax has been forced to kill."

Forced? "I don't want to hear this, Nell. I'm sure you've come up with a million and one excuses in your head. You're a sympathetic person."

"I am," she agreed. "I do know that people who commit crimes almost always have some kind of a reason. Most of them aren't justified, but how can we judge a person if we don't know the whys? How can we learn how to stop another crime if we don't know the impetus for the behavior?"

She wasn't buying it. "I don't need to know about his shitty childhood."

"Jax would love to know."

"You're not going to confuse me and get me to agree with you."

"That's not what I'm trying to do at all. I'm trying to explain the situation to you because I don't think anyone else will." Nell frowned.

It was apparent she wasn't getting out of this conversation. She could walk away, but in the past Nell had proven quite adroit at getting her way. It was best to listen to her and then move on or else she could find herself with a protest going on outside her cabin. "All right. Tell me this magical story that will make everything okay."

"There's no magic in this story," Nell said. "There's pain and loss. I think Henry told me because he knew it would soften my heart knowing what those young men have been through. Jax has no idea what his name is or where he comes from. He doesn't remember anything past the last eighteen months of his life."

"Bullshit." Did they all think she was an idiot?

"No. Henry wouldn't lie about this," Nell insisted. "Jax and his brothers—she called them his brothers, you see—they were all born in a laboratory. I call it that but in so many ways it wasn't a birth. It was the death of the men they'd been."

She didn't understand a thing. "In a lab? Was he involved in some sort of experiment? Did he volunteer to test some weird drug?"

"No one would volunteer for this." Nell's armed tightened around the puppy like he was a security blanket. "Dr. Hope McDonald was a pioneer in the field of mind alteration and conditioning, though you won't see her best work in any medical journal. She worked at The Ranch for a time, developing something the CIA had an interest in. Have you ever heard of time dilation? Neither had I. It's a way to trick the brain into believing more time has passed than reality. She developed two drugs. One erased all personal memory. The subject retained knowledge of certain things—how to brush his teeth, what a cup was called. Muscle memory was retained. The subjects who had been trained to fight could still do so. But all memory of family and self was gone."

232

She tried to process Nell's words. It didn't make sense. "Why would anyone want to do such a thing?"

"I have a theory. She needed test subjects for her time dilation drug. That particular drug could be used to do an enormous amount of good. Think about a young cancer patient. Give her this drug and the right stimulus and she lives a full life in her head. Give it to a scientist and he has more time to research. I know it sounds odd, but the mind is an incredible thing. But there are darker purposes to a drug like that. Torture could last longer, leave the victim with minor wounds but the memory of terrible pain."

River shivered despite the warmth of the afternoon. "Someone tested this drug on Jax?"

"Yes."

She didn't want to believe it. She wasn't sure she did, but Nell wouldn't lie. Had she been deceived? "So they gave him this time dilation drug and then tortured him and then erased his memory so he couldn't remember what happened to him?"

"Not exactly," Nell said. "I don't know all of the details, but I know his memory was erased again and again. The only one who remembers a substantial amount of his time with Dr. McDonald is a man named Theo Taggart."

"Taggart?"

Nell nodded. "Yes, he's Ian's half brother. He spent over a year in the doctor's tender care. He wrote up what he could remember. Henry let me read it and now I'm going to do the same for you. A copy is in the bag with the tea. Theo talks about how they were beaten and forced to comply. They were tested against each other. The doctor used sophisticated psychological techniques to train the men to obey her orders. I know we all want to think that we would be the one who didn't break, but read his report and tell me you wouldn't. I can't imagine what he went through."

"You're telling me Jax became a criminal because some crazy lady told him to?"

"I know it sounds terribly outrageous, but it's also true." Nell kissed the top of Buster's head and set him down. The puppy immediately started chasing a butterfly. "Jax was born in a lab fully grown. All he's known in his life is pain and forced compliance, and yet he was gentle with you."

A shiver went through her. If it was true…some of the things he'd said made sense. His awkwardness. The weirdness of his "brothers."

Nell walked back to her bike. "I'm not telling you you should do anything. If you don't care about Jax, then it's good that you broke it off with him. You're the first woman he's ever had a relationship with. When you think about it, he was a virgin. I'm sure he'll recover. After all, he spent years being tortured and he's still capable of love. He could have kept it at a one-night stand and moved on to the next woman, but I think what he craved was a connection with someone who spoke to his soul."

"I don't know that I can forgive him." Even if everything Nell said was true, he'd still lied to her. He'd still put her in jeopardy.

"You don't have to forgive him to want to make sure he's safe." Nell popped up her kickstand. "He's going into those woods tonight. He's going alone. I think he doesn't care if he lives or dies."

"Why would he do that?" He had no training. He wouldn't know what to do.

"Because Ezra thinks The Ranch holds the secrets of who his men are. Or were. Of who their families were, where they came from. He thinks there might even be a cure waiting for them there. What would you risk to potentially regain your memory? Your father died, but he's still there in your mind. He's still with you in every memory of a birthday or driving lessons or quiet time spent together. You still have him. The Lost Boys have nothing."

The Lost Boys. That's what Heather had called them. Solo. Damn it. She had to keep up.

Lost. They'd lost their pasts. Did Jax have to lose his future?

She couldn't be with him again. He'd lied. He might have had a reason to lie, but he'd done it even knowing what that would mean to her.

She opened the bag and found the tea. It wouldn't hurt to read the report. It wouldn't change anything.

"Come on, Buster." She would make some tea and see if anything this Theo Taggart person said made a lick of sense.

And then she would start the packing process because Jax had made it impossible for her to stay in Bliss. What a lifetime of memories of her dad couldn't do, a few days of loving Jax Seaborne had. She couldn't stay here anymore because there were far too many ghosts.

Chapter Fifteen

"There are so many dicks. So many dicks."

Jax agreed with Robert's horrified whisper as he stood on the grand lawn at the Mountain and Valley Naturist Community. It was late afternoon and everything was ready for him to walk into those imposing mountains. According to Solo this was the best way to walk into the national forest land unnoticed by any prying eyes. The Naturist Community was private and everyone here had been vetted carefully. There had been only one new member accepted in the past year and he was apparently solid.

And by "naturist" they really meant a bunch of naked people. The community practiced a nudist lifestyle.

"How do they keep their dicks so pasty white? The white guys, I mean. The black dudes have appropriately colored dicks, but how are the white guys dicks so white when they walk around in the sun with them swinging like that. Not that guy. His dick is smart. It burrowed in away from the sun." Tucker's eyes were wide as he looked around.

"Could we not stare at the dicks?" Henry sputtered the question out as though they'd finally found something that shocked the guy. "It's considered impolite to stare."

Ezra shook his head. "I don't know, man. It's not like a locker room where you tend to put a towel on as quickly as possible. These guys are playing horseshoes with their penises hanging out."

"This is a lifestyle," Henry said, sounding as prim as a guy who'd killed a shit ton of terrorists could sound. "It's not something to be mocked."

"I wasn't mocking," Robert replied. "I certainly wouldn't mock that guy. That's not a dick. It's a third leg."

Jax was fairly certain Robert was talking about the guy who owned Trio. He was talking animatedly with the man who ran the community, and there was no way to politely avert one's eyes from a cock that big. How did the guy stand up when he had an erection? It had to take most of the blood in his body.

"I thought this would be hotter," Owen said. "Where are the women?"

"The ladies are having tea," Henry explained. "Nell found a lovely Darjeeling when we were in Colorado Springs and she's sharing it with her women's group."

And if the women's group gathered here, they were likely all au naturel.

Owen stood a little taller. "I like tea. And I'm Scots and everything. I could bring an international flair to the ladies' group."

"I can bring a sharp knife to your abdomen," Henry replied, his eyes going all John Bishop on Owen.

"Or I could go back and play poker with Dante and Sasha. Sasha thinks he's smart but he always farts a little when he's bluffing. The man has guilt gas." Owen slapped Jax's shoulder. "Don't get eaten by a bear. Or eat stuff that could kill you. Or get lost and end up in Canada."

Owen hadn't spent much time on geography. "I promise."

Tucker turned serious. "And if you have to make the decision between that data and your life, well, I know I would rather have an alive brother than information about a bunch of people I don't know. Be safe out there."

Robert joined them. "I'll be monitoring the conditions as much as I can. I wish you would let me go with you."

This was the best course of action. "You need to be seen around town, and someone needs to figure out where Green went. Concentrate on tracking him."

They'd discovered Levi Green had left his motel room. The manager had said he hadn't bothered to check out, simply packed up and driven away in his Benz. He was out there somewhere and he would be watching. Or he had someone else watching.

He knew what Ezra was worried about. Not that Ezra had mentioned his concerns to the rest of the group, but Jax had briefly overheard him arguing with Big Tag. Ezra thought his ex-wife had set up that whole scene with Green the previous evening in order to throw him off the fact that she was working with him. Ezra didn't trust his ex-wife as far as he could throw her, or so he'd said. Jax wasn't sure about that. He sided with Tag. Big Tag had told him he thought Solo was trying to get her man back. He'd said he knew what a woman in love looked like and told Ezra to not be surprised if she's spent years anally plugging herself as a beautiful way to remember their love.

Sometimes he did not get Big Tag's humor.

Robert shook his hand. "Will do."

Tucker was next to step up for a big good-bye, and Jax had the sudden feeling he was like Dorothy ready to click his red shoes together. He'd talked to his own personal lion in Owen. Robert was totally the Tin Man, and there was Tucker. The Scarecrow. He absolutely would miss Tucker most of all.

Where was Buster when he needed him? That pup could be his Toto. Come to think of it, his hiking boots kind of had a red tinge to them.

Kayla would be proud him using his newfound pop culture knowledge.

"Do you have everything?" Tucker fussed over him, checking his backpack. "I put the MREs in. The good ones. No meatloaf. It's disgusting. And I gave you the last of the good jerky. Now remember to boil the water before you put it in the MRE. Should I have included a thermometer? How will you know if the water reaches the proper temperature?"

"Because I have eyes and can see it boil." Damn, Tucker

238

needed a girlfriend. Even the blow-up kind. He'd heard there were robotic women on the way. He would order one super needy and let Tucker expend all his mother hen on her. "I'm good. I've checked my pack twice."

"I've checked it, too. He's got everything he needs, and I made sure he knows how to use it." Solo strode up, carrying a rifle in her hands. "And here's this, as advertised. It's got a scope on it."

Ezra held a hand out. "I'll check it first."

She sighed. "There are no bugs on it and no locators. It's just a rifle. There are wolves out there and bears, though the rifle will probably just piss off the bears."

"I'll see about that," the boss vowed, stepping away.

Solo nodded Henry's way. "Did you find that map you made?"

"I have it," Jax replied.

The way Henry explained it, when he'd first moved to Bliss, he'd surveyed the area around his cabin thoroughly to a mile and a half radius all ways. The area Jax was interested in was roughly four miles due east of Henry's place, but because of where he was going in, he had to hike along a good portion of the area Henry had mapped. He'd gone over all of it including getting back to the place where Solo had told him to camp the first night.

In the morning he would have roughly half a mile of mapped territory and then it would be all him and a compass and luck. Not that he'd had much luck lately.

He would be alone and could be for days. He wasn't sure if that would be a good thing for him or if he would spend the whole time going over and over his mistakes with River. At the end of this mission, he would either walk out of the woods with what they needed in his hands or he would likely die in the forest.

It was funny, but he cared about dying now. He hadn't when he was in the facility. He'd survived because some instinct told him to. Even while he'd been living in The Garden, he hadn't truly given a crap if he lived or died. He'd enjoyed having friends and watching movies with Kay and trying new food, but the core of him had been empty, a vessel that didn't know what it meant to be full.

Sometime during the day, he'd realized it was okay that she couldn't love him. He loved her and that was what he'd needed. He'd spent all his time and energy on forcing her to see him, but seeing her, really knowing her, had been the best part of his life.

"Jax and I went over everything," Henry said. "He'll be good for tonight and tomorrow morning. After that, he knows the direction he needs to go. He's got a grid map and he's going to search as thoroughly as he can. You've given him markers to use."

Solo had spent time in the woods. She'd described a lot of the territory to him and a few of the markers he needed to look for to know he was going in the right direction.

"I still wish I could have gotten River to at least talk to him," Solo said. "She knows that forest better than anyone. A lecture from her would have made me feel better about sending him in alone."

"I'll be fine." The way she'd spoken made him wonder. "Did you try to see her? Was she okay?"

He already missed her like he'd lost a limb. He could feel her close, but knew she was gone. He wondered how long it would take before it truly settled in his bones that he wouldn't hold her again.

"I went by her place but her Jeep wasn't there," Solo admitted. "When I went to the office I was told by Andy I wasn't welcome anymore, and Ty had already boxed up my desk. I know she was in there, but I can't force her to talk to me. Although I do actually have a small interrogation facility in California."

Jax stared her down. "You are not taking River anywhere."

Solo's face went all innocent. "It's nice. It's done in soothing colors and everything. You know for a dude who spends an awful lot of time in dungeons, you are judgey."

He didn't care what Solo thought of him as long as she didn't think she could force River to do something she didn't want to. "River is out of this. We leave her alone now."

He slid a look Tucker's way and his friend nodded. Tucker would make sure no one went after River in his absence. He could count on Tucker to ensure she was safe.

Tucker's face suddenly screwed up in a mask of horror. "Oh, I didn't want to see that much of Big Tag."

Well, at least they knew where Big Tag had been spending his off time. And he knew why Ezra hadn't been worried about the newest member of the community. Big Tag walked up completely naked, no shame whatsoever.

"You guys ready?" He put his hands on his hips as he surveyed the group.

Solo gave him a grin. "Someone remind me to high-five Tag's wife. Damn."

Ezra frowned, pointedly ignoring his ex. "Dude, where are your pants?"

Big Tag did not care. It was obvious in his casual shrug and the way he let it all hang out. "Back in the locker room. Charlie's coming in for the weekend. She should be here soon and I wanted to greet her properly. Alex and Eve are watching the kids. Kala and Kenzie are going to 'help' with the new baby." Tag snorted. "I can't believe they bought that. Anyway, we're going to have some fun while we're here. So Jax, don't fuck up and make me leave my lounge chair. Charlie and I will either be here, in Talbot's playroom, or hanging in the bunker with Mel and his girlfriend Cassidy. I think Charlie can handle Mel's tonic. He doesn't believe me. Do you think if she does it will prove to him that I'm married to an alien? Huh. I hadn't thought about that. Either way, I think it's going to be amusing."

"You know you're here to work, right?" Ezra asked pointedly. He handed Jax the rifle back, having obviously decided it was device free.

Tag held out an empty hand. "I don't see a paycheck there. Do you?"

Jax secured the rifle to his pack. Tag had done way too much for them. Tag had saved them and housed them and given them something to do. Hell, it had been Tag who had given him a name. He stepped up, holding out a hand. "Don't worry about it. You and Charlotte have fun. I'll take care of this part."

Big Tag shook his hand. "Be careful out there. Keep that walkie on you. You have a sat phone if you run into trouble. Charlie and I will monitor it. Don't forget to hook it up and charge it on the solar charger."

"Yes, Dad." Though he was fairly certain whoever had donated the sperm that created him probably wouldn't have hung around his son with his dick swinging.

A chuckle came from Tag. "Yeah, that's precisely why I'm bringing my wife up here. I'm way too much in dad mode and she's got so many kiddos hanging off her she needs to remember she's a woman, too. I also think having Charlie around town will sell the story that we're about to pull up stakes better than anything. Levi might believe I think there's nothing dangerous happening because I brought my wife in. He's an idiot. The dangerous stuff is why I bring her in. If the shit hits the fan, I like having my Charlie covering my back."

Hearing the way Tag talked about his wife made him miss River. They'd only had a couple of days together, but she'd found a place in his heart. Yeah, he hadn't known how dumbass he would sound. Even in his head.

And he didn't give a fuck. River was important to him. When he was done with this job, he would find a way to watch over her. He couldn't be with her, but he could still care for her. He could make sure she was okay.

Solo watched him as he hefted his backpack over his shoulders. "I wish you would change your mind. I have a pack in my SUV. I can come with you right now."

But this was his journey. "I'll be fine. I think I used to do this. I'm not afraid of the woods. I think I'll be good out there. It's weird but sometimes we know how to do things we knew from before."

"Like muscle memory?" Solo asked.

"Sometimes it goes beyond muscle memory," Ezra replied.

"We're fairly certain Tucker worked in some part of the medical profession," Tag added.

"Yeah, like the evil part." Tucker put a hand on Jax's shoulder. "I'll see you soon. Robert and I are supposed to go into town and have a beer and talk to someone named Callie about how depressed you are and how you won't come out of your room."

Robert chuckled. "Yeah, the big guy over there who owns

Trio told us she's the best about getting the gossip flowing. It would be like telling Big Tag at Sanctum."

Tag frowned, his eyes flaring, and then he calmed and nodded. "Yeah, that's accurate."

Solo turned back to him. "I still wish you would let me go. Even if you come from a background where you've hiked a lot, it doesn't mean you know these woods. You need someone with you."

"I think he's got someone," Ezra said. "You can stand down. I don't know why she changed her mind, but she's got this."

Jax turned to see what Ezra was looking at and he saw her, his world narrowing to one woman. River walked toward him, a big pack on her back. She wore dark green pants and her hiking boots, a white tank covered with a plaid flannel shirt. Her dark hair was in a high ponytail. She was more beautiful than any woman he'd ever seen.

Andy and Ty walked along either side of her. Andy had keys in his hand and Ty was carrying Buster. The puppy started to wriggle and squirm and bark as they got closer. River nodded and Ty let the puppy down.

It was weird how happy it made him to see that ball of fluff run his way. He'd bought Buster to impress River, but he'd gotten caught in the trap of caring for another creature. He knelt down and swore the dog had grown in the day since he'd seen him last.

He picked the puppy up gently, looking into his eyes. "Hey, buddy. Did you miss me? Did Mom take care of you?"

River was here. Something infinitely warm settled deep inside him. She'd come when he needed her, even when she was angry with him.

He cradled Buster to his chest, letting the puppy lick him in a fury of doggie affection. That was when he saw River's eyes go wide and realized she'd caught a glimpse of Big Tag's...well he couldn't call it Little Tag. That did not suit the monstrosity Tag was wielding. It was also Sean Taggart's nickname and he doubted the badass chef would be happy to share it with Tag's dick. Jax moved in front of the big guy, cutting off River's view.

"Nice work," Tag said under his breath. "Use the time you

243

have with her. You can convince her. And be safe, man. I'm going to go. I've got a wife to impress. I've still got this body even after three kids."

"I don't think that's how the childbirth thing works," Tucker said.

"Don't tell Charlie," Tag replied, his voice trailing off as he strode back to the horseshoe pitch.

Solo's head shifted. "That man looks just as good leaving."

There was no way to miss the way Ezra turned a brilliant scarlet. "It looks like you're in good hands, Jax. I think I'll leave so I don't mess up Solo's view."

Tag was right. Ezra's butt was super hurt.

Solo watched him leave, but quickly shifted her attention to River. "I'm glad you changed your mind."

River's hands were tight around the straps of her pack. "I'm not here to make things right between us. Don't expect forgiveness or some grand reunion. I'm here because it's important. Jax, I'm not getting back together with you."

"You lied to her," Andy said, his tone snide. "I tried to talk her out of this, but she's stubborn."

"What Andy is trying to say is you should know if you do anything to her out there, we'll come after you," Ty finished.

Both of River's male friends were looking at him like he was some kind of serial rapist looking for his next victim. He ran his hands over Buster's fur, waiting for the rage to start. It always seemed to be there, that volcanic emotion threatening to burst forth at the earliest opportunity. Especially when someone looked at him like he was nothing. Not this time. They were watching out for her. He got that.

Funny, he hadn't gone after Levi Green, either. He should have joined in with Ezra, pounding his fists on the guy, taking out all that anger, and yet rage hadn't been the emotion he'd felt.

She'd changed him. Or rather caring for her had changed him.

Tucker was getting his "don't fuck with my brother" face on. Jax shook his head. "It's all good. I won't try anything. I'm grateful she's willing to guide me."

"I'm doing it because I read that file on you," she explained.

Solo's eyes went wide. "Where did you get a file on him? Is Levi back? River, you can't believe a thing he says. He'll twist the truth. It's what he's good at."

"Mr. Green isn't the one who gave me Theo Taggart's file," River explained.

He'd read Theo's file. When they'd been rescued, one of the first things required of each of the former captives had been to make report of everything they could remember about what happened to them. They'd then read each other's files. Theo had been Dr. McDonald's golden boy, the only one who hadn't been carefully selected. McDonald had chosen Theo for emotional reasons.

He didn't envy Theo for his past. He did envy the man's bright future with his wife, Erin, and his son, who'd been born while Theo was in captivity.

"Then who gave it to you?" Solo demanded. "Taggart? If Beck is passing around classified files, they will come after you all."

Henry had the dippiest smile on his face. "I wondered why she insisted on going for a ride alone. It was my Nell. She can't stand to see two soul mates separated."

"This is serious." Solo's head dropped back on a groan.

"Yes," Henry replied. "It is. If she's still trying to bring people together, there might be hope for us."

River moved closer to him as Solo started to argue with Henry about the misuse of classified documents. "Do you think there might be a cure out there?"

"No," he replied because he would never lie to her again. "I don't think Dr. McDonald was at all concerned with cures. She wanted us like this. What I might find is research that could lead to a cure, or I hope I can find files on us."

"She was very detail oriented," Robert said, his tone solemn. "She would have known where each subject came from and have a comprehensive history on each. If we've got family, their information might be in that lab."

"And if we know more about the therapies and drugs she used on us, we might be able to figure out a way to bring back more of

245

our memories," Tucker explained. "We've all started having flashes. I think she couldn't completely eradicate that part of the brain without losing more than she wanted to. She needed her subjects to remember things like how to speak a language, how to do daily things. I think she severed connections. But that doesn't mean the memories aren't still there."

"And you think someone else might try to get this information." It wasn't a question. River stared up at him with somber eyes. "They could start the program again."

"They could make more of me." And that would be a shame. That would be dangerous. He'd been dangerous, and the thought of another hundred men like him out in the world kept him awake at night.

Her eyes closed briefly but when she opened them, he could see the will there. "Then we should find this place. But I'm serious, Jax. This is not about you and me."

"If I am what you say I am, if I was using you, then you have nothing to worry about. I've got what I want. I have you guiding me. I don't need anything else from you." It occurred to him that Tag was right. She was here. She'd come back, and it hadn't all been about fighting for what was right. She wasn't willing to risk her life merely because she was trying to save some unknown generation of people who might or might not come up against Dr. McDonald's vision.

She'd come for him. She'd come because she'd needed a reason.

He had no doubt that she would keep her distance, protect her heart, but deep down she couldn't let him risk his life alone.

"And if you're not what I think you are?" She finally met his eyes and he could see the trepidation there.

"If I love you, if I did everything I did because I wanted you and nothing else, then you should go home and let me go alone because I'll try my hardest to win you back. I'll do it because my life has been short and you're the first thing that made me want to live. You are the sun in the sky, River. If I'm *that* man, you're in trouble." He had to warn her. It would be smarter to simply agree with everything she said, but he wasn't doing that to her. Of course, she had given him an option. "But then you know who I am so you should be safe enough."

She went still and he worried he'd pushed her too far, but she took a long breath, as though coming to a decision. "I do know who you are and I know what I'm doing. Let's go. We're wasting daylight."

She took Buster from him and gave the pup a cuddle, whispering to him that she would be back and he shouldn't mess up Ty's place too badly. She kissed the top of his furry head and passed him to the man who would watch over him while they were gone.

And then she walked off, following the path that would lead them into the woods.

His own personal yellow brick road.

He nodded to Ezra and his friends and followed.

Chapter Sixteen

She was making a terrible mistake.

River knew it the minute he'd looked her in the eyes.

I'll do it because my life has been short and you're the first thing that made me want to live. You are the sun in the sky, River. If I'm that man, you're in trouble.

She sat in front of the small fire she'd made, his words echoing in her head. He'd looked so open in that moment it had been hard to believe he was lying.

But she wanted him to be lying. If he was lying she didn't have to face the fact that maybe what he'd told her had been false, but what he'd felt had been true. She would have to decide if she was brave enough to risk her soul again. But that wasn't all. She wanted them all to be lying to her because what Theo Taggart had gone through had been nothing less than pure hell on earth. The idea that Jax had been through something similar made her heart twist.

She didn't want to feel for him. She wanted to be numb again because when she was numb she didn't feel pain.

And you don't feel joy, baby girl. You don't get one

248

without the other, but life means nothing without joy. It means nothing without pain. I wouldn't take back loving your mother for anything. She's gone now, but loving her was the joy of my life and that's worth the pain.

She shoved away her father's words. It was the place, that was all. This had been one of her dad's favorite camping spots because it was off the beaten path. He'd brought her here many times. When he wasn't working, he would take her out in the woods and they would spend weeks camping and studying nature and simply existing in what he called the world's best hotel. That was why she felt restless. There were ghosts here.

"Are you all right?" Jax sat across from her.

She was far from all right. They'd hiked in silence all afternoon and well into the evening, him following behind her. He moved more quietly than she would have expected for such a large man. Sometimes she'd looked back to make sure he was still there and every single time she'd caught him staring at her with a sad look on his face.

The path Solo had chosen to get them out under cover had included a couple of decent climbs. Nothing that would require climbing gear, but it had been hard physical work. Jax had been good at it, his body moving with ease, hands knowing where to grip to haul himself up. He'd done this before. That was another lie.

Or he didn't remember and this was one of those muscle memory things Nell had talked about.

When they'd reached the campsite, he'd been helpful and quick to learn. He'd had both tents up before she could make the fire. They'd eaten MREs while talking about innocuous subjects like how she would train Buster and how he was going to buy Tucker a plastic blow-up doll to love.

But now she couldn't escape the questions she really wanted to ask but wasn't going to. Nope. She was treating him like any other client. She wouldn't ask Joe from Wisconsin personal questions. Of course, Joe from Wisconsin usually brought along his Jane or his kids or his friends, and they would bear the burden of campfire talk.

"How much time do you remember?" The question came out before she could think to hold it in. She didn't need to know more about him. She needed to do her duty so she could sleep better at night knowing she'd helped.

After she'd read Theo's account of his captivity and torture, she'd known she would guide Jax to The Ranch. She wouldn't be able to live with herself if she didn't try to help.

Because that's life, baby girl. It's tough, and no one person can save the world. There's so much bad out there that it's overwhelming. It's easy to throw up your hands and give in. But faith—real faith—is knowing you can't save it and still trying any way. If we all would just try, maybe the world would be a better place.

She wished she would stop hearing her father's voice.

"Time is hard for me. I think I've been alive for about three years. I guess the better term would be aware."

The words gutted her and yet Jax said them without emotion. "You don't know for sure?"

He sat back against the log he'd dragged up to their makeshift campsite. "Sometimes it seems like I was born a few days ago but other times it feels like I spent decades there with her. With Dr. McDonald. Sorry, I have to remind myself not to call her Mother."

That was what Theo had said. Hope McDonald had twisted the idea of maternal love. She was a psychopath who hadn't known how to love at all.

Jax stared at the fire as he continued. "I remember waking up and not understanding where I was. There was this godawful bright light and the room I was in was pure white. She was there. She seemed kind at first. I was sick from the drugs and she helped me. Sasha was there, too. I think he was the first of us. Well, the first one who survived. I don't know about Robert. He was with the other team. They moved around more than we did."

Theo and Robert and a man named Victor had been another "team," one McDonald moved around South America and Asia. They'd been forced to commit crimes to fuel her business, to stay alive.

"Didn't you ask yourself where your family was?" River

asked. She didn't understand completely. It was hard to comprehend what they'd been through.

"I didn't remember whether I had a family or not. The doctor told me I'd been in an accident and that Sasha was my brother. He was nice to me in the beginning. We only had each other and Dante until she brought in Tucker and a guy named George. There were others, but I was close to Tucker and George."

"But not Sasha and Dante?"

He hesitated, as if trying to figure out how to reply. "I was at first, but then she started the training."

Did she even want to know this? It would be better to leave the knowledge as academic, mere words on a page. If she listened to Jax's story, it would be real, visceral. If she listened to him, she would empathize with him.

"Did you ever come here with your dad?"

She'd taken too long, been quiet and given him a chance to turn the tide of the conversation. "I want to hear about the training."

He brought his eyes up. They glowed in the light of the fire. The shadows made the planes of his face seem even more stark and masculine than usual. "I would rather hear about your father. The training wasn't pleasant."

"Why did the training hurt your relationship with Sasha and Dante?" If she started talking about her dad she might lose it. She needed to find a way to stay centered. She'd thought about climbing into the tent she'd bought, but it was still early and she worried she would lie in there thinking about the fact that it was big enough for two, and Jax was huddled in Henry's old tent.

He was silent for a moment and his eyes strayed back to the fire. "The training came in different forms. She would pit us against each other. She had handlers. That's what she called them. They were guards meant to keep us in line. At first the training was the same thing you would find in a gym. We would work out for hours every day. Then it turned into a competition. She would put us on the treadmill and whoever fell off first lost."

"Fell off?"

"Oh, yes, if you stepped off the treadmill, you were beaten

251

physically. If you fell off, you were beaten, but at least you got to eat that night. I remember several times when one of us would urinate on the treadmill because we knew if we stopped for a break she would remind us that she was in control and that we would do Mother's will. I have a couple of scars from passing out and banging around on the thing. She would sit and watch us for hours, taking notes. They controlled the machines and we would try to keep up."

Her heart threatened to crack. "You competed against Dante and Sasha?"

"Often," he allowed. "I would beat them and they didn't handle it well. And then there was the ring. When there were enough of us, she would make us compete to see who would be the alpha for the week. The alpha got the best food, the choicest place to sleep, sometimes women. Theo's group was more advanced than we were, or perhaps McDonald simply preferred them. She trained them differently from what Robert's said. I think they were her elite soldiers. We were her pack of trained dogs. That's what she wanted. A pack of loyal dogs to do her bidding."

"You're not a dog, Jax."

His lips turned up slightly. "I don't think that it's so bad to be a dog. I know Buster's pretty happy. Like all things in life it depends on who takes care of you, on who teaches and cares for you." The smile faded. "We were trained on weapons once she decided we were sufficiently loyal. I was a problem child. I required an enormous amount of correction. Sometimes she would have me beaten when I hadn't even done anything wrong. She told me I was the stupidest of her sons and I lived on her sufferance. Sometimes I'm almost sure she hated me."

She gasped as she realized where the scars on his back had come from. Somehow she'd convinced herself he'd been in a terrible accident. It had been easier to think that it had happened at once, and then he'd been in a hospital with drugs to numb his pain. But his scars came from a thousand cuts, dealt out over time until he likely couldn't recall a day without pain.

Something was opening inside her and it threatened to take over. She couldn't do it, couldn't let herself be ripped open by his pain.

"You survived," she said carefully, tamping down the emotions roiling through her. "You were lucky."

"I was very lucky," he agreed. "She picked the wrong man to get obsessed with. If she hadn't come after Theo Taggart, I wouldn't be here. His bad luck was my salvation because Big Tag wasn't going to stop until he got his brother back. I won't even go into Erin Taggart. She scares me a little. But that day…she would be offended, I'm sure, but that day when Theo's family came for him, she was an angel. A foul-mouthed angel who talks to her gun a lot, but an angel."

She wanted to get him away from the brutal times, but she still had some questions. "You don't remember girlfriends?"

A sly smile crossed his face. "Are you asking if I remember sex?"

Heat flashed through her system and she wasn't sure if it was pure embarrassment. There was some arousal in there, too, since he'd said the word sex and in her mind that word had a definition. Jax Seaborne *was* sex to her. "I was curious. You said they would bring in women. I think Tucker mentioned hookers. I thought it was weird at the time, but now it makes sense."

"Oh, sweetheart, those were hookers brought in by Big Tag," he corrected. "They were nice women. They were kind to us. The women McDonald would bring in were almost always murdered as a way to keep us in line. I never had sex at the facility. Even before I realized what was happening, I couldn't touch anyone in there."

River stood up. She couldn't breathe. He had to be lying to her. He had to be. "They killed women?"

"Not all of them, but occasionally after the alpha of the week would sleep with his prize, he would wake up to a dead body and be told he'd killed her in the night. It happened to George and he didn't speak or eat for two weeks. He believed them. He believed he killed that woman. Now we know it was the handlers who did it. We were given drugs to make us sleep through anything, and that was when they would sneak in. It was a way to remind us not to get too close to anyone from the outside. Not that we knew anyone from the outside." Jax considered her for a moment as she

253

paced in front of the fire. "This bothers you."

"Of course, it does. I'm human."

"I've known plenty of humans who didn't care."

Because the only people he'd known were evil doctors and minions and men who were desperate to survive.

"River," he said quietly, "I'm lying. It didn't happen, sweetheart. It's a well-crafted fiction. You were right. It was all a way to manipulate you. I'm sorry. I shouldn't have done that."

She stared at him for a moment. "You're lying now. Why?"

"Because I just realized I don't want to make the world any worse for you. There are some things it's better not to know. There are some things that should be hidden. I've learned a few truths about the world in the last few days. Pain is relative. My pain can't be compared to yours. Pain is real to the person feeling it. It shouldn't be held up like it's a contest."

Oh, but he would win. "Jax, what you went through was horrific."

"And I'm sure losing your father was horrific, too. At the end it's all nothing but pain unless we learn something from it. I wish I'd been honest with you. I wish I'd met you that first night and told you that I don't remember ever being with another woman, that in all the ways that count, I was a virgin until you. I wish I'd given you that."

Tears pulsed behind her eyes. God, what kind of a person was she? She hadn't cried at her own father's funeral but here she was, wild emotion threatening to spill over. She turned and strode away, needing to breathe. It was too much. Far, far too much.

She leaned against a big pine tree, the fire behind her, Jax behind her.

The air held the promise of snow to come in a few weeks. The rains they'd had would soon turn powdery and white. It already capped the mountaintops and the blanket would soon flow all around her. In a few weeks, Ty would go part time and he would stay at the lodge. She would have to decide what to do with the rest of her life.

Where would Jax be? On the run? Alone?

She'd been his first lover. His only lover. Who the hell was this man? Could she believe him?

She heard the quiet crunch of boots against the forest floor. "I want to be alone, Jax."

"I won't say a word," he promised. "But I have to watch over you. I won't ever bother you again, but you should know I'll always be there for you. If you ever need me all you have to do is call. We change phones a lot out of necessity, but I'll keep the one you have the number to. I'll have it with me and I promise I'll always have it charged and I'll answer it."

I'll always be there. I won't let you down, baby girl. You're the most important person in the world to me.

Her father had said those words to her and he'd been standing in almost the same spot where Jax was. She remembered it like it was yesterday. It had been right after her mother had died. After the funeral, her father had packed them up and they'd hiked until she couldn't walk anymore. She'd fallen to the forest floor, exhausted. He'd built a fire and they'd looked down on the valley below.

That's Bliss, he'd said to her that night. *It looks peaceful from up here. It looks like nothing bad ever happened, but even Bliss has its troubles. Wouldn't know joy without pain. Wouldn't be Bliss without sorrow. The key to living is to accept the pain for what it is—a reminder. Yeah, your momma is gone, but that doesn't mean we stop living. She's up there waiting and watching. Death is nothing but a reminder to live, to love while we can.*

But his death had been so painful. His death had been a slow wasting away of his vibrancy, his love, his light. Her precious father had been reduced, made small by a disease that ate away at everything he was.

A sob came from her throat and Jax was suddenly beside her.

Jax, who had been through so much. All he'd known in his short life was pain and horror, and he still said he loved her.

She'd spent a lifetime loved by a man who taught her everything he'd known with patience and a gentle hand, and it hadn't been until this moment that she could feel anything but relief at his death.

255

He was gone. He was gone and she didn't know where he was. His body was in the ground and his soul…

"River, don't cry. It's over."

She shook her head. He didn't understand. She felt for him. She did, but there was more to the emotion coursing through her. "I…my father…"

"He's still here with you," Jax whispered. "Nothing is ever truly lost."

She shook her head. "You can't know that."

"I can. God, where is this coming from? I can hear the words in my head, but I don't know where they come from," Jax whispered. "Nothing is ever truly lost. When a flower dies, it seeds the earth with its beauty. It's not lost, merely transformed."

She glanced up and his eyes were shining in the moonlight.

God, he was everything he'd said he was. He was broken and yet there was something so beautiful about him. Somehow he'd put himself back together.

"He's here, isn't he?" Jax asked. "You feel him in the forest."

She nodded, too overwhelmed to speak. Her father was here. He'd been waiting for her, waiting to show her the way back to herself. He was in the trees—the aspens that shook and shimmered and the pines that split the sky. He was in the wind that brushed her face.

The cycle of her father's life had closed, but his love…oh, that wasn't a circle. That was an infinite line reaching to the past, to her grandmother and great grandfathers and beyond. It would stretch into the future, connecting her children to him and her grandchildren to her until there was love as far as she could think.

That was her father's legacy. His soul couldn't be judged by the way he'd ended, only by the way he'd lived. That death had been a falsehood, a lie meant to trick her into thinking the world was empty. Or perhaps it was a test. A test of patience. Of kindness in the face of misery. Of bravery. It was hard to love. Love hurt, and it was also the only reason to live.

"Go ahead, River," he whispered. "Cry. It's good to cry. Will you cry for me? I can't. It's there. I can feel it, but it won't come out. I think she burned it out of me, but if I had someone who could cry for me, I think it might be all right."

It was all she needed. The dam burst, volcano exploding in a riot of grief. She'd lost her father twice. Once to death and then to her stubborn refusal to mourn. Mourning was a beautiful thing, a tribute to those who had passed, a time to remind herself to live, and she'd skipped that step. She'd allowed herself to get stuck in the pain, to never let herself feel the joy.

She sobbed, her knees hitting the dirt, but Jax was there with her. His strong arms wound around her, and she wept against his chest. He smoothed back her hair, rocking her but saying nothing. He allowed her to mourn, to keen and cry and finally to miss him. Oh, it felt so fucking good to miss him, to yearn for her father.

And Jax. She mourned for him, too. For all he'd lost. His past. He didn't know if anyone out there loved him, wished he was with them still. He was alone in the world. He'd been born into pain and yet he'd found a way to love.

Could he love her? Could she be brave enough to love him even knowing it would end? He would leave. He had to. He would be on the run for the rest of his life potentially. He couldn't stay. Did that mean he wasn't worth loving?

She cried for what they could have been.

Slowly, she came back to earth, a peace settling over her. Her chest ached with how hard she'd cried, but it was the best of aches, the kind that told her she was finally healing.

"Tell me I don't have to let you go." He was sitting with his back to a tree, her in his lap.

She could hear the beat of his heart. It was too much. She couldn't make any decisions tonight. "Would you hold me for a while? I don't know where we're going, but I want you to hold me."

His arms tightened, and she felt him sigh as if in relief. "Always. When I'm gone, I want you to remember that I'm always holding you in my mind. You are the best thing that ever happened to me."

She cuddled close, emotion threatening to overwhelm her again.

She fell asleep that way, her head against his shoulder, his arms wrapped around her. Not unlike the way she'd slept that night when her father had taken her into the woods. Safe. Warm.

Loved.

* * * *

She was surrounded by death. It was there in the mist.

Jax. She screamed his name, the word echoing through the forest, mocking her. She knew she should be quiet, but he'd been gone so long.

He appeared before her, a sad smile on his face. He said not a word but reached out for her, his hand touching her cheek.

This was good-bye, she realized. Still, her body lit up from that touch and she knew no one would ever move her the way he did. She didn't even know his true name, didn't know if he had a wife waiting for him, had loved ones at all, but it didn't matter because in that moment she knew he was the only man for her. Somehow the universe had meant him for her, had conspired and twisted the world so they would meet and love and be torn apart.

He drifted back into the mist, the gray cloud swallowing him whole.

Her heart felt constricted, like her chest was too small to contain it and would burst and bleed and cover the forest floor if she didn't find him. She ran into the mist, her vision going hazy. She couldn't tell where she was going. It was too thick. That mist clung to her and it was as if it was a living thing. That mist was emotion, creeping into her skin, making her scared and pitiful.

She could stop, the mist seemed to whisper. Go no further and everything will be all right. Stay where you are. You'll be safe here.

But there was no safety for Jax. There would be no respite, no haven.

Footsteps echoed and she took off in the direction she thought they were coming from. The woods could be deceptive, sound pinging off trees and bouncing around like a ball she was trying to catch.

She couldn't leave him. He would be alone out here. He would have no one. He would wake up again and realize his past was gone and this time, she would be part of that past. She would be erased from his memory, no longer even able to give him comfort in the form of reminiscence. It couldn't happen. He couldn't wake up in that white room, cold and alone. He wouldn't survive it this time.

She ran, heedless of where she was going, praying her instincts could lead her to him.

She caught sight of him ahead as the mist seemed to fade and she realized he was surrounded by wolves. He stood there, in the middle of the clearing she'd played in as a child. It was deep in the woods, past all worn trails. It was a secret place, the furthest she was allowed to go because...her mind threatened to warp. Something about the clearing. Danger. She wasn't supposed to go past this point.

Here and no further.

The wolves circled him and she realized he was holding Buster. Buster barked and snarled at the pack as if he understood the danger they were in, but Jax's eyes were on her.

She started to move toward him and suddenly she was a child again, looking up into her father's eyes.

No, sweetheart. You can't play here. It's dangerous. Stay in the light and you'll be fine.

But Jax was in the darkness. As she stood there, she watched the shadows take him...

River turned over, a gasp coming from her chest as the dream ended and she realized where she was. She was in her tent, the one she'd bought at the big box store. It took her a moment to catch her breath and orient herself.

Jax had carried her to her tent, gently easing her in. He'd been on his hands and knees when he'd zipped her into her sleeping bag,

259

and with shadows playing around him, he kissed her forehead. She'd thought he would crawl in next to her, but he'd left and she hadn't had the energy to argue.

She sat up and realized the fire was still going, larger than it had been before. She scrambled out, hoping it hadn't gotten out of control. She hadn't told him how to put out the fire. He wouldn't know all the steps that went into making sure everything was properly doused and safe. If the embers weren't all soaked, they could catch fire again. It had rained recently, but any fire was dangerous in woods like these.

She stopped as she realized he was still sitting there. He relaxed against the log he'd dragged over, his head tipped back toward the sky.

"I thought you were sleeping," he said, still looking up. "I'm sorry if I woke you."

She noticed he'd dragged his sleeping bag out and laid it outside the tent he was supposed to be using. "You couldn't sleep?"

She wouldn't tell him about her dream. It was too close to the surface. He'd been there, in danger and out of reach. She couldn't go where he was. River shook it off, concentrating on the man in front of her.

They had few days left and he looked so remote. She couldn't stand it. It had been stupid to think she could hear his story and not get close to him again.

"There weren't any stars in London," he said. "Well, they were there, but not like this. And we weren't allowed outside in the facility. I'm afraid the tent feels too much like a cell to me. I'll stay out here with the stars. They feel…familiar to me."

How terrible was it to know he should remember and never be able to catch it? She settled in next to him, looking up at the sky, trying to see what he was seeing.

A blanket of stars, diamonds shining down on them.

"Dante told me they were dead," he said, his voice flat. "I was on the rooftop at The Garden, trying to see them through the fog, and he said I shouldn't bother because they were nothing but dead suns. The light takes millions of years to get to us. A lot of the stars in the sky went nova a long time ago. That makes me sad."

It would have made her sad mere hours before, but she had a different perspective now. Funny what a good cry and strong arms around her could do. It had restored her, made her more faithful to who she was at her core. Almost two years she'd spent in the prison of her father's disease, but there was light. It came from the stars. It came from the people around her. It came from him.

It would light her way home if she let it.

"It shouldn't make you sad. Everything dies, but it's like you said. Nothing is lost." It was funny how easy it was to think of her father now. "My dad would take me out here and we would do science experiments. One time he brought me and Ty and our friend Lucy overnight and we had a telescope. He told me the same thing Dante said except with a different twist. He said wasn't it amazing that even after all that time, their light was here, still traveling, still moving. Though the sun was gone, its light is used to mark the path for sailors, to illuminate our darkness, to give us something to dream about. Nothing is lost, merely transformed."

"I love you, River."

She was silent for a moment and then realized the truth. She'd loved him from the moment she'd seen him, that connection sparking to life. "I love you, too, Jax."

He turned to her, a sad smile on his face. "I wish I knew my name."

But he had a name. She'd been wrong in her dream. He had a true name. "It's Jax. You're Jax, and that's all you need to be."

He was quiet for a moment, though his hand slid over hers, connecting them again. "The others worry they left people behind. I don't think I had anyone."

"You did. I know you did." She knew it deep inside. Now that she'd cast off the weight of her past, she could see him as he was. Lovely. Amazing. She threaded her fingers through his, loving how warm he was. "I think you had parents. A mom. A dad. Maybe both. I think they loved you so much that love imprinted on you and even when the memory was gone, the love remained. It protected you. It shielded you like nothing else could. That love was there when you needed it. You came out whole, Jax."

"No, I'm broken." There was a hoarseness to his voice.

She shook her head and made her decision. She needed him to believe. She let go of his hands and straddled him, looking him straight in the eyes as she cupped his face. "You might be broken, but you're whole. We're all broken. Some of us forget to pick up our lost pieces and tape them back into place. But you didn't, baby. You somehow held yourself together. You found brothers to care about and protect. You didn't give in to the darkness. You should be a monster, but you're not. You should be shut down and twisted, angry at anyone who didn't go through what you did. But you saved me. You loved me."

"Love you," he corrected as his hands came up to cup her hips. "I'll always love you. But I don't think I can stay with you. I really am a wanted man. I would bring that down on this town if I stayed. They'll come for me, but I need you to know that no matter what happens, I'll love you. I'll die some day loving you."

"Because I was your first?" She had to ask. It didn't make a difference, but she wanted to know. There could be other women for him.

"Because you're my only." He put his hands on her back, drawing her down. "Because my love for you won't die, it'll merely transform. When I'm gone I want you to feel my arms around you. I want you to know that I'm waiting for you, for the day we'll be together again. In this life or somewhere else. I know it because this feeling can't be wrong, and it can't be destroyed. It's forever."

The world went watery as she lowered her mouth to his. Emotion overwhelmed her for the second time. This wasn't about mourning, though. This emotion was the relief and joy of a soul finding its mate. She'd been wrong when she'd said he was whole. Jax himself might be whole but he wasn't complete without her. He was a part of her soul now, the part that had faith, the part that believed, the part that loved.

She kissed him as the stars above lit the night.

Chapter Seventeen

Jax kissed her with everything he had, her body against his warming him in a way no fire ever could. He'd followed her all afternoon and late into the evening. He'd held every moment as precious, hoarding them like a man who knew he would need them to get through all his lonely days without her.

This, oh, this, he would dream about forever.

He'd meant something to her. When she'd cried in his arms, when she'd wailed and wept and let her grief rise to the surface, he'd known what he'd been born to do. Not born in that sterile lab, but born to a mother who'd loved him. Born and named and raised to take all the love he'd been given and pour it into this woman. His woman.

He realized it in that moment. Love was like the other things he remembered. It wasn't something a drug could take from him. It had been written into his DNA by people he couldn't name, but he was grateful. He wasn't some animal born in a lab. That had been done to him. He'd been a choice, a gift to his mother or father or whatever person out there who had loved him so much he could go through the fire he'd been through and still be open enough to love River.

"Don't cry, baby." Her fingers came up, whisking away tears. "That's my job."

But it felt good. He would never cry in front of anyone else, but it was okay with her. She was safe. He could give her his every emotion and she would hold them to her heart. "I love you."

She leaned over, kissing his tears away.

Everywhere her lips brushed his skin, he seemed to light up from within.

"I love you, too." She moved to his jawline, kissing him all along his cheek and down to his throat. "I'm sorry I reacted the way I did. I should have listened to you."

He needed to make a few things plain. He gently dragged her up and looked in her clear green eyes. God, he would never get over those eyes. "You should have run as fast as you could. I lied, baby. I might have reasons for it, but I lied to you, and I won't ever do it again. You had every right to be angry with me and I'm so grateful for your forgiveness. Thank you for giving me another chance, River. Thank you for giving me a few days with you."

He didn't want to leave her, but when Ezra pulled them out, he would go. It was dangerous to stay in one place for long, and he'd already brought Levi Green into town. He'd put Henry and the rest of them in danger.

"Make love to me," she said. "While you're here, I want you to make love to me as often as possible, and then promise me when you're done you'll come home."

She was his home. Not some place. Not a space on the earth, but a woman. "I'll sneak back and see you as often as I can, but I won't put you in danger." And he had to disappoint her. "I can't make love to you. Not all the way. I didn't bring condoms. I didn't think you would come with me and I wasn't planning on trolling the woods for ladies."

He expected her to laugh, but she grew solemn. "Make love to me."

"But I…" The gravity of her request hit him.

"Make love to me, Jax," she said, her voice sure. "It's a risk I'm willing to take. And I'm not talking about the risk of getting pregnant. I'm talking about the risk of not getting pregnant. I want it. I want something of you I can love and adore and raise to be as amazing a man as his dad."

"Or hers." He hadn't thought about kids until he'd met her. He dragged her down to meld their mouths together.

It was stupid. It was a bad time. He might not survive to see his child grow up.

What was faith for if he never took a chance? He'd been through all that pain. He had to grab joy where he found it.

He kissed her, his tongue tangling with hers. Over and over he caressed her lips, memorizing her taste for all time. He sank his hands into her hair, pulling it free from the knot she'd wound it into. It spilled over his skin, raining down on her shoulders. When she came up for air, there was pure desire in her eyes and it made him feel larger than he'd been before.

She leaned back, undoing the buttons of the flannel shirt she wore. She slipped it off and tossed it away from the fire. Her skin was golden in the light cast by the campfire. If he had a million days with her, this was what they would do. They would live a life here in Bliss. They would roam the woods and after they'd settled their little ones down for bed, he would take their mother by the light of the fire, showing her over and over how much he needed her, how she was the center of the universe. No sun could hold a candle to her.

She dragged her tank top over her head and unhooked her bra. He sat back, watching her, accepting her gift to him. Every inch of skin she uncovered was a present, an offering of self, and he would never refuse it.

"I never saw anything as beautiful as you."

She grinned, a light expression he hadn't seen on her before. He'd put that smile on her face. "You haven't been out much, babe."

He cupped her breast. "I don't need to. I know perfection when I see it. And this is perfect."

He loved the way her eyes went dark, the lids coming down like they were too heavy to stay open. Desire sparked off her, hardening his cock. The time they'd spent apart had been roughly a day, and it had been far too long. A minute without her was an eternity.

Her arms wrapped around him and he was lost in her. His whole body responded to her touch and scent, to the taste of her. The idea that he didn't have to wear a condom nearly fried his brain. His cock had never been this hard, never wanted so much. He ran his hands down her back as he kissed her again. He smoothed his palms down to the cheeks of her ass and tilted his pelvis up, letting her know where he wanted to be. Inside her. Deep inside her.

Her hands found his shirt, dragging it over his head. There was a chill in the air, but he didn't feel it now. All he felt was her heat, the warmth of her love. He kissed his way down her cheek to her neck, loving the way her head dropped back and she moved restlessly on his cock. If he didn't have his pants on and he'd managed to get hers off, he would already be inside her.

Fuck, he might spend the rest of his time here inside her.

It would make it hard to find what he was looking for, but he was willing to try.

He kissed his way down to her breast. How had he lived without her breasts? They were utterly perfect. They fit in his hand and god, he loved to tug her nipples in his mouth.

He licked at her, feeling the way she shuddered against him and arched her back. He took her offering, sucking that first sweet nipple between his lips. He tugged on it, pulling it between his teeth and biting down lightly.

Her moan went straight to his dick. She rubbed against him, her hips moving in time to the rhythm they created. He couldn't help but match her, his pelvis grinding up against hers as he licked and bit and sucked her nipples. He traced her areola with the tip of his tongue before sucking her deep.

Her hands found his hair, fingertips running over his scalp and holding him to her. He growled and twisted, turning her onto his sleeping bag. He hadn't meant to use it that night, had known he couldn't sleep, but now he was happy it was here. He would take her under the stars, by the light of the fire.

He rolled her on her back and kissed his way down her torso. He let his hand drift down under the waistband of her pants, delving into her underwear. His body tightened further as his finger slid over her pussy. Wet and ripe, she was ready for him. He touched her, sliding over her eager clitoris and dipping inside her pussy.

He could smell her, the intoxicating scent of her arousal mingling with the woodsy fire. He dragged her pants down, taking the panties with them. He got to his knees, looking down at her and memorizing the sight. She was stunning, her beauty emblazoned on his brain. She lay back on the sleeping bag, her hair flowing around her, her skin glowing from the warm campfire light. Need was in her eyes. Need for him.

He took her ankles in his hands.

"Jax." His name was a plea on her lips.

He spread her legs, making a place for himself between them. He leaned back over, laying kisses on her belly, working his way down. She would be so beautiful pregnant. He would do anything to be there, to take care of her, to hold her and protect her while they waited for their baby. "Yes?"

"Please come inside me." Her legs moved restlessly around him, stroking against him.

"I will." But not the way she thought. He couldn't get enough of her. He would never get enough of her.

He spread her legs wide and put his nose in her pussy, inhaling her sweet scent.

"You kill me when you do that," she said on a low moan.

He suckled her clit.

"Jax, let me up."

He didn't want to do that. He hadn't even started yet. He thrust his tongue into her, fucking her gently.

"Jax," she groaned, her hands in his hair, tugging lightly. "Babe, let me show you something. You are the best lover I've ever had, but you've only been doing this for a couple of days. Let me show you something. Let me teach you."

That got him moving. Was he doing something wrong? He thought she liked it when he put his mouth on her.

She scrambled up, getting to her knees and wrapping herself around him. "I want to show you something. I want to show you

267

how we can take care of each other at the same time. First I need you to take your pants off. I want you naked. I love your body, Jax."

There was no deception in her eyes, no sympathy for his ruined flesh. All he could see in her was honest desire. It made his hands move to the fly of his pants, unhooking and pushing them off his hips. He kicked them off and toed out of the socks he was wearing so he stood in front of her completely naked. He towered over her, but it struck him that he was the supplicant. He might be taller, broader, physically stronger, but he needed her. He needed her to feel complete, to feel at home in a world he didn't always understand.

She looked at his chest, her hands going straight for the largest of the scars. She smoothed her palms over them and then kissed each one, little butterfly wings on his flesh. Her head came up, eyes lighting with excitement. "I didn't think about how much you don't know or can't remember. Jax, we can have so much fun with this. I've never been the one with more experience. I can show you things. Dirty things. Sexy things. Lay down."

He wasn't sure he liked being out of control, but it was obvious his dick couldn't care less. His dick poked her in the belly.

She seemed to sense his hesitance and her eyes softened, hands on his waist. She rubbed against him. "Please. When we're done, you can take me any way you like, but try this with me. I want to do everything with you. Sex wasn't great until I met you. Let me share this."

He couldn't possibly deny her. He got down on the sleeping bag, laying himself out while she stood over him. It wasn't something he would do for anyone else. He couldn't make himself vulnerable to anyone except her. He looked up at her, taking in the sight of her body. She was his forest nymph.

He expected her to get on top of him, to take his cock, but instead she turned.

"Have you ever heard of a sixty-nine?" The question was asked in a husky tone.

His cock nearly went off then and there. Yep. He'd seen some porn. "Are you going to sit on my face, baby?"

"Sort of." She straddled him, giggling as she moved a bit awkwardly. "I'm sorry."

He gripped her hips. Fuck, he loved this view. Her pussy was right there, and he could see the gorgeous globes of her ass. He ran his hands up and down her backside. "Don't ever say you're sorry for giving me this. This is the best present ever." That was probably not the way to put that. "I mean except for your love, of course."

Heart over pussy. That's what Kay had taught him, though it was hard to remember that lesson because her pussy was right there.

He felt her whole body move with the force of her laughter. It was so good to hear her laugh, to know he'd brought her respite.

That was when she put her mouth on him, kissing his cock and taking the base in her hand.

He took a deep breath, his body lighting on fire as she licked at the head of his dick.

"See, this is fun, babe." She hummed the words on his cock as she ran her tongue over his sensitive flesh.

He gripped her ass and gave back. He speared her with his tongue, diving deep into that body he loved so much. Pleasure swamped his senses. He could feel her mouth sucking at him, pulling his cock inside. Her teeth scraped lightly along his skin, making him shudder. He matched his pace to hers. She sucked him deep. He drilled his tongue inside her. She blew on his cockhead. He suckled her clit.

It was a contest, the best kind. Which one of them could bring the other the most joy. He was determined. He would win this one.

He brought his hand up, letting his thumb find her clit. He pressed down, rotating as he tongue fucked her.

She cupped his balls as she deep throated him. How she took him to the root he had no idea, but his eyes threatened to roll into the back of his head, his balls getting ready to shoot off.

That was not happening.

He twisted his thumb and his tongue was coated with her orgasm. Her body shook and she lost her rhythm, gasping and moaning against his dick.

It was his time to take over.

He flipped them over, taking care to keep her off the grass. He eased her over and got to his knees. There was the most sweetly satiated look on her face as she opened her arms to him.

The air was heavy again, filled with the knowledge that this was forever. No matter what happened, he would love this one woman. He would love her and want her the rest of his life.

He would never have met her had he not been taken. He had no idea what his life had been before, but it wouldn't have included River. Perhaps the man he'd been wouldn't have seen her value, gotten trapped by her unique beauty. All that mattered was the fact that he had her now. He loved her now. She was part of his soul.

"Come here," she whispered. "I need you inside me. Always."

He lowered himself down, mating his body to hers. He rubbed his cock along her soaked pussy, covering himself with her. He kissed her as he thrust up, connecting them.

This was what he'd needed. He stopped, holding himself up over her and letting her get used to his size. Her legs wound around him and he stared down at her. "I could stay like this forever."

Her hands ran up his back, the look on her face as old as time. His seductress. "I think you should move, babe. Take me higher. You're the only one who has ever been able to do this to me." She squeezed her pussy around his cock. "Come inside me. You feel so good."

She was the one who felt good. He couldn't hold back an instant longer. He moved his hips, finding the rhythm they'd built before. Her legs were tight about him, forcing him to thrust up even harder. He could feel her nails in his back. He welcomed them. Those were marks he would be proud to bear. He worked over her, every thrust taking them both higher. He couldn't take his eyes off her. They connected, their bodies and eyes and souls all meshing.

In the end, he couldn't hold out. He couldn't stay in that place forever, but he could give her something. She tightened around him. When she called out his name, he went over the edge with her.

The orgasm took over his whole body and she felt like the only thing real in the world. He clung to her, riding the wave. Nothing had ever felt as good as River's body milking his cock. Her muscles held him tight until he had nothing left to give her and he collapsed.

Peace seemed to surround him as she ran her hands soothingly over him. She kissed his cheek and jaw and neck like she couldn't stop herself.

"I owe Nell Flanders," she said, her voice husky. "I'm making that lady some amazing vegan cookies."

He would give up meat for her. "I'll help. I owe her, too. God, I love you." He kissed her again, rolling to the side and drawing her close. "And I owe your father for teaching you all about this place. I love it out here. I feel at home."

Most of that was because she was here, but something inside him had changed the minute they'd landed in Colorado. Something had sparked inside him. He was comfortable here, like he'd found an old sweater he'd forgotten about, the one that warmed him best.

She laid her head on his chest. "Me, too. I love my cabin, but I always feel more centered out here. I wonder why I didn't come here after he died."

He knew. "You weren't ready."

"I wasn't. It's funny how now I can remember Dad without the pain. It's there, but it's not the whole of my emotions. I can remember how awesome it was to be his daughter." She sniffled, and he tightened his arms around her. She could cry all she liked. He would hold her. "He took me out here all the time. He said this was my playground."

She sat up all of the sudden, her eyes wide.

"What's wrong?" He reached for her hand.

"Oh, Jax, I think I know where The Ranch is."

271

Chapter Eighteen

River moved through the heavily wooded area, looking for landmarks. She knew most of them in this forest. They were everything from the ranger way station, where they stored emergency stashes of water and supplies, to certain trees. She always knew she was close to Creede when she got to the massive tree they called The Bear's Scratching Post due to the deep gouges in its trunk. She knew she was coming out on the southern side of the forest when she found the pond on the edge of the Harper Stables. Of course, she always stopped when she saw the sun gleaming off that water because it could be dangerous to walk up to that pond if the person hiking didn't want to see how well the Harper twins loved their wife, Rachel. Those three spent a lot of time naked in that pond. But that wasn't what she was looking for today.

Where was it?

"You know the trees?" Jax asked the question carefully, as if he wasn't sure she was being serious. Sometimes he had to figure out if people were joking, she'd discovered.

And sometimes he thought she was just plain crazy. It was okay. He wasn't the first to look at her like she was weird when she walked up to trees and ran her hands over their trunks. She studied the tree. "They don't allow any cutting in this part of the woods. These trees have been here for thirty or forty years. Somehow even when we have big fires, they seem to miss this place. I played here a lot as a kid."

This part of the forest was familiar to her, though in a vague way. It wasn't a part of the forest she would take clients to, not even small, well-trained groups. It was overgrown and there were no trails. Jax had been forced to use those muscles of his to move several major boulders that had fallen down the mountain. They were at the base of one of the mighty mountains here. They were at over eleven thousand feet at this point, and the mountain climbed another three thousand above them.

"You had an interesting childhood," he said with a smile that didn't quite reach his eyes.

He'd been quiet all morning. Not that he hadn't been affectionate. He'd made love to her twice since her revelation. He'd held her hand when he could and when they stopped to rest, he would pull her onto his lap and kiss her senseless. But there was no denying her lover had something on his mind.

Probably the fact that if they were successful, he would have to leave.

"I had the best childhood." It was easier to look back now and smile. It was as if a veil had been lifted and she could see past her grief and anger to the reality. Her father was more than those last few terrible months. She was satisfied now. Satisfied that she'd done right by him, that her pain had been in service to their connection.

Love wasn't safety and sex and fun. Love was about the work put into a relationship. It was about the risks one took, and one of those risks was always death. Hell, it wasn't a risk. In the end it was a certainty. She would lose him one day. Even if they had fifty years together, death was inevitable, and the fact that they'd had a life together wouldn't make it easier.

They would be torn apart. Whether it was by the danger to him now or death or some random act no one saw coming. They would not get out of this life together, and there was no guarantee of some magical place that would reunite them.

273

And yet she believed. There was the certainty of pain, and yet she was going to love that man because it was what she'd been born to do.

"I like hearing your stories," he said, clearing the way.

"It's been a long time since I liked telling them. It feels good to talk about my dad." She stopped, hearing something moving to her left.

Jax went perfectly still and suddenly there was a semiautomatic in his hand.

It was a reminder that this was no fun hike. She was silent for a moment and watched as a bunny hopped out of a bush, looking up at them as though surprised and then bounding away.

She breathed a sigh of relief. "It's okay. There's a lot of wildlife out here. I haven't seen anything that makes me believe that people have been through here in the last couple of days."

"You can tell?" His shoulders were still stiff, a sure indication he was on his guard.

She nodded. "Oh, yes. People leave lots of signs. If someone wanted to follow us in here, they could. We've been careful. We've picked up all our trash, but there are always traces left behind."

"I haven't heard anything out of the ordinary," he said. "I doubt Levi Green would trudge through the woods. He wouldn't mess up his expensive loafers."

She'd spent a good portion of the morning questioning him about the CIA agent who had almost wrecked her life. Jax didn't know a lot about him, but he had several strongly held opinions about the man's ancestry.

"Might he post a guard?" It had been bugging her. "There's all this classified information out here and no one's guarding it?"

"I'm sure there's security, but it likely won't be human. I think they'll have some kind of surveillance, but if they post guards they have to get them in and out. Regular traffic would invite local questions. Local questions would lead to national ones," Jax explained. "And you have to understand that Levi Green isn't in charge of The Ranch. He's doing the bidding of his bosses."

From what she understood now, there were several factions in the Agency and they warred against each other as much as they did enemy intelligence agencies. She wondered what faction Solo belonged to. "And they don't want anyone to know about what we're doing here. Even if we get in and steal the information?"

"In this case secrecy is more important. I think they also believe if that intelligence gets out there, it'll actually be easier to get their hands on it. They don't have to brief the president on the fact that it's been there all along. They can say some bad guys had it and they liberated it. If you think about, we're kind of doing their bidding."

"They're underestimating you." Those men would fight like hell to keep that knowledge from getting into the wrong hands.

"I hope so. I have to wonder how Levi got here so quickly," he mused, leaning against a massive boulder, his pack at his feet.

He looked relaxed again. She'd been surprised at how easily he moved in the woods. He might not remember his past, but she would bet he'd been an accomplished hiker. Though his body was relaxed, there was a stony expression on his face and she could guess why. "You think it was Solo."

He shrugged, a negligently graceful movement of his shoulders. "No matter what she said, I think she would likely have informed her bosses. What else could it be? We took serious precautions coming out here. We left under cover. We made sure no one was following us. Obviously it wasn't like we flew out of Heathrow. We went in a private jet and had three of the best hackers in the business cover our tracks. No one knew where we were going. The Agency should think we're still sitting on our asses at The Garden."

"That doesn't mean she's against you." She'd been angry with the woman she'd called Heather, but the purging of the previous night had made her look at everything with new eyes. "I hope not everyone in the CIA is some kind of drooling villain."

His lips curled up slightly. "Not at all. Hence the factions. Levi Green works for a particularly bloodthirsty one. I think the worst part is they truly believe they're doing what's best for this country. They believe sacrifices must be made. Of course, they're not the ones sacrificing. It's why Ezra left, though he has his

275

secrets, too. I don't know who Solo is working for. I only know Ezra doesn't trust her, and she's the most likely suspect to have given away our position."

"Like I said, she could have done it because she had to, not because she was trying to bring you all down. She was a good friend to me. She didn't have to be. I would have kept her around anyway. As long as she'd done her job, she would have had all the access she needed to keep an eye on Henry and make her assessments. But she did far more. She helped with my father. She held my hand at his funeral. She was my friend."

"Then I'm glad she was here," he said, his expression warming. "I'll think about it. I don't trust her right now, but part of that is Ezra's influence, and he's conflicted to say the least. Did you know she'd been married?"

"She talked a lot about her ex-husband and how she was still in love with him." Now all the pieces had fallen into place. "She said he left her after she got his brother killed."

"I can't help much there," he replied. "Ezra plays things close to the vest. I had no idea he'd been married. He hasn't dated in the time I've known him, and the man could walk into a sex club and not be tempted."

Jax would know because apparently he'd lived in one for a while. The Garden, she'd learned the night before, had been his haven after Taggart had liberated him from the crazy evil doctor's lab. The Garden was also a BDSM club, but then he'd likely be going straight to another one. They were going to retreat to someplace called Sanctum when they were done with this mission. The idea that the man had been surrounded by willing women and hadn't taken a single one boggled her mind. She looked at him and all she saw was how gorgeous he was, how intensely sexy the man could be, and she couldn't help but wonder. "He's not the only one who doesn't get tempted. Why didn't you take comfort from them? I'm sure there was some woman who would have been happy to have you in her bed."

"They felt sorry for me," he replied, his eyes losing a bit of their light. "I wanted more, and besides, I did find comfort. I found friends. I had people who cared about me, though not like you do.

It's different. I think I always knew something like this was out here. I wanted it to be special and it was."

She dropped her pack and strode to him, plastering her body against his. How would she ever live without this feeling? "It is special. This thing between us, it's everything."

He held her close and kissed the top of her head. "I'm glad I waited."

She was, too. Still, she was worried about a few things. "So you said they'll have security. How will we get in? They don't have like lasers and stuff, right? I'm sorry. I know I sound crazy but I'm imagining this Indiana Jones thing where we pull a file and a boulder rolls out to squash us."

His laughter echoed through the forest. "I watched that one. No, I don't think they've got it rigged like that. They'll be much more high-tech, and from what I understand they didn't have a ton of time to set booby traps. We'll be dealing with tech, and I have something to help with the problem."

"What's that?"

"They'll have to have everything operating remotely. I'm sure they'll have drones over the area frequently. I have a device that will scramble any Internet or satellite connections to the facility and for a few miles around it. Well, except for mine, of course. I've got a sat phone I can call back to base on and I've made sure the program I'll run won't interfere with the frequency we're using. The communications blackout won't last forever. Whoever is monitoring it will try to counteract. I've modified it to switch frequencies every few seconds, but if whoever they have on the other end is good, they'll figure it out in twenty minutes tops. Then we'll have maybe another thirty or forty minutes for them to reach us if they've got a chopper around here."

That wasn't a lot of time. They would have to move quickly. If she could find it.

"I need you to promise me something." He stared down at her for a moment. "If someone comes for me, I want you to run."

The idea turned her stomach. She couldn't leave him alone. Not again. "I can't do that."

"You have to. If anything happens, you run and hide and get

back to Bliss. Find Ezra or Big Tag. They can start the search."

He truly believed someone was coming for him. Maybe not today, but someday. It was there in his grim stare. He wasn't sure how many tomorrows he had. No one ever was, but his worry was more immediate. It was real, and she would have to sit up nights wondering where he was in the world.

"Hey, I'm sorry. I don't want to bring you down." He kissed her forehead and sighed, hugging her tight. "I just want you to be ready in case things go bad."

She had a pistol in her pack. She should move it to her pocket. It wouldn't do to tell him, but she had zero intentions of leaving him behind to save herself. They were in this together. Men had weird ideas, and in this case she would ask forgiveness and not permission. "I will be."

She would be ready to defend him, to protect him. She would be ready to give him her all.

He stared down at her. "Can I ask you a question?"

She nodded, hoping he wasn't going to ask something like "are you lying to me about running when I tell you to."

"Is it a good time? I mean…how likely is it?"

Her heart softened. It had been an impulse to tell him to make love to her without condoms the night before, but she didn't regret it. And she wouldn't lie to him. "It's not a particularly good time, but you never know."

He frowned for a moment. "It's not a particularly good time because you could be pregnant or because you aren't?"

She went on her toes and brushed her lips against his. "Because I'm probably not. I don't think I'm ovulating, babe. I wish I was. I really do."

He dropped his forehead to hers. "I worry I'm being selfish."

He had every right to be selfish. "You're not. But you are being pessimistic. I know that's pretty hypocritical of me since I haven't exactly had a sunny outlook on life the whole time you've known me. However, *this* is more like the real me, the one I was before my dad got sick and my ex turned out to be an ass."

A smile crossed Jax's lips as though he was thinking about something nice.

"You're thinking about him in jail, aren't you?"

"I am," he agreed. "I think he's likely scared and miserable and worried he's going to have terrible things happen to him."

She had nothing to say to that. She knew she should be more sympathetic, but she was with Jax on this one. "We have some money to distribute."

"I'm already working on the problem. I've got a list of his known aliases. We'll make things right." He kissed her forehead again, though this time she could feel him ramping up the heat.

Her whole body responded. "Do you want to park it here? I know we still have the whole afternoon, but we're both tired. I saw a spot that would be big enough for a campsite."

Especially now that they wouldn't need two tents. She fully intended to zip them in together tonight.

His hands managed to find her ass. "I'm not that tired."

She lifted her face to his, her body starting to hum, and that was when she saw it. A rock peeked out a mass of bushes. A moment from her childhood flashed through her head. There had been far less brush around it. She had scaled it, scrambling up and scraping her knees. She'd held a stick up like it was a sword and proclaimed that she was the queen of everything she could see.

She'd looked out over the clearing and she'd run out like she was leading an army.

Her father had stopped her at the opposite tree line. Before she could move into the shadows, he'd caught her up in his arms.

No, sweetheart. You can't play here. It's dangerous. Stay in the light and you'll be fine.

Stay in the light.

What had Jax said?

If they post guards, they have to get them in and out. Regular traffic would invite local questions.

The Ranch had been closed for years. What would have been the easiest way to get people in and out? They would use the same roads the rangers used. They would likely bring them in when the rangers had supply runs or present them as environmental scientists or researchers. No one would question that. But they would need to use roads for much of the trip.

279

"What is it?" Jax was staring the same direction.

"I think we're close." She moved away from him, trying to put together the map in her head. Bliss was to the south. The only way to get in from there was to hike in, but there were several places along 149 where a larger vehicle could go off road. The Wheeler Geologic Area was straight to the east.

It had been three years, but the signs would remain. Three years and a couple of good rainy seasons would guarantee that there would be growth, but the road would still be there.

"My father wouldn't let me go past that tree line." She pointed to a spot outside the clearing. The meadow was still green and a few arnica flowers remained, their bright lemon-yellow pedals like beams of lights. "I was just a kid but I remember how upset he got once when he found me exploring back there."

"Maybe he was afraid of bears. We're pretty high up."

"No, this was different." Her father knew they always ran the risk of running into bears or cougars or wolves. He wouldn't have had that slightly panicked look as he'd carried her back to the sunlight. She walked out into the meadow. Where would one hide a whole facility in the middle of the mountains?

Inside one of them, of course.

"No one would question blasting back then," she said. "Back in the mid-century, they were building roads and they would blast off the sides of mountains to do it sometimes." Excitement thrummed through her because she was sure they were close.

"Help me up." She pushed past the brush to start to climb up what her father had called his thinking rock. It was flat on top, but hard to climb because of it roundness.

Jax simply lifted her up and placed her on top. He then hefted himself up like it was no big deal.

So damn sexy.

She looked out over the meadow. Looking at it with adult eyes, she could sense the eeriness of it all. A sunlit meadow surrounded by dark forest. She could be standing in perfect light one moment and doused in shadows the next. Her father had been afraid of whatever was in those shadows. "We have to search the tree line. I think it's there."

He shook his head. "This isn't where my research showed the glints of metal. If anything, I would say it's on the other side of the mountain. That's where I thought we were heading."

And they had been, until she'd had the dream. "It's here. I know it is. Do you trust me?"

He took her hand. "Always. I'll grab our packs. We'll start a search."

He hopped down and she looked over the land. His secrets were here. She could feel it.

* * * *

Jax looked down at the ground River was kneeling on. She was incredibly excited about some grooves. They'd been searching for a good three hours, painstakingly moving through the tree line that separated the meadow from the base of the mountain above them. His quads were getting a workout, moving up and down the slope looking for the hidden entrance.

"It's faint, but do you see how the ground slides off slightly here. Someone cleared a path years ago. I think someone even leveled this part off. This was a road once," she said.

When he looked closely, he could see the difference. She was right. At one point someone had built up the path. He paced to the other side, to the spot where the hard-packed dirt descended slightly. This had been a decently wide road. Not wide enough for two lanes, but large trucks might have gotten through. "This couldn't be from three years ago."

She shook her head. "No. This is old, but think about the history of The Ranch. It was originally built as a shelter during the cold war. There would have been secrecy around it, but they wouldn't have been able to hide the fact that they were doing something back here. They would have to have brought in large construction equipment. It would have been easy to keep people out of the area though. If they came in somewhere between Bliss and Creede, there's not a lot of population to worry about."

"And when they switched the facility over to a black ops site, they could have used a couple of Jeeps to move people in and out."

281

"And potentially helicopters from time to time," she added. "The meadow would be a perfect place to drop off. There's a similar spot on the north side of the mountain that would be even less likely to have a stray hiker around. I say we follow this road."

His yellow brick dirt road. He took her hand and they started along the path. Now that he was looking at it from this vantage point, it was easy to see the path. At some point someone had clearly cut the trees. Nature had made a resurgence, but the trees along the road were obviously younger than the ones around them.

When they got to the end of this road, he would have to leave her. Levi Green showing up had made that plain to him. Whether it had been Solo who tipped the man off or cosmic good luck on Green's part, he wouldn't stop. He would hound them all.

He had to find a way to leave River out of it.

And he would have to find a way to come home to her if he could.

Despite what she'd said, he still felt selfish. The idea of getting her pregnant, of having some piece of him survive if the worst happened…he didn't even have words to describe how that made him feel. But he couldn't leave River alone with a baby.

He brought her hand to his lips and then let it swing back down.

"Jax, we're going to find a way," she said as though she could read his thoughts.

"I know." Sometimes a little lie wasn't the worst thing.

"You don't, but you will," she promised. She stopped, pointing ahead. "Do you see that?"

He stared for a moment and then saw the glint of something distinctly not natural up ahead. It was nothing more than a flash as the sun struck it, but it was enough to have them both jogging up the slope. There was no more road to follow this way. His boots found purchase and he followed behind her. Despite the gravity of the situation, he couldn't help but admire how good her ass looked. She wore a pair of cargo pants that somehow managed to be perfectly functional and sexy as hell.

He didn't want to let her go. Not ever. Maybe they were wrong and this was one major wild-goose chase. Maybe they could stay here in the woods and never come out. They could live together in the forest, away from the rest of the world. As far as he could tell, the world was shitty without her.

She reached the place where they'd seen the glint of metal and strode up to the tree. There was a large spike sticking out of it. "I think this is a marker. I don't know why else it would be here."

He trusted her instincts. "Let's canvass the place then."

She stood there for a moment, looking around. "We need an entry. I think what we're looking for is inside this mountain."

He wasn't sure. He'd seen the aerial views. He was fairly certain the pictures hadn't been of that spike. He was starting to worry they were on the wrong side of the mountain.

Of course, if they were that would mean getting around to the right side of this monster, and that would take a few days. A few days where he would have to be with River twenty-four seven. He would have a few more nights with her. It wouldn't be so bad to be on the wrong side of the mountain.

"There it is," she breathed.

And he saw it. Up ahead of them was a cave. He would think they might be heading into some bear's home except he could see the bars crossing the entrance. Someone had tried to cover those iron doors with vines and foliage, but at some point they'd dropped away.

This was the entrance to The Ranch.

River rushed forward, scrambling to get to the cave.

He followed, overtaking her. "I'm going first. I don't know what kind of security they have."

She let him move ahead of her.

He glanced around, looking for anything that might come out of nowhere to get them. There had to be motion detectors somewhere. They wouldn't leave it completely without defense.

He found what he was looking for about fifteen feet off the ground. Shit. There was a camera pointed right at the cave entrance. It was likely on a long-term battery and connected to a satellite. He was glad he hadn't let her run ahead of him or she would already be on their radar.

He had to protect River at all costs.

She followed the line of his gaze and cursed under her breath. "I might be able to climb up there."

And potentially break her legs if she fell. "No. I'll take care of it, but you have to know the minute I take it down, we're on a clock."

"We're in the middle of nowhere," she replied. "How fast can they possibly act?"

He set his pack down and pulled out the rifle Solo had given him. It would be easier to work with than the pistol he had. He attached the scope because he didn't want more than one attempt at this. "Well, they had an agent embedded in your company, so I think they probably work pretty fast."

"Good point," she replied. "Though I suspect it would be hard to have someone show up here quickly if we trip an alarm." She put a hand on his arm, looking at him with worried eyes. "Jax, we should think about this. What if we can't get that door open? We'll have to break in. It looks like someone attached it to the actual mountain. We may have to chip away at the rock, and that could take a while. I don't have anything we can use. Maybe we should go back and come in with the proper tools."

He liked her idea because it would give them more time together. Unfortunately, he couldn't be sure there weren't more cameras and they hadn't been caught. The truth was they were already on a timer and it was ticking away.

He got to one knee, brought the scope up, lined up his shot and pulled the trigger.

The camera blew apart in an instant.

"So we're a no on getting the right tools," River said, shaking her head.

He was already reaching back into his pack. He'd come ready for this job. He pulled out a lock picking set. "I got special honors in lock picking class and no, you do not want to know what happened to the guy who finished last."

It had been Tucker, and he'd had the holy hell beaten out of him. Jax still felt guilty at times for winning that particular "class."

"You think you can get that sucker open?" River followed behind him.

"I'm more worried about the inner door." He got down on one knee, selecting a pick and torque. The lock was quite large.

"There's another door?"

"There's always another door, and the next one won't look anything like this." He'd been in enough secret labs to know how they rolled. This first door was merely a deterrent. The second would be the one to keep them out. And then there would be more inside. There would be any number of obstacles, the worst being time.

He would give them an hour. If they hadn't found what they needed, he would get her out of here. He couldn't risk that someone would show up.

The lock was surprisingly easy to pick. Two minutes and they were in.

They moved from the sunlight into shadows and a chill went up his spine.

River's hand slid into his as they made their way into the cave. "This place feels wrong. I know it's my mind playing tricks on me."

"Or intuition," he replied.

"This is not what a cave normally looks like. It's far too clean." She touched the side. Roots were starting to press through. "Someone used to clip these."

Something moved up ahead and River jumped. He moved in front of her and then stopped when he saw the flash of eyes staring back at him. "Well, they couldn't keep everything out."

She sighed in relief behind him. "Possums get in everywhere. Be careful. She might have babies, and that's when she'll get vicious. She's a smart girl. Not a lot of predators can get through those bars."

The possum hissed at them as they carefully moved around her nest. He saw something else that didn't belong here. A red light flashed at the back of the cave.

A clicking sound echoed lightly and then he could see again. A beam of light shone on the metal door that covered the back of the cave. This was the door meant to keep people out and secrets in.

"Shine that light on my pack, baby." He got to one knee and reached for his laptop and a connector cable.

River moved the light with him, illuminating his space as he found the electrical box and popped it open. He found the input and connected to the computer that ran the facility's major systems.

"What are you doing?" River asked, her voice hushed in the gloom of the cave.

"I'm attempting to take over the system." He looked down at the screen. Password. "I've spent the last couple of weeks writing a program to break in. I worked with a woman who used to work for the Agency. She's a brilliant hacker and she knows their systems better than anyone else." The light went green. Chelsea Weston was fucking brilliant. "And we're in."

"Just like that?"

He had total control in a few keystrokes. They would be able to move through the facility freely. And there were a couple of options he hadn't counted on. "I can do one better than merely getting in. Apparently there's still a generator."

He touched the key and the lights sputtered on. There was a screeching sound as their furry friend obviously took exception.

"Sorry, buddy," River said. "We'll be done soon."

He hoped they would. "Now comes the hard part."

"Because we're not sure which lab she worked in?"

He disconnected and shoved his laptop back in his pack. The lights were all on. Now he had to hope no one was home.

Chapter Nineteen

River shivered as cool air hit her skin. It had been warm outside, but they'd moved into something completely unnatural. The air was stale, but Jax had gotten it moving. The lighting was far too bright.

Everywhere she looked was white. Pure white. So white it was an absence of color, of anything at all, really.

"Is this what your lab was like?"

Jax had gone silent, moving through the outer spaces carefully. He insisted on going first always. Every door he managed to get open, he would step into and then give her the go-ahead to follow him.

Some had been seemingly innocuous, nothing more than rows of microscopes and refrigeration units. Almost all of them had computers that had been left behind. They'd found what looked like a pharmacy complete with a sign left behind saying it would open again at eight a.m.

One had been terrible. They'd left the animals behind. Now they were nothing but bones in cages, but her heart had ached at what those creatures had suffered. Darkness and hunger with no way to save themselves.

Like Jax.

"Yes, it was a lot like this," Jax said, his voice steady as he managed to open another door. "I bet she modeled her other labs on this one. It looks like we hit the break room. It's good to know the fuckers got their cappuccinos."

The break room was pristinely kept and luxurious in a way most offices couldn't be. The bistro tables were straight out of a fine dining establishment and the coffee machines would make any barista proud. There was a chalkboard that proclaimed today's breakfast would be eggs benedict or steel cut oats with a choice of toppings.

It was good to know the evil doctors knew how to live well.

"I don't suppose you got cappuccinos." There wasn't any dust. It was odd. It looked like the place was ready for use, waiting for someone to come in and sit down and enjoy some coffee.

"Caffeine wasn't good for us. That's what Mother said. We were on very strict diets. No dairy. No sugar. Very few carbs. You think I'm ripped now, you should have seen me then. We weren't allowed to go over two percent body fat."

She hated the fact that his voice had lost any animation. He was back in hell and it was up to her to remind him he didn't have to stay here this time. She moved into his space, putting her hands on his waist. "I think you're sexy just the way you are. In fact, I could fatten you up a little bit. I'll make you all kinds of sweet stuff and then you won't be so fast when you try to run away from me."

A smile slid across his face. "I would never run from you."

He kissed her swiftly and moved on again, but at least the terrible bleakness had been wiped from his eyes.

She followed behind him. "I think we might have come in the back entrance."

They'd passed a bunch of storage rooms and she'd noticed a row of clipboards with lists of supplies on them, waiting to be checked in. They'd moved through the building, past what looked to be living quarters. She'd gone through some of them, but couldn't find one that had anything to do with the woman who'd tortured Jax. He'd explained that it was possible she wasn't in the facility when they evacuated. All they'd found was some rooms with left behind makeup or clothes. No random notes that might tip them off as to who had stayed here.

"I think so, too," he replied, moving to the opposite side of the break room. "If she truly did base her European lab on this place, the real treasure trove should be through the doors and to the left."

She followed him out, hating how eerie the place was. Their footsteps echoed over the concrete floors. She couldn't help but wonder how many men like Jax had been through this place, had their lives ripped away in the name of science and security.

They found the first of the larger labs and Jax took a deep breath. "This is it. Not this one probably, but this is the first of ten separate labs. Five on the left and five on the right. She would have used one of these if she had a base here. We'll have to search every one."

He connected his laptop to the high-tech looking keypads and the doors suddenly swung open.

Damn but he was one sexy computer nerd.

Twenty minutes and five of ten rooms later and he was a frustrated computer nerd. He stared at the screen in front of him. Whoever had worked here had left behind a large mainframe computer Jax had been able to connect to.

It hadn't given him what he wanted.

"It looks like they were working with something cellular here. I don't understand all the medical stuff, but they were definitely interested in manipulating the human genome," he muttered.

The dark aspects of the place had been made incredibly clear. Jax had taken one look at lab two and backed out, closing the door as quickly as he could. She'd gotten a glimpse of bio hazard suits and shuddered.

She didn't like to think about what these scientists could do to DNA.

Jax unhooked his computer and glanced down at his watch. "We have to leave soon."

He stood and strode to the hallway.

"We're fine. We can stay the night here if we have to." She couldn't let him leave without trying everything they could.

"They'll be here soon. I want to avoid whoever comes out

here to fix that camera. It could be anyone. They've likely got someone embedded. Probably one of the rangers. The nearest station is an hour away. I gave us forty minutes when we started and our time is almost up."

"Then we should each take a room and search it."

He stopped, his hand on the next door. "No. You stay with me."

He was so frustrating. "We can cover more ground apart."

"Or we can stay together and…that's all I've got. We're staying together."

"Look, I'll leave the door open and everything will be fine. I'll call out if I find something." She wasn't taking no for an answer. She knew damn straight why he was insisting on leaving early. It was to protect her. If he were here alone, he would likely still be searching hours from now. "There's more at stake than just me. Let me help. I can't be the reason Robert and Tucker never find out who they are. Dante and Sasha deserve to know why they were taken, who's waiting for them."

His jaw hardened, but he nodded. "Leave the door open and you yell if you find anything that vaguely looks like it could have something to do with us. You've got five minutes in that room and then we meet back out here. Is that understood?"

He could go all military on her when he wanted to. "Sir, yes, sir."

"That means something else in my world," he said with a shake of his head. "Go."

She was in the lab in a shot, propping the door open with a stool from the tall rectangular desk she found at the front of every lab. She hooked her thumbs under the straps of her pack. She'd wanted to leave hers at the entrance, but Jax insisted they carry them.

Her shoulders were starting to ache.

This was the largest laboratory she'd been in yet. The others had been one room with several desks, a shared workspace. The test animals had been held in another part of the facility. This one was different. It seemed to have several rooms in it. She walked into the large space at the front. Two hallways branched off. This space had two desks, a large refrigeration unit, and a wall of what looked like different microscopes. There were stools in front of each.

She moved to the hall to the left and found another refrigerator, though this one looked more like something one would find in a home. A note was stuck to the front.

Don't take my fucking yogurt.

Good to know. Across from the fridge was a set of glass doors and what looked like a surgery. A medical bed was in the center of the room, a massive surgical lamp above it. A chill went through her when she saw the bed was equipped with restraints.

Was that dark stain blood?

She turned away and forced herself to walk down that hall. She stopped when she came to the cells.

There was no other word for it. Those three glass rooms with cots and toilets were cells. The doors were closed and that could only mean they were on a different grid from the rest of the facility.

She walked up, putting her hands on the glass and looking inside. The bed was unmade, blanket thrown back and pillow dented. There was a robe draped across the end of the bed and slippers that looked like they could fit Jax's massive feet. Had he been trapped in here? Had this been the first home he could remember?

Her heart ached at the thought that he'd potentially been "born" here.

It was very much like he'd described the lab in Europe he'd been rescued from.

"Jax." She shouted out his name. "I think this is it."

She turned and realized how far back she'd gone. He probably couldn't hear her. The hallway seemed to make a loop around the back of the lab. She followed it around. There was another room. This one looked like it was equipped for training. There were weights and mats on the floor.

She walked through the hall, calling for him again.

And then she noticed the door to her right.

It was the only room that wasn't bright white. Set against the rest of the lab, it looked almost like a hole she could fall into. She stepped to the edge of the room. It was dark inside. She felt around and found a light switch, illuminating a cozy-looking office with an antique desk and chair. They were ornate, completely out of synch with the rest of the place. There was nothing modern about this space.

River walked in, her hands going to the bookshelves. They contained row after row of medical tomes. Books about neurology and memory seemed to be the doctor's favorites, though she had several journals detailing the latest surgical techniques. On the ornate desk sat a framed picture. A blonde woman stood in her black cap and gown, a doctoral hood around her shoulders. She stared out at the camera, a smile on her face that didn't quite reach her eyes. She was flanked by a pretty woman with laughing eyes and a large man River recognized from his many appearances on news shows. Senator Hank McDonald.

This was the place. This was where she'd plotted and planned to change the lives of the men she called her "boys."

She felt sick, but there was a sense of urgency running through her body that kept the anxiety tamped down.

She pulled the small USB drive that was connected to the laptop on the desk, shoving it in her pocket. She opened the desk drawer and found a leather-bound journal with notes written in a precise feminine hand.

Harvey has proven to process the first round of drugs far too quickly. His brain reforms connections after a few days without his dosage. He remembered yesterday. I might have to terminate him. I can't have Daddy getting upset with me.

Harvey. That had been Jax's name. God, he'd been here. He'd been in that damn cage and she'd been mere miles away going on with her life. She'd been marrying that idiot and getting her heart broken while the love of her life had been treated like an animal in here. How many times had she hiked these woods and never known this was here?

She flipped the page again.

I might have to leave The Ranch. Something's happening

with the group funding. The CIA might have good facilities, but they can't compete with the company I work for. Kronberg Pharma is very interested in my research. They sent me a new surgeon to work with. Dr. Reasor is young, but ambitious. He's got a genius-level IQ and absolutely no morals whatsoever. My kind of guy. We'll see what happens. If he proves unsuitable I wouldn't mind making him a subject. It would be fun to see if I can break that brilliant mind of his. If I get a whiff that he's planning on stabbing me in the back, I'll show him how my drugs work firsthand. Until then, I'll let him do my dirty work. He looks rather cute with bloody hands.

Every word she read made her ill. She picked up the journal, reaching around to tuck it into her pack.

There was a drawer of file folders along the back wall. She opened one. Thick files of medical charts were neatly organized in alphabetical order. She pulled the first one. It was labeled *Albert*.

River slapped the file folder on the desk and opened it.

"Albert" had been a twenty-eight-year-old homeless veteran McDonald had found on the streets of Denver. The doctor had researched the man. His legal name had been documented as Stephen Wells, a former private first class who'd been honorably discharged due to his PTSD.

The bitch had the gall to write a note to her partner in crime.

Dr. Reasor, take a look at this one. He'll thank us for helping him forget.

It was there written on a perky pink sticky note.

The file contained an autopsy report detailing how Stephen Wells had died. He'd had an allergic reaction to the drug, causing his heart to stop.

Owen, she'd been told, had a bad reaction, too. His skin still bore the scars, but he'd lived.

Jax could have died. It would have been so easy for him to die here.

She needed to find the Harvey file.

She turned back to the file cabinet and there it was. Harvey. She couldn't read it. Not now. Now that she had it in her hand, all that mattered was checking for the others and getting the hell out before someone showed up.

"Jax! I found it." He should be the first one to look through that file. Not her. He needed to read it and decide what he wanted the others to know.

He would read it by their fire tonight. They would hike as far as they could and then hunker down until morning. He would read his file and she would be there to support him no matter what it said.

She flipped through but there was no Sasha. No Robert or Tucker or Dante. Were those the right names? Or had they been like Jax? Had they chosen new names?

She had to find Jax. She started through the door and stopped because she wasn't alone.

Solo stood in the middle of the lab, a gun in her hand.

* * * *

Jax didn't like that River was across the hall, but she was correct about the fact that they could get more done.

Something didn't feel right though. Something felt off.

He looked back and the door to the lab across from him was open. He watched as River moved around inside.

She stopped in the middle of the room, staring at the bank of microscopes.

A cold chill crept along his spine and suddenly he couldn't breathe. He stepped back into the hall. He couldn't get stuck. This place brought back so many terrible memories.

His short life had been full of them. But now he would focus on the good ones. When he left, he would concentrate on remembering everything about River.

He turned and forced himself to walk into the other lab.

He knew immediately this wasn't the one he was looking for. There were white boards covered in equations. He didn't understand the math at all.

But he lifted his phone to take a picture of each of them. Dante was some kind of mathematical genius. Perhaps he could decipher what was happening in this small lab.

Despite what he'd told Ezra, he'd never intended to not document what he could about The Ranch. The information could be invaluable. He'd already copied what he could from the mainframe. They would have the names of the scientists who came through this facility and they could watch them. They could be the check the Agency needed. They could find the factions inside the CIA who were working for the greater good and feed them information.

Allies. If they had allies on the inside, he might be able to find some kind of a life. They might all have a chance at something vaguely normal. For him that meant a chance with River.

He moved to the next lab and found it empty. Nothing but clean white space.

Two more to check and then they would be out of here. He would have to hope that they could use the information they'd found as leverage because it appeared the whole op was a bust on the personal front. He'd seen no evidence that Dr. McDonald had ever been here, though he knew she had. She must have pulled out before the shutdown. Or been smart enough to see it coming.

He couldn't help but think back to those cages. All those dead animals, used and abused and left behind because they didn't matter.

He could have met the same fate. He could have been nothing but bones, having suffered starvation and dehydration. He could have died knowing no one cared, that he didn't matter.

He was probably going to have a lot of dogs. River should know he might end up being that dude who brought home all the strays because he knew what it meant to not have a home.

"Jax."

He stopped inside the lab at the far end of the hall. The door had closed behind him and he could barely hear his name being called.

He rushed to the door, throwing it open and then shrinking back because he saw something he hadn't expected to see. Someone was moving down the hall, a shadow turning from the break room to the hallway. She came into view, a Ruger in her hand, moving with the surety of a well-trained operative.

Son of a bitch. He should have listened to Ezra and not his own stupid instincts. He backed away, closing the door silently behind him. He had to get ready. He eased the heavy pack from his back, gently putting it on the ground. He would move far better without it.

Now that he thought about it, he had a lot of information on his system. She would want that. The least he could do was make it hard for her to get it. They'd already discovered the bench seating in the labs had storage underneath.

Solo would need to move quickly, too. She wouldn't want to be caught by whoever came from the security force the Agency had hired or her faction would be outed. She would likely take his pack and run. Not that he intended for her to leave this place alive.

She was threatening River and he couldn't abide that.

As quickly as he could, he shoved his laptop into the storage space, grabbed the other item he would need, and zipped his pack closed, hoping beyond hope that she didn't inventory it before she ran.

He had a little time. She would need to check the labs they'd come through before. She seemed like a cautious agent. He would wait until she went into one and then find River. He would stash her someplace safe and face the agent alone.

But before that he had to get a message out.

He glanced out his door as unobtrusively as possible. Sure enough, Solo was slipping into the first lab at the end of the hall. It was one of the larger labs. It would take her a minute or two to sweep it.

That gave him time.

He pushed the button on the satellite phone that should connect him to base. If everything worked according to plan.

"Jax? Is that you?"

The dulcet tones of Charlotte Taggart's voice gave him great comfort. She was a woman any man could count on. "We've been compromised. Tell Ezra Solo is here and I'm going to try to take her out."

He heard Big Tag curse in the background.

"Message received," Charlotte replied. "Look, something's going on. We're sending a chopper your way. The Agency is on the move. Hunker down if you can and wait for Ezra."

"What do you mean you're sending a chopper? How do you know where I am?" It didn't make sense.

"Jax!"

Fuck. "Charlotte, I have to get back to you."

There was no way Solo hadn't heard that. He could hear it through a closed door and Solo was far closer to River than he was.

He let the phone drop even as he could hear Charlotte asking for more information.

He gripped his semi and moved across the floor to the door. Opening it slightly, he could see Solo was already walking through the door.

His heart had started to race. What the hell was Solo going to do with River? She wasn't the one Solo wanted. The best-case scenario was that Solo would take River hostage and exchange her for himself. He would do it. He would make the trade and then fight like hell when he knew River was out of danger.

And if they found the doctor's formulary and decided he was the best test subject around because they already knew he wasn't allergic to it? Well, then he would do anything he could to remember her, to hold on to any tiny piece of her.

Theo Taggart had done it.

In that moment, he realized he hadn't loved anyone before. The barest memory of Erin had survived because Theo had loved her so fucking much. He knew it wasn't scientific. It wasn't logical, but somehow Theo's love for Erin had survived.

And he would do the same. He'd always thought that if the needle was coming for him again, he would find a way to permanently end himself.

He wouldn't because now he had something to live for.

Jax took a deep breath and moved as quietly as he could across the concrete floor. He had to get in behind Solo.

"Jax, I found it!"

He could hear the light in her voice, the triumph of discovery.

They'd gotten so close. They'd almost had it.

He couldn't let River be taken.

"River, don't panic," Solo was saying. She sounded the slightest bit breathless. "Where's Jax? I need to talk to him."

"How the hell did you find us?" River asked, her voice shaking.

He moved through the doorway. They weren't in the main room of the lab, but he could easily hear their conversation now.

"I wasn't following you," Solo replied. "I was following someone else. Come on. We need to move. We need to find Jax and get out of here now."

"I don't think I should go anywhere with you," River said, but she was obviously moving because he could hear her more clearly now.

They were coming toward him. He moved to the hall on the opposite of where they were coming from.

God, he couldn't breathe in here. This was it. He knew it instinctively. River had found the place where he'd been born.

For a second his vision flashed white and he couldn't see a thing, couldn't feel anything but cold. The drug always felt like ice in his veins.

He moved until he was sure he was out of sight. He would come up on them from behind. That would give him the best chance at taking out Solo and saving River. The minute Solo went down, he would pick up everything they had and run because he didn't doubt for a second she would have backup.

"You have to come with me." Solo stepped out and then stopped as a sound pinged through the air. Her white T-shirt bloomed with red and she got the strangest look on her face. "Motherfucker."

Andy stepped into the room, a gun with a suppressor in his hand. "Sorry, Solo. Guess you aren't as good as you used to be. And River, you will definitely be coming with me."

Chapter Twenty

River dropped to her knees beside Solo, her heart in her throat.

What the hell was happening? One minute she'd been sure Solo was going to kill her and the next it was Solo on the floor, a bullet in her chest. Had it gotten her heart? She looked down and blood was staining the white cotton of the T-shirt Solo wore.

She took a deep breath. Ty had taught her a thing or two. She needed to stanch the bleeding first.

"Tell Beck, I'm sorry," Solo said on a breathy gasp. "I'm sorry for everything. Please, River, tell him."

"You can tell him yourself." She started to reach for the knot at her waist. Her flannel shirt would have to work. She needed to stabilize Solo and get search and rescue out here.

"Don't make a move or I'll put a bullet in you, too." Andy stood over her, that big gun in his hand. Fucker was supposed to be a pacifist. He had lied on his resume in more ways than one.

"She's dying." She had no idea how long Solo had, but it wasn't much time. She needed real medical help. It no longer mattered that the woman had lied to her. All that mattered was she'd been a friend. It was obvious now that she'd come here to try to prevent Andy from springing his trap.

Andy shrugged. "I don't care. I'm here to do one job and one job only—and that's to get everything you have back to my boss. You see, unlike you, my boss is clever. He knew this group would make a run for The Ranch. He's known since Taggart saved them that one day they would come here and he would use them to further our interests."

"Didn't recognize you," Solo managed to say between pants. She put a hand against her chest and winced.

"I'm not Agency," Andy replied. "My boss knew you were here. He also knew you would be on watch for a while. I didn't meet Agency standards. Apparently I'm not good enough for those fuckers, but Levi saw something in me."

She should have known that man would be behind everything. "How did he know where we were?"

"Guess he's just smart."

"I don't understand how you got in. We locked the door behind us." Jax had been careful. Andy wasn't. Solo had dropped her gun when she'd been shot. She'd fallen forward and the gun was now at her side. River could feel the metal against her knee, but Solo's body covered it.

"You came in the back entrance, the supply entrance, if you will," Andy explained. "There's another way in. Given the direction you would have to come in from, I assumed you would enter through the back. I waited at the front. When the cameras went off, I knew we were a go. I was going to give you time to find what I needed. I was told not to enter unless I had to, but guess who strides right in and she had a key. Who you working with, Solo? Who is so deep at the Agency that he has a key to The Ranch?"

"Wouldn't you like to know?" Solo spat.

He stared down at her. "In fact, I would. I would love to know exactly who you're working for. I think I might get brownie points with the boss. Maybe I should take that key and see if I can find someone who can figure out where it came from."

Solo tried to move, but she only managed to get an inch or two away before she stopped. "Don't you fucking touch me."

"I would touch you all I like but you're not my type. I like my females a little less aggressive than you." Andy pointed the gun straight at Solo's head. "Now, River, you can come with me and we'll go find your boyfriend or I'll put a bullet through her right now."

She couldn't sit here and watch as Andy killed Solo. "Please let me try to stabilize her."

She needed time. Jax was out there and he would figure this out. He would come for her. He wouldn't leave her here. No way. She would have to find a way to save him because he would absolutely offer himself up in exchange for her.

Solo had managed to get up on one elbow, but it obvious she was spent. "He won't let you do that. And he'll kill you the minute he has a chance."

"Or I can take him down and we'll get out of here," a heavenly voice said. She looked back and Jax had his gun up, Andy in his sights. "Get behind me, River. We're leaving and if Andy makes a single move, I'll kill him."

"Only if I don't get you first, asshole. This room is tight and I wouldn't be surprised if the walls are perfect for ricochet," Andy said, his lips curling in a smarmy smile. "If you start a firefight, I promise I won't care who I take out. You want to take that chance? I don't think so. You see, I think you're the dipshit who fell in love with his mark. I think River's woe-is-me thing got to you. River's pathetic, by the way. I told the boss exactly how to get to her. And then she proves to be even more pathetic because she went back to you. You don't learn, do you, River? You were supposed to stay away from him. My boss wanted to keep the balance, but since you wouldn't play the game, we'll take the information instead and blame it all on you. I personally think this worked out for the best."

She definitely learned to vet her employees better. That was for sure. Jax moved in front of her, putting himself between her and Solo and Andy.

It gave her a chance to get her shirt off and hold it to Solo's chest. It looked like it hadn't hit her heart. She'd moved enough that it was a bit above her heart, but it seemed like she was working on one lung. Solo groaned as River pressed down.

"It's going to be okay." She wasn't sure how they would get out of this, but they had to. She couldn't have come this far only to

301

get gunned down by an asshole on the wrong side of a moral argument inside a bureaucracy.

Solo leaned back, shaking her head. "No, it's not, and I probably deserve this. Tell Ezra I was working with the good guys. Please tell him. I love him so much. He was the best thing that ever happened to me."

"Why don't you take your girl and walk out," Andy offered.

"I don't believe you." Jax's whole body was tight.

She had the feeling if he hadn't been worried about ricochet, he would have already shot the bastard. The odds weren't likely, but she knew Jax wouldn't put her at risk. She had to find an advantage.

She knew what it was, but it had been forever since she'd fired a damn gun, and Jax was in her way.

Solo's eyes met hers and she squeezed River's hand, nodding as though she knew exactly what she was thinking.

"I don't care about you or River," Andy was saying. "Like I said, I did everything I could to make sure you didn't find The Ranch. Now, I only care about the data. You two are responsible for everything that happens. Leave your stuff behind and I'll let you walk out the same way you came in. I've got transportation arranged. By the time you get back in, the damage will be done."

He would have taken the prize and pinned the blame on Ezra Fain and his Lost Boys. It wasn't hard to figure out what Andy's plans were. They would be locked out without Jax's computer and there would be a mountain between them and the front entrance. They would have to run because there was zero way Levi Green didn't pin Solo's murder on Jax.

She held the flannel over Solo's wound with one hand and with the other started to reach for the gun.

Jax moved over, stepping right into the potential line of fire. "We'll do it. We'll leave everything behind and walk out of here."

"We can't leave Solo." How could she simply walk away?

"Yes, you can," Solo said, her skin turning ashen. "But you have to be careful. He'll try to kill you."

"River, I need you to get up and move behind me," Jax ordered. "We're going to walk our way back. Drop everything and stay behind me. I'm not taking my eyes off this fucker."

"Jax, I found your file." They couldn't leave without it. She hadn't read it.

"You're more important," Jax replied.

"Go." Solo squeezed her hand again. "It's okay. Just promise me."

The whole world went blurry. "I promise."

The gun was in her hand. Andy's eyes were still on Jax. She eased the safety off.

She would have one shot at this. Literally. If she didn't kill Andy on that shot, he would fire back.

"Let River go first," Jax said. "When she's outside, I'll follow her."

Andy sighed. "You're not going to make this easy on me, are you?"

Andy fired, the *ping* splitting the air.

Jax fired back and that sound roared through the small space.

River stood, firing Andy's way. The recoil put her on her ass. She fell to the floor and everything went silent.

"River?" Solo was trying to get up.

Jax was on his feet, moving toward the place where Andy had fallen. "Stay down, Solo. I think he's dead."

He kicked Andy's gun away. River managed to get to her knees, breath sawing in and out of her body. Was it over? Had they gotten him?

Jax was standing over Andy's body, his head hung low.

"We need to get Solo out of here." They couldn't leave her behind. She could go and find a way to patch her up. Jax would have to use his sat phone to call for help. They needed a helicopter.

Jax turned and River felt her eyes widen in horror again. His shirt was covered in blood. He held a hand to his gut and fell to his knees.

* * * *

He knew he'd been hit the moment he pulled the trigger. In the split second before, he'd seen it in Andy's eyes that he'd been

303

done playing with them. He'd known that he had seconds before Andy would kill both him and River. Andy had never meant to allow them to leave. He would have taken everything they'd found and left three corpses behind.

Levi Green had been smart. He'd found the perfect asshole to do his bidding, but it wasn't going to work out for him. River was going to live. River was going to get out of here and she would take the information back.

She would make things right. For everyone but him.

Although when he thought about it, she'd already made things perfect for him. He'd gotten to love her and know what it meant to be loved.

"We need to get Solo out of here." She was on her knees, trying to get to her friend.

He hated the fact that it was going to end like this, but he couldn't see a way out. They were miles from anyone who could help them. He'd been hit in his gut, right below his ribcage. There was a bullet in his liver. He wouldn't go fast, but he would go.

He turned and saw her. So fucking gorgeous. And she'd been smart, too. She'd gotten Solo's gun. He wasn't sure which shot had taken out Andy, but he was glad she'd been quick.

He felt like hell. It was weird. He didn't feel the bullet. What he felt was nausea and a light-headedness he couldn't shake. He couldn't stay on his feet a second longer. He stumbled and hit his knees. Pain suddenly wracked through him. There it was. It had taken his brain a while to process the horror done to it.

"Jax," she breathed his name and scrambled to get to him.

How long would it take? Fuck, he couldn't do this to her. "Baby, I need you to get the sat phone. It's in the last lab on the left."

"Do you mean this?" a new voice asked.

He thought he'd been sick before. The sight of fucking Levi Green striding in made the world spin on its axis. Green was dressed all in black, from his black boots and pants to the bulletproof vest he wore over a T-shirt. And he wasn't alone. The five men who walked in behind him were dressed identically. Each held a SIG Sauer in their hands, flanking around Green like they were his security detail. Jax knew they weren't. They were some kind of elite unit Green had put together, very likely off the Agency's radar.

Levi Green sat Jax's backpack down with a thud before moving into the anteroom of the lab.

Green stood over them, surveying the damage. His face was a perfect blank as he looked down at Andy's body. His eyes flared when he saw Solo.

He moved to her side, kneeling down. His voice went low and soft as he reached down and gently smoothed her hair back. "Tell me, Kim. Who did this?"

Jax tried to get in front of River, but they were surrounded. He got the feeling if Solo said the wrong thing, they might be the next to go.

Solo shook her head. "You did, fucker. Sent that asshole in."

Green stood and nodded toward one of his men. The man immediately was at Solo's side, pulling up her shirt and shouting orders for one of the other men to find a medical kit.

Green looked down at Andy's body. "I would kill you myself if you were alive. No one hurts her except me." His eyes came up. "This is McDonald's lab, isn't it? I never thought I would see the inside of this place. I really thought I'd done my job and scared you away." He shook his head as he looked around. "This turned out even better."

River was behind him, her hands keeping him upright. "Please, help us. He's been shot."

"Well, that's what happens when you invade government property," Green replied with a tsking sound. "You know what you've done here is criminal."

"What was done here by the doctors is the criminal act," River argued.

"I disagree." Green stood over them. "What was done here was important work. The research done here will keep our country strong."

"It was torture," River replied.

"You say tomato," Green shot back.

Jax shook his head. "It's not going to work, baby. He's not

305

going to let us live."

A single brow arched over Green's right eye. "Know everything, don't you, Jax?"

There was one thing he was certain of and he had to find a way to avoid that particular outcome. "I know you can't let us live."

"Really? Now, the way I see it, I actually *should* let you live. It works out better for me. If I let you live, the Agency then believes you're the ones who have the intelligence. My boss is covered and you're the bad guys. If I leave your corpses here, that will make the other factions ask questions. They'll want to know who killed you and if said killer now has all that important data. If I let you live, they'll have a target and it won't be me. You can tell your story around the world, but they won't believe you. I assure you according to everything they'll find on me, I'm in Seattle at the Four Seasons meeting with a woman I've been fucking on a regular basis for the last three years. The Agency loves predictable schedules, you see."

He wasn't sure he believed that Green would let them live. It was likely a tactic. "Solo could tell."

If they let her live. He rather thought things would go better for Solo than it would for him. Two men worked over her, wrapping her up. They'd found some kind of medicine and another man ran in carrying a medical kit.

"Solo can't say a word," Green said with a frown as he watched them work. He glanced down at his watch. "Not if she wants to keep her job and her secrets. She doesn't want anyone to know she was here any more than I do. She'll have a hard enough time explaining her injuries. I would love to know who she's working for, but I know the rules of this game."

"This isn't a game," River said and he could hear the tears in her voice.

Green looked down at her with something akin to pity in his eyes. "Everything is a game, dear. The only people who refuse to admit that are the losers. Right now, I've got ten men working to get absolutely everything they can from this place. We'll strip it clean and the Agency will be forced to come to the conclusion that former operative Ezra Fain has gone bad."

"Ezra isn't trying to do anything but find out how to help his men," Jax managed to say.

"Ezra is a dreamer, a ridiculous idealist. You're beyond help," Green said with a sad shake of his head. "The truth is you don't want to know what your pathetic life was before. No one is looking for you. It's precisely how McDonald got away with what she did. No one cared about you."

"They do now," River said.

Green's face went blank again. "Yes, and that is a problem for me. Is she stabilized?"

The man standing over Solo nodded.

"Excellent. Take her to the helo. I'll be right behind you. Start it up because I already sent out the signal and they'll be close behind us." Green watched as two of his men eased Solo onto a stretcher and lifted her up. He took her hand when they stopped beside him. He brought it to his lips. "You have to know no matter what game we're playing, you're the queen and I will protect you. Beck wouldn't do this for you. Beck would likely leave you there to bleed out. Think about that."

He watched as her middle finger came up.

Green simply laughed. "Your recalcitrance does nothing to make you less attractive to me. This thing with Beck is nothing more than a fond memory. He's not coming back to you. I'll be with you in a moment."

He nodded and the men took Solo out.

He was getting weak. His arms wouldn't come up anymore. He tried, but he couldn't move. Fuck, he didn't want to die here. Maybe River could drag him outside and he could die in the woods where he'd loved her.

He didn't want to leave her.

Green got to one knee in front of him. "I'm taking the data, but I need you to understand that I play fair when I can. What happens next is called forced reciprocity, and I want you to remember it. My men have already found your laptop. It was clever to hide it, but they're very thorough. We have Dr. McDonald's files, including the one on you. I'm going to offer you a choice."

"River lives." It was the only choice he cared about.

Green rolled his eyes. "How very earnest of you. River was always going to live. It would be a little like kicking a puppy. Not that I mind kicking them. It teaches them how the world works, but I have to maintain a certain balance. You see, I happen to think that Taggart would come after me hard if he finds a bunch of corpses of his little buddies and their girls. I know Beck…I mean Ezra…would come after me if I left Solo here for him to find. I lied to her. No matter what he says, I knew he was still obsessed with her when he spent months chasing her double around the world. He's going to lose that game. I'll get the girl in the end."

He was so fucking tired. He couldn't quite process what Green was saying. "River lives."

Green sighed. "Yes, River lives. River lives and you will, too, I hope. I don't need Taggart on my ass. I'm giving you a choice, Jax. This is what I meant by reciprocity. You see, I'm going to do you a favor and I think you won't come after me. I think you'll take my offer and run for the rainbow you all seem to be looking for."

"Please help him." River was crying behind him, her arms around him and tears hitting his neck.

Green ignored her. "Here's your choice." He held out his hands and suddenly he was holding a manila folder in one hand and a piece of paper in the other. "This is your file. I found it where your girlfriend dropped it. This file will tell you who you are. Where you came from. You can have it or I can give you the name of a doctor who worked with McDonald before her death. She's a neurologist, specializing in Alzheimer's and other memory-based illnesses. I believe she helped McDonald with her drugs, teaching her how to break the connection in your brains. She also might be the key to a cure. She might not be. Or I could be lying completely because I'm a sadist and I think it's fun to watch you squirm. It's a leap of faith when you think of it."

"Name." He wasn't even sure he would make it. He would take any leap he had to in order to help his brothers.

"I thought you might say that." He slipped a piece of paper

into Jax's pocket and held up the file. "I'll keep this. I think it might be fun to know something you don't know. Good luck. I need to head out. Can't have Solo dying on me. Tell your boss I have his queen and I intend to treat her well."

He stood back up and gestured to the men he had working the lab. He let out a high-pitched whistle and his men proved they were well trained.

Through his weakness, he saw the men had stacks of files and one was carrying a laptop. One of the men dropped Jax's backpack in front of him. They'd obviously gone through it and decided they didn't need the extra weight.

They'd lost everything.

"You can't leave us here," River pleaded.

"I can and I will." Green gave them a jaunty salute before reaching down and plucking a pin off Andy's dead body. "Can't have anyone figuring out I had a body cam on this guy. You're lucky I did. Good luck, you two. Hey, when you crazy kids finally procreate, think about Levi for a boy. It's a good name and I kind of made this whole thing happen." He glanced down at his watch again. "Better go or I'll cross paths with the cavalry. Keep him alive, River. They'll be here soon."

Green turned and walked out the door, his men following behind.

And he was left alone with River. "Get the name, baby. Get it out of my pocket. It's important that you tell Ezra and Big Tag everything that was said here today."

She eased him down to the floor. Even with her moving as carefully as she could, his body still screamed out in pain. God, he hated this part. He hated feeling so out of control, but there was nothing to do. He couldn't make her more afraid than she already was.

Her gorgeous green eyes loomed above him, tears making them shine like crystals. "Please hold on. I'm going to figure out how to deal with this. First I have to stop the bleeding."

He had a nice-sized hole in his abdomen. He was fairly certain he would keep right on bleeding until he had nothing left. He forced his arms to work, reaching for her one last time. "No, you need to take the name Green gave me and run. I need to know you're all right."

She frowned down at him. "So you can die in peace?"

The expression deepened, and he got the idea that saying yes would piss her off more. "I need to know you're okay, baby. I need to know you're out there in the world living a life. I need to know you'll remember me."

Tears dripped from her eyes and she squeezed his hand. "I'll never forget. Never. But I won't have to because we're getting out of here." She crawled over to his pack and pulled out the sat phone. "How do I use this?"

He managed to force his head up to see the phone. And the problem. "He took the battery, baby. It's useless."

He could see the scenario play out. River would live. He would die here and Levi Green would craft a narrative where Andy had been working for Ezra. He'd likely already laid out a nice trail. Ezra had been burned by the Agency, left on his own when he wouldn't fall in line. Now he would be hunted by them. He was in the same place as the rest of the Lost Boys.

But Green would get his balance because he wouldn't tip anyone off as to where Ezra was. He had what he wanted. He had the intel. He didn't need the war that would go along with turning them in because he would be starting that war with far more than Ezra Fain and a couple of Lost Boys.

He would be taking on McKay-Taggart, and it was obvious Levi wasn't ready to do that.

Yet. Green had an end game, but Jax wasn't sure what it was.

"Tell Tag Levi Green has a plan," he managed. "Tell him to research the name I was given, but to be cautious. Green will be watching. He didn't give it to us out of the goodness of his heart."

She set the phone down and shook her head. "No. I'm not leaving you. There's a surgical unit. I can figure this out. I can get you stable and we'll move you. I'll go to the ranger station and get help."

"I won't be here by the time you come back." It was at least three hours hike to the nearest station and then there would be all the red tape that came with a rescue. He gave it another hour, hour and a half tops before a cleaning crew showed up. He wouldn't make it. He was weakening by the moment. "Baby, take care of Buster."

"No." She dropped to her knees again. "You can't leave me."

But he'd always been destined to leave her. "I love you, River. You made it worthwhile. You made me happy to be alive."

Tears dripped from her eyes. "Please don't leave me."

The floor underneath him vibrated slightly. Was that a function of his death? Was his body shaking and he couldn't sense it?

Fuck, he didn't want to leave her, but the world was starting to blur.

She stood up and he heard voices.

"What the fuck did they do to you, man?" Tucker was here. "We're going to need to stabilize him. Does anyone have a knife? I've got to get this shirt off him. It looks like a GSW to the upper right quadrant, doc."

A man with short red hair was suddenly staring down at him. "We can't move him. This is happening here. Jax, my name is Dr. Caleb Burke. I'm going to give you something to put you out and then I'm going to try to save your liver. Make the choice right now. Make the choice to live."

The world seemed to be spinning. Nothing seemed real, but then he saw her face and it stopped. He focused on her as he felt something jab into his arm.

Remember her. Remember River. She was all that mattered.

The world went dark, but he wasn't alone this time.

Chapter Twenty-One

River paced outside the small OR. It had been hours since they'd gotten to the tiny hospital in Del Norte, CO, but Jax was still in surgery.

"I brought you some coffee." Robert held out a Styrofoam cup. "I didn't know how you like it."

"Black is fine. Thank you." She took a long drink. It tasted like motor oil, but that didn't matter. All that mattered was what was happening behind those doors.

"Tucker says he was stable during the helo flight," Robert said, leaning against the door.

That flight had been the most tense forty minutes of her life. After Dr. Burke had gotten Jax stable, he'd decided to move him. He needed to remove a portion of Jax's liver and resection some of his lower bowel.

She'd explained that unless he wanted to do it surrounded by a CIA crew who would likely arrest or shoot them all, he'd better do it in an actual hospital. Dr. Burke liked field surgery way too much in her opinion.

Still, she would have done anything to ensure Jax lived through this. That moment when she'd realized he'd been

312

shot…she'd been ready to lie down and die with him.

She wasn't letting him go. Not to death, and certainly not because some crazy doctor lady thought he would be fun to experiment on.

"Dr. Burke thought he was stable enough for the helicopter ride." She sat down on the couch in the small waiting room. "What happened? How did they know where to go?"

She was calm enough now that she could ask a few questions.

The door came open and Ezra, Big Tag, and Henry strode in.

"Is he okay?" Ezra walked right up to her, his eyes tight with obvious anxiety.

Did he know about Solo? "Jax is in surgery right now."

"And everyone else?" Ezra asked.

Stubborn to the end. "Andy's dead and Solo was stable the last time I saw her. But she did take a bullet to the chest."

"She was alive?" The question seemed forced from his mouth.

"She was alive. Levi Green took her with him."

Ezra nodded and stepped back, like he knew all he needed to know. "Well, it's good to know Levi takes care of his people."

Ezra was working under a mistaken impression. "She didn't want to go with him. She came to try to get us out of there before Levi showed up. She knew he was coming for us."

"Yes, because she knows Levi quite well. He's her lover," Ezra said. "They're playing a game with us."

"Or she is what she says she is and she's trying to make it up to you," Big Tag pointed out.

Ezra took a seat opposite from them, completely ignoring Big Tag's opinion. "River, I need you to tell me everything that happened."

"First tell me how you found us." She still couldn't believe it happened. One minute she'd been crying over Jax and the next, she'd had hope.

"Levi Green called me," Big Tag replied. "No idea how the fucker got my number. He said he was on his way to The Ranch but there'd been trouble and I should get my guy out because the Agency was on its way. He also said I should send a doctor. Then he texted me longitude and latitude and I sent Owen and Tucker into town. Nate Wright let us borrow the county emergency rescue helo and Henry got Doc Burke to go with them. I would have gone, too, but they needed to run light."

"We're lucky Owen, Tucker, and Burke aren't in custody right now," Ezra complained.

"And that's probably why he called me," Big Tag shot back. "He knew you would be far too stubborn. Green is an asshole but he's played fair about this so far. He didn't want the Agency getting their hands on Jax, either."

"Because then they would have listened to him about Green being there," Henry pointed out. "Jax doesn't have the information, I assume. Did Green take it all?"

River nodded. "We found the files. I found a diary of sorts, too."

"On who? Who were the files on?" Robert asked. The question was asked in a soft tone, but his hands were knotted on his lap.

She didn't have good news on that front. "Just Jax. Or rather, Harvey. I was going to take them all. I didn't know if she changed your name when she rebooted you, so to speak."

Robert sat back. "She didn't. I was there several times when she wiped Theo's mind. He was always Tomas. I'm fairly certain I was always Robert. I don't know about Dante and Sasha. They were held with Jax. It's possible she treated the other team differently."

"What you're saying is Levi has all the files." Ezra seemed impatient to get to core of the problem. "You found everything we needed and Levi has it all now."

She nodded.

Ezra cursed and stood up, striding out the door.

Big Tag sighed. "Don't mind him. He's worried about his wife."

"I bet Levi will send an update if only to fuck with Ezra's mind," Henry said, sitting back. "Do you know anything about why those two hate each other?"

Big Tag shook his head. "No idea. I never worked with either one of them, and we both know I didn't go through the same training they did. I was recruited from Special Forces." He looked up and suddenly there was a bright smile on the man's face. "Ah, there's my girl."

"And mine." Henry was beaming, too.

A gorgeous amazon with strawberry blonde hair walked in beside Nell Flanders. "We got here as soon as we could. I have Sasha and Dante cleaning up the cabin. We'll leave for Dallas as soon as Jax can fly. What crawled up Ezra's butt and died a painful death? He was not pleasant to me."

Big Tag held out a hand, drawing the redhead onto his lap. "I'll kill him for you, baby. River, meet my wife, Charlotte Taggart. Charlie, this is the reason Jax lost his damn mind and probably why he got shot. It's a pattern. Fall in love, get your ass kicked and hard."

Owen was grinning as he walked in. "Precisely why I'll avoid the condition altogether. I'm too much man for one woman. Besides, I don't like getting shot."

Nell sat down beside River. "Are you all right?"

It was good to have a friend around. She slipped her hand into Nell's. "I will be once Dr. Burke walks out here and tells me Jax is going to be fine. That's what I need."

He was going to walk through those doors any minute now.

Any minute.

"Charlie, I've got an assignment for you," Big Tag was saying. "I need you and Chelsea to put those old skills to work and dig up some information on Kimberly Solomon."

Charlotte wrapped an arm around her husband's shoulders, looking perfectly comfortable in his lap. "Ezra's ex-wife? I can do that. It'll be fun. Are you looking into why Levi Green seems to think she's a prize of war?"

"Absolutely," Tag said.

"There's something going on here, something under the surface, and I don't think Ezra will come clean," Henry agreed. "He's too close to this. We need to figure out why Green is playing things the way he is."

"He said something about forced reciprocity." She hadn't understood it at the time, but then she'd been busy trying to hold

Jax together.

Henry laughed, but it wasn't an amused sound. "That's why he did it."

"Of course, that's why he did it," Big Tag replied.

Robert leaned forward. "Are you saying Levi Green thinks because he called us and told us where to find Jax that we'll give him a free pass?"

Tag sighed and seemed to find comfort in his wife's presence. "He thinks I won't send an assassin after him. He's also sending a message. He knew where we were going. He knows how to get to us and all he took was data. He's telling us he'll play nice as long as we will."

She couldn't think that Levi Green viewed humans as anything except pawns. "Jax wanted me to tell you that he thinks Levi has an endgame in mind. Whatever that means."

"It means Jax is thinking ahead," Tag replied. "I suspect he told you to tell me because he was certain he would die and you would live on."

Charlotte slapped at her husband's chest. "Don't you make fun of the emotional stuff. I'm pretty sure you didn't take my near death on the yacht with a sigh and a shrug."

"Baby, I knew nothing as wimpy as some water could take you out," he replied. "I just sat back and waited for Satan to ship you back to me with a note requesting I not send you to him again. Jax was overly dramatic about it, I bet. He was probably all 'you're best thing that ever happened to me' and shit."

He had been. But it was easy to see the way Big Tag's hands had pulled his wife closer. She was starting to understand these guys. Sarcasm was a tool. It was how they showed they cared. She would bet if Big Tag didn't give a damn, he likely wouldn't say anything at all.

"So it was all a bust," Robert surmised.

Not entirely. She'd retrieved the note from Jax's pocket. "Levi gave Jax a choice. He could have the file on himself or the name of a doctor McDonald worked with. And I read enough of her journal to have some things we can investigate. She was working with a man named Dr. Reasor. She described him as being young and particularly ambitious. He was there when she started her experiments on Jax. I think Jax might have been her first subject. Well, the first one who lived. I know Sasha was there when he woke up, but from what I can tell, she rebooted Jax a lot. He was her problem child."

"Dr. Reasor?" Owen asked, paling a bit.

Robert shook his head. "It's a coincidence."

"We don't know that," Owen argued.

Tag sat forward. "Reasor and Razor are awfully close, but it doesn't mean Tucker was working with her."

River gasped. "Tucker? Tucker was Dr. Reasor? She mentioned she used him on the really bad stuff because he liked getting his hands bloody. That's not Tucker. He's sweet. Of course she also mentioned that if he got out of line, he could be her next patient."

"No one mentions this to Tucker," Tag ordered. "Charlie?"

"I'll get with Chelsea and see what we can find out," she promised.

She couldn't believe it. It was like Robert said, a coincidence. She stood up and reached in her back pocket and pulled out the note. "Have you ever heard of a Dr. Rebecca Walsh? It says she's in Toronto."

Taggart held his hand out and she handed him the note. "No, but I'll have Adam find out everything he possibly can about her. It'll be a trap, but we might need to follow the trail. We'll regroup in Dallas and figure out what our next move is."

Robert sighed and let his head fall back. "I can't believe we went through all of this and we came out of it with one name and it's from the evil guy, so we can't trust it. Why would Jax do that? Why wouldn't he take his file?"

"Because Levi mentioned she might be the key to a cure." Because Jax would never put himself above others. He was a hero. He was definitely her hero.

She started to sit back down and that was when she felt it. Oh, she'd forgotten all about it. They'd taken everything she'd put in her pack. They'd taken the files she'd dropped when Solo had been shot. Jax had lost his computer and all the data he'd collected, but they hadn't searched her personally. When she'd first walked into McDonald's office, she'd found the doctor's laptop and taken the USB drive. She'd shoved it in her pocket. "I might have something better than that note."

Robert's head came up and everyone was staring at her. She pulled the drive from her pocket. "Is that what I think it is?"

"I found it connected to the laptop in McDonald's office," she said.

Taggart's eyes lit up. "And we all know the good doc liked redundancies. I believe that's her backup. River, you are my favorite of all the chicks I don't sleep with."

Charlotte hit him again.

Taggart shrugged. "Well, when was the last time Serena brought me a shit ton of intelligence? Phoebe spied *on* me, never *for* me. Avery makes some delicious cookies, but I think data on the crazy person who tried to kill my brother wins."

Before she could say anything else, the door opened and Tucker walked in with a smile on his face. "He's going to be okay. Doc says in a few weeks, he'll be as good as new. One of us can go back and sit with him. He's unconscious but Dr. Burke says it's fine."

Every eye was on her, but she was already moving. That was her place and no one else's. They might be his brothers but she was going to be his wife.

She walked through the door, determined that nothing would separate them again.

* * * *

Jax came awake, the white light stirring him to fear. He was back. He was back in the bad place. He was supposed to remember something. His head was foggy and his body ached like a motherfucker. What had happened?

River. He was supposed to remember River. He couldn't let them take her memory away. He could survive as long as he knew she was out there, alive and happy.

"I'm here, babe." A warm hand found his. "Don't move too

much or you'll tear your stitches."

His stitches? He forced his eyes open and there she was. The pain seemed dim compared to the smile she gave him. "River. You're here."

She nodded. "I wouldn't be anywhere else. And you need to understand right now that I'm coming with you to Dallas and wherever you go afterward. I know you have to stay with the group for now, but the group just got a little bigger."

"You're not bringing the dog," a grumpy voice said.

"I am so bringing the dog," River replied, though she never stopped looking into his eyes. "Ezra thinks Buster will cause problems on the road, but I don't care. He's our mascot now."

"Ezra thinks Buster will pee all over the nice private jet the billionaire loaned him and then the billionaire won't loan him a jet anymore." Ezra's face came into view. "Good to have you back, Jax. And to have you conscious again. You were out for fourteen hours. Time to get a move on."

"He's resting," River insisted.

He wasn't going to get a word in edgewise. "What happened? I remember Levi showing up and I thought he was going to kill us."

"He just stole everything we found and pinned the whole theft of government property thing on us, so there's probably another warrant out for your arrest," River admitted. "Not that Nate's going to rush in here. We've got a day or so before he thinks we could get in trouble. He can work it from the Bliss end, but he can't promise that if your picture gets out in Del Norte that law enforcement here won't rat you out."

Then he would end up back in a cage and that wasn't happening. Not when River was here and they were whole.

Mostly.

"I'm ready to go." He would walk to the plane if he had to.

Ezra smiled down at him. "You have some time. We're not going anywhere without you, man. And apparently we're not going anywhere without the dog." He shook his head. "I'm going to go let the rest of the guys know. They moved you into a private room this morning, but they still don't want more than two of us in here at a time. River won't give up her spot."

"Nope." She sat down in a chair beside his bed, her hand still in his. "You'll pry me out of here over my dead body."

"Then I'll send them in one at a time," Ezra promised. "But I'll give you two a minute before I do. And Jax, good work, man. You handled everything as well as any operative could. I'm proud of you."

Jax breathed a sigh of relief. If Ezra wasn't trying to murder him, it couldn't have gone too badly. He'd been shot and then some crazy-eyed guy had told him to make the decision to live and he had. He'd held on to the memory of River and she'd gotten him through. "Where the hell am I, baby?"

She kissed him, butterfly busses across his face. "You're in the hospital in Del Norte. Levi Green did exactly what you said he would. He put us in his debt. He called Big Tag and gave him our location. Big Tag said he's seen enough to know to send a doctor along. But he couldn't have done it without Levi's help. Although, when you think about it, Levi was the reason you got shot in the first place, so I don't think we owe him anything."

He definitely didn't owe that bastard a thing, but he bet Green's offering would keep the peace. For now.

"River, have you thought about this? What will happen if you come with me?" He wasn't sure he was strong enough to tell her she couldn't come with him. But he had to point out the problems with her plan. He had to make sure she understood the dangers.

"What will happen is I get to be with the man I love." She gave him the sweetest smile. "That's all that matters. And you should understand that if you think you can get away from me because you have this misguided sense of self-sacrifice, you should know that I'm a fairly good tracker."

As she'd proven. She'd found The Ranch. "I'm just sorry I couldn't save the information. You gave that to me, baby. I wish I'd been able to secure it for all of us."

Her smile went wide. "I smuggled out the USB attached to McDonald's computer. It was in my pocket. Big Tag says it's a gold mine. And some guy named Adam Miles says he thinks there's enough data that he can figure out who you are."

He wasn't sure he wanted to know. "Will you still love me if I have a wife and three kids?"

"You don't, baby. They would have looked for you." She turned serious. "I will love you no matter who you are. I'll love you forever."

He took her hand and put it to his heart. He couldn't ask for anything more.

Chapter Twenty-Two

Dallas, TX
Two weeks later

He was feeling pretty good for a guy who'd lost part of his liver. Of course he'd gained something else. He'd gained a wife.

He'd married River the previous weekend after he'd been given the go-ahead to actually get out of bed. He'd needed a cane to prop himself up, but he'd stood in Big Tag's backyard and said his vows in front of all his friends and their canine ring bearer. That had probably been a mistake since Buster had taken off in the middle of the hastily put together ceremony. Only the Taggart twins had saved the day, corralling the dog and finding the wedding rings in their sandbox.

It had been a good day. They'd found out River's ex, Matt, had pled to multiple charges and would spend time in jail. They'd started giving money back to his victims. He'd learned nothing felt better in the world than doing good with his wife by his side.

He glanced down at his ring. Something about it gave him incredible comfort. He needed it now because he was sitting in the conference room at McKay-Taggart waiting for Adam Miles to come up from his office downstairs.

He was about to find out who he was. Or rather who he had been.

River put a hand on his. "Are you ready for this?"

He was. He was ready because his past didn't matter. His future was sitting right beside him. "I'm good, baby. I'm more concerned about Dr. Walsh."

He'd spent the last week researching Rebecca Walsh. She was a wunderkind neurologist. At the age of thirty, she was one of the top researchers in her field, but then she'd graduated from Harvard at the age of fifteen and Johns Hopkins three years after that. She was an honest to goodness Doogie Howser, and she might also be responsible for the worst parts of Dr. McDonald's work. Her fingerprints were all over McDonald's writings. They had authored several papers together and Hope had often called on the young Becca Walsh for help.

Dr. Walsh now worked with a pharmaceutical company in Toronto and her work sounded eerily like McDonald's. She was researching the ways the brain made connections and how it stored memories. She was researching how those connections were broken. Oh, she said she was working to find a cure for Alzheimer's and other degenerative neurological diseases, but Jax wasn't sure. There were questions about her finances that needed to be answered.

And then there was the fact that Hope McDonald had sent Dr. Walsh a package right before her death. He'd hacked the good doctor's email. McDonald had asked Walsh to keep it for her and told her it was important.

He would like to see that package.

The door opened and Adam Miles walked in carrying a box, followed by another man, a man Jax hadn't expected to see.

"Hello, Ten." Jax stood up and held out a hand. "I thought you were in Africa."

He'd met Tennessee Smith and his wife, Faith, several times while he was staying at The Garden. Dr. Faith Smith had been a revelation. He'd been reluctant to meet the woman since she was

Hope McDonald's sister and daughter to Senator Hank McDonald, who had known and approved of his psychotic daughter's experiments.

Faith was different. Faith was kind and patient. She worked for charities around the world. It had been hard at first, but he'd had to admit that she wasn't her sister.

Tennessee Smith was a former CIA operative. He'd been crucial to the mission that ended in Jax and the rest of the Lost Boys being liberated.

He owed Ten.

Ten shook his hand and introduced himself to River. Adam sat down at the head of the table, a mysterious smile on his face. He placed the box on the table to the side.

That smile made Jax's gut tighten. That smile told him Adam knew something.

He sat back down. "How is Faith?"

Now that he was here, he was beyond nervous. It wouldn't change anything. He was married to River and he wasn't going to leave her. If he found out he had a wife somewhere, he would try to do right by her, but he wasn't the man she'd married. If he had a kid…he would do everything he could to have some kind of a relationship. God, what would River think if he was a bad guy in his former life?

Like Tucker might have been. They weren't planning on mentioning Dr. Reasor to Tucker, but Adam and his group were looking into the mysterious man who was mentioned in several of the computer files River had smuggled out on that USB drive.

He had no idea how Tucker would take it if he turned out to be Dr. Reasor.

He shoved that worry aside for another day. They had plenty to do before they headed to Canada. In a few weeks they would all be in Toronto setting up for a new mission. Even River would play a part.

"Faith is waiting out in the lobby," Ten said in his slow Southern accent.

"Why doesn't she come in?" He started to get up. He didn't mind Faith sitting in on this meeting.

River put a hand on his arm. "Give it a minute, babe. You need to know a few things before you make that decision."

River knew? He turned to her. "He's already told you?"

Adam nodded. "I wanted her to be aware of what I'm about to tell you. Your past is complicated, and it might be upsetting."

River's hand slid over his, tangling their fingers together. "It's going to be okay. I think you're going to be fine with this, Jax. I think, in some ways, what's in that box will give you peace. And how you handle the other news, well, I'm with you any way you want to go, but remember we only get so much time here. We need all the love and family we can get."

What the hell did that mean? "Just tell me."

Adam opened the box and pulled out a picture. He slid it across the table. "Your name is Jason Reynolds. You were born to Pamela Reynolds thirty-two years ago in a tiny town in rural Oregon."

Thirty-two. He was thirty-two years old.

He stared down at the picture. A pretty blonde woman was holding up a tiny baby boy and beaming for the camera. That woman was in love with her child. It was there in her eyes.

And his eyes watered. His mother. His mother had loved him.

He'd said he didn't want to know, but now that the picture was in front of him, he had to know. He'd had a life. "What did she do? What other family do I have?"

He could have brothers and sisters. He could have aunts and uncles.

Adam held up a hand to slow him down. "First off, let's put your mind at ease about a couple of things. You aren't married. No kids."

He sighed in relief. He'd hated the thought of someone out there he owed responsibility to. "I'm married now." He touched the photo as Adam laid out several more. This was his life, laid out in photographs. There was him as a grinning toddler, his mom holding him up and pointing to the camera. There he was wearing a Little League uniform, his smile gap toothed. Photo after photo chronicled his life. "Where did you get these? How did you find out my name? Is she alive? I'm sorry. I know I'm asking too many questions, but my mind is a little blown right now."

Adam sat back. "No problem. I can answer all of those for you. The drive River had in her pocket contained a ton of personal files including photographs, but those look personal, too. We have to keep going through them. She had several scholarly papers she was working on and all of her email correspondence. She was likely trying to back them up when she was forced out of the facility. The file contained emails and private thoughts. Unfortunately, it didn't contain her formulary, but that's why you're investigating Dr. Walsh. The emails indicate they were working closely together. However, there was enough information on the files River smuggled out to extrapolate what happened to you. It was never said outright in her emails, but I know how McDonald found you and why she chose you for her experiments. Your mother was born on the East Coast. She was an only child. She went to Georgetown and majored in political science. From all the information I've gathered, I believe she intended to go to law school, but she took a year off to intern in DC."

"What happened?" He shook his head, the truth completely evident. "I happened."

"Yes," Adam agreed. "Your mother left DC a few months before her internship was up. She had one remaining family member, an aunt, who lived in Oregon. Your mom moved out there, had you, and opened a business. She ran a nursery. Pam's Plants and Nursery. She won small business owner of the year three years in a row."

"That's why I know so much about flowers," he murmured, his eyes on the photos. She was lovely, his mother.

"I suspect so," Ten continued. "I'm sorry to say but she died in a car accident when you were eighteen. You went into the Marines."

"Where was my dad in all of this?" There were no men in the pictures. Just him and his mom.

"That's the complicated part," Ten said. "There's no father listed on your birth certificate, but the hospital bill was paid in full, and not by your mother. It was paid for in cash."

"That's unusual." Jax was starting to see an emerging pattern.

"So my mom had an affair in DC, likely with a married man. I'm not going to judge her. She was young. She was probably vulnerable. I'm surprised she kept me."

"I believe there was some pressure on her not to," Adam allowed. "But she did. From what I can tell, she took a check for thirty thousand dollars from a DC lawyer and she left and never returned. She raised you and by all accounts, she was happy."

A terrible thought hit him. "Was the car accident really an accident?"

Ten waved that off. "There were witnesses. It was raining and an oncoming truck lost control. It was truly an accident, Jax. You mourned her, but you went into the Marines and you had a good career there. I've got your records. You were well liked by your fellow Marines and your commanding officers. In fact one of them kept this box. Before your last deployment, you decided to give up the apartment you were living in. He said you were going to figure out your next move when you got back. He was storing your stuff in his garage. When you died, he gave away the clothes and stuff, but for some reason he couldn't get rid of that box."

River's hand was suddenly on his back and she leaned in. This was the bad part. Whatever they said next would rock his world.

"Died?"

Ten looked grim. "According to the military records, you were killed in a helicopter crash on your way back to your unit in the Middle East. There's only one problem with that report. Everything was filed properly. Your death is on record and you were buried. There's a record of you getting on the chopper. But we can find no evidence that you were ever on the plane to Riyadh. We know you flew home six months before. You had arranged transport, but there's no evidence you got on the plane. As a matter of fact, we believe you were in Houston the day you went missing."

"Why would I have been in Houston?"

"Apparently someone gave you one of those genetic tests for Christmas two years before," Adam replied. "You had taken it and gone so far as to make an account with the company. I think you were looking for relatives. By the way, I'm surprised to find out

327

you're a full tenth Native American. You don't look it at all."

"Adam, focus," Ten said, his voice tense.

"Fine, anyway, one of the services this site provides is to match your DNA if you opt in," Adam continued. "They send you updates, like so and so is a ninety-eight percent match to be your first cousin or third cousin or so on. Two weeks before you went to Houston, you received an email from the site stating that they had found a potential close family match. You shared 1705 centimorgans over fifty-two segments with this woman who had also uploaded her data. You sent her an email and were invited to Houston to meet her."

His whole body went tight. "Who did my mother intern for?"

"Senator Hank McDonald." Ten affirmed Jax's fear.

"I went to meet Hope McDonald?"

Ten shook his head. "You went to meet Faith. She was the one who had the account, but while she was in Africa, she let her sister handle everything. You have to know Faith never got your email and Hope and her father shut down her account. She didn't know, Jax."

Senator McDonald had been on the senate Armed Services Committee. He had deep ties to the CIA. It would have been easy to fake his death. He had no other family except his Marine family. He'd been like a lamb to slaughter. "I assume the senator didn't want it to get out that he had a bastard."

"Jax," River began.

He shook his head. "I can guess what happened from there. I walked into my half sister's home, she gave me the drug, and I became one of her first experiments."

"Yes," Adam agreed. "There's no record of you after that."

Ten leaned in. "Jax, Faith is out in the lobby. She wants to see you. She's eager to have you as a brother, but I have to ask if you can accept her. She's not like the rest of them. If she'd had any idea, she would have moved heaven and earth to find you. She feels guilty. She thinks she's the reason you're here."

She *was* the reason he was here, but he understood that could mean several different things. She could be the reason he'd been tortured and lost his memories. She could be the reason he was on the run.

Or she could be the reason he'd found River. She could be the reason he'd found his true home.

It was all in how a person chose to see things.

He stood up, his decision made.

"Jax?" Ten stood, too, his anxiety obvious in the way he held his hands in fists at his sides. "I'm asking you not to take this out on her."

He was halfway through the doors when he heard River's reply.

"He would never do that," she said.

Faith was standing in the lobby and her eyes widened when he strode out. Her eyes were red. Had she been crying? Had she been crying for him?

Did she want a brother? Because he damn straight wanted a sister.

He walked straight up to her. "Hi, sis."

She gasped out a choked cry and threw herself into his arms. "I'm so sorry, Jax. I didn't know."

She would have been there that day in Houston. He could see it plainly. If she'd been the one to get his email, she would have met him at the plane and welcomed him with open arms. She would have asked him everything, trying to learn what she could about her brother.

He let go of all his anger. River had taught him it had no place in the face of love. Love was everything. He would take all the love he could get.

He let go and turned out slightly, though he kept an arm around his sister's shoulder. "River, come meet Faith."

Faith brought River into the circle. "I wish I'd been at the wedding."

"I have lots of pictures," he assured her. He smiled down at River. "I thought I didn't have a lot to give you. But I can give you a sister-in-law."

Faith's smile was brilliant. "And a nephew. And we're adopting. I'm so glad to have an aunt and uncle from my side for them."

329

Ten stepped up. "And you have a brother-in-law you will always be able to count on. Always."

Jax shook his hand as Ten mouthed the words *thank you*.

But there was nothing to thank him for. He was the one who had been blessed.

River moved into his arms. "Should I call you Jason now?"

He held her close. "Nope. I'm Jax forever more. You think you can handle that?"

"Absolutely." She went up on her toes and kissed him.

"Let's have a family lunch and I'll fill you in on everything else we know," Ten offered.

He followed his new family out, eager to learn more about his past life. But he was more eager to enjoy his new one.

* * * *

Three weeks later

Owen stared at the picture on the screen. Dr. Rebecca Walsh. She wore a white lab coat, her hair pulled back in a severe bun. She wore a pair of glasses and her eyes were serious as she stared at the camera, but there was beauty there, too.

He'd watched videos of the woman. She was awkward until she started talking about her research, and then her face would light up.

Could such a pretty face hide evil intentions?

"I've got our base of operations ready," Ezra was saying. "We leave for Toronto in two days and then we'll have about a week's set up before we make contact with the subject. We're relatively certain she's never met any of you. She was never at The Ranch, and according to all our records, she never traveled to the bases Dr. McDonald kept you at. We believe they worked together remotely. We know they met a couple of times, but I don't think McDonald would have brought her experiments with her. Does anyone remember Walsh?"

They sat in the conference room of McKay-Taggart. They'd been working here and living in Adam Miles and Jake Dean's guesthouse for three weeks, but it was almost time to start the new op.

The thought of getting back to work made his blood pump again. He wouldn't tell anyone, but he was bored. They'd been hanging out at Sanctum, but he couldn't get the vision of the doctor out of his head. Something about the woman…

Which proved his instincts were shite. They could take his memories, but they couldn't take away his awful taste in women.

Apparently in his past life he'd fucked about any woman who would let him, and definitely a few he shouldn't have. He had the scars to prove it.

Tucker shook his head. "No. She's pretty, but she doesn't look at all familiar to me."

"Me, either," Robert agreed.

The rest of his team shook their heads.

"If she does recognize one of you, we'll have more information than we did before. But this is precisely why we've got Owen running point on this. There's no chance she's met him," Ezra explained. "How are we on logistics?"

"I managed to find two apartments in the same building as Dr. Walsh. River and Jax will take the one on the same floor, and Owen and I will move in downstairs," Robert explained. "Tucker has been accepted as an intern at the institute, and Dante and Sasha have jobs there, too."

"As janitors," Dante complained. "This is a terrible job. Why does Tucker get to be in the smart job?"

Tucker leaned over. "Do you know how to read a CAT scan of the brain? Know what the limbic system is and how it affects long-term memory?"

Dante frowned. "No. But I suppose I do know how to clean toilet. I will thank Dr. McDonald in hell. I want an assignment where I am allowed to kill many people. I do know how to do this."

Sasha sat back. "Don't worry about it, Dante. We will likely be the ones killed since we're walking into a trap."

They weren't the most optimistic of chaps. "We'll be fine. We know Levi Green will be watching us. We'll be ready this time."

Ezra chuckled. "Well, we'll certainly try. And if anyone sees my ex-wife, run the other way."

He wasn't sure Ezra was thinking clearly when it came to the woman they all now called Solo. He'd talked to Jax about his experiences with her. Owen thought she might be working an angle none of them had thought of yet.

But that would play out as it would. In the meantime, he had a woman to figure out.

Dr. Walsh.

Becca.

He sat back as Ezra and Robert continued, but his mind was on the woman. It all came down to her. She might be the key to getting his memory back.

Was she an innocent pawn? Or the devil herself?

He meant to find out.

* * * *

Owen and all the Lost Boys will return in *Tabula Rasa* coming February 26, 2019

Author's Note

I'm often asked by generous readers how they can help get the word out about a book they enjoyed. There are so many ways to help an author you like. Leave a review. If your e-reader allows you to lend a book to a friend, please share it. Go to Goodreads and connect with others. Recommend the books you love because stories are meant to be shared. Thank you so much for reading this book and for supporting all the authors you love!

Tabula Rasa
Masters and Mercenaries: The Forgotten, Book 2
By Lexi Blake
Coming February 26, 2019

Owen Shaw and his "brothers" lost everything, their entire existence erased. Science had robbed he and all the Lost Boys of their memories and their past, but not their future. Hunted by every intelligence agency in the world, they are focused on two goals: find a cure for what was done to them and ensure that the technology that ruined their lives doesn't get out into the world. Rebecca Walsh might be the key to achieving both. Owen has been studying her closely, living in her building, and he cannot resolve how such a beautiful, giving woman could have helped design the evil process that destroyed his past.

Dr. Rebecca Walsh has dedicated her life to researching the secrets of the mind. Her atmospheric rise in her field was fueled by the horror of watching her mother's agonizing journey into madness at the hands of a disease with no cure. She vowed to never rest until she finds it. But obsession takes a heavy toll, and when Owen moves into her building she realizes how much of her life she has missed out on. Owen opens her eyes to a whole new world, filled with joy, laughter, and possibly love.

Owen and Rebecca grow closer, unraveling more about each other and the mysteries surrounding her connection to Hope McDonald. As the sinister forces working against the Lost Boys descend on Toronto, secrets long buried are uncovered that could shatter the bonds holding the Lost Boys together and cost Rebecca her life.

Discover Lexi Blake writing as Sophie Oak

Texas Sirens

Every girl dreams of her alpha cowboy, the one who sweeps her off her feet. In Texas Sirens, every girl gets two.

Set in both small Texas towns and cosmopolitan cities, Texas Sirens features beautifully broken heroes and heroines who discover that unconventional love is their best chance at happily ever after.

Small Town Siren
Siren in the City
Siren Enslaved
Siren Beloved
Siren in Waiting, Coming September 4, 2018
Siren in Bloom, Coming November 6, 2018
More coming in 2019!

* * * *

Nights in Bliss

Bliss, Colorado, is home to nudists, squatchers, alien hunters, a bunch of ex-military men, and a surprising number of women on the run. Bliss is a place where cowboys hang out with vegan protestors, quirky is normal, and love is perfectly unconventional. So grab a chair and settle in. If you can forgive the oddly high per capita murder rate—and the occasional alien sighting—you'll find that life is better in Bliss.

Each Bliss story is a standalone, though found family is important so expect the characters to stick around, playing a part in each novel.

Three to Ride
Two to Love
One to Keep, Coming August 7, 2018
Lost in Bliss, Coming September 25, 2018
Found in Bliss, Coming October 9, 2018
Pure Bliss, Coming December 4, 2018
More coming in 2019!

About Lexi Blake

Lexi Blake lives in North Texas with her husband, three kids, and the laziest rescue dog in the world. She began writing at a young age, concentrating on plays and journalism. It wasn't until she started writing romance that she found success. She likes to find humor in the strangest places. Lexi believes in happy endings no matter how odd the couple, threesome or foursome may seem. She also writes contemporary Western ménage as Sophie Oak.

Connect with Lexi online:

Facebook: Lexi Blake
Twitter: authorlexiblake
Website: www.LexiBlake.net

Sign up for Lexi's free newsletter.

85932035R00201

Made in the USA
Middletown, DE
28 August 2018